THE
Reluctant
DAUGHTER

What Reviewers Say About Lesléa Newman

"Lesléa Newman is as fine a writer as we (women, lesbians, Americans, humans—pick one or more) have... The merely good would simply not be acceptable from her pen."—*Bay Area Reporter*

"A constant gift provided by Ms. Newman is her ability to look reality in the eye. This is not a woman who minces words."
—*Mama Bears News and Notes*

"Newman's humor is cosmic."—*A View from the Loft*

"Newman has an easy narrative style, sometimes breezy and an obvious affection for our strange and wonderful community... Newman has a way of softening pain to enable the reader to look at difficult issues."—*Outlines*

"Some of her stories are humorous, some are fervent; each is a gem, polished to brilliancy without being overworked."
—*Southwest Book Review*

"When Newman is at her delicately nuanced best, she is very good indeed...She captures the humor and pain inherent in the human condition."—*Booklist*

Selected Titles by Lesléa Newman*

NOVELS

Good Enough to Eat

In Every Laugh a Tear

Jailbait

SHORT STORY COLLECTIONS

A Letter to Harvey Milk

Secrets

Every Woman's Dream

Out of the Closet and Nothing to Wear

Girls Will Be Girls

She Loves Me, She Loves Me Not

The Best Short Stories of Lesléa Newman

POETRY COLLECTIONS

Signs of Love

Still Life with Buddy

The Little Butch Book

Nobody's Mother

CHILDREN'S BOOKS

Mommy, Mama, and Me

Daddy, Papa, and Me

The Best Cat in the World

A Fire Engine for Ruthie

The Boy Who Cried Fabulous

Heather Has Two Mommies

*For a complete list of Lesléa Newman's titles,
visit www.lesleanewman.com

Visit us at www.boldstrokesbooks.com

THE
Reluctant
DAUGHTER

by

Lesléa Newman

2009

THE RELUCTANT DAUGHTER

ISBN 10: 1-60282-118-6
ISBN 13: 978-1-60282-118-7

This Trade Paperback Original Is Published By
Bold Strokes Books, Inc.
P.O. Box 249
Valley Falls, NY 12185

First Edition: September 2009

CREDITS

EDITOR: Stacia Seaman
PRODUCTION DESIGN: Stacia Seaman
COVER DESIGN BY SHERI (GRAPHICARTIST2020@HOTMAIL.COM)

Dedication

for my mother
and her mother
and her mother
and her mother…

If you want to understand any woman you must first ask her about her mother and then listen carefully.

—Anita Diamant, *The Red Tent*

I T TOOK ME half a century to find my mother.

My mother wasn't lost like the poor child whose sad face graces the poster hanging outside the convenience store that I pause to study every time I dash in to buy a carton of half-and-half for Allie's morning coffee. Nor was she lost like the small gold Jewish star my parents gave me to wear around my neck when I turned sixteen that slid off its chain one day when I wasn't looking and disappeared as completely as an ice cube melted by the sun. No, I've always known exactly where my mother is: sitting in the living room of the split-level house I grew up in on Maple Drive, a quiet tree-lined street in Oakwood, New York, a suburb smack dab in the middle of Westchester County. I can locate my mother any time I want to, but that doesn't matter. She is still missing in action. At least to me. My mother and I are so estranged, she doesn't even know that we're estranged. It's not that we don't communicate with one another. We speak on the phone once a month, sometimes once every other month, sometimes once a season. I am always the one to break the silence between us and dial my parents' number, usually during a weekday when I know my father isn't home.

It's never my idea to give my mother a ring. The thought would never even occur to me on my own. If it weren't for Allie, years could easily slip by without my mother and I having a conversation. But Allie, my sweet, kind, wonderful, not to mention drop-dead handsome as a butch can be Allie, can't seem to mind her own damn business and leave well enough alone.

It can happen on a Tuesday. Or a Thursday. At around three

o'clock, I'll climb into our just purchased, "previously loved" station wagon and drive toward Main Street to do some errands. Allie and I reside in a quaint, liberal college town on the southern tip of Maine called Paradise, and it pretty much lives up to its name with the smell of the ocean permeating the air all year long, the beauty of the landscape equally breathtaking during all four seasons, and on top of that, the many shops that hang rainbow flags in their windows, letting both the locals and the tourists know that ours is a gay-friendly town. I pull into a parking space right in front of our organic food co-op, unsuspecting, maybe even humming to myself. It's a glorious spring day and I'm generally a happy, humming type of person. After I shut the ignition, I pocket my car keys and reach into my shoulder bag for my list of things to do: *Pick up dry cleaning, drop off vacation photos…* As I scan each item planning my route, my eyes catch on something. Three little words scrawled in Allie's small slanted southpaw handwriting that make my heart beat faster. Not "I love you," which is written at the very bottom of the page underneath *buy battery for alarm clock*. No, the three little words that stop me cold, inserted between *don't forget kitty litter* and *mail car payment*, are "call your mother."

"You call your mother," I say aloud. It's a mean thing to say even if Allie is miles away at the lumberyard she manages and cannot possibly hear me. Allie would give anything to call her mother, but the woman died two decades ago, when Allie was barely twenty-seven. Allie is an only child and her mother was her only parent. They left Puerto Rico when Allie was five, first living in the Bronx with some friends they knew from the island, and then moving up to New England because Allie's mother wanted her daughter to breathe fresh air, live among grass, trees, and flowers, and be close to the sea. Allie says her mother loved her more than life itself, and she never felt like she was missing anything by not having a father, siblings, or any kind of extended family. Until her mother died, that is. After Allie lost her mother and before I came along, Allie was all alone in the world. And even though Allie is once again a part of a family of two, a family she and I have created, she still misses her mother terribly. Every year on November 11, the anniversary of her mother's death, Allie wakes up in tears, rises without a word, and lights a pure white seven-day candle in her mother's honor. Allie and I got together four years after her mother's death and at that point, she couldn't even mention her without breaking down completely. Things are better now, but still, Allie's voice shakes and her eyes grow moist whenever she speaks of her mother.

Call your mother. I stare down at the words, seething. Isn't it enough that I'd sent the woman a Mother's Day card last week after spending the better part of my day off choosing it? I'd walked up and down this very street, going into the drug store, the stationery store, the bookstore, and several overpriced galleries and gift shops, browsing through racks and racks of frilly pink cards that said things like, "God couldn't be everywhere so He invented mothers." Oh please. I could hardly stomach reading that card, let alone bringing it up to the cashier and paying for it. The only card I seriously considered purchasing was one picturing an endless field of day lilies that read, "If I had a flower for each time I thought about my mother, I could walk in my garden forever." Well, that's certainly true, I mused, as I stared at the card in my hand, but then again the thoughts that run through my head on a regular basis are hardly complimentary and if my mother is anything, she is smart—smart enough to know that much and decode my hidden meaning in two seconds flat. I put the card back and looked at dozens of others, all the while knowing I would never find what I was searching for. A card that said, "Mom, I'm sending you this purely out of obligation," or "Mom, I know you did your best, but it wasn't good enough," or "Mom, we're both getting older. Do you think we'll ever heal our relationship?" But since they don't make Mother's Day cards for daughters like me—daughters who feel too hypocritical to send a "you're the greatest mother in the world" card but can't quite bring ourselves to boycott the Hallmark holiday altogether either—I do what I do every year: buy a card with a photo of a bright yellow sunflower or a vase of peach-colored roses on the outside, and on the inside where it is blank, I write, "Dear Mom, Have a wonderful Mother's Day. Love, Lydia." And that's the end of that.

Except now on top of sending a card, Allie wants me to make a follow-up call, too? "Alicia Maria Taraza, I can't believe you did this to me." I rattle the folded-up to-do list in my hands, though it is really Allie that I want to throttle. Without meaning to—or perhaps on purpose—my dearly beloved has ruined my day completely. Anybody who knows me at all knows that my day will certainly be ruined if I do call my mother. And now if I don't call my mother, my day will still be ruined because I'll feel guilty. As charged. Guilty of being the world's worst daughter. *You can't even pick up the phone and call your own mother, bring a little happiness into her life, make her day? How can you be so selfish, so self-centered, so self-absorbed, so self-involved?*

"Don't forget self-cleaning, Mom," I say, answering my mother's voice, which is ricocheting around my head like a cold metal ball bouncing about a pinball machine. I get out of the car and fume through town, marching in and out of shops and checking off the errands on my list. I'm in a bad mood when I return to the station wagon, and the sight of the yellow parking ticket wedged behind my windshield wiper puts me over the top. "Damn it, Allie, you're paying for this," I say, snatching up the ticket. "It's your fault I forgot to feed the meter. If you hadn't messed with my list..."

I'm still muttering to myself when I pull into our driveway. At this point even I know I'm not really mad at Allie, who is only trying to help, after all. I hang up the dry cleaning, put the kitty litter in the closet, and then go in search of Mishmosh, so named for the cacophony of colors splayed across his fat little body. According to our vet, only one in about three thousand calicos is male, and though Mishmosh came from very humble beginnings—Allie and I found him mewling behind a Dunkin' Donuts dumpster covered with fleas and powdered sugar—he never lets us forget how lucky we are to reside with such a rare creature who allows us to wait on him hand and foot. I find His Highness sprawled belly-up in the middle of the queen-sized bed he begrudgingly shares with Allie and me, soaking up a spotlight of sun and getting his orange, brown, and black fur all over our vintage white chenille spread.

"Wake up, Mishmosh. I need you." He opens one eye and throws a look in my direction that clearly says *don't even think about disturbing me* but nevertheless allows me to lift his limp body and drape it over my shoulder for moral support. He even purrs in my ear as I flop down on the maroon tweed living room couch, prop my feet up on the oak coffee table Allie made for my last birthday, and dial my parents' number.

"Hello, Lydia." My mother answers on the first ring. She never sounds surprised to hear from me, no matter how long it's been since I've called. Her voice is pleasant as though this is something ordinary, just a daughter calling her mother on a weekday afternoon. "How are you?" my mother asks, and then before I can answer, says, "I got your card. Thank you."

"You're welcome."

That taken care of, I'm ready to hang up the phone, but my mother has other plans. I hear the click of her lighter, and the inhale and exhale of smoke, which means she's settling herself in for a nice little chat. Since we really don't have anything to talk about, I know she will turn to the one subject that can always be counted on: the weather. "So is it raining by you?" she asks as if on cue.

"A little."

"By us, it's pouring, I'm telling you, what a rainy spring we're having. It rained so much in April—well, you know what they say, April showers bring May flowers—but it's the middle of May and it's still raining and the poor flowers are drowning, so enough already. And it was such a wet winter, besides. So much snow we had. And ice. I don't mind the snow so much, but the ice storms are really the worst. Your father even stayed home one day, the driving was so terrible, and you know how bad it has to be before he'll miss a minute at work. God forbid some nut should be out in such miserable weather to pick up his dry cleaning and find the shop closed. And now this rain. They say it's supposed to stop tomorrow, but what do they know? Bunch of dummies, those weathermen, they're always wrong. How you can keep your job and be wrong ninety-nine percent of the time is beyond me…"

As my mother rambles on, barely pausing for breath, I feel myself careening toward the altered state I always drift into when I speak to her on the phone. Or rather when she speaks to me. During these conversations I don't say much. I slump down on the sofa, cradle the receiver between my neck and shoulder, and enter some sort of fugue state. Sometimes, like now, I study the ends of my hair, searching the dark strands for split ends, a habit I gave up as a teenager. A habit I *thought* I gave up as a teenager. I sigh a lot. My mother doesn't notice.

As she talks on and on, I picture my mother sitting in one of the two matching forest green recliners in the living room, the cordless phone in one hand, her cigarette in the other. On the end table beside her there is a cup of coffee gone cold. At her feet is a pile of magazines; on her lap are a pack of playing cards and the remote control for the TV. She is wearing a blue velour bathrobe and matching slippers even though it is the middle of the day. The window shades of the room are pulled down, the burglar alarm is activated.

Even two hundred fifty miles away, I can barely breathe.

Eventually my mother ends her filibuster on the weather and asks, in a cutesy voice, "So how's by you? What's new like this?"

"Nothing," I reply automatically. It's the same one-word response I've given to this question for more than thirty years now, ever since I left home for college, my ticket out.

"Nothing?" my mother repeats, a hint of hurt in her voice. I'm sure she knows that something must be new in my life; after all we haven't spoken since the middle of January. "Are you still teaching?" she asks.

"Yes," I tell her for the hundredth time. I've been a tenured professor for over a decade now, but my mother always thinks I'm on the brink of being fired. "In fact, I proposed a new course for next year and it looks like it's going to be approved. It's called—"

"Did I tell you Selma Appelbaum's youngest daughter finally got married?" My mother interrupts me, proving what I knew all along: she couldn't care less about my academic career, she was just making polite conversation. "Last weekend, the wedding was. You remember Karen."

"No, I don't."

"Yes, you do."

"No, I don't."

"You do, Lydia. Think for a minute. They lived right around the corner from us, Karen and her sister Sharon, remember? She was the skinny one, Karen—who would ever dream it would take her so long to find a husband? For a while her parents thought maybe she'd turn out, you know…like you. But thank God, last year she finally met someone."

They thought maybe she'd turn out like you: a happy, healthy lesbian living with the woman of her dreams in Paradise. She should be so lucky, I think, as my mother drones on.

"They went all-out for the wedding, over three hundred people were there, can you imagine? Her father probably had to mortgage his teeth for her dress alone, but no matter what he paid, it was worth it, she looked gorgeous. She always had a lovely figure, Karen did, not like her sister Sharon, who could still stand to lose a few pounds. You remember Sharon."

"No, I don't."

"Sure you do. Who could forget Sharon and Karen? Well anyway, the wedding was very unusual, the color scheme was bright fire engine red, I couldn't get over it, whoever heard of such a thing? The groom's mother, who was no Slenderella, believe me, looked like an overgrown tomato and…"

While my mother proceeds to trash every member of the bridal party as though she were auditioning to be Joan Rivers' co-host on *Fashion Police* the morning after the Oscars, I can't help but wonder what she would say about the outfits Allie and I wore at our wedding, which took place fourteen years ago and to which my mother was not invited. Allie, with her short sharp hair slicked back and her dark eyes shining with joy, looked positively dashing in an off-white satin shirt with wide Spanish sleeves tucked into black tuxedo pants complemented by brand new spiffy patent leather shoes. And I felt quite glamorous standing beside her with my dark curly hair piled on top of my head, wearing a cream-colored suit with a fitted jacket, knee-length pencil skirt, and matching pumps with ankle straps and four-inch heels that made me almost, but not quite tall enough to look my betrothed in the eye. Allie and I tied the knot on our second anniversary, and though the state of Maine refused to grant us our civil rights and call our union a marriage, I refused to call the event anything other than a wedding. For my money—and we spent plenty on the reception hall, the food, the cake, the flowers, the rings, and the deejay—it was a wedding like any other, legal status be damned. I knew that Sunday in September would be the happiest day of my life and though Allie tried, I could not be convinced to invite anyone who would be one iota less than overjoyed to be in attendance. And just as I knew without the slightest doubt that I wanted to become Allie's unlawfully wedded wife and spend the rest of my days, not to mention my nights with her, I was equally certain that a public declaration of our love and devotion would not be met with a rousing "Mazel tov!" from my father and mother or any other member of my family.

It's not that they don't like Allie. My parents like her just fine. Actually I'm pretty sure they like her better than me. It's that to this day, they have not gotten comfortable with the fact that they have a lesbian for a daughter. I keep thinking they're getting better, but then something happens. The last time Allie and I visited my parents was about a year ago, and things were going along relatively well—in other words, nothing disastrous had occurred—until we made the mistake of accompanying my father to the grocery store to pick up the cheesecake my mother had ordered to serve that evening for dessert. While waiting on the bakery line, we ran into a young family that had just moved into the neighborhood. My father put his arm around my shoulder, saying, "This is my daughter, Lydia," and then introduced me to the husband, wife, and two young children who were strapped inside their double stroller happily munching away on sugar cookies shaped like dinosaurs. Then there was an awkward pause, and just as I was about to introduce Allie, my father stepped in and did the honors. "And that's her roommate," he said, gesturing toward Allie and shocking us both. And though I explained the error of his ways several times, he refused to acknowledge that he'd done anything wrong. So I in turn refused to speak to him for the rest of the afternoon.

"Anyway, it was a very lovely evening," my mother says now, wrapping up her report of the Appelbaum affair and bringing me back to the present. "Why it took so long for a pretty girl like Karen to find a man to marry, I couldn't tell you, but all right, as they say, all's well that ends well. She's not forty yet so if they hurry things along, they still might be able to have a child, or I guess they could always adopt, plenty of people do. Aaron seems like a very nice guy—oh, I forgot to tell you, that's the best part: the groom's name is Aaron, can you believe that, Karen and Aaron? I'm telling you, everybody's already joking they should have a boy and name him Darren. And then someone said—oh, wait. Hold on a minute, Lydia. I have another call."

My mother's voice disappears and I shut my eyes, exhausted. I feel like I could sleep for days. My breathing slows and I adjust Mishmosh to use him as a pillow. But before I drift off, my mother gets back on the line.

"It's the plumber. I've been waiting for him to call all afternoon. I'll speak to you later." My mother hangs up the phone, and I, who have been known to rant and rave for hours about the rudeness of call waiting, thank God for this brilliant invention that lets me off the hook.

❖

"IF YOU DON'T have anything nice to say, sit next to me," read the cocktail napkins stored on the third shelf of my mother's pantry next to an oversized box of pink Sweet'N Low packets. I suppose this would be funny if it weren't also true.

Once a year I make my annual pilgrimage to my parents' house. Allie comes with me, knowing that if she doesn't, I'll be that much more of a basket case when I return. She's a real trouper, my Allie. I'm sure she could name at least a thousand other things she'd rather be doing on the Sunday of Memorial Day weekend, other than driving four and a half hours to share a meal with my parents and then driving four and a half hours back. Especially since it's turning out to be such a lovely afternoon, sunny and breezy and perfect for digging in the garden, which Allie loves to do. But Allie doesn't complain. Instead, she steers the car around the post-winter potholes that have turned the streets of our neighborhood into an obstacle course and waits until we've merged onto the highway to give me a pep talk. "Remember, it's only a movie," she says, taking her eyes off the road for a split second to glance in my direction.

"Now showing: *Night of the Living Dead*." I move my hand in front of me as though I were outlining the title on a marquee and then reach down for my purse, which is parked next to my feet. For about the twenty-seventh time since Allie backed out of our driveway, I pull a compact out of my bag, flip it open, and stare at my reflection. My mother will scrutinize my appearance like she's looking into a mirror, and the less I give her to criticize, the better. I run my fingers through my unruly dark curls, which have been recently shaped and trimmed to just barely graze my shoulders, wipe an imaginary smudge of mascara off my cheek, and stare into my own eyes, which are light brown and flecked with gold, just like my mother's. There is an expression in them I rarely see. I look scared. Small. Vulnerable. Whenever I feel like this, I remind myself that I'm a strong, independent woman. A professor of Women's Studies who has been voted teacher of the year at Paradise College. Twice. A loving and beloved spouse. A good friend. A respected member of my community. None of that matters today. Today I am a frightened child who can't do anything right. Who looks wrong, acts wrong, *is* wrong.

All too soon our southbound car ride comes to an end and we turn the corner onto my parents' street and pull up to the curb in front of the neatly trimmed shrubs that stand guard in front of their split-level home.

"The credits are rolling," Allie whispers, giving my hand a squeeze as I reach up to ring my parents' doorbell.

"Hello, hello." My father opens the front door before I have a chance to push the buzzer. He looks so much older than he did last time I saw him, it takes a minute for my eyes to adjust, as if I've just stepped out of a very dark room directly into sunlight. The lines creasing my father's forehead are deeper than I remember, and his cheeks are more sunken in than they were a year ago. My father has always been tall and slender, unlike the women of the family, including me, who tend to all be under five feet tall and "pleasingly plump." And he has always been a snappy dresser. After all, as the owner of a chain of dry-cleaning and tailoring shops, it's part of his job to look his best. But today the royal blue shirt and gray pants he is wearing seem empty, like they are fluttering off a hanger he is handing over the counter to a customer instead of covering his skin and bones.

"Doris, c'mon. Lydia and Allie are here," my father calls upstairs. The three of us crowd the front hallway waiting for my mother to appear.

"I'm coming, I'm coming." My mother's disembodied voice precedes her down the stairs. A minute later her descent is announced by a creak: the dreaded third step from the top that always gave me away on weekend nights when I snuck into the house after midnight. As a teenager, I thought of it as the third rail, because stepping on it and inciting my father's wrath was as good as committing suicide.

"Hi, Lydia." My mother makes her entrance waving the lit cigarette wedged between the second and third finger of her right hand like Bette Davis in an old black-and-white 1940s movie. She moves in close to kiss the air next to my cheek, then turns her head to take a puff and exhale without blowing smoke in my face, which she knows would only start a fight. "Hello, Allie," my mother says, barely glancing at my butch, who got a new haircut especially for this occasion and spent close to an hour picking out and ironing the perfect outfit, a black button-down short-sleeved shirt tucked into tan khakis. My attire, on the other hand, is examined within an inch of its life as my mother looks me up, down, and back up again, until I feel like I am something to buy that she doesn't think is worth the price. I am wearing a plain black skirt and a white cotton summer sweater with lace around the collar and cuffs. Nothing she could possibly criticize.

"Have you lost weight?" my mother finally asks as she stubs out her cigarette in a porcelain ashtray shaped like an upturned hand resting on a little table by the front door. This is her usual greeting and is somewhat of a trick question. If I had lost weight, which I haven't—nor do I want to—my mother would shower me with praise. Since I am still a perfect size fourteen, just as I was last time I visited my parents, my mother's question is her way of voicing her disappointment without seeming rude. There is no good way to answer this question. If I lie and say yes, my mother will mutter, "Hmmm." Translation: *Are you sure? You don't look any thinner.* If I tell the truth and answer, "No," my mother will say, "Too bad," and nail me with one of her withering looks of disapproval. Rather than fall into either of these traps, I plead the fifth and say nothing.

"Vamos. Vamos." My father interrupts the awkward silence that has descended like a cloud and gestures for us to get going. Whenever my father is around Allie, he feels compelled to dredge up a word or two from the Introduction to Spanish class he took in high school fifty-seven years ago as a nod to her Puerto Rican heritage. He removes my mother's spring jacket from the hall closet and waves it in front of her. *"Toro, toro,"* he sings out as if my mother is a bull. My mother turns around, backs up, and slides her arms inside the sleeves. She looks shorter than I remember, and is dressed in a black pantsuit with a long jacket that she probably thinks hides her hips and gives her a slender appearance. But all it really does is make her look like she's going to a funeral.

"Where are we off to?" I ask my father as we step outside and my mother lights a fresh cigarette.

"How do you like my Caddy?" he replies, gesturing toward the gleaming black sedan parked in the driveway. My father, who grew up so poor he never thought he'd be able to afford a bicycle, let alone a car, takes great pride in trading up for the newest model every year. He explains all the car's special features to Allie and me in great detail, like a salesman on his first day at the job, while my mother finishes her cigarette, tosses it on the ground, and grinds it out underfoot. Only after we all duck inside the car and buckle up, my parents in the front seat and Allie and I, like two overgrown children, banished to the back, does my father answer my question. "We're going to Monticello's for an early dinner," he informs me as he looks over his shoulder to back out of the driveway. "Jack and Crystal are meeting us there."

Allie squeezes my shoulders, which are now hunched up around my ears; she knows I am making a supreme and heroic effort not to

groan out loud. I haven't seen my cousin Jack in ages. For good reason.
My cousin Jack is the only child of my mother's twin sister Beatrice,
who died of complications following a car crash many years ago when
Jack and I were both sixteen. My mother and her sister were the kind
of twins who did everything together. They wore matching outfits all
through their childhood, they went out on double dates, and they both
married good-looking grooms at a double wedding (my uncle Benny
resembled Marlon Brando in his younger years; my father has aged
handsomely and looks a bit like Gregory Peck). My mother and her
sister even got pregnant at around the same time. There's only one thing
the twins did differently, according to family lore: my mother married
a *mensch* and my aunt Beatrice married a *schmuck*.

From the beginning my uncle Benny was a drinker and a gambler,
not to mention a womanizer. My aunt Beatrice lay in a coma for months
after the accident and he didn't even have the decency to wait until
she actually stopped breathing before running off with another woman
practically half her age. Of course Jack came to live with us when his
mother died, so overnight he became the son my parents always wanted
and the sibling I'm glad I never had. A sibling who called me "fatso"
and "frizz bomb" and thought there was nothing funnier in the world
than blowing into the crook of his arm to make farting noises whenever
I walked by. A sibling who monopolized our only television by sitting
in front of it every night and turning the channel knob until he found a
football, baseball, basketball, or hockey game to watch. A sibling who
always had first dibs on my father's car over the weekend. A sibling my
mother adored and doted on, cooking his favorite meals, giving him
money to buy comic books and records whenever he wanted, ignoring
how messy his room was, the floor strewn with dirty clothes, candy
bar wrappers, soda cans, and album sleeves. And it did me no good to
complain about Jack's behavior or privileges. "Jack's going through a
hard time," my mother reminded me every other minute. "It wouldn't
kill you to think about someone other than yourself for a change and be
a little nicer to him once in a while."

Jack and I overlapped in my parents' house for two miserable
years—our junior and senior years of high school—and then I left for
college and he stayed. And stayed. Jack made one attempt at college
life, going to some big university out west somewhere, but he either
dropped out or got thrown out—no one's quite sure which—halfway

through his first semester. And so Jack flew back to the Pinkowitz nest and lived with my mother and father until he was thirty. Rent-free, I might add, even though my parents made me pay room and board for the lousy—and I do mean *lousy*—three months I lived with them the summer after I graduated from college. When I pointed out how unfair that was, my mother reminded me that life wasn't fair and that the very least she could do was put a roof over her poor motherless nephew's head and put some food into his poor motherless mouth. I think of Jack as my "brousin," a cross between brother and cousin, much like brunch is a cross between breakfast and lunch. Except brunch is something to linger over and enjoy; being in Jack's company is something to get over and done with as quickly as possible. Jack hasn't changed much since his brief college career; he still likes to "party," as he puts it. A lot. As does his trophy wife Crystal, who is a dozen years younger than he is, or possibly more since she refuses to divulge her exact age. The last time I saw the two of them was a year and a half ago at their daughter Bethany's bat mitzvah.

Jack is richer than God, though I can never figure out what he actually does for a living. When asked, all he'll say is that he's in "the industry," meaning he works in show biz. Jack and Crystal own a very expensive suburban house forty minutes away from my parents, a swanky apartment on Central Park West, and a summer home in the Hamptons, right on the water. All bought without the benefit of an undergraduate degree, let alone a doctorate, as Jack likes to remind me. Though Jack is hardly religious. As I recall he got kicked out of Hebrew school for coming to Shabbat services several weeks in a row wearing a T-shirt that said "Moses was a basket case." When the time came for his only daughter to be called to the Torah, Jack did not hesitate to pull out all the stops.

Crystal and Jack sent out the invitations to Bethany's bat mitzvah in March, a good six months before the big event. I remember the day ours came. Allie had Mishmosh on her lap in a pillowcase with his hind legs sticking out so I could trim his back toenails, something he hates for me to do. The doorbell rang, startling Mishmosh, who leapt six feet in the air, scratching both of us in the process before dashing under the bed, where he stayed for several hours.

I opened the door, already annoyed at whoever had rung the bell, to see a man standing before me in a white tuxedo. White jacket and tails, white pants, white shirt, white cummerbund, white shoes, white tie. Behind him, parked on the street in front of our tiny humble home, was a long white limousine.

"Allie, get out here. Quick," I called over my shoulder.

"Wait a minute. I'm bleeding," she called back.

"I don't care. You have to see this." I didn't know why this gentleman was at our front door—had Allie entered some type of sweepstakes?—but I knew this was a sight I'd probably never see again in my lifetime, and I wanted Allie to see it, too.

"Miss Lydia Pinkowitz?" the man asked.

"Ms.," I replied.

"What the—?" Allie came up behind me, pressing a towel against her gouged thigh.

The man in white brought a round silver tray out from behind his back and lifted its cover with a flourish. "My compliments," he said with a little bow.

On the tray was an ivory-colored envelope. The names *Lydia Pinkowitz* and *Alicia Taraza* were written upon it in a delicate, elegant hand.

"It's too beautiful to open," I said, my voice a reverent whisper. The man bowed again and retreated to his vehicle. "You do it," I said to Allie as the limo pulled away.

We went back into the house and Allie slit open the envelope carefully, using a wooden letter opener that had a peacock carved on its handle. "Oh no," she said. "You're not going to be happy."

And I wasn't. The card Allie pulled out of the envelope informed us that Jack and Crystal Gutman had invited us to their daughter Bethany Joy's bat mitzvah. And with this much advance notice, it was pretty hard to think of an excuse that would get us out of it. The reception was a huge affair held in Scarsdale in the backyard of some movie mogul that Jack knew, under a tent large enough to shelter a three-ring circus. Bethany was the star of the show, and she had prepared for the part by spending hours at a nearby spa where experts had given her a full body seaweed scrub along with a manicure, a pedicure, and a makeover, and done her hair up in such an intricate style, she told me she had to sleep sitting up the night before so she wouldn't ruin it. Everyone was dressed in their glittery sequined best, and there were so many people there, I hoped Allie and I would simply blend into the crowd and not be noticed. But no such luck. The minute we arrived, Jack rushed over to us, slung his arm around my shoulder as if we were the most intimate of friends, and gave me a sloppy wet kiss on the cheek. Then he pulled me away from Allie to ask in a hushed voice if I wanted to "party" with him and some members of the band. When I politely declined his offer, Jack blew up. "This is the thanks I get for waiting around all afternoon for you to finally show?" he yelled loud enough to make several people turn their heads in our direction. "Lydia, you are the most ungrateful person I have ever met." And before I had a chance to respond, he threw both hands up in the air and without another word to Allie or me, stomped away in disgust.

So I am polite but distant when I greet Jack and Crystal at the restaurant. Partly because I am not thrilled to see them, and partly because I have already started leaving my body in order to get through the evening. No one says much as we stand around the parking lot waiting for my mother to finish smoking the cigarette she lit the moment she stepped out of the car. When she is done, we enter the restaurant single file with my father leading the way. He stops in front of a small wooden podium and announces with great authority to the maître d' standing there, "Max Pinkowitz, table for six." The gentleman scans his list, checks something off, and immediately takes us to a table in the middle of the room, but before Allie can sit down, I clutch her arm to stop her.

"What's the matter?" she asks.

"You'll see," I say, and sure enough, just as I expected, my mother tells the maître d' that she doesn't like the table he's shown us. When asked what's wrong with it, she shakes her head as if the answer should be obvious and says, "Just bring me to the table you were saving in case I didn't like this one."

Much to my amazement, this ploy always works, and tonight is no exception. Without losing his composure, the maître d' complies and we move *en masse* to a better spot: a quiet, round table tucked into a cozy corner. Everyone looks to my mother for approval, and after a minute she says, "It's all right," in a voice that conveys it isn't, but she supposes it's the best they can do.

A shell of myself sits down at the table between Allie and Jack, who is wearing jeans and a T-shirt under his open dinner jacket that reads "Red Sox Suck" in defiance of the restaurant's dress code and the fact that Allie is a rabid Red Sox fan. Jack has a short, squat, neckless wrestler's body and though he's never played a sport in his life, he likes to dress like he's just come from the gym. I'm surprised he's not wearing sweatpants. He has quite a collection of T-shirts; I remember the one he wore to the reception following his daughter's bat mitzvah that read, "Who is this teenager that keeps following me around and calling me Dad?" Crystal, who sits on Jack's other side, was an aspiring actress and model before she married my cousin (Jack likes to boast that he turned her from a model into a model wife) and she still likes to dress as if she is about to be discovered by a talent scout and whisked away to Hollywood. Tonight she is wearing a sleeveless hot pink dress that ends at least a foot above her bony knees with shoes, purse, and earrings the size and shape of donuts to match. Her jet black hair is short and sculpted into dozens of stiff spikes; she looks like a porcupine that fell into a vat of India ink. To her left is my father. My mother sits between my father and Allie. I glance around our happy little circle once and then busy myself with unfolding my napkin and draping it over my lap.

Soon our server, an extremely handsome young man with light blue eyes and deep dimples in his cheeks, arrives to get this party going. "My name is Sebastian and I'll be taking care of you this evening," he says, putting a basket of bread in the middle of the table. Then the poor fellow, who cannot possibly know what lies in store for him this evening, takes a step back, flips open his order pad, and starts reciting the daily specials. Crystal, who is already chatting on her cell phone with someone, interrupts his mouthwatering description of a wild mushroom and pumpkin risotto entrée to ask about the cream of asparagus soup.

"Oh boy, here she goes," Jack mutters in a stage whisper, throwing his hands up in the air as if to say, *What can I do?*

"Is it made with heavy cream, light cream, half-and-half, or milk?" she asks.

"I have no idea," Sebastian informs Crystal.

"Well, find out," she says, and then throws Jack a look. "What?" she asks, her voice sharp with annoyance. "It makes a big difference in the calories."

"Whatever," says my cousin. His wife goes back to her phone call as Sebastian leaves in a huff. In a minute he returns and lets us all know that the soup is made with heavy cream.

"Not worth the calories. Which is just as well because that means I can have an entrée," Crystal says, staring pointedly in my direction to let me know that if only I followed her fine example, someday I could look anorexic, too.

"Would you care for something to drink?" Sebastian addresses Crystal, his voice a bit curt but still this side of polite.

"I'll have some red wine," Crystal says. "Something very dry."

"Shall I bring a bottle for the table?" Sebastian asks.

"No," Crystal answers. "Just bring a bottle for me."

Crystal goes back to her phone call as the rest of us order drinks and appetizers: shrimp cocktails, goat cheese and walnut salads, and bowls of the very fattening cream of asparagus soup. When Sebastian takes our entrée orders, Crystal, who is finally off the phone, punches my father on the shoulder. "You're paying, right, Uncle Max?" she asks. "Then the hell with my diet. I'll have the lobster."

Sebastian makes his escape and my mother dives into the bread basket. She chews with her mouth open, looking around the table. "Say something," Allie whispers to me, as if I had a clue as to how to get the conversation rolling.

"So, Jack," I say, mostly to placate Allie. "Have you bought a home in the Hollywood Hills yet?"

Jack tilts his head at me puzzled, as if I'd just asked him to buy Allie and me a home in the Hollywood Hills. "Now why would I want to do that, Lydia?" he asks in a mocking tone that more than implies that he thinks I have a huge ball of cotton stuffed inside my skull instead of a functioning brain.

"Because you work in the industry?" My voice goes up at the end of my sentence like an insecure teenager who turns everything she says into a question.

"Lydia, New York City is the capital of the world," Jack tells me as though he were explaining to a child that the earth isn't flat. "I haven't been to L.A. in years. And anyway, just because you're bisexual doesn't mean I have to be bi-coastal."

Like that makes any sense. I know Jack makes these ridiculous comments just to see if he still has the ability to annoy the hell out of me, and the last thing I should do is give him the satisfaction of knowing that he hasn't lost the knack. But I am as incapable of keeping my mouth shut as he is. "Jack, I am not bisexual," I inform him for the ten millionth time.

"Oh, and by the way, how's Tommy?" Jack asks. "You know, your high school *boyfriend*?"

"Oh, he was such a nice boy," my mother chimes in. "How is he? Do you ever hear from him?"

I shoot Allie a look that says *this is all your fault* before I address my cousin. "Jack," I say, as if his very name leaves a bitter taste in my mouth. "Thomas and I dated for about ten minutes tops, plus, as I've already told you at least a hundred times, he came out a year before I did. He and his boyfriend just had a civil union ceremony in Vermont and are just about to adopt a baby and—"

"Can I have the butter please?" my mother asks a little too loudly. Clearly she has had enough of this conversation. Jack passes her a dish full of butter pats shaped like seashells and shakes his head at me like he doesn't believe this cockamamie story about Thomas. It is completely beyond Jack's capabilities to accept the fact that a woman can be perfectly happy without a man. I make a mental note to myself to dust off my old T-shirt that reads "A woman without a man is like a fish without a bicycle" and give it to him for his next birthday.

"Jack." My mother finishes buttering her bread and pops it into her mouth as she watches the server refill my father's water glass. "I can't believe your hair."

As my mother swallows, we all swivel our heads in Jack's direction. I know what's coming next. As a homage to the adolescence he wishes he never had to leave behind, Jack wears his long straight hair in a stringy ponytail that drips down his back all the way to the belt loops of his scruffy jeans. Jack's hair used to be dark as chocolate syrup; now it's the color of milk gone sour. Jack's ponytail drove his own mother crazy for many years and now my mother, as a way to honor her dead twin sister, feels obligated to nag Jack about his hair every chance she gets.

"All that long white hair." My mother shakes her head. "I don't know where you get that from. It doesn't run in our family. It must come from your father's side. My sister, may she rest in peace, never had gray hair. I don't have any gray hair." My mother pats her wavy coif, which we all know she's been dying for at least a quarter of a century. "And look at my daughter." My mother points across the table with another slice of bread she's fished out of the basket. "She doesn't have any gray hair either."

Allie and I exchange glances. I'm forty-eight years old. Of course I have gray hair. Not that you'd ever know, thanks to my fabulous hairdresser.

My mother registers the look that passes between Allie and me—I never could pull anything over on her—and raises one finger, its nail shiny and red, aloft in triumph. "Aha!" she crows. "You *do* dye your hair. Whatever happened to 'I'm never going to dye my hair. Gray hair is natural.'" My mother imitates the holier-than-thou tone of voice I used to argue this point with her when I was a fourteen-year-old born-again feminist. I realize she has been waiting thirty-four years to hurl these words at me. No wonder she didn't start in with Jack about cutting off his ponytail. My mother and father socialize with Jack and Crystal all the time, which means my mother has ample opportunity to pick on Jack. Since she rarely sees me, I am her chosen target for the evening.

Before I can respond, not that I plan to, Sebastian returns with our appetizers. Crystal tells him she doesn't like her wine, even though she's drained more than half her glass.

"It's not very dry. And besides, I'd rather have white," she says, shrugging off Sebastian's glare and Jack's groan. "Hey, lighten up, people. It's a woman's prerogative to change her mind."

Sebastian bristles visibly, snatches Crystal's wineglass off the table, and leaves without a word. One second later, Crystal's cell phone blares out the opening notes of Abba's "Dancing Queen" and she lifts it to her ear and scurries away.

"Who keeps calling?" I ask Jack.

"How should I know?" he answers. "Ask Crystal." Which I don't bother doing when she returns ten minutes later, just as our food arrives.

As in many posh New York restaurants, the dishes are enormous. Sebastian removes our bread plates to make room for our entrées. He sets a dish practically big enough to sit upon in front of each one of us before departing. Immediately sounds of clattering silverware fill the silence among us. We are all grateful for something to do, except for Crystal, who does not touch her lobster.

"Crystal, c'mon, eat something," Jack coaxes her with his mouth full. Crystal responds by downing the wine that's left in her glass in one long gulp.

Jack persists though he knows it is futile; his wife never eats in public. "Crystal," he says. "When was the last time you ate?"

"Passover," she snaps at him, licking a drop of wine off her upper lip.

"Why did the waiter take away my bread?" My mother, mouth full of salmon, has just noticed her bread plate is missing. Or she is sick of Crystal being the center of attention. Or both.

No one responds to her question, however, and just at that moment, Sebastian reappears. "How is everything?" he inquires politely.

"Very, very good," says my father, who likes to make everyone happy, but my mother does not share his attitude or his opinion.

"Why did you take away my bread?" my mother asks in a belligerent tone.

Sebastian looks at her, baffled. "If you want more bread, I'd be happy to bring you more bread," he finally says. "All you have to do is ask."

"I don't want *new* bread." My mother speaks to Sebastian slowly, as if he has trouble understanding English. "That's not the point. I was still eating my *old* bread. You shouldn't have taken away my plate until I was finished with it."

"Would you like me to go find your old bread?" Sebastian asks in a sincere tone, as if this really were an option. "Would that make you happy?" I am truly impressed with the way he keeps even a hint of sarcasm or nastiness out of his voice.

My mother, not knowing what to make of this, glares at him, and Sebastian, who clearly isn't easily intimidated, glares right back. "Oh, never mind," she finally says, turning away and dismissing him with a wave of her hand. But then she turns back and adds, "What do you know anyway? You're young yet. Clueless. But don't worry, darling. You'll learn," she says, pointing a finger at him, her voice more ominous than comforting.

Allie taps my leg under the table. "Stay with me," she whispers, sensing I am far away. At this point I am hovering somewhere up near the ceiling, watching the show going on beneath me. If I could, I'd burst through the roof of the building and sail away like a red balloon come loose from a child's fist. I imagine myself a red dot getting smaller and smaller, then disappearing altogether. But my mother's harsh voice brings me back down to earth.

"She doesn't need more wine." My mother spreads the flat of her hand over the top of Crystal's glass.

"You're right," Crystal tells my mother sweetly. "I'll have a martini instead," she barks at Sebastian. "With extra olives."

Sebastian takes his leave again. I consider running after him. To apologize for my family. And to reassure him that he'll get a big tip. (My father is very generous in that department.) But I am glued to my seat and my mouth is taped shut. Paralyzed. Mute. Trapped.

"You know, Lydia," Crystal says, addressing me for the first time all evening. "The reason I married your cousin is because on our first date he showed me a picture of his handsome father and I thought as he got older he'd start to resemble him." Crystal pauses and an image of Jack's father, my uncle Benny, rises in my mind. I haven't seen him since I was a teenager, but still, I distinctly remember his strong, muscular build and chiseled, brooding face.

"It's a shame," Crystal goes on, "that good looks always skip a generation." She takes a sip of the drink Sebastian has just plunked down in front of her. "Just my luck. Instead of turning out like his sexy father, he's starting to look more and more like pudgy cousin Lydia every day." She reaches over and pinches Jack's flabby cheek.

"Crystal." Allie half rises out her seat and I'm half afraid, half hoping she'll deck her. "That's a terribly cruel thing to say."

"It isn't cruel," says Crystal matter-of-factly, "if it's true."

Just when I think things can't get any worse, the evening's entertainment begins. Middle Eastern music drifts through the room like smoke and out of nowhere, a belly dancer appears. She is scantily clad in a silver bikini top and sheer, low-slung harem pants to match. Her outfit is complete with three-inch silver heels, which even I, in my semi-comatose state, can't help but notice and have to admit are an interesting touch.

My father and Jack rotate in their seats to watch the dancer gyrate around the room. Crystal places two fingers into her mouth and whistles loudly, like she's calling over a hot dog vendor in a ballpark. "Over here, over here," she yells, beckoning the woman toward us with both hands and pointing to my father. Jack shakes his head and rolls his eyes as the woman shimmies closer to our table. *This we need like a hole in the head,* I think, which is something my mother would say if she wasn't chomping on a string bean she's snatched off my father's plate. But my mother doesn't need words in order to be understood. As the belly dancer nears us, my mother shoots her the look that Jack and I used to call her Evil Eye. It's a look that speaks volumes. A look full of fury and disgust. "Don't you dare come one step closer," the Evil Eye says. "You should be ashamed of yourself. Get out of my sight. I'm warning you…" It's a look that was directed at me during my childhood many, many times.

The dancer spins on her silver heels, and leading with her rippling belly, slithers off in another direction. I watch her go, wishing I could follow.

Crystal slumps back in her seat and all is quiet for a blissful moment. Then my mother speaks. "Crystal," she says in a seemingly innocent voice. "How's my favorite great-niece?" My mother is being sarcastic, since Bethany is my parents' only great-niece, but I doubt that Crystal in her inebriated state understands that.

"Why don't we call her and see?" Crystal reaches for her phone, but Jack grabs her hand to stop her. "She's fine," he says quickly. A little too quickly.

"Why didn't she come have dinner with us?" my mother asks.

"She had plans." Jack shrugs. "You know how teenagers are. The last people on earth she'd want to spend any time with are her own two parents."

"Is she behaving herself these days? Or is she still cutting school?" My mother shakes her head. "You know, she probably wouldn't get into so much trouble if you didn't spoil her the way you do." My mother considers herself an expert on parenting, since after all, she raised me. "The latest computer, a cell phone, her own charge cards…you give her everything she wants. That's no good for a child."

"Excusez-moi." Crystal grabs her purse and leaves the table in a flash of pink, swaying her hips back and forth as if she is still at a fashion show waltzing down a runway. Jack scrapes back his chair and trots after her.

My mother watches them go, her bottom lip curled in disapproval. "They've always spoiled Bethany rotten," she says. "Ever since that child was a baby." I can't even pretend to be interested in this conversation, which I've heard many times before, but my mother doesn't care. Allie and I, along with my father, are her captive audience. "You know Jack works ten, twelve hours a day and Crystal is never home either. I don't know what she's so busy with besides getting her hair done and going to her exercise classes, but I'm telling you, it isn't right. A mother should be home with her child. Otherwise the child doesn't even know who her parents are."

Out of the corner of my eye, I see my father ogling the belly dancer who is dangling a cluster of grapes in front of a lucky man seated at a nearby table.

"Crystal would wait until Jack got home at six or seven o'clock or even eight o'clock at night and then they'd all sit down to supper, though you could hardly call it that. Frozen pizza, TV dinners, take-out from a deli, sometimes just cereal—you know Crystal is so concerned about her figure she hardly eats, let alone cooks—and then they'd let Bethany stay up for hours, until nine, ten, eleven o'clock, even when she was just a baby. Of course they hadn't seen her all day, so you could hardly blame them. But still, it isn't right." My mother picks up her fork and taps it against the side of her plate. Ever since smoking inside restaurants became illegal in the state of New York, she's been at a loss as to what to do with her hands after she's finished eating. "My daughter was in bed at seven o'clock every night," my mother informs Allie.

"That would be yours truly," I explain, just in case Allie has gone brain dead and doesn't know this.

My mother ignores me. "I closed the door to her room every night exactly at seven o'clock because by that time I'd had enough. And then I wouldn't open her door again until seven o'clock the next morning. I thought that was fair: twelve hours for her and twelve hours for me. I figured what's the worst that could happen?" My mother shrugs. "She couldn't kill herself there all alone in her room. In the morning I'd open the door and she'd be fine. Crystal would never listen to me when Bethany was young. If she had, she wouldn't be getting into so much trouble now. Girls are very hard to raise, believe me, I know. Much harder than boys. They say it's the hormones, but that's just B.S., pardon my French. There's no one meaner, nastier, or more self-centered than a teenage girl. That one wouldn't lift a finger to help me," my mother says, lifting her own finger to point at me. "If I asked her to wash out a plate, a cup, God forbid she should rinse off a spoon, you'd think I was

LESLÉA NEWMAN

asking her to scrub the floors on her hands and knees with a toothbrush, the way she carried on. 'You're ruining my life!'" my mother yelps in a high-pitched voice, glaring in my direction. "And I'll tell you another thing." She leans closer to Allie and puts her hand on her arm. "You know that old saying, spare the rod and spoil the child? It wouldn't be so terrible if Jack hit Bethany once in a while either. Even big as she is. My husband wasn't afraid to give my daughter a good *zetz* when she deserved it..."

"That would be me," I mumble again as my mother balls up her fists and punches the air.

"...and it didn't hurt her one bit." My mother sits back, satisfied. I can feel Allie looking at me, not knowing what on earth to say. But I can't help her out here. I am too busy staring at the lump of cold mashed potatoes on my plate. Believe it or not, the food is shaped exactly like Abraham Lincoln's head. For some reason this inspires me to try and remember the words of the Gettysburg Address: *Four score and seven years ago our fathers brought forth on this continent a new nation, conceived in liberty and dedicated to the proposition that all men are created equal...*

I am thoroughly impressed with myself until I remember that the text of the Gettysburg Address was given as a typing test every year in high school, and in fact my fingers are pounding out the letters now as if the table we are sitting at has a keyboard on top of it.

"Look at her, she still leaves half her dinner over." My mother continues talking about me as though I am not here. "You have to teach your children that money doesn't grow on trees. And not only that, it's a sin to waste good food. She was such a picky eater, that one, especially breakfast, that was the worst. You'd think I was torturing her, with the fuss she made. I'll tell you, when she was little I made her sit at the kitchen table and eat everything on her plate. I didn't care how long it took. I didn't care how cold it got. I didn't care if she put it in her mouth and spit it out, I made her put it in again..."

"Would you care for some coffee or dessert?" Sebastian, who is clearly a glutton for punishment, is back at our table. And now even if I'd wanted dessert, my mother's rehashing of my childhood has completely taken away my appetite.

"I'll have coffee," my mother says. "And wrap that up." She points to the untouched lobster on Crystal's plate. "I'll have that for lunch tomorrow. I'll make a salad. And throw in those potatoes, too."

"Ooh, good idea, coffee," says my father. "And I'll have a little piece of cheesecake."

"No you won't," my mother informs him. "First of all, there's no such thing as a *little* piece of cheesecake. And second of all, you don't need it."

"All right, Doris," my father sighs. He knows what my mother is really saying: if she can't have a piece of cheesecake because she's supposed to be watching her weight, she'll be damned if anyone else at the table will enjoy a slice of her favorite dessert.

"I'll have Mexican coffee. With an extra shot of tequila." Crystal and Jack are back, dashing my hopes that they'd snuck out the back door and left for the evening. Jack orders a glass of Jack Daniel's, which he jokingly refers to as his namesake; Allie and I pass.

Sebastian disappears and then returns with drinks for Crystal and Jack, and a large carafe of coffee for my parents. He pours them each a cup and then, eager to be done with us, leaves the large silver carafe on the table. I watch my mother and father sprinkle pink packets of Sweet'N Low and pour cream into their coffee cups as conversation comes to a complete halt. Which frankly is fine with me. But not fine with my mother.

"You have something on your sleeve," she says to my father.

"Where?"

"By your elbow."

My father lifts his arm and twists it, attempting to see what my mother is talking about. "Where, Doris? I don't see anything."

"It's on your other elbow. Here." My mother dips her napkin into her water glass and starts wiping my father's sleeve.

"Doris, don't rub it! I've told you a million times, dab, don't rub." My father snatches his arm away from her. "I'll take care of it when we get home. Please."

My mother shrugs and places her napkin back on her lap. "Pardon me for living. I was only trying to help."

"That type of help only makes things worse." My father pulls at his sleeve to examine it, then lowers his arm and picks up his coffee cup. He empties it in one loud slurp, pours a second cup for himself, and swallows that in one gulp as well before filling up his cup again for the third time.

"I'll have more coffee, please." My mother's tone is surprisingly pleasant as she addresses my father, a hundred times more pleasant than it's been all evening. She lifts her porcelain coffee cup from its saucer and waves it toward him like a white flag of surrender.

"Of course, Madame." My father often reminds my mother that you get more flies with honey than vinegar (to which my mother always responds, "Who wants flies?") and I can tell he is pleased that she has decided to change her tune and be nice to him for the rest of the evening. He slugs down his third cup of coffee and then lifts the carafe and turns it upside down over my mother's cup. Nothing comes out. "It's empty," my father announces.

"Of course it's empty," my mother says, suddenly furious. "You had to drink all the coffee," she snarls at him, punctuating her words with a loud clink as she places her cup back on its saucer. "You couldn't leave some for me. Not one lousy drop."

"Grrr." My father puts the carafe down, balls up his fists, and starts jabbing the air. "Put 'em up, Doris. C'mon, put 'em up."

"Don't do that!" The feminist inside me who's been asleep this entire evening bursts out of my throat, startling everyone. "Violence against women is never funny," I announce. "Even as a joke."

"You see what I've had to put up with for all these years?" my mother asks, aligning herself with me for the first time in my entire life. Then she turns to my father. "I'm telling you," she says, shaking a finger at him. "Enough is enough."

This is an inside family joke. My mother is quoting an elderly friend of my parents who divorced her husband after being married to him for sixty-three years. When my mother asked her why she wanted out so late in the game, the woman simply replied, "Enough is enough."

"You can always come live with us, Uncle Max," Crystal says. "Right, Jack?"

Jack drains his glass. "Sure. Whatever."

"Over my dead body." My mother makes sure she has the last word. "Which might be sooner than you think. But never mind that. Just remember Max: even though I won't live forever, I *will* haunt you forever."

Sebastian takes this as his cue to deliver our check. My father looks it over, adding up the bill in his head. After he's done calculating, he glances up and for some reason catches Allie's eye. *"Mucho dinero,"* he says with a sigh.

Allie reaches for her wallet. "I have some *gelt*," she tells him.

My father's mouth drops open and I can't tell if he's feigning shock because a Yiddish word I taught Allie flew out of her mouth so easily, or because someone has actually offered to help him pay the bill. Then he laughs, waving away Allie's offer like it's a major annoyance, and slaps his American Express card down on the table. Crystal stands, takes a wobbly step, and collapses back into her chair. Jack slings Crystal's fat pink purse over his own shoulder, and pulls his wife to her unsteady feet. Allie scrapes back my mother's seat and takes her elbow to help her up. My mother fumbles in her pocketbook for a pack of cigarettes, sticks an unlit one between her lips, and then places one hand on the table and leans her weight on it while she catches her breath, something I have never seen her do before.

"I'm fine," she says, sensing I'm about to ask if she's all right. "I know this is news to you, but I'm not as young as I used to be. It just takes me a minute." Sebastian returns, scurries away with my father's credit card, and just as quickly scurries back. My father signs the bill and leads us all to the door. As we pass Sebastian, he winks at me. It's then that I notice the tiny upside-down pink triangle decorating the lobe of his left ear.

"Doll," he says, his hand heavy on my shoulder, "if you give me your address, I'll be sure to send you a sympathy card."

❖

THE NIGHT IS dark and still as if the whole world is holding its breath, watching, waiting, not daring to make a sound. A round white moon hovers in the empty sky like an unblinking wary eye. From far away comes the distant sound of glass breaking. At first it's a soft sound, a pleasant sound, like the tinkling of some wind chimes hanging from a neighbor's front porch. Then the sound grows more insistent, louder. Glass, lots of glass, an endless amount of glass; windows and doors of stores, exploding and collapsing into the street. Shards glistening like stars. Jewish stars. Yellow Jewish stars. People are running, screaming, their eyes wide moons of fright, their mouths black holes in their shattered faces. Buildings are on fire, orange flames licking the sky, and a river pours down the street. A red river. A river of blood.

I know exactly what is going on and where I am. *"Kristallnacht, Kristallnacht,"* I mutter, my voice cracking with terror.

Allie is awake and shaking me in an instant.

"Lydia. Lyddie. Shh." She smoothes my hair away from my face and gathers me into her arms. "It's okay. I'm here. I'm right here. It was only a dream, Lydia. Shh."

Allie turns on the reading lamp on my nightstand and I look over her shoulder. I'm home. Safe. Everything is in its proper place: the photo Allie took of a pink and blue Bar Harbor sunset is hanging on the wall over her dresser; our dirty clothes are piled in the wicker laundry basket next to the door; the spider plant that always needs watering is hanging in the window; Mishmosh is snoring softly on the jumble of blankets down by our feet.

"Want to tell me about it?" Allie asks, laying us both down softly.

"I don't remember."

"You were saying something about Crystal. Crystal not…Crystal knocked…"

"Crystal knocked?" I don't remember dreaming about Crystal. But then the nightmare flashes through my mind again and I understand what Allie is trying to say. Try as she might, Allie never can pronounce the guttural "ch" sound so commonly used in Yiddish. And German.

"Kristallnacht," I tell Allie as the dream comes flooding back in its entirety, making me shudder. And then, being a teacher, I can't help but explain. *"Kristallnacht.* I've told you before, Allie. It's a German word and its literal meaning is 'crystal night,' but the more common translation is 'the night of broken glass.' It's the night that officially began the Holocaust, November 9th, 1938. Synagogues were destroyed, buildings were burned…"

"Hush, *habladora.*" Allie, knowing I am capable of digressing into a long, detailed lecture on the Holocaust, even upon waking from a nightmare, gently interrupts me using her favorite endearment, the Spanish word sounding so much sweeter than its English equivalent, motor-mouth. "It's okay. It's over. It was just a dream."

"But what do you think it means?" I ask her.

"Crystal night? *Kristallnacht?*" Allie tries her best to pronounce the word correctly, but the last syllable comes out like the prelude to a spit. "Isn't it obvious?"

"Explain it anyway." I don't want to hear what Allie has to say so much as I need to hear the sound of her voice pouring over me like a waterfall. I burrow my head into the warm, soft spot between Allie's shoulder and neck to listen. Mishmosh, annoyed at all this middle-of-the-night activity, but still, never one to miss out on an opportunity to cuddle, climbs up my side and settles his abundant weight along my hip like a large furry heating pad.

"The way I see it," Allie pushes a stray strand of hair away from my forehead and lovingly tucks a dark curl behind my ear, "*Kristallnacht* was the beginning of the end for the Jews," she says, stroking my back as I stroke Mishmosh.

"Not all the Jews," I mumble into her soft skin. "Some of us are still here."

"Yes, Professor Pinkowitz," Allie chides me. "Crystal Night, which occurred on Sunday, May 29th, 2005, was also the beginning of the end."

"The end of what?" I ask her.

"The end of dealing with your family. For a while, anyway."

"Really?" I push back to look into her dark Spanish eyes. There is so much love there, I almost start to weep. "But Allie, you're the one who always wants me to be in touch with them. You're always telling me I should call them, send cards to them, make more of an effort…"

"I know," Allie says. "I'm sorry, Lydia."

"*You're* sorry?" I frown at her. "It's not your fault, Allie. If anyone should apologize, it's me. I'm the one who made you take me down to see them."

"But it was my idea," Allie insists. "I always think that visiting your family isn't going to be that bad and then it isn't that bad. It's worse."

"You really think so?" I sit up and prop my pillow behind me. "Whenever I try to explain to people why I can't stand seeing my family, they never get it." Mishmosh resettles himself on my lap as I lean back with a sigh.

"I guess you had to be there," Allie says, as if she's talking to a group of people who don't laugh after she's told them about a situation she thought was funny.

"I mean, there's just no room for me in that family. I can't be *myself* with them," I say forcefully, as if I'm arguing the point with Allie, even though she's clearly on my side. "It's not even that they don't accept me so much, it's that they don't care about me. I don't even *matter*." I thump Mishmosh on his hefty side for emphasis. "Think about it, Allie. Did my mother ask me even one question about my life? No, she did not. Oh, wait, let me correct myself. She did ask me one question. She asked me if I'd lost any weight. Can you believe she still won't let up about that?" I don't give Allie a chance to answer before continuing my tirade. "And I hate the way she talks about me like I'm not even there. Plus, her memory of my childhood is completely different than my memory of it. *I* never washed a dish or a cup or a spoon? Are you kidding me?" My voice rises with a note of hysteria. "*I'm* the one who did the supper dishes every night. *I'm* the one who made the beds every morning. *I'm* the one who did the laundry, *I'm* the one who vacuumed, *I'm* the one who dusted. What do you think turned me into such a goddamn feminist?"

"Okay, okay. Lydia, calm down. I believe you. You don't have to convince me." Allie sits up, too, and puts an arm around my shoulder.

"It's like they shun me, Allie," I say, still feeling the need to explain. "I mean, they don't give me the silent treatment—that would be too obvious. It's more insidious than that. My mother talks to me, all right, but she doesn't ask me anything about my life because clearly my life isn't worth knowing about. She acts as if I haven't done one single thing since I left home thirty years ago. So it's like I'm sitting there and I'm invisible at the same time and I just can't take it anymore."

"You're not going to take it anymore," Allie says firmly. "You're going to give yourself a break. You're not going to visit them, talk to them, or even think about them for a while. Doctor's orders, Lydia. It's too painful for you."

"It really is," I whimper like the hurt child I am, despite my grown-up status.

"Come." Knowing there aren't any words that will make me feel better, Allie pulls me close and hugs me tight. I sink into her embrace, and Mishmosh, disgusted that I can't keep still so he can sleep, uses my legs as a springboard to leap onto my dresser, where he hopes to catch some shuteye.

"All right now?" Allie asks after a little while has passed. When I nod, she reaches behind me to turn off my reading lamp. We lie down together and I roll onto my side and close my eyes. Allie kisses my cheek and bids me good night. "I don't want you to lie there tossing and turning and thinking," she warns gently, knowing me all too well. "Especially about your family. Shut down your brain and get a good night's sleep, Lydia. I mean it. Okay?"

"Okay," I whisper, but before I can drift into dreamland, Allie, without meaning to, undermines her own suggestion by uttering a phrase that makes me instantly think of my mother. "I'm serious, Lydia," Allie murmurs into the darkness. "Enough is enough."

❖

MOTHERS, MOTHERS EVERYWHERE, as far as the eye can see. Now that I've decided not to think about my own mother, I see other mothers everywhere I look. Buying fruits and vegetables at the supermarket with their babies waving chubby arms about and gurgling in backpacks strapped behind their shoulders. Lifting weights at the gym with their newborns napping in car seats/baby baskets parked down at their feet. Strolling around campus hand in hand with their pint-sized offspring skipping beside them when I stop by once a week to pick up my summer mail. It seems like all winter long the mothers of Paradise were in hibernation and now that summer's here they've come crawling out of the woodwork with their infants, toddlers, pre-schoolers, kindergarten-through-sixth-graders, tweens, and teenagers in tow. And both the mothers and their offspring love interacting with me. They smile, they strike up conversations, some even flirt.

"Who are you making eyes at?" a woman standing in front of me at the post office asks the little boy squirming in her arms. There I am minding my own business at the post office, waiting to mail an article about the rising popularity of drag kings on college campuses to a stuffy academic journal that I'm sure will never accept it, when a toddler dressed all in blue, bats his long eyelashes at me, grins, and then buries his face against his mother's chest. A minute later he lifts his head, peers up at me, and starts playing peek-a-boo all over again.

"He likes you." The boy's mother turns around and smiles at me, then speaks to her son. "Don't you, Matthew?"

Matthew responds by kicking his mother in the kidneys several times with great enthusiasm. As she shifts him around in her arms like a lopsided bag of groceries, I feel obligated to return the compliment.

"He has beautiful blue eyes," I say, which is true.

"He gets them from his daddy," the woman says proudly. "Don't you, sweetheart?" Matthew doesn't answer, just blinks at me again. The woman laughs. "He's going to be a real lady-killer," she says, taking a step forward as the line moves ahead. As a card-carrying feminist, it takes everything I have to restrain myself from challenging the violent implication of Matthew's mother's word choice, not to mention the assumption that her bouncing baby boy is going to grow up to be a healthy, happy heterosexual. But I know from past experience that if I do open my big mouth, the only thing I'll accomplish is proving what most people already think about feminists: we're a bitter, angry lot with absolutely no sense of humor.

"Do you have any children?" The woman smiles at me again as her question cuts through my thoughts like a knife.

"Who me? Oh my God, no." Without thinking, I laugh at the very idea, and then watch the smile on the woman's face freeze before her expression transforms into a look of sheer horror. Luckily the postal clerk calls out "Next!" rescuing the poor thing from the nutcase standing behind her who obviously doesn't understand that being a mother is the most wonderful thing in the world.

I have never wanted to be a mother. Growing up, I had no interest in playing with dolls, though my bed was covered with a legion of stuffed animals: dogs, cats, elephants, lions, tigers, and giraffes, each one named, fussed over, and adored. As a teenager, I just couldn't understand the attraction of motherhood. "Why should I gain fifty pounds, get varicose veins and stretch marks, spend hours in pain giving birth, and then take care of someone for eighteen years who is only going to grow up and hate me?" I asked my best friend Colleen, who came from a large Irish family and not only wanted to be a mother, but wanted a dozen kids. At least.

When Allie and I got serious about each other, which, in true lesbian fashion, happened on our second date, I knew I had to bring up some difficult issues. Untangling myself from her steamy embrace, I said the four words nobody likes to hear: "We have to talk."

"Did I do something wrong already?" Allie asked, her voice full of concern. We had just left the crowded dance floor of a club that dubbed

Tuesdays "alternative lifestyle night." Among a horde of sweaty gay men and lesbians doing the hustle (it was the tail end of the eighties, after all) Allie plastered her body against mine, belly to belly, and taught me her favorite Latin dance. "You can't have a Puerto Rican girlfriend if you don't know how to merengue," she said, showing me how to move my hips and guiding me across the floor. When the song ended we continued dancing out the door and began making out like two teenagers before we even hit the street. Allie led me to a bench in a nearby school yard, sat me on her lap, and glued her lips to mine. If I thought I had been living in Paradise before, now I knew I was in Heaven.

But before I could let things go where they were heading and where I certainly wanted them to go, there were a few things I had to find out. So though I didn't really want to, I made myself slide off Allie's lap, took her hand in mine, and began the conversation.

"Alicia Maria Taraza," I said, the newness of her name a delicious treat on my tongue. "Are you non-monogamous?"

"Hell no," she said, giving me a look that would become very familiar over time and which basically meant, *what are you, loco?*

"Excellent." I made an imaginary check mark in the air. "Next question: if we ever decided to live together, would you insist on having a Christmas tree in the house?"

"Well…" Allie pretended to think the matter over. I knew, and she later confessed, that she wasn't pondering how she felt about Christmas trees; she was trying to figure out the answer I wanted to hear so she wouldn't say the wrong thing and blow her chances of having her way with me that night.

"It's not that important," Allie finally said. "Christmas was never a big deal in my house. I mean, we had a tree and everything, but the biggest holiday for Puerto Ricans is Three Kings Day. Could we celebrate that?"

"Sure," I said in the spirit of compromise. I wasn't all that familiar with Three Kings Day, so it didn't carry the oppressive weight of Christmas, a holiday that grated on my Jewish nerves from the day after Halloween when the first red-and-green store displays went up, right up until New Year's Eve when they were finally taken down.

"Anything else?" Allie asked, already moving in for another kiss.

"There is one more little thing," I said, trying to make light of the next question, which was the real deal-breaker. "How do you feel about having children?"

"Having children," Allie repeated, nodding. "Well, let's see." Since Allie hadn't known me long enough to know what I wanted her to say, she had no choice, really, except to be honest. "If I wound up with someone who really wanted kids, I would never stand in her way of having them. But it's certainly not in my game plan."

"Hooray!" I threw myself into her long, strong arms and gave her a kiss that let her know she had passed the pop quiz I had sprung upon her with flying colors.

I always thought one of the perks of being a lesbian was not having to become a mother. But lately it seems that Allie and I are the only ones who feel that way. Every time I turn around, another birth announcement arrives in the mail. A friend who just turned thirty breaks down in the baby food aisle of Price Chopper and convinces her lover it's time to pick out a sperm donor and start inseminating. A colleague smack dab in the middle of menopause adopts a little girl from Guatemala. A woman Allie works with and who holds a very special place in our hearts since she set us up on our first date many years ago decides to "try out" motherhood by becoming a foster parent to a twelve-year-old. If I have to buy one more copy of *Heather Has Two Mommies* for a pair of new lesbian parents, I swear to God, I'll scream.

And I do scream one hot Saturday night during the first weekend of August when Allie and I go to a potluck dinner given by two women on her softball team. Over hummus and tabouli and more variations on macaroni salad than I thought possible, a group of lesbians sit on the floor and passionately discuss the consistency of their children's "poop" in relation to the pros and cons of cloth versus disposable diapers. These are the same women who not too long ago spent their Saturday nights arguing about world politics, social injustice, and articles from the latest issue of *Ms. Magazine.*

"Gag me with a pacifier," I whisper to Allie, who simply gets up to help herself to another slice of strawberry rhubarb pie. As I wait for her to return, a little girl named Aurora wearing a pink T-shirt that has the words "Future President" emblazoned across her future chest comes flying into the room and flings herself into one of her mothers' arms with a piercing, wounded shriek.

"What happened, honey bear? Did you fall down? Did you hurt yourself somewhere?"

Aurora nods tearfully and points to her head.

"Oh no, not your little head. That must have really, really hurt. Let Mommy make it all better. Here." Aurora's mother gathers her daughter onto her lap, kisses the top of her head, and then cradles her so lovingly, I have to turn away as a memory from over forty years ago enters my mind and fills my eyes with tears. I also fell and bumped my head one day when I was Aurora's age and Colleen and I were playing jump rope outside. But when I burst into the house sobbing, my mother did not tenderly embrace me. She barely looked up from the soap opera she was watching, and when she did and saw no blood dripping down my face or broken bones poking through my skin, she said, "Lydia, you're fine. Nothing hurts. Stop crying. Don't be such a baby." And when I only howled louder, my mother snapped, "Lydia, stop crying right now or I'll give you something to really cry about." Which, I have to admit, was a very effective parenting technique: I shut up immediately. As does Aurora, who is now snuggled up against her mother's chest, the picture of contentment. Aurora's mother rests her cheek against her daughter's silky blond hair and rocks her back and forth, humming softly. Then, with a look of utter bliss on her face, she catches my eye and says to me, of all people, "You don't know what love is until you become a parent."

"*I* don't know what love is?" I ask Allie the moment we get into the car. "*You* don't know what love is? Only parents know what love is? How dare she?"

"Of course we know what love is," Allie says, looking over her shoulder to back away from the scene of the crime.

"I just can't believe she said that. What did, what does…" I'm so mad I'm sputtering.

Allie drives with one hand on the wheel, the other stroking my arm in a vain effort to soothe my ruffled feathers. "Of course that was an obnoxious thing to say." Allie slows for a stop sign. "But the woman can't help herself, Lydia. All new mothers are like that. It's called milk mind."

"Are you defending her?" My voice rises and it is then that I scream.

"Wow." Allie pulls over to the curb and stops the car. "What the heck, I didn't need that eardrum anyway," she says, shaking her head to clear it. "Lydia, c'mon now. You can't take everything personally. Can't you see when somebody says something like that, it's more about her than it is about you? Obviously *she* never knew what love was until *she* became a parent."

"Yeah, yeah, yeah." I know Allie is right. But still, the comment rankles me. It's there in my head the next morning when I sit down in my study to check my e-mail. And what do I find waiting in my inbox? A slide show of not one, not ten, not thirty, not seventy-five, but one hundred and one photos of Colleen's youngest child—her fifth!—for me to peruse, admire, and purchase if I so desire. Serves me right for booting up my laptop on a Sunday morning instead of relaxing with the *New York Times* crossword puzzle, a steaming cup of hazelnut coffee, and a chocolate-covered biscotti or two.

As I mentally scold myself, I hear Allie's footsteps coming up the back stairs from her basement workshop. "Are you finished sanding the tables?" I ask her, referring to some furniture she is building for our local battered women's shelter.

"Almost," Allie answers as she comes into the room and leans over my desk. "What'cha looking at?" Her white T-shirt is covered with sawdust like a donut sprinkled with cinnamon and she smells just as tasty.

"Baby pictures," I say, rolling my eyes. "Colleen's too old to pop out any more so now they're adopting. She's from China."

"She's a cutie," Allie says, and then notices the look of dismay on my face. "What? Don't tell me you're annoyed that Colleen adopted a baby, Lydia. Please. What kind of feminist are you?" I scowl at Allie, who knows that to me this is the ultimate insult. "C'mon. Lydia," she coaxes. "You told me that all Colleen ever wanted was to be a mother, so doesn't she get to make that choice? And besides, I'm sure she and her crew are giving little…" Allie narrows her eyes at my computer screen. "…Mei Lin a very good home."

"You're right," I admit, studying the drooling little girl, who looks like every other drooling little girl I've ever seen, more or less. "But honestly, Allie. How would Colleen feel if I sent her one hundred and one pictures of Mishmosh?"

Allie chuckles. "Try it and see."

"Maybe I will." I lean back in my chair and contemplate the

possibilities. "Mishmosh sleeping on his back, Mishmosh sleeping on his stomach, Mishmosh sleeping on his left side, Mishmosh sleeping on his right side, Mishmosh sleeping on the bed, the sofa, the kitchen table…"

"Mishmosh chewing up the plants, Mishmosh dumping over the garbage, Mishmosh sharpening his claws on the living room rug…" Allie ticks off his less-than-fabulous attributes as the little devil comes trotting into the room. He marches straight toward me and bumps his enormous head against my shin, which is his way of asking for affection. It's barely ten o'clock and it feels like the temperature has already hit eighty-five, but Mishmosh doesn't care. The warmer it gets, the more attention he craves; I don't know why. Allie, who also has a tendency to feel frisky in the heat, jokes that it's his Puerto Rican side.

"Hey, he's not that bad," I remind Allie. "Come up, Mishman." I pat my legs and eighteen pounds of cat jumps onto my lap, turns in a circle, and then collapses into a purring heap. "Look how adorable he is," I say to Allie. "He's as cute as that baby any day."

"Of course he is. Plus he outweighs her at least two to one." Allie scratches Mishmosh under the chin, then leans down to squash him between us, forming what is known in our household as a "Mishmosh pit." After listening to him purr for a minute, Allie straightens up. "I wouldn't tell Colleen that you think her new kid can't hold a candle to our cat, though."

"No, I guess not." I hit my Return key and Allie and I both stare at another picture of Colleen's daughter that pops onto my computer screen. She's wearing a tiny T-shirt that says "Spit happens," which makes me groan and Allie snicker.

Allie heads back to the basement and I turn away from my email and open a new empty page on my laptop. I'm supposed to be writing an article—just because I have tenure doesn't mean I can slack off in the publishing department—and besides, I need something new to present at the Women's Studies conference I'm attending this fall. But my mind is as blank as the computer screen before me. "What's wrong with me, Mishy?" I ask the purring puddle on my lap, who responds by swiveling his ears back and stretching his toes. "Any idiot can write an article." It's something my mother said to me years ago when I was home visiting and still foolish enough to believe I might be able to convince her to give up cigarettes though she'd been smoking since she was fourteen years old. I doubt I really thought my argument could persuade her; rather I felt some sense of guilt about my mother's bad habit since she told anyone who asked that the only reason she still smoked was because her daughter made her nervous. So during this particular visit, I was telling her about a new form of hypnotherapy that was supposed to be very effective. She pooh-poohed the idea, of course, and I foolishly defended it. "Mom," I said, "I'll send you the article I read about it and you'll see. It was published in this really great holistic health magazine called—"

"Lydia," my mother interrupted, looking me right in the eye. "Any idiot can write an article." So much for asking what she thought of the article I'd written about Jewish feminist rebels from Lilith to Emma Goldman. I'd sent the academic journal my work had been published in to my parents months earlier but neither of them had ever mentioned it. For a while I had an index card with my mother's words tacked to my bulletin board to look at whenever I was having trouble with my writing, figuring if "any idiot can write an article" I could, too. But Allie thought the message wasn't exactly a loving one and made me take it down.

"Maybe I have Purina Cat Chow mind instead of milk mind," I say to Mishmosh, scratching him under the chin. Since motherhood seems to be in my thoughts so much lately, maybe I should write about that. But I'm not really thinking about motherhood; I'm thinking about non-motherhood. Am I the only woman left on the planet who doesn't have a burning desire to be called Mommy? And even if I were the last non-mother (un-mother?) on earth, who cares? I'm happy with my life and my choices. Aren't I?

"Aha!" I say, startling Mishmosh, who jumps off my lap and heads for the doorway, his tail swishing in anger. Halfway there he stops, stretches his front paws forward, and raises his rear end toward me, making sure I am aware of his extreme displeasure before leaving the room. As I watch him stalk off in search of quieter sleeping quarters, I realize that Allie is right—Allie is always right—there is a reason why all these women having babies annoys me so much. The thought hits me as hard and fast as a bucket of ice water thrown in my face: somewhere, deeply buried beneath my steely feminist core, I don't believe I'm a worthwhile human being because I am not a mother. I am so stunned by this realization, I know it must be true.

"But how can that be?" I ask the walls, which unfortunately do not answer. Do I really think that all the academic work I've done, all the political activism I've been involved in, all the teaching, the writing, the research, all that adds up to *nada* just because I've never warmed a bottle of formula, rocked a crying baby at three o'clock in the morning, or changed one single cloth or disposable diaper in my entire life?

In an effort to banish this realization as quickly as it arrived, I start typing furiously. And what appears on my computer screen is a list of childless (child-free?) women who pop randomly into my head, all of whom I admire. Oprah Winfrey, the goddess of daytime TV. Marilyn Monroe, the sex goddess of the fifties. Katharine Hepburn, the goddess, period. Georgia O'Keeffe, whose artwork hangs on my walls; May Sarton, whose journals line my bookshelves; Julia Child, whom I hereby dub Julia Childless and whose cookbooks gather dust in my kitchen. Celia Cruz, the Queen of Salsa and Allie's favorite female vocalist. Allie herself. My great-aunt Selma, who never married and whom my parents always talked about in whispers as though being a "spinster" was a fatal disease. My high school English teacher Miss Hennessy, who wore pantsuits and men's shoes and was rumored to live with another "old maid" on the outskirts of town. Mishmosh's vet, who calls herself Dr. Cynthia and owns a big farm with horses, cows, dogs, cats, ferrets, and a parrot named Wynona. Frida Kahlo, Susan B. Anthony, Mother Theresa, Rosa Parks…

And then there are the lesser known women whose stories I've been collecting for years. It's one of my Sunday morning rituals, along with sleeping in for an extra hour, eating something that involves chocolate for breakfast, and doing the crossword puzzle in the *New York Times*. Every Sunday when I am well rested and well fed and before I feel ready to try and figure out a six-letter word for "whine" (snivel) or remember who played the title role in the 1944 film *Laura* (Gene Tierney), I turn to the last page of the first section of the paper and comb the obituaries in search of a woman who is survived by "several nieces and nephews" or who died "surrounded by many loving friends." And there's always at least one. A women who was active in the arts, in social services, or in the world of business. A women who lived to be one hundred and two and swore the secret to her longevity was drinking a glass of red wine and smoking a fat cigar every evening before she went to bed. I love these women and faithfully clip their death notices every week and file them away. I look at them often, and feel comforted to know that they lived *New York Times*–worthy lives even without perpetuating the species. If they can do it, I can do it, I think as I open the top drawer of my desk to take out a thick folder of yellowing newsprint. "At least I'm in good company," I tell myself just as Allie comes back upstairs and pokes her head into my room.

"Now what are you doing?" she asks, standing in my doorway with a piece of folded sandpaper in her hand.

"I'm making a list of women who never had children but still led a worthwhile life," I tell her, adding Gloria Steinem—how could I have possibly forgotten her?—to my list.

"*But* still led a worthwhile life?" Allie tilts her head to the side and stares at me. "*But*? Lydia, do you feel okay?" Allie steps into the room and presses her lips to my forehead, checking to see if I have a fever.

"Of course I feel okay."

"Then what's going on?"

"I don't know." I save my document, titling it "Women Who Don't Know What Love Is" in honor of the remark Aurora's mother made last night. "Maybe I'm missing out on something by not having a baby."

"Whoa. Close that folder and shut down that computer." Allie waits until I put my laptop to sleep and then takes me by the hand and leads me away from my desk through the kitchen and out the door into our backyard. "Sit down." She parks me at the picnic table in the middle of the lawn and goes inside to get us some iced tea.

"Bring out my sunhat," I call after her, squinting in the bright midmorning light. While I wait for Allie to return, I feast my eyes on her magnificent garden. Our yard is the biggest on the block and the main reason we bought this house, so that Allie could continue her mother's tradition of growing the most beautiful flowers in the neighborhood. Allie works the same magic on her garden that she works on me; tiger lilies, daisies, irises, roses, bleeding hearts, and other plants and shrubs I can't even name all blossom magnificently under her touch.

"Here." Allie returns, plops my straw hat onto my head, and hands me a tall glass. "Bottoms up." She clinks her drink against mine before taking a long sip. "Now Lydia," Allie says. "Either you're having heatstroke, menopause has finally kicked in and your hormones are making you crazy, or alien beings have entered your body and taken over your brain. Which is it?" Allie pulls a lawn chair up next to me, drops into it, and leans forward, her elbows on her knees and her eyes full of concern.

"I don't know," I say again. I don't seem to know anything lately. "Allie, look at me. I'm forty-eight years old—"

"Forty-nine next weekend," Allie reminds me. "And we've got big plans, remember?"

"I remember," I say, with an obvious lack of enthusiasm.

"What?" Allie asks. "Did you change your mind about going away for a romantic weekend? Do you want a party instead?"

"No, Allie."

"Then what's the matter?"

"It's just that…" I shoo away a fly that has perched on the rim of my iced tea glass. "I'm about to turn forty-nine and what have I done with my life? Nothing."

"You're kidding, right?" Allie's look of concern has crossed over into worry. "Do you want me to go back in there," she points toward the house, "and print out your résumé? Do you want me to pull out all the letters you've gotten from former students saying how having you as a teacher changed their lives? Do you want me to tell you once again all the ways that you've changed *my* life?"

"Oh, Allie, what does it all add up to?" I ask, looking down at my lap. "Even Jackie Kennedy said the accomplishment she was most proud of was the way she raised Caroline and John."

"Lydia, maybe it's time to lift the embargo. What do you think? Maybe you should call your mother." Allie folds her arms across her chest and sits back, bracing herself for my response.

"Why would I want to do that?" I ask Allie in a voice that conveys I'd rather swallow my own kneecap. "And anyway, you're the one who said I should take a break."

"Break time's over," Allie announces, like we're co-workers who have to get back to our jobs. "It's been a few months, Lydia. You can't ignore your family forever. And who knows? Maybe they've missed you. Maybe things have changed."

"I doubt it. Nothing ever changes."

"The only thing constant is change," Allie reminds me, though I'm hardly in the mood for platitudes. She studies me for a minute, lost in thought, and then leans forward with a look on her face that says she's figured it all out. "Listen, Lydia," Allie says. "Think back to when you first came out as a lesbian."

"What in the world does that have to do with anything?"

"Just work with me here for a minute, okay?"

"Sure." I can't for the life of me make sense of this segue, but I'm happy to go along with it. Anything to get Allie off her "call your mother" kick. "Go on," I tell her.

"Remember when you first came out and you threw away all your skirts and heels, buzzed your hair, and took a car mechanics class?"

"Of course I remember." I look at her. "So?"

"What happened after that?"

"You know what happened, Allie."

"Tell me anyway."

"I met you. And I grew my hair out, started wearing dresses again, bought lipstick and lingerie, and made you lemonade while you changed the oil in my Toyota."

"Because..." Allie prompts me even though the answer is a no-brainer.

"Because," I tell her what she already knows, "I realized I didn't want to *be* a butch, I wanted to be *with* a butch."

"Exactly." Allie raises both hands in the air, palms to the sky as if the connection is obvious. "Don't you see, Lydia?"

"See what?"

"It's the same thing now. You don't want to *be* a mother, Lyddie. You want to *have* a mother."

"Allie, that's ridiculous." I slam both fists down on the picnic table. "I'm forty-eight years old, for God's sake. I'm way too old to need a mother."

"No, you're not. And Lydia, you don't need *a* mother. You need *your* mother."

"Allie, she's the last person I need. I'm an adult. I'm not a child anymore."

"You may not be *a* child, Lydia, but like it or not, you're still *her* child." Allie looks me in the eye. "You'll always be her child, Lydia, trust me on this. I know what I'm talking about." Allie glances at the big maple tree on the edge of our lawn, then lowers her gaze and says softly, "Take it from me, Lyddie. You're never too old to need your mother."

"Oh, Allie." I reach forward to pull her into my arms and offer comfort. But it is Allie who gathers me up and hugs me tight, because in the end, I'm the one who bursts into tears.

❖

"SILENCE IS GOLDEN, so let's get rich." It's a game I thought my mother invented but as I got older, I saw that it was something all mothers knew about. I imagined they all went away to motherhood boot camp or the University of Motherhood where they learned to say things like, "Try it. How do you know you don't like it if you won't even try it?" And, "The reason is because I said so." Or maybe it was all just hardwired into their DNA.

When I was growing up, my mother, like many of the other mothers on our block, took her turn picking up some of the neighborhood kids from Hebrew school. And after being cooped up for two hours on a Monday or a Wednesday afternoon staring at letters that went the wrong way and looked like the scribbles we made way back in kindergarten, my classmates and I, crammed into the backseat, were ready to let loose.

"Mrs. Pinkowitz, Steven hit me."

"I did not, Mrs. Pinkowitz. Mindy's lying."

"I am not."

"You are, too."

"I am not. Ow!"

"Mom, Steven pinched Mindy. He did. I saw him."

"I did not!"

"You did, too!"

"Hey, that's my lunchbox. Give it to me."

"Make me."

"Mrs. Pinkowitz…"

"That's enough," my mother said, the ever-present cigarette stuck between her lips moving up and down with her warning. Though my mother did not speak loudly, hers was the voice of authority and it quieted us instantly. In the silence that followed, she inhaled sharply, and a blue cloud of smoke rose and encircled her head, reminding me of the halo of dirt that always surrounded Charlie Brown's messy friend, Pig-Pen. "We're going to play a game now." My mother glanced at my friends and me in her rearview mirror. "It's called 'Silence Is Golden, So Let's Get Rich.' Whoever stays silent the longest wins."

"But Mrs. Pinkowitz…"

"No talking." My mother glanced at us again. "Anyone who says one word will walk the rest of the way home."

Steven and Mindy and I looked at each other, our eyes wide. Would my mother really throw us out of the car and make us walk miles through the streets of suburbia where occasionally older kids rode their bikes but no one had ever been known to walk? Too scared to call my mother's bluff, we clapped our hands over our mouths and stifled our giggles. Mindy didn't even say anything when Steven popped open the clasp on her Mary Poppins lunchbox and ate the Twinkie she had been saving for later all afternoon.

We are still playing "Silence Is Golden," my mother and I. It's been almost five months since that fateful dinner with my parents and Jack and Crystal, and I haven't spoken to anyone I share a gene pool with since.

"But isn't that what you wanted?" Vera asks as we slide our lunch trays down the cafeteria line, trying to decide between burnt soy burgers and some kind of stew made mostly from vegetables left over from last night's dinner. The food is always awful at these regional Women's Studies conferences, and though each year Vera and I threaten never to return, we faithfully make our way to whatever school is playing host—this year it's a small private college in upstate New York—mostly because it gives us a good excuse to hang out together and catch up with each other. Vera lives and teaches in Philadelphia, is twenty years my senior, and was my mentor a lifetime ago when I was a lowly grad student, hardly daring to take my own academic work seriously. After all this time, I'm still amazed that Vera considers me her colleague; though I've called her by her first name for almost two decades now, part of me will always think of her as "Dr. Rosenbloom."

"How's this?" Vera leads me to a table at the far end of the cafeteria to give us a little privacy.

"Perfect." I sit in the corner with my back to the wall and unwrap my packet of plastic utensils, not in any rush to return to the conversation we had started while choosing our food. Vera takes her time as well, making small talk about the weather—it's unusually chilly for Columbus Day weekend—and salting her food in an attempt to make it edible.

"You look great," I tell her, impressed as always with the way Vera presents herself to the world. Her sleek silver hair is cut in a fashionable asymmetrical bob and she wears a clunky necklace of black and white zebra-striped beads that few women her age—or any age—could get away with. I met Vera in my militant baby dyke, pre-Allie days when all I wore were torn jeans, flannel shirts, and work boots or baggy sweaters, sneakers, and army pants. The minute I walked into my first Introduction to Women's Studies class and caught sight of my glamorous professor clad in a semi-clingy sweater dress, back seam stockings, and two-inch heels, I was intensely suspicious of her. How could someone who looked like she had just sashayed off the pages of a fashion magazine be a tried and true feminist? But Vera proved to be a brilliant teacher; she put my doubts to rest and taught me a thing or two about the tyranny of political correctness all at the same time.

A few years later when I ran into her at a conference similar to this one, Vera was even more delighted than my mother to see me wearing a skirt. "Let me guess," she said. "You found your butch." I smiled and blushed a deep red, answering her question without saying a word. Vera celebrated my coming out as a femme ("And with a name like Pinkowitz, how could you be anything else?" she asked) by presenting me with a button that proclaimed, "I may wear high heels but I can still kick ass." Needless to say, we've been fast friends ever since.

I can always count on Vera to stand out amidst our Women's Studies sisters, most of whom dress in drawstring pants and Birkenstock sandals. Today she has on a long gray riding skirt with a soft-looking black cashmere sweater and a matching cropped suede jacket, which I dutifully admire.

"Check these out." Vera lifts the hem of her skirt to show off her footwear. Vera is a shoe freak and has been known to arrive at a three-day conference with seven pairs of shoes.

"They're gorgeous." I gaze at her black and white cowboy boots with lust in my eyes. Like Vera, I love shoes almost as much as our other common vice: chocolate. "Are those snakeskin?"

"Lizard." Vera lowers her voice to a whisper, though no one could possibly hear us over the din of two hundred scholars, students, and professors chatting about curriculum and complaining about the food. A sound, incidentally, that both of us adore.

"You don't look so bad yourself," Vera comments, giving me a thorough once-over. I am wearing a hot pink fuzzy turtleneck sweater over black wool slacks and black leather ankle boots. "You've aged about two minutes since the last time we saw each other."

"Vera, that was only a year ago."

"Still," she says. "You could easily pass for a student. It's hard to believe you're going to turn fifty next summer."

"Hey, don't rush me," I say, sawing my soy burger in half with my serrated plastic knife. "I've still got a good ten months to go before I kiss my forties good-bye."

"So how are you going to celebrate the big event?" Vera wants to know.

"I'm throwing the party to end all parties. Saturday, August 13th, one o'clock, in our very own backyard. So mark your calendar," I point at her with my knife, "now."

"Got it," Vera assures me, tapping the side of her skull where that magnificent brain of hers resides. "I wouldn't miss it for the world."

"Good. And speaking of birthdays," I lift a forkful of wilted lettuce drenched in Day-Glo orange dressing, "isn't somebody turning seventy at the end of this year?"

"Nobody sitting at this table." Vera glances at the empty chairs beside us and shakes her head. "Why don't we change the subject, Lydia? Ask me how my workshop went."

I let it go—Vera never was one to make a fuss over her own birthday—and oblige her. "So, Vera, how did your workshop go?"

"Lydia, I thought you'd never ask. It was excellent." Vera swallows a bite of stew and screws up her face at the taste. "I had about thirty women there—most of them undergraduates—and after I got them all riled up about the terrible oppression of prescribed gender roles, we spent the entire time trying to come up with a definition of 'butch' and 'femme' that didn't include the words 'masculine' and 'feminine' and which we all could live with."

"Wow, that must have been challenging." Vera loves to fan the flames of feminist fury and I can just imagine my former mentor in her glory, striding down the aisles between her students' desks, pacing back and forth as she pondered their comments, and then marching to the front of the room to grab a stick of chalk and write key words on the blackboard in a furious staccato. "What did you finally come up with?"

Vera holds up one finger while she gulps her water. "We went back and forth a hundred times and then just as we were about to give up any hope of reaching a consensus, a woman remembered something she had read somewhere and everybody loved it. So, our definition of butch is," Vera pauses for dramatic effect, "iron-covered velvet. And our definition of femme is," she looks pointedly at me, "velvet-covered iron."

"Ooh, that's good. That's very good," I say, pushing my tray away though most of my lunch is still on it.

"How did your workshop go?" Vera abandons her food as well, and reaches into her shoulder bag at the same time I unclasp my purse.

"What do you have in there?" I ask as she digs around.

"Toblerone. Bittersweet," she says, breaking off a piece for me. "And you?"

"Godiva." I pull out a small gold box and offer her a truffle. Vera and I both learned a long time ago that the only way to get through these conferences is to avoid the coffee altogether and fortify each other with chocolate. "I think people liked my workshop. I got the idea one day when I was reading an article in *Good Housekeeping*—"

"*Good Housekeeping*? Good God." Vera raises her eyebrows, pretending to be shocked. As if I don't know she has a lifelong subscription to *People* magazine.

"Which I was browsing through at the dentist's office," I say in a feeble attempt to defend myself. "Anyway, it was about women caught between raising their young children and taking care of their aging parents. I thought: What about women who don't have children or parents? I did some research and decided to focus on Gertrude Stein, who had no kids and whose parents died when she was a teenager. Plus since the personal is always political, I spoke about my own experience, of course."

"Of course." Vera fixes me with her piercing blue eyes. "But Lydia, you do have parents."

"Sort of," I say, though I know Vera won't let me get away with that.

Vera nibbles on her chocolate and gives me a look that means we are now about to have a Serious Conversation. I squirm in my seat just as I did years ago when she called on me in class and I knew that whatever answer I came up with wouldn't be good enough for her. Vera is well aware that she is the kind of professor whom students constantly complain about while they have her as a teacher, and endlessly praise in hindsight because she makes them think and work so hard. Vera never lets her students—or her friends—get away with anything.

"Tell me more about what's going on with you and your mother," Vera says, still fixing me with her eyes. It is then I remember that in a former life before she became a professor, Vera ran a very successful full-time therapy practice and still sees a few clients on the side.

"Where do I begin?" I ask, and just as I get the words out, two young women approach our table hand in hand. *Saved by the baby dykes*, I think as one of them steps forward, pushes a hank of green-and-magenta-striped hair out of her eyes, and waits to be acknowledged.

"Hello," Vera, ever the gracious one, says, though she stops short of inviting the couple to sit down. But the woman nearest us ignores her and stares pointedly at me. "Don't you know who I am?" she finally asks, her tough exterior shattered by the note of disappointment in her voice.

I wrack my brain while looking her up and down. Along with the in-your-face hairdo, she sports black-painted nails, deep purple lipstick, and wears a short gunmetal gray skirt, torn fishnet stockings, and a leather bomber jacket that is positively swimming on her. I'm sure it belongs to the ultra butch watching from a distance who is at least twice her size. She's probably a former student, but her face is not in the least bit familiar. "I'm sorry," I offer a weak apology. "I'm at that age where I can't even remember my own name half the time and—"

"Rebecca." She cuts me off with an impatient wave of her hand. "Rebecca Pearl. From Oakwood. My family lives across the street and down the block from you."

"Rebecca Pearl?" I still look at her blankly.

"Don't you remember?" Her voice is almost pleading now. "You used to babysit for me when I was about five. Remember? I was always asking you to play Barbies with me, and you wouldn't unless I agreed that Barbie could discover the cure for cancer or something instead of just marrying Ken…"

"Oh my God." I look closer, and sure enough, underneath the heavy-duty eyeliner, I can just make out my former neighbor's innocent little face. "I remember now. You're Becky Pearlman, right?"

"Sort of," she says, "I used to be, but I dropped the man. In more ways than one."

"Little Becky Pearlman," I repeat in wonder. "How do you like that? Sure I remember now. So you're, what? About thirty-two, thirty-three? Are you a student?"

"Yeah, I'm kind of on the twelve-year plan, and this semester I'm finally getting my degree."

"That's great," I tell her, and then remember my manners. "Vera, this is Becky—"

"Rebecca."

"Sorry. Rebecca. I used to babysit for her and her sister. How is Ruthie?"

"Ruth's okay, though she just got divorced and is back living at home with my parents. Lee and I were just there last weekend." Rebecca looks back toward her girlfriend, who acknowledges us with a curt nod.

"Really?" I ask, my curiosity piqued. "How does your family feel about you being a lesbian?"

"Oh, they're cool. Whatever makes me happy and all that. You know. My mom's kind of taken up the cause; she's a member of PFLAG and everything. There's a Westchester chapter and she goes to all the meetings but she's the only person from Oakwood there. It's a pretty heterocentric place," Rebecca explains to Vera, in case she doesn't know. "Oh, and guess what," she says, turning back to me. "While we were there, my mom and I bumped into your mother at Stop & Shop."

"You did?" I can just imagine the look my mother would have given the punked-out Rebecca. It wouldn't have been pretty.

"Yeah, in the spaghetti aisle. I told her I was really excited about coming to this conference and that you were going to be presenting. And my mother—you know she's a librarian, right?—said that she had just read some really great article you had written about gay rights in South Africa."

My eyes widen. "I bet that went over well," I murmur to Vera. Then I look back up at Rebecca. "What did my mother say?"

"It was so weird." Rebecca shifts her weight from one combat boot to the other. "She didn't say anything. She just turned around and walked away. Left her cart there and everything."

"Are you kidding?" I am vaguely aware that I am not acting in a very professional manner here, but right now I don't care. "Are you sure she didn't say anything?"

"Nope. Nothing."

"Nothing? Not one word? Like, I don't know, good-bye?"

Rebecca shakes her multicolored coiffed head.

"Wow." I lean back against my chair and stare at the soggy mess on my lunch tray, which blurs in front of my eyes. I thought my mother was way past the point of doing anything that would shock me, but this dramatic display of rudeness is a bit over the top, even for her.

"I'm sorry," Rebecca says, as if she needs to apologize for my mother's behavior. "Maybe I shouldn't have told you. I think my mom even went over the next day with some PFLAG pamphlets, but your mother wouldn't speak to her."

"It's very nice to meet you Rebecca, Lee." Vera, trying not to appear impolite, nevertheless practically shoos the two women away from our table. After they're gone, she takes my hand and asks gently, "Lydia, are you all right?"

"Let's take a walk." I stand abruptly and gather my tray. All of a sudden the loud bustling cafeteria feels confining, as does my turtleneck sweater. Either my emotions are getting the better of me, or I'm finally having my first hot flash. I expect it's the former, though I'd be a lot happier if it were the latter.

We discard the remains of our lunch and exit the building. Crisp fallen leaves crunch beneath our boots as we stroll across the campus quad, past the ivy-covered brick buildings and shedding trees. Squirrels chase each other through the grass, other conference attendees walk in groups of twos and threes; some smile and wave to us as they pass. Vera takes my arm as we amble along, not because she needs it for support—at sixty-nine she is far more spry than I am—but because she knows *I* need the support. Vera has been hearing about my mother for just about twenty years now. We discuss her latest escapade concerning Rebecca and her mom, and then I bring Vera up to date on my current situation, ending with the unexpected and surprisingly deep hurt I feel at my mother's participation in the silence between us.

"Why doesn't she call me?" I ask Vera, whining like an adolescent who has been sitting by the phone for days hoping to hear from her latest crush. "I know she never calls me, but still, it's been almost five months now and I thought surely she'd pick up the phone before Rosh Hashanah to wish me a happy new year or after Yom Kippur to see if I'd had an easy fast."

"Maybe she'll send you a Chanukah present," Vera says, turning left and leading us past the college library. "Though as I recall, you weren't exactly thrilled with what she got you last year."

"Can you blame me?" I laugh bitterly. "As if Allie and I would ever wear matching blue polyester sweatshirts with wide-eyed kittens chasing butterflies painted on them. What are we, the Bobbsey twins?" The surly voice of my inner teenager bursts out of my mouth.

"Well, she knows you like cats, Lydia," Vera says, stopping us both in our tracks. "And at least she included Allie."

"Vera, when was the last time you saw me wearing something blue? Never." I supply Vera with the correct answer. "Let alone something made of polyester. Don't you see? My mother bought me something that she would like, not something that I would like."

"What do you want from the woman, Lydia? Two years ago, if I remember correctly, she sent you a check and you weren't happy about that either."

"A check," I say, my voice full of disgust. "What am I, a charity? She doesn't even know her own daughter well enough to pick something out for her."

"Sounds to me like she's damned if she does and damned if she doesn't." Vera starts walking again, and since her arm is still hooked through mine, I have no choice but to follow. She leads me to a wrought iron bench near the campus greenhouse and sits us both down.

"So, you're not talking to her, which theoretically should make you happy, but obviously doesn't," Vera says, summing up our conversation as if it's the end of a fifty-minute hour. "Seriously, Lydia." Vera looks at me with those piercing blue eyes that always demand the absolute truth. "Your mother is how old? Seventy-two?"

"Seventy-three."

"So she's not exactly young."

"Vera, she's not exactly old, either. She's practically the same age as you are."

"Still, life holds no guarantees," Vera reminds us both. "Your mother's been a chain smoker for what, about fifty years?"

"Fifty-nine, but who's counting?"

"You are," Vera points out. "Lydia, all I'm saying is, one never knows what's around the next corner. So don't stand on ceremony. If you want to talk to her, call her."

"But Vera, we've been having the same exact boring conversation since the day I left home. I just can't take it anymore."

"So talk about something else."

"I can't."

"Have you ever tried?"

"Not for a long time."

"Uh-huh." That's all Vera has to say to let me know that she wants details, so I supply them. "It was exactly twelve years ago, when my friend Vincent died. You remember?" Vera nods and squeezes my arm tightly against her side. How could she forget? Vera spent hours on the phone with me, listening to daily reports about Vincent's decline: the burgundy KS lesions splotched all over his face, the thrush in his throat that made it impossible for him to swallow, the numbness in his feet and legs...

"The day he died was a gorgeous hot August afternoon, just about a week before my birthday. Allie was off fishing with some friends, you were in Europe, and my therapist was on vacation. I had been expecting him to go for weeks, but still when he did, it was such a shock, I was a total wreck. So in a moment of weakness, I called my mother. I know, I know, what was I thinking, right?" I look at Vera, who understands that the question is better left unanswered. "So the conversation was going on the way it usually does, with my mother talking about the weather and someone's grandchild who just got engaged, and the new tiles she'd picked out for the bathroom floor. I just couldn't take it anymore, so I interrupted her by blurting out, 'Mom, I'm really upset. My friend Vincent just died of AIDS.' And she said, 'I'm sorry to hear that.' Which you would think is an appropriate thing to say, *if* you didn't know my mother. After a few seconds of silence, she said, 'Lydia, let's talk about something pleasant. What else is new?' Don't you see, Vera?" My voice chokes with pain. "My mother wasn't sorry that my friend had died.

She was sorry *to hear* that my friend had died. She didn't want to talk about it. She wanted to keep things light, change the subject, know what else was new. What else could possibly be new? Vincent had just *died*, for God's sake."

Vera slips her arm out from my elbow and takes my hand gently in hers. "I'm sorry, Lydia," she says softly.

"What are *you* sorry for, Vera?" I ask, my voice rising sharply. "Why is everyone always apologizing for my mother?"

Vera doesn't respond and we sit side by side in silence for a few minutes until the quiet is broken by a man yelling at the top of his lungs, "Stella! *Stella!*" Out of nowhere, a floppy-eared beagle I presume is Stella bounds across the grass toward us, her tail wagging furiously and a noisy jangle of metal tags dangling from the red collar around her neck.

"Come over here, Stella, you silly puppy." Happy for the distraction, I lean forward to grab hold of her collar with one hand while letting her lick the fingers of the other. Stella's owner approaches us to reclaim his dog, and thanks me as he clips on her leash and leads her away. As Vera and I watch them go, the sun ducks behind a cloud, casting us in a shadow that makes me shiver.

"First I'm hot, then I'm cold..." I try to lighten the mood between us. "Is this what menopause is going to be like?"

"It was so long ago, I hardly remember." Vera waves her hand through the air, feigning nonchalance. "Have you had your first hot flash yet?"

"I'm not sure," I say. "My body's gone kind of haywire and I'm a lot warmer in general than I used to be. Especially my feet."

"That's only the beginning, Lydia. When you have your first hot flash, believe me, you'll know." Vera unbuttons her suede jacket and shrugs it off. "Are you still chilly? Here." She drapes it over my shoulders

"No, that's okay." I wiggle out of her jacket and hand it back.

"Lydia, take it. For God's sake, I'm trying to *mother* you." Vera does not hide the frustration in her voice as she arranges her jacket across my back once more. "You know," she says thoughtfully. "That could be part of the problem."

"What do you mean?"

"You say you want your mother to know you, but how can she if you don't let her? Yes, she failed you when Vincent died, but have you let her in since then?"

"Vera, how can I? I took a risk and look where it got me."

"Lydia, I understand how much she hurt you, but that was twelve years ago. Everyone deserves a second chance."

"Second chance? Ha. Try eight-hundred-and-forty-seventh chance. And that's being conservative." I wait but Vera does not laugh or even chuckle. "Vera, I know it isn't all my mother's fault and that every relationship is a two-way street. I've learned at least that much for all the years I've spent in therapy." Vera still does not crack a smile. "But how can I fix things between us if she won't talk about anything besides the weather? It's always been like this. I've been trying to talk to her for years. For *decades*."

"Decades? Hmm." Vera lapses into silence and I watch her out of the corner of my eye, well aware that she is pondering what I've just told her in order to put together her assessment of it. And a minute later, she proves me right. "Lydia, I'm not going to deny the pain your mother has caused you over the years," Vera begins. "And in a perfect world she would take the first step. She would call you, she would apologize to you, she would express a desire to make things right. But you and I both know that's not going to happen."

"I'll say."

"Lydia." Vera speaks my name in her no-nonsense voice, which is even more intimidating than my mother's. "All that happened a long time ago. You haven't had a real conversation with your mother in decades, as you say. So the question is, why hasn't anything changed?"

I watch two dried-up leaves whirling in the wind at my feet for a minute before I answer. "I don't know, Vera. I really don't," I tell her. "When I was younger, I tried to have a better relationship with my mother, but I just couldn't get through to her. Even as a kid I knew that things weren't right between us and once I asked her to come to counseling with me but of course she wouldn't. So as I got older, I just stopped trying. It hurt too much, and in a lot of ways it was easier to learn how to take care of myself. It's like somewhere along the line, my mother and I made this unspoken agreement to never dive below the surface and talk about anything that mattered. You know. Don't ask, don't tell."

"In other words, you gave up on each other."

I think this over. "I suppose so."

"How sad," Vera says and if I didn't know her better, I'd think she was being sarcastic. "Lydia, I'm going to be tough with you here."

I smile ruefully. "I wouldn't expect anything less."

"Good. So listen to me. It's time for you to grow up. You have to be the adult here. I mean it. You're not a child or a teenager anymore. You are an adult and you have to start relating to your mother like one."

"Meaning?"

"Meaning you have to step outside yourself and develop some compassion for your mother. She's a woman, Lydia, with her own history and hurts and issues. She had a childhood which I doubt was easy, she married young, and if she has even half the brainpower of her daughter, I'm sure she was bored out of her mind being a 1950s housewife. And then her twin sister died, which is a tremendous loss…" Vera pauses to let this new take on my mother sink in. "She's a whole person, not just the mother of Lydia Pinkowitz, you know."

"Of course I know that, Vera."

"You know it up here, Lydia," Vera taps my forehead lightly. "But do you know it in here?" She pokes my chest right over my heart. "Anyway, the point is, you have to decide whether or not you want to have a relationship with the woman who happens to be your mother. And if you do, you have to take some risks. And if you don't, you have to let go. Which clearly you are not capable of doing. Don't give me that look. I'm not criticizing you." Vera, who can often read my mind, is quick to clarify. "I'm complimenting you. I think it's a good thing that you can't give up on your mother. But that being the case, you have to try to change things. I know it would be taking a big risk, but Lydia, look at all you're risking by not taking that risk." Vera's baby blues bore into me. "And believe it or not, Lydia, I truly think your mother will be grateful. She's a mother; she wants to mother you. And you're not letting her. And I'll tell you something else." The left side of Vera's cheek twitches like it always does when she comes up with a particularly brilliant idea. "You think of yourself as a motherless child. But did it ever occur to you that the woman who gave birth to you might very well think of herself as a childless mother?"

"Isn't it time to head back for the afternoon session?" I jump up so quickly, Vera's jacket slides to the ground. "There's a talk on Elizabeth

Cady Stanton that a former student of mine is giving and I don't want to miss what she—"

"Wait a minute." Vera bends for her jacket and tugs my arm to make me sit back down. "Lydia. I love you like a daughter—"

"I know you do."

"—and I'm only talking to you like this because I don't want you to make the same mistake that I made."

I turn to give Vera my full attention, knowing from her tone that what she's about to say is very important.

"I never told you what happened when my mother died," Vera says, looking off into the distance. "A few months before she passed away, she said something extremely nasty to me. I don't even remember what it was now; it could have been any number of things. It was probably something about Serena. I know my mother blames me and my lousy parenting skills for the fact that her oldest granddaughter had a silver ring in her eyebrow and a tattoo of a snake curling around her forearm." Vera pauses, still staring at the distant hills surrounding campus, and I let my eyes follow her gaze. Vera and I have taken many road trips together and sometimes our most intimate conversations have taken place as we sat in her car side by side, staring straight ahead just like this.

"Maybe my mother had a little too much to drink that night," Vera continues, "and told me yet again how she wished she had a normal—read: married daughter. A daughter who wasn't crazy enough to be a single parent by choice. '*That* you call a choice?'" Vera asks, infusing her voice with the old-country Yiddish accent of her mother. "Or maybe she was just being her usual thoughtless, judgmental self and was criticizing what I was saying, what I was wearing, what I was doing, or the newest way I was messing up my life." Vera shakes her head as if to banish her unpleasant memories. "The point is, I stopped speaking to her. And she died before we had a chance to reconnect."

"Oh, Vera." I reach for her hand. "You never told me that."

"It's not something I like to think about, much less talk about," she says, still gazing across campus. "Believe me, never in a million years did I ever dream that my last words to my own mother would be 'Mom, I've had just about enough of you.'"

"Ooh." I wince as though someone accidentally-on-purpose stepped on my heart.

"I know." Vera nods and turns to look at me. "I would just hate for the same thing to happen to you, Lydia. It's a terrible feeling. Plus as a therapist, let me tell you it's a lot easier to do the work while your parents are still alive." Vera lets out a deep breath, squeezes my hand, and stands. Without another word we make our way back to the conference slowly, walking side by side like two draft horses hitched to an old creaky wagon, dragging an impossibly heavy load.

❖

PAVLOV'S DOG HAS nothing over our telephone. Talk about a conditioned response: the minute Allie or I even think about having sex, the damn thing knows and starts to ring. And tonight with the street noises outside our bedroom window muted by a thick covering of January snow, it sounds even louder than usual, almost like a scream.

Allie detaches her lips from one of her favorite parts of my body with a groan. "Just ignore it," I whisper, pretending I don't have one ear cocked toward the answering machine.

"Okay." Allie happily goes back to what she was doing, but at the sound of my father's voice—so familiar and yet so strange and unexpected—we both sit up and strain to listen.

I am out of bed in a heartbeat, my bare feet padding across the cold wooden bedroom floor. Stark naked, I hurry through the living room and into the kitchen, but before I can snatch up the phone, I trip over Mishmosh, who appears out of nowhere and inserts himself between my feet mewling for a snack.

"Mish!" I scold him as I catch myself on the kitchen counter and hear the last few words my father utters before he hangs up.

Allie is two steps behind me, carrying our nerdy, matching terrycloth slippers and robes. "What did he want?" she asks, making sure I am covered and warm before dressing herself.

"I don't know." I press the rewind button as Allie picks up Mishmosh. The three of us huddle in the dark kitchen, listening.

"Lydia, it's uh…it's Dad." My father's voice sounds tired as he falters. "I'm calling to tell you that your mother is fine."

"What?" Allie asks, confused. "Why would he call to tell you that your mother is fine?"

"Hush." I quiet Allie and rewind the tape. "I'm trying to listen."

"…to tell you that your mother is fine," my father says again. "The doctors here say everything is fine and she's going to be fine, so there's nothing to worry about. I'll call you tomorrow." Then there is a pause. "Okay," my father says quietly, more to himself than to me. And then he hangs up.

"Oh my God." I stare at the answering machine as if it can live up to its name and answer the questions spinning around my head. What's happened to my mother? Where is she? What doctors? What's wrong with her? Allie lowers Mishmosh to the floor with a gentle thud and tries to lead me toward a chair but I insist on staying where I am and listening to the message again.

"Do you want a glass of water?" Allie asks. "How about a cup of tea?"

"No thanks." I switch on the light and play back the message one more time, writing it down on the back of the envelope that contains our electric bill. "How can my mother be fine at the same time that she's going to be fine?" I ask aloud. "If everything *is* fine, there's no need to use the future tense, as in 'she's *going to be* fine.'" I underline the offending phrase as if I'm correcting a poorly written essay handed in by a Women's Studies 101 student. "And if there's nothing to worry about," I continue editing, "then there's no need to *say* there's nothing to worry about. So obviously, there really *is* something to worry about."

"Why don't you just call him back?" Allie, ever the practical one suggests. She hands me the phone and I dial my parents' number but nobody answers.

"Where would they be on a Sunday night at…" I look at the digital clock on the microwave oven. "…thirteen minutes after eleven?" Because I was born on a Friday the thirteenth, I have always considered thirteen my lucky number, so I take this as a positive sign: just as my father said, my mother is and/or is going to be fine.

"Your father said, 'the doctors here,'" Allie reads the note over my shoulder. "Do you think they're at a hospital?"

"This is ridiculous," I say, my voice rising. "Why didn't he leave his phone number? Who leaves a message like this? I mean, what does he think, I can just roll over now and go back to sleep? My family is so damn dysfunctional." My voice sounds shrill even to my own ears, but righteous anger is the only way to dissolve the hard knot of fear that's starting to form in my stomach.

"Lydia, let's not panic yet." Allie sits down and pulls her chair close to mine. "Try dialing star-sixty-nine and see if you can find out where he was calling from."

I do as I am told and my father's cell phone number comes up. Allie looks pleased: problem solved. Except my father doesn't answer when I dial the number. I leave a message for him to call me immediately.

"So all we have to do is wait," Allie says, folding her arms and leaning back, in it for the long haul.

"Not quite." I place the cordless phone on the kitchen table softly as though I don't want to wake up anyone who might have the good sense to be asleep at this hour. "My father's technical skills leave a lot to be desired. I'm sure he has no idea how to get into the voice mail on his cell phone."

"Why don't you call Jack?" Allie suggests. "He might know something."

"Jack." Just saying his name makes me want to crawl back into bed and pull the covers over my head. For a week. But Allie's right; maybe he does know something. "Can you get my address book?" I ask Allie.

"Where is it?"

"In my pocketbook. On the couch in my study." I don't have the strength to move.

Allie leaves the kitchen and returns holding my purse at arm's length. "No way I'm going in there," she says, dangling my bag out in front of her. "That thing bites."

I smile to show Allie that I appreciate her attempt to make me laugh, even at a time like this. Allie, a true butch from her steel-toed boots to the top of her buzz cut, has never carried a pocketbook and finds them a bit intimidating. "That thing is like a black hole," she once said to me, pointing. "It sucks up everything in its path. I'm afraid if I ever went in there, I'd never get out."

Taking my bag from Allie, I reach in, find my address book, and flip it open to the page that has Jack's information on it. I also fish out my cell phone and dial his Westchester number first, then his Manhattan number, and finally his number in the Hamptons. To my great surprise, all three of them have been disconnected.

"That's bizarre," Allie says. "Are you sure you have the right numbers? Maybe you're dialing wrong because you're upset."

"Do you want to try?" I ask, not masking my annoyance. I hand her the phone and not surprisingly she comes up with the same results: *The number you have reached, 212-555-7347, has been disconnected. No further information is available. The number you have reached...*

"What do you think happened?" Allie puts down the phone, admitting defeat.

"Will you feed him?" I nod my chin at Mishmosh, who has been sitting in front of his bowl patiently waiting for a handout ever since his two human can openers leapt out of bed. As Allie tends to him, I think out loud. "These are pretty old numbers. When was the last time I called Crystal or Jack?" Truthfully, I can't remember ever speaking to either one of them on the phone. "I bet I know," I say to Allie's back as she stands at the sink, rinsing off the cat food fork. "Jack probably doesn't even have a land line anymore. You know how he likes to be on the cutting edge of things. He probably went totally cellular years ago." I scowl at my cousin's inconvenient hipness. "Now what?"

"Now we have milk and cookies," Allie says, standing up and moving toward the cabinet over the stove.

Has Allie gone mad? I watch her, incredulous. *Who can eat at a time like this?* As Allie sets a box of Oreos, a carton of milk, and two glasses down on the table, I wonder what she's up to. Is Allie actually hungry? Having a sugar craving? Or such a creature of habit that she has to indulge in our usual post-coital snack even though she's been cheated out of an orgasm or two?

"Here." Allie dips an Oreo into a glass of milk until it is nice and soggy, just the way I like it. "C'mon, eat something."

"No thanks," I say. "I'm not hungry."

"Have it anyway." Allie extends the cookie toward me. "You need a little *nosh*." At the sound of the Yiddish word uttered so lovingly, my heart cracks open and I finally understand. Allie isn't doing this for herself. She's doing this for me. Allie can't make it—whatever *it* is—go away, but she can take care of me, nurture me, in this simple way, the way that she knows best.

I accept Allie's offering, a little smile playing across my lips.

"What?" Allie asks, smiling too, and dunking a cookie for herself.

"Alicia Maria Taraza." I take a bite of softened chocolate wafer. "Are you trying to mother me?"

"*Mother* you?" Allie, who often says she has all the maternal instincts of a piña colada, is insulted to the core. "Lydia Marilyn Pinkowitz, I am not trying to *mother* you," she says in a huff before gentling her voice. "Silly girl, I'm trying to *baby* you."

"Oh," I say softly. And then I crawl onto her lap and let her.

❖

IGNORANCE IS BLISS, *ignorance is bliss...* It's twenty past eight and I'm still in my bathrobe, sitting on the couch in my study with my hands clasped in my lap and my eyes closed, the phrase repeating itself inside my head over and over like a mantra. Every so often—usually during times of crisis—I remember the Zen phase I went through years ago after attending a Women and Buddhism conference, and decide that meditation is the answer to all my problems. So I set the timer on the microwave oven for thirteen minutes, sit up tall and straight, and try to quiet my mind.

Ignorance is bliss, ignorance is bliss... The three words are stuck inside my brain like a song fragment from one of the scratched-up records I listened to as a teenager. Bliss would be nice, serenity would do, I'd even settle for fairly calm at this point, anything to replace the anxiety that has lodged itself in my gut like a stone and won't go away until I find out what has happened to my mother, who I'm sure would be very surprised at my reaction to all this. "Why, Lydia," I can just hear her saying, one perfectly manicured hand fanned across her ample chest. "I didn't know you cared."

Even though my thirteen minutes of meditation aren't over, I open my eyes to peek at the clock hanging over my bookcase. It's half past eight and still my father hasn't called. Damn. What is wrong with him? How could he leave me hanging like this? I blow a long, loud puff of air out of my mouth and mutter a few expletives under my breath. So much for serenity, acceptance, and being in the moment, I think as I shut my eyes again and try to focus. Thankfully the microwave timer buzzes just as I exhale.

"Are you cooking something?" Allie appears in the doorway dressed in jeans and a brown corduroy shirt, cradling her Monday morning cup of coffee.

"No. Meditating." I open my mouth into a giant yawn. "Or trying to, anyway."

"No word, huh?" Allie and I both glance toward the phone on my desk. "Have you tried calling?"

I nod. "No answer."

"Did you send Jack an email?"

I nod again. "No response."

"Well then, you might as well enjoy the calm before the storm." Allie lifts her mug and, peering over the rim at me, takes a noisy sip. "Why don't you go back to bed and rest a little? It's January, remember? Semester break. You're supposed to be on vacation."

"You're right." I stretch my arms overhead and let out another huge yawn. "Maybe I will get back into bed. If Mishmosh will be kind enough to share it with me. I didn't get much sleep last night."

"Call me if you hear anything." Allie turns and I follow her into the kitchen where she laces up her work boots, zips her jacket, and gives me a kiss good-bye. As soon as she leaves the house I head toward the bedroom, but the moment the door clicks shut I reverse direction and go back into my study just as we both knew I would.

I am incapable of going back to bed once I'm up, or napping during the day; work is how I relax. It's one of the many ways I take after my father. Another trait we have in common is that we are both early birds, up with the sun. Unlike my mother, who is not fully human before ten o'clock in the morning. Growing up, it was my father who greeted me downstairs on school days and made sure I got out the door in time to catch my bus. He danced around the kitchen frying eggs, pouring orange juice, and singing off-key Broadway show tunes, pretending he was Yul Brynner in *The King and I* or Robert Goulet in *Camelot*. This was all too much for my mother, who never joined us for breakfast during the week. On Saturdays and Sundays she managed to drag herself downstairs at a fairly decent hour, groaning, "Coff*eeee*," the last syllable dragged out into a desperate moan. "Doris, you made it," my father always cried with delight, happy as a puppy to see her. He'd pull out a chair, help her slump into it, and once she was settled, start singing, "If Ever I Would Leave You," or "Younger than Springtime," further aggravating my mother, who longed for nothing more than dead silence. Which is exactly what I don't want right now.

"Ring, Pavlov," I command the telephone. It doesn't obey. Maybe it will if I start thinking about Allie and me and the things we almost did last night. I squeeze my eyes shut and try to come up with a good sexual fantasy but my heart isn't in it and besides, it doesn't work. Nine o'clock comes and goes. As does nine-fifteen. Where could he possibly be? "Is it too much trouble to pick up the goddamn phone and let me know you're okay?" I say aloud. Oh great. Now I'm beginning to sound like him. Whenever I stayed out past my curfew or committed some other infraction against my parents' many rules, which was more often than not, it was my father's job to reprimand me. During my teenage years, "just wait till your father gets home" was my mother's standard greeting whenever I walked through the door.

Nine-thirty arrives and departs, followed by ten o'clock. I manage to throw a load of laundry into the machine, choke down half a piece of toast, and check in with Allie twice. I download my email hoping for a note from Jack, but finding none, I log onto the Internet to look up all the hospitals within a thirty-mile radius of my parents' house. Many phone calls later I learn that no one by the name of Doris Pinkowitz has been admitted in the past forty-eight hours to any of them.

While I'm sitting at my computer, I decide to go over the syllabus for the new course I'll be teaching this spring: American Women's Contemporary Fiction from 1970 to 1999. The reading list still has some holes in it. I can't decide which book of Toni Morrison's to teach, *Sula* or *Song of Solomon*, and there isn't time for both. I wander over to my bookcase where the well-worn novels are leaning against each other on the middle shelf like two old friends. Was it Colette or Virginia Woolf who said that reading a novel before noon was her favorite guilty pleasure? I can't remember. My favorite guilty pleasure is sitting on the couch in my study reading a novel before noon on a weekday in my bathrobe with a large cup of hot chocolate steaming at my side. I indulge myself and it works: after only fifteen minutes I am so involved with *Sula* and her problems that when the telephone does ring, I almost don't bother answering it. But then with a jolt I remember my own problems and jump up to get the phone.

"Lydia, it's Dad."

"Dad, what's happening? Where are you? Is Mom all right? Why didn't you leave me your number so I could call you back? I was so worried, I didn't sleep all night."

"Lydia, calm down. C'mon now. Your mother is fine. I told you so on the message. And you know if you want to reach me, all you have to do is call the office. They always know where I am."

Oh right, the office. How could I forget? My father's secretary knows his whereabouts but his own daughter doesn't have a clue. *And whose fault is that*, the little voice in my head named guilt asks. To shut her up, I continue blasting my father as I pace around my study. "Dad, why did you wait so long to call me this morning?"

"Lydia, please. I'm doing the best I can here. And besides, it's barely eight o'clock."

"Eight o'clock?" I stop in my tracks and glance at the clock on the wall which reads two minutes past eleven. Am I dreaming? Or in a time warp? "Dad," I ask, "where are you?"

"We're in Los Angeles," my father answers.

"Los Angeles?" I keep repeating my father's words like a deranged parrot. "What are you doing in Los Angeles?"

"We were on an Elderhostel trip, Lydia. I told you we were going."

"No, you didn't." Has my father forgotten we have not spoken to each other in eight months?

"Sure I did. It's the trip Selma and Harry Appelbaum took last year, remember? They couldn't stop raving about it. Every day they give you a different program: Jewish history, Jewish theatre, Jewish literature, Jewish art...I must have told you about it."

"No, Dad, you didn't tell me about it."

"Lydia, I'm sure I told you. You must have forgotten."

"I didn't forget. You didn't tell me. Never mind." I can't believe we've been on the phone for less than two minutes and already I'm arguing with him. I collapse onto the couch and lean forward, holding my head in my hand. "Dad, just tell me what's going on."

"Your mother caught something."

My father says this casually, as if he and my mother were on a fishing boat and she hooked a bluefish or a flounder. I wait for him to elaborate, but he doesn't so I ask, "Dad, what did she catch?"

He sighs as though he isn't sure whether or not it's a good idea to tell me. "Some type of respiratory thing," he finally says. "You know how these trips are. You're with a bunch of *altercockers* all day long, on the bus, off the bus, everyone coughing, sneezing, spreading their germs around like wildfire. But don't worry, Lydia, the doctors say she's going to make a full recovery. There's nothing to get excited about. Your mother's going to be fine."

"Can I talk to her?"

"We're not at the hospital right now. We're at the hotel."

"Who's we?"

"Jack is with me. Hold on, I'll get him for you."

My head snaps up. "Dad, wait. I don't want to—" But my father has already put down the receiver and gone in search of the last person on earth I feel like talking to right at the moment. Or at any moment.

"Lydia." The way Jack says my name I can tell he's as pleased to be speaking with me as I am to be speaking with him.

"Jack." I answer in kind. He says nothing until I ask the obvious. "What's going on with my mother?"

"Well, for starters, she's in intensive care—"

"What?" I shriek. "I thought my father said she was fine."

"Sure she is, Lydia. As fine as anyone who had to be carried out of a lecture about Jews and musical theatre called 'Give My Regards to Tevye' in front of two hundred and fifty people and rushed to the emergency room—"

"What?" I shriek again. "They had to carry her out of a lecture?"

"Relax, Lydia. It was the best place it could have happened. An auditorium full of Jews, are you kidding? Uncle Max said when he stood up and yelled, 'Is there a doctor in the house?' about ninety-seven people rushed over to help."

"Oh my God." I can't believe what I'm hearing. "Jack, please tell me—" My voice breaks with sobs that have risen unbidden from my throat and I can't form another word. I cover the mouthpiece of the phone with my hand while I take a few deep breaths to calm myself down.

"I told you we shouldn't have called her," Jack says, presumably to my father. "Lydia, try to keep the hysterics to a minimum, okay? We've got enough to worry about here."

I want to reach my hands through the telephone wires across three thousand miles, wind his greasy white ponytail around his neck several times, and strangle him with it, I really do. But he has important information that I am desperate to find out, so I force myself to remain civil. It's a huge effort. "Jack," I ask in a shaky voice, "can you please tell me exactly what happened? Starting from the beginning?"

Jack lets out a deep sigh to let me know I couldn't be imposing on him more if I were asking him to fly to the moon and back merely by flapping his short, hairy arms. Nevertheless, he's a decent guy, so he'll be kind enough to fill me in. "Lydia, our parents—"

"Whoa." I'm on my feet pacing around the room again. This is too much. When did they become *our* parents? "Hello, they're *my* parents, Jack, remember? They're your uncle and aunt."

"Oh excuse me, Professor Pinkowitz. I forget how fussy you always get about using just the right word."

"Speaking of the right word, it's *Dr.* Pinkowitz," I inform him, knowing but not caring that I am being an asshole.

"Whatever." I can practically see Jack rolling his beady little eyes. "Well anyway, Lydia, they're my parents, too. My godparents. In case you've forgotten, let me refresh your memory: my mother is dead and my father the schmuck is AWOL and has been since I was a teenager. Aunt Doris and Uncle Max are the only family I have."

"They're still not your parents," I say stubbornly.

"Lydia, they think of me as their son."

"Says who?" I can't quite believe we're having this long overdue discussion now of all times, but apparently we are.

"Lydia." Every time Jack says my name he utters the three syllables with a new degree of exaggerated patience, as if the longer this conversation continues, the stupider I get. "Do I have to spell it out for you?"

"Yes, Jack, I guess you do."

"Who did they call when they really needed someone? Not their darling daughter, that's for sure." Jack pauses to let his words sink in. "In case you haven't noticed," he continues, his voice triumphant, "they didn't call you. They called me."

Tears sting the corners of my eyes, and I wipe them away with the sleeve of my bathrobe. Jack knows he just delivered a knockout punch, but I refuse to go down without a fight.

"First of all, it's *whom*," I say, unable to stop myself. "*Whom* did they call. Not *who*. And second of all, they probably called you because you're so familiar with L.A.," I add, even though my words sound lame, even to me. "You know, because you work *in the industry*." I emphasize the irritating phrase my cousin is always throwing in my face.

"Lydia, I haven't worked in Hollywood for a long time. I'm based in New York, remember? And besides, we're not exactly sightseeing here."

"Well, I don't care. They're still not your parents. They're mine," I declare like a two-year-old who has just snatched a box of crayons back from a thieving playmate. I can't believe the words that are coming out of my mouth—me, the champion of chosen families who has actually delivered a paper on the subject entitled "Creating Families in Creative Ways." I'm eating my words and they're making me sick to my stomach. And to top it all off, I still don't know what's happened to my own flesh and blood.

"Jack, I'm sorry," I say even though I'm not. But I know if Jack gets any madder, he will simply hang up the phone. "Can you just tell me what's happened to her?"

"I accept your apology," Jack says, his voice smug. "Wait, Uncle Max is telling me something. Hold on."

If he were really your parent, you'd call him Dad, not Uncle Max, I think, further proving Jack's point—I am always making a big fuss about using the correct word. Or words. As if in a case like this it really matters.

Jack takes his time coming back to the phone; I know he is enjoying this new power he has over me and wants to milk it for all it's worth by withholding information for as long as he possibly can. I lie back against the couch exhausted, pull a section of hair forward, and examine it strand by strand, searching for split ends.

"We have to go in a minute." Jack's voice reappears, jarring me away from my old habit. "Visiting hours start at eight o'clock, and we want to get over there and grab a quick breakfast in the cafeteria before we go up to see her."

"Jack, I still don't know what's going on. You haven't told me anything and all my father will say is she's going to be fine. Can I get some more information, please? Like, is there a name for what she has?"

"Bronchitis." Jack throws me a bone.

"Oh." I sit forward and breathe a bit easier. "That's not so bad."

"It is on top of her emphysema."

"She has emphysema? Since when?"

"Since who knows when? She smokes like a chimney, Lydia. Or I should say smoked."

"She stopped smoking?" This is the most shocking news I've ever heard in my entire life. Jack might as well have told me that my mother grew another head or just ran the New York Marathon.

"She quit a few months ago. When she broke her arm. It was too much trouble to light her cigarettes. You know how she is, Lydia." Jack finally acknowledges that I am somewhat familiar with my own mother. "When her mind is made up, her mind is made up. So that's what happened. She quit cold turkey. Just like that."

"Wait a minute. My mother broke her arm?" I keep repeating Jack's words back to him, hoping that by doing so I'll be better able to absorb them. "When did she break her arm? Why didn't anybody call me? What happened?"

"She fell. Her arm's fine now. That's the least of her problems," Jack says curtly.

"Jack." I am gripping the phone so hard, my hand is beginning to cramp. "Why didn't you call me when my mother broke her arm?"

"Because Aunt Doris told me not to. She said she didn't want to bother you."

"Bother me?" I collapse against the back of the sofa again, stunned. "She really said she didn't want to bother me?" Closing my eyes, I swallow hard. "What about my father?" I ask, grasping at straws. "He didn't want you to call me either?"

"Nope," Jack says, not masking the triumph in his voice. "In fact, Uncle Max specifically told me not to call."

"And if he told you to jump off the Empire State Building you'd do that, too?" I leap to my feet, furious again. "Jack, can't you think for yourself for once in your life?"

"Lydia, I'm a trustworthy guy. I work in the industry, remember? People tell me all kinds of things in confidence and that means my trap stays shut. I have never, in my entire life, broken anybody's trust and I don't intend to start doing so now. Especially for you. Uncle Max told me not to call you when your mother broke her arm so I didn't call you when your mother broke her arm. Case closed."

"Jack." I force his name between clenched teeth. "I am not one of your fucking clients, okay? I'm your..." I pause, searching for the right word. "...relative."

"Lydia, I can see that the only person you care about in this family is you. Oh poor, poor Lydia, she doesn't know what's going on, no one fills her in." Jack's voice drips with sarcasm and I imagine him raising his arms to imitate a violin player in a show of false sympathy. "Well, maybe if you cared a little more, you wouldn't be so left out of the loop. We could have used your help, believe me, when Aunt Doris broke her arm. Crystal was there almost every day cooking, cleaning up…"

"I'm sorry she had to go through that," I say to Jack, but I don't mean Crystal. I mean my mother. I'm sure she was less than thrilled to have Crystal taking over her kitchen. And God only knows what she served my parents for dinner—Cap'n Crunch cereal with 2% milk and a celery stick on the side?

"You know, Aunt Doris acted kind of strange when Crystal was there," Jack says, his tone of voice a tad less hostile.

"Strange? How so?"

"She acted like someone who knew she was dying."

"Dying? What do you mean?" The contents of my stomach lurch again and I sink back onto the couch.

"I mean one night Crystal came home wearing a mink coat, and this was some piece of fur, let me tell you. Even though the sleeves were too short and it was too big around, it didn't matter. She still looked like a million bucks in it. Hell, anybody would."

I silently marvel at the way Jack manages to compliment and insult his wife all at the same time.

"So," Jack continues, "I said to her, 'What's with the mink?' and she said, 'Aunt Doris gave it to me. She said it was the most beautiful thing she owned and she wanted me to have it.' Now, Lydia, doesn't that strike you as strange?"

"Very," I say, taking a deep gulp of air. I know that coat. I remember the day my father gave it to my mother; it was a present for their twentieth wedding anniversary. I was fifteen years old and had just become a staunch vegetarian, and it took everything I had not to squirt ketchup all over the gift that made my mother swoon with delight. Why was she giving away her most prized possession now? And to Crystal of all people? Not that I would ever wear a mink coat, which is something my mother knows. But still, if it was the most beautiful thing she owned, the thing she treasured most of all, why wouldn't she save it for me? Am I really such a horrible daughter?

"Yes, yes, yes," Jack says, as if to answer the question floating around my head. But he is talking to my father. "I'll be right there, Uncle Max. Listen, Lydia, I have to go."

"Can you please put my father back on the phone?"

"Mission impossible. Uncle Max has left the building."

"Jack—"

"Lydia, don't bust my chops, all right? I have to go."

"Can you at least give me the name of the hospital my mother's in?"

Even though I can tell he doesn't want to, Jack gives me all kinds of phone numbers, which I hastily scribble on a pad: the hospital, the hotel they're staying at, his cell phone, my father's cell phone, which of course I already have, not that it did me any good. Now I feel a little calmer; at least I can call the hospital and speak directly to my mother.

"Thanks, Jack," I say, heading toward my desk, eager to hang up the phone. But just before I say good-bye, my whole body starts to tremble, and I realize that once I hang up, I'll be losing my lifeline to her. My mother. And imperfect as she is, she's the only one I've got.

"Jack," I say, my voice small and vulnerable. "Do you thinks she's going to be okay? Or is my father just saying she's fine because he needs to believe it?"

"Lydia, what am I, a doctor?" Jack asks, but his voice has softened a bit, too.

"Isn't there anything else you can say to me?" I plead, as tears start to fall.

"Yes, there is," Jack says, sounding harsh again. "Get your ass out here, Lydia." He pauses and then screams, "Now!"

❖

I AM GOOD at many things; being a daughter is not one of them. A good daughter would have hung up the phone after speaking with her cousin Jack and immediately made plane reservations. A good daughter would already have her suitcase packed. A good daughter would not be sitting on the couch in her study with her cat's head resting on her lap, staring out the window at the falling snow and asking her mother to die.

"Mom," I say aloud. "I've never asked you for anything, but now I'm asking you to do just one tiny little thing for me. Please don't make me come out there. If you really loved me, and you're going to die anyway, you'd do us both a favor and just go now, no muss, no fuss, no cross-country plane trip. I know it's an unusual request, and not exactly a nice one, but still, I'm asking you politely. Please? Pretty please? Pretty please with sugar on top?" I wait for the phone to ring again, this time with the hospital on the other end delivering the sad news, but the only sound in the room is the loud jagged purr of Mishmosh snoozing happily beside me.

I sigh and stroke the soft fur between his pointy little ears. I'm going to have to go out there. I know this. Why would my mother start making things easy for me now? And besides, don't I deserve the final deathbed scene that I've fantasized about a million times? It's so familiar to me, I don't even have to shut my eyes to conjure up an image of my mother lying in a coma, her ability to speak gone, but her razor-sharp hearing completely intact. And finally, I get a chance to deliver the speech I've rehearsed in my head so many times.

"Mom," I say, imagining myself pulling a chair close to her hospital bed and taking her hand. "I need you to know how much you've hurt me over the years. Everything I did was wrong, and every time you criticized me—my weight, my hair, my clothes, my friends, my career choice, my 'lifestyle,' as you call it, my failure to give you a grandchild—I felt like a wooden pencil you were breaking in half with one quick snap. You never held me when I was a child. You never gave me a hug. You never told me you loved me. You never said you were proud of me. You never made an effort to get to know me or let me get to know you so we could be part of each other's lives. You never sent me a newspaper clipping or a recipe in the mail, you never called me just to say hello and that you were thinking of me like other people's mothers do. Nothing I have ever done has pleased you. Nothing I have ever done has been good enough for you. We've never had a heart-to-heart conversation. I have basically lived without a mother for forty-nine years, and I don't think there are words that can say how much pain that has caused me, and how deeply I have ached for you every single day of my entire life."

Whenever I come to this part of the fantasy, whether I am in my therapist's office, driving my car, or falling asleep beside Allie, I always start to cry. And today is no exception. But as I'm wiping my wet cheeks with the sleeve of my bathrobe, something unusual happens: I get mad.

"*Now* you're going to die?" I thump the arm of the sofa and yell so loudly that Mishmosh springs off my lap as though he's being scolded. "*Now*, before we have a chance to work anything out, *now* you're going to leave me? How dare you?" I scream as Mishmosh scurries from the room. "You have some nerve," I mutter, a phrase my mother has often said to me. "Some goddamn nerve."

My outburst energizes me enough to cross the room, pick up the phone, and call the hospital number that Jack gave me. I stare out the window at the fat, lazy snowflakes drifting through the sky as I am put on hold once, twice, three times before I finally reach a nurse named Angelina who tells me that no, I can't talk to my mother; she isn't well enough to speak on the phone. And contrary to what my father so desperately wants to believe, she is not "fine" at all. Angelina's official diagnosis is that my mother is "not so good."

"Do you think she's going to die?" I ask the question I do and do not want answered.

"I can't say," Angelina replies, which I take to mean she isn't allowed to say, not that she isn't capable of making a judgment call.

"If she were your mother, would you come?" I ask, tearfully. Despite Jack's order to get my ass out to the West Coast pronto, like a good Pinkowitz, I'm not going anywhere without a second opinion.

Angelina hesitates before saying again, "She doesn't look very good," and that she can't say much more than that. If I want, I can call back later when the doctor makes his rounds, but there's no guarantee he'll have time to speak with me.

After I hang up I dial the lumberyard, but one of Allie's coworkers tells me she's too busy with a customer to come to the phone. And my therapist, believe it or not, is out on maternity leave. Vera is next in line.

"Lydia, what a nice surprise," she says, her voice more relaxed than usual. "God, it's nice to be on break, isn't it? I'm still in my bathrobe and it's almost time for lunch, how do you like that?" Vera, who is even more of a workaholic than I am, chuckles, pleased with herself. "Is this how the other half lives? You know, much as I love teaching, I could get used to being a lady of leisure. How about you?"

"Vera," I say, which is all it takes for her to know that something is terribly wrong.

"Lydia, what's the matter?" Vera asks, the lightness instantly gone from her voice.

"It's my mother," I wail, and then tell her everything.

"Oh, Lydia, you poor thing," Vera clucks with so much tenderness, I almost go over the edge completely. But that would never do, so I change the focus of our conversation and tell Vera about my mother's mink coat, which, as Jack was only too happy to mention, now belongs to Crystal instead of me.

"But Lydia, you would never wear something made of mink," Vera responds, stating the obvious just as I knew she would.

"That's not the point, Vera," I say, relieved to let my anger flow. "She still should have given it to me. And for your information, I had big plans for that coat. Remember the article I sent you years ago, about that vegetarian woman who inherited a bunch of furs from her mother and made them into teddy bears, and then started her own company? I was going to send my mother's coat to her so she could make something out of it for me. I know it's hypocritical since I'm a vegetarian and everything, but still, the animals are dead already, it's not like I'm killing them all over again, so—"

"Lydia, please. Stop already. Enough about the coat." I can tell by Vera's voice that her patience is wearing thin. "You need to deal with what's going on with your mother. What if this is the end? If you don't go out to L.A., you'll spend the next forty years sitting in your therapist's office trying to resolve your guilt. You have to get on a plane, Lydia, and the sooner, the better."

"All right, all right," I mumble into the receiver. Even though I'm not surprised at what Vera is saying, I don't have to pretend to be happy about it. But if I'd wanted someone to give me permission to not go to California, I wouldn't have called her. I would have called…whom? I can't think of one person on the planet who would tell me what I want to hear: *It's okay, Lydia. You don't have to go see your dying mother. You have much more important things to do, like work on another article that no one will ever read, clean out the junk drawer in the kitchen that's been bothering you for years, sit around in your bathrobe and watch your cat's toenails grow, pick at the split ends of your already damaged hair…*

"I know this will be hard for you." Vera's acknowledgment cuts into my thoughts. "But it's also an opportunity. Think about what you want to tell your mother. These might be the last words she ever hears you speak."

"I have nothing to say to her," I lie, and even though Vera doesn't believe me, she allows me to steer our conversation in another direction. I ask Vera what she's going to do during intersession and she tells me she's going off to Albany in a day or two to see Serena and help her celebrate her upcoming birthday. Vera can't believe she's old enough to have a daughter who's about to turn forty; I can't believe Vera's daughter, or anyone's daughter, would want her mother around on such a momentous occasion. I tell Vera I don't want to interrupt her visit with Serena but she insists I can call her any time. "If my cell phone is turned on, that means I'm open for business. I hardly sleep anymore anyway," Vera reminds me. "It happens to women of a certain age, Lydia. Ever since menopause I've been waking up at four o'clock, five o'clock... Six in the morning feels like the middle of the day."

"Thanks, Vera. I just may take you up on your offer."

"You're welcome, Lydia. And listen, think about what you want to say to your mother. There has to be something."

We hang up and I stay where I am for a moment, berating myself for not telling my dearest friend the truth. But how could I tell Vera what a horrible creature I am? Only a truly evil person would be pleased at the thought of guilt-tripping her own mother during the last moments of the poor woman's life. No, only Mishmosh and my therapist, who gets paid to tell me that I'm not rotten to the core, are allowed to know that there have been many times in my life when I have actually looked forward to the time I would become an "orphan." People feel sorry for motherless daughters; people judge daughters who don't speak to their mothers while they're still alive. I have always suspected that various people, including Vera, Allie, and maybe even my therapist, secretly think that my failed relationship with my mother is all my fault. Even though they would never say so, of course.

But sometimes other people say things. Not directly, but still, I get the message. As I make my way into the kitchen to see if Mishmosh is ready for his midmorning snack, I remember a conversation I had with my young colleague Emmeline right at the beginning of last semester when she was a newly hired faculty member in the Women's Studies department.

It was a Friday night and Emmeline asked if I wanted to go somewhere and have a drink with her. What she really wanted to do was cry on my shoulder as she told me the long, sad saga of her recent breakup, which was the main reason she was so happy to accept her new faculty position at Paradise College. It gave her the perfect excuse to abandon the city where she had just finished grad school and move three hundred miles away, leaving behind the louse who had dumped her without any warning and completely broken her heart.

"Emmeline, have one of these," I'd said, urging her to eat a cracker spread with Brie to soak up the Merlot she was guzzling like cherry soda. "I know it's hard, but you'll find someone else."

"That's easy for you to say. You've been with Allie what, ten years, twenty years?"

"Something like that." I left the exact number of years Allie and I have lived together vague on purpose. No need to rub it in.

"Well, I'll tell you one thing." Emmeline drained her glass and set it down on the table with a thunk. "The next person I go out with won't get very far unless he or she gets along well with his or her mother."

"What do you mean?" Normally I would have teased Emmeline about the grammatical awkwardness that she, being bisexual, was forced to employ, but her comment hit home and brought me up short.

"I mean," she waved her empty glass toward our server, "if you can't have a healthy relationship with your own mother, I don't see how you can have a healthy relationship with anyone else."

"Is that so?" My voice was colder than the ice cubes chilling the Amaretto I was sipping. "I guess that means my relationship with Allie isn't as healthy as I thought."

"Really?" Emmeline asked as our server whisked away her empty glass, reassuring her she'd be right back with another. "You mean to tell me that the Queen of Feminism has a few issues with her mother?"

"A few? A few hundred maybe," I said with a huff. "Entire theses could be written on the subject."

"Tell me about it." Emmeline leaned forward, eager to take the focus away from the tired old subject of her failed love life. "Is it because you're a lesbian?"

"No. Or at least not totally." Suddenly I felt like having another drink, too, so when our server returned with Emmeline's glass of wine, I asked her to bring me a second cordial. "I mean, that didn't help, of course, but my mother and I didn't get along from the day I was born. In fact, according to family lore, my very first word was 'no' and it all went downhill from there." I sighed the sigh that always escapes my lips whenever I talk about my mother. "She always takes every choice I make personally," I went on, aware that I was starting to whine. "I became a vegetarian not because I loved animals but because I hated her cooking. I became a lesbian not because I loved women but because I didn't want my life to turn out like hers. I left New York not because I loved New England but because—"

"What did she say when you came out as a lesbian?" Emmeline interrupted.

I shrugged as if it were no big deal. "Nothing."

"Nothing?" Emmeline's eyebrows rose. "What do you mean, nothing?"

"I mean," I held up my right hand and placed the tip of my index finger against the top of my thumb to form the shape of a big fat goose egg, "nothing. Literally. I sent home a letter, thinking that was the kindest way to come out to them, you know, give my parents some time to sit with the news and absorb it before we talked. And believe me, I spent weeks on that letter. I must have written fifty drafts." I picked up my freshened drink and downed it. "One week went by, then two, then three, then an entire month. I was beginning to think that maybe my letter had gotten lost in the mail. But no such luck." Emmeline waited while I lifted a cracker to my mouth and bit into it, hard. "So I called and asked my mother if she had gotten my note and she said yes. I asked her why she hadn't phoned me. And she said, 'I didn't call you because I didn't want to have this conversation with you.' So I said, 'Well, guess what, Mom. We're having it.' And she said, 'No, we're not,' and hung up the phone."

"She hung up on you? Wow." Emmeline was properly shocked. "Did you call her back?"

"No, why would I? So she could just hang up on me again?"

"What about your father?"

"We've never talked about it either." I reached for another cracker, pushed a gooey lump of Brie onto it, and shoved the whole thing into my mouth.

"Well." Emmeline sipped her drink thoughtfully. "I don't know,

Lydia. Maybe you're the exception that proves the rule. Most mothers love their kids no matter what. They can't help it. It's instinct. I mean look at that awful killer, Jeffrey Dahmer. He chopped up young boys and put them in the freezer, and even *his* mother wept when he died."

Mishmosh wanders into the kitchen and meows loudly, startling me back into the present. "Am I really less lovable than a serial killer?" I ask my furry friend as I dump the contents of a can of Nine Lives into his bowl. "What's so terrible about me?" I wonder aloud as he frantically gulps mouthfuls of tuna as though he hasn't eaten for two days instead of two hours. "There has to be something."

There's only one way to find out, the voice of reason, which sounds an awful lot like Vera, whispers in my ear. I try to ignore it, and make myself a cup of tea. But when I lift the kettle to fill it with water, I notice that my hand is shaking. Not only that, my whole body is trembling again just as it was when Jack and I wound up our conversation a few hours ago.

"Maybe I should take a hot bath to get the chill out of me," I say to Mishmosh, but instead of heading for the bathroom, I go back to my study, sit down in front of my computer, and bring up the home pages of several different airlines. With my belly still trembling, I book an early morning flight for tomorrow, lay out the clothes I'll need to take, and then dash out to the supermarket. By the time Allie gets home from work at quarter after five, my bags are packed, my electronic ticket is printed out, and all our kitchen counters are strewn with enough cans of cat food to get Mishmosh through the rest of the winter and enough cereal, eggs, frozen dinners, and canned soup to feed Allie and her entire softball team between now and next July.

"What's all this?" Allie asks as she comes inside, stamps the snow from her boots, and shrugs off her jacket. "Are we expecting a storm?" Allie knows how I love to panic shop when bad weather is predicted.

"I'm going to California," I announce, filling Allie in on the day's events and all I've found out about my mother.

"Okay, then. We need to make a list." Allie sits down at the kitchen table and grabs a pad and pen, getting right down to business. "Let's see. We have to call someone to take care of Mishmosh, find someone to drive us to the airport, change the message on our answering machine…"

"Whoa. Slow down, Allie." I turn to face her, a roll of paper towels clutched in each arm. "I didn't say *we* were going to California. I said *I* was going to California."

Allie adds another item to her list before looking up. "What do you mean?" she asks. "Don't you want me to come with you?"

"Come with me?" I open a cabinet door and shuffle things around. It never even occurred to me to ask Allie to fly to California. "Why in the world would you want to come with me?"

"Oh, I don't know," Allie says, her voice overly casual. "I wouldn't mind taking a break from the cold, and I hear L.A. is nice this time of year."

"Allie, what's the matter?" I stow the paper towels, shut the cabinet door, and lean back against it with my arms folded, frowning. Sarcasm is so contrary to Allie's nature that whenever she attempts it, I know something is bothering her. But it usually takes me a while to figure out what.

Allie busies herself with sorting the day's mail into three piles of letters, bills, and magazines, before she answers. "Lydia, why do you think I'd want to come with you?" She opens the latest issue of *Woodworker's Journal*, flips through a few pages, and then slaps it shut. "I want to be there for you. I want to support you. We're a team, remember? We're in this together."

"Oh." I cross the room and perch on her lap, sidesaddle. "That is so sweet of you," I say to her and I mean it. But I also know this is one journey I have to take alone. "I won't be gone long," I tell Allie, despite evidence to the contrary: the one hundred forty-seven dollars' worth of groceries that have yet to be put away. "And we can't really afford two plane tickets to California."

"I don't care about the money," Allie says, knowing I don't either. "Lydia, don't you need me?"

"Of course I need you." I place my hands on Allie's shoulders and lean back so I can stare into her dark Spanish eyes. "I need you here to keep the home fires burning. So you'll be ready to take care of me as soon as I get back."

"Will you at least call me every day?" Allie asks, wrapping her arms around me.

"Of course," I say. "I'll call you every minute. It's three hours later there, right?"

"No, three hours earlier. Here." Allie unfastens her watch and buckles the thick black leather strap around my wrist. "Keep my watch on East Coast time and your watch on West Coast time. That way you won't get mixed up."

"Allie, I can't take your watch." I stare at the new butch/femme display at the end of my arm: Allie's treasured gold-faced timepiece that once belonged to her grandfather, and my delicate white wristwatch with glittery rhinestones on its face instead of numbers. "What if I lose it?"

"You won't lose it," Allie assures me. "I want you to take it. So you won't forget me."

"Forget you? Don't be silly, Allie. Maybe you're afraid that you'll forget me. Here." I jump off her lap and dig into the right front pocket of my jeans for my good luck charm: a dark mahogany wooden heart the size of a newborn's fist. Allie made it for me during the wee hours of the morning that followed our first date because after she took me home she was so wound up she couldn't sleep. So instead she cut and carved and sanded until she came up with a tiny heart, smooth as a piece of sea glass, to fit in the palm of my hand. A small token of her affection, she'd said when she presented it to me on our second date, which occurred less than twenty-four hours after our first.

"I can't take your heart, Lydia," Allie tries to protest.

"Too late," I reply, placing the charm in the center of her upturned hand and closing her fingers around it with a kiss. "You already have it."

Allie pockets the trinket and then stands up and hugs me. "I'll miss you," she says, holding me close. "But I'm proud of you, Lydia. You're doing the right thing. You're a good daughter."

"No, I'm not," I mumble into her chest. "I'm a lousy daughter."

"You're not a lousy anything," Allie insists, kissing the top of my head.

"Well, I'm certainly not a good daughter. Not by a long shot," I insist, stepping out of Allie's embrace to resume putting away our groceries. "I'm nowhere near anyone's definition of a good daughter."

"You're not a bad daughter either," Allie argues, handing me a hunk of Swiss cheese and a carton of half-and-half.

"Then what kind of daughter am I?" I ask myself more than Allie as I stash our dairy products, shut the refrigerator door, and then stare at its blank white surface searching for the answer. I mull over my question like it's a crossword puzzle clue that's got me stumped. But not only don't I know how many letters I need to describe the type of daughter I am, I don't even know if such a word exists.

Allie puts the rest of our food away in silence; she knows how important words are to me, and that I won't be happy until I find just the right one.

"Ambivalent?" I say the word aloud in a voice full of, well, full of ambivalence. "Maybe that's it," I say to Allie's back as she stacks cat food cans high on a shelf. "Though I'm not really ambivalent. I am taking action. But not because I want to. Because I feel obligated to."

Allie doesn't comment and another minute of silence goes by before a new word hits me. "Dutiful," I say, trying on the word for size. "I'm a dutiful daughter."

"A beautiful daughter." Allie nods thoughtfully. "I'd say that's just about right."

"You would." I smile. But dutiful isn't it either. Dutiful sounds so meek, so obedient, so submissive, so nauseating. I close my eyes to concentrate harder, and as I do so the perfect word appears behind my eyelids as clearly as if it were written in big white letters on the blackboard in front of my classroom. "Reluctant," I proclaim to Allie, opening my eyes. "I'm a reluctant daughter. One who wants no part of this, but nevertheless is forcing herself to go along with it. But not willingly. Re-luc-tant-ly," I say, enunciating each syllable. "Kicking and screaming every step of the way."

❖

MY MOTHER LIKES to say, "If you want to make God laugh, tell Him your plans." And much as I hate to admit that she's right about anything, I have to give her this one. As recently as two days ago, if anyone had asked me, "What are you doing on Tuesday?" I never would have answered, "Flying to L.A." Yet here I am, all buckled up with my carry-on bag and pocketbook stored underneath the seat in front of me, waiting to take to the sky.

Somehow, despite my last-minute reservations, I manage to wind up in a row by myself. Already bone tired, I curl up in the plaid blue blanket the flight attendant begrudgingly fetches for me, shut my eyes, and try to sleep. But it's no use. I can't sleep and cry at the same time and I can't stop crying.

What is wrong with you? I berate myself as the plane starts to taxi. Honestly, what is the big deal? Yes, your mother may be dying, but so what? You've lived without her all these years and you've managed just fine. What will you be losing? A phone call every other month, if that, and a visit once every spring. Your mother knows nothing about your life, you know nothing about hers. You gave up on each other a long time ago. You're pretty much strangers. So you're not really losing her—you never really had her to begin with.

As the plane picks up speed and leaves the ground, I cry even harder. Soon I am joined by a child across the aisle from me whose steady sobbing builds into a loud wail that quickly explodes into an unrelenting, screeching crescendo. If I wasn't staring at the little girl with my very own eyes, I would swear her screams were those of someone being tortured, not someone whose parents are frantically waving cookies, juice boxes, and stuffed animals in her face, practically turning themselves inside out in their desperate attempts to soothe her. *Poor kid*, I think just as a woman in front of me pokes her head into the aisle, catches my mascara-streaked eye, and says in a voice full of sympathy, "Poor mother."

I look away without giving her the understanding smile and nod I'm sure she's expecting since I, like she, am clearly old enough to have had the experience of dealing with an in-flight out-of-control child. But I have never been in this mother's or any mother's shoes, and I am too worn out to politely pretend otherwise. Instead, I stare out the window at the clouds we have just broken through and out of nowhere I remember an article in the paper I recently read about a five-year-old who really was being tortured. By his mother. And in a very sick way I had envied his broken nose, cracked ribs, and split lip. At least his wounds were out there, visible for all the world to see, and it was obvious that he couldn't possibly have done anything to deserve them. When I got to the middle of the article and read that the first words out of the boy's mouth when he woke up in the hospital were *I want my mommy*, I couldn't read any more.

"I want my mommy," I whisper, wiping the tears from my cheeks with the corner of the scratchy blue airline blanket that is failing to keep me warm. As we race across the sky and the screaming little girl finally quiets down and falls asleep, I try to fill the bottomless hole of grief inside me with everything the flight attendant has to offer: a can of ginger ale, a granola bar, two bags of pretzels, and a bruised apple. Which doesn't help matters at all; I still feel sadder than ever, and now on top of that, I feel sick. Trying to distract myself with the latest issue of *People* magazine, a crossword puzzle, even the airline's overpriced shopping catalog proves futile; I am unable to focus on anything except my mother. I almost wish I had seatmates beside me to ask if I'm traveling for business or pleasure, to chat about the weather, even to show me pictures of their children and grandchildren that I could pretend to admire.

Be careful what you wish for, I remind myself after I board my connecting flight in Chicago and find myself wedged into the middle seat between two passengers in the dreaded last row of the plane right near the bathrooms. To my left, in the coveted window seat, sits a surly teenager wearing frayed denim shorts and a tiny purple T-shirt that ends several inches above her waist in order to show off the silver ring glittering in her navel. When I smile at her she bares her teeth for an instant and then tilts her head so that her long dark hair falls between us like a curtain at the end of a play. A minute later she pulls a copy of *Cosmo Girl* out of the backpack at her feet and, angling her body away from me, makes a big show of flipping through the pages of her magazine while loudly cracking her gum.

I get the message and turn to my right. The woman in the aisle seat is clearly someone who still dresses up to travel. She is all decked out in a long floral skirt and fuzzy pink sweater, and the perfume she is drenched in smells like the lilac bush in our backyard that blooms every spring, sending Allie into a full-blown allergy attack. Her freshly styled lavender-tinted white hair floats above her head like a dollop of whipped cream, and I bet she is probably the last woman on earth, other than my mother, who still refers to the place where she gets her hair done as a beauty parlor. Her hands are dotted with brown age spots and lined with raised blue veins, and she wears quite a bit of jewelry. Several heavy gold bangle bracelets adorn both her wrists, making soft clinking sounds against each other whenever she moves, and in addition to the requisite gold band on the fourth finger of her left hand, she sports three other rings, two decorated with emeralds and one boasting several diamonds.

I am just about to say something to her when the pilot gets on the intercom to tell us that we are next in line for takeoff. As soon as the plane starts its noisy race down the runway, my neighbor opens a thick book on her lap and moves aside a shiny red ribbon that had been holding her place. She traces a line of print with a pearly white polished fingernail and silently mouths the words on her page. Being naturally nosy, I sneak a peek at her reading material and confirm my worst suspicions: it's a Bible. King James Version, New Testament. Oh great. I better not whip out my copy of the latest volume of *Dykes to Watch Out For*, which I brought along to take my mind off my troubles. Life is so ironic, I think as we bump into the air and take flight. Of course the radical lesbian would get seated next to the nice conservative Christian lady. It's the way of the world. If our plane crashes, this woman might be the very last person on earth I ever speak to. Or I ever don't speak to, since we have yet to start a conversation.

Leaning forward to pluck the airline's in-flight magazine out of the seat pocket in front of me, I glance to my right again, and as I do so, I see a teardrop fall on the tiny print of my neighbor's reading matter. A sinking feeling descends upon me as I scan the table of contents of my magazine. Can't I just pretend I didn't see that? The last thing I want to do is take care of somebody else right now. Right now I want somebody else to take care of me.

Another tear plops onto my seatmate's page. I look up to the ceiling, hoping that the plane has sprung a leak, but no such luck. I'm a New Yorker, I don't get involved, I remind myself, but then I hear Allie's voice—always the voice of reason—pointing out that I haven't lived in New York for over two decades. And besides, New Yorker or not, I hate to think of myself as the type of person who can ignore a woman around my mother's age sitting on an airplane, quietly weeping.

I wait until a flight attendant offering headphones for the in-flight movie passes by and then, resigned, I reach down for my purse and pull it onto my lap. "Here," I say to the woman on my right as I dig out a packet of tissues. "Would you like one of these?"

"Oh, thank you," the woman says. "That's very sweet of you, honey." And with that one word, I'm caught, hook, line, and sinker. Whenever a woman of a certain age uses an endearment to address me, the hard casing around my heart melts away and I become putty in her hands.

The woman dabs at her runny eyes and I root inside my pocketbook again to offer her a mirror. Having just spent the better part of my Chicago layover reapplying my makeup in the crowded airport bathroom, I have enormous sympathy for my new friend. When she is satisfied with her appearance, she crumples the tissue, tucks it inside the sleeve of her sweater, and closes her Bible softly. I take this as a signal to begin our heart-to-heart.

"I'm Lydia," I say, holding out my hand.

"Very nice to meet you, dear. My name is Edith. Edith Donavon." Edith takes my extended hand but instead of shaking it, she grasps it firmly and lowers it onto her lap.

"Do you want to tell me what's troubling you?" I ask, finding that I'm actually curious to know.

Tears well up in Edith's eyes again. "It's my husband," she says, her voice cracking on the word. "He was supposed to be on this flight."

"Where is he?" I ask, though I think I can guess the answer.

"He died last week." Edith sadly confirms what I suspect.

"I'm so sorry to hear that," I say, using my free hand to get Edith another tissue. She is crying freely now, her lips trembling and her breath coming out in short whispery gasps.

"I'm sorry." Edith squeezes my hand and then releases it to blow her nose.

"No need to apologize," I tell her, bending down to put my purse back on the floor in front of my feet. "It's all right to cry."

"That's just what my doctor says. He told me to cry whenever I want to, for however long I need to. He told me I can't keep all this bottled up inside me or I'll burst wide open."

"That's exactly right," I say, in what I hope is a soothing voice. Then a thought occurs to me. "Your husband was supposed to be on this plane? Then I must be sitting in his seat."

This brings unexpected fresh sobs from Edith. "No." She hiccups the word. "That wasn't his seat. He was supposed to be underneath."

"Underneath?" Now I'm totally confused.

"Yes." Edith plucks the tissue packet out of my lap and helps herself. "We were flying him home to bury him."

"And he's not on the plane?"

"They lost him," Edith wails, losing it herself. Her face crumples and loud sobs escape from deep inside her. I am tempted to gather her up into a hug but we are both buckled up tight, and there is the hard armrest between us besides.

"Don't worry, they're going to find him." A woman in the aisle seat two rows ahead of us turns around and states this with confidence in a loud, brassy voice. "And if they don't, we're going to sue the pants right off them, aren't we, Mama?"

Mama? My mouth drops open and I stare at the woman who is still pivoted toward us in her seat. Though her style looks young—red hair hanging halfway down her back, gold hoop earrings large enough for small birds to perch upon, and a low-cut yellow sweater—the lines on her face lead me to believe her age is close to mine.

"Is this your mother?" I ask, incredulous.

"Yep, that's my mama all right," the woman answers in a jovial tone.

"Here, let me change places with you." I am already bent in half, gathering up my things from in front of me on the floor.

"Thanks but no thanks. I'm fine right where I am."

"What?" I glance around to see if anyone else has heard what I've just heard, but all the passengers within earshot are either absorbed in the movie on the screens over our heads, playing video games on their laptops, or hunched over fast asleep.

"Your mother is very upset," I hiss to Edith's daughter. "Don't you want to sit with her?" I can't believe I'm speaking about Edith as if she isn't right beside me.

"No way." The woman dismisses my question with the wave of one hand. "I've taken care of her my entire life. Now somebody else can have a turn."

I fall back in my seat, stunned. My feelings are hurt on Edith's behalf, but she doesn't seem fazed by her daughter's comments in the least.

"That's my Iris, named for the flower," Edith says, with unmistakable pride in her voice. "Isn't she a riot?"

"She's a riot all right," I murmur as Iris, satisfied that I am once again engaged with her mother, nods and then swivels around to face front.

"Something to drink?" A flight attendant whose eyes and eye shadow are both as blue as the sky we are zooming across hands Edith and me plastic cups and soda cans. She hesitates for a moment, then pushes her cart forward, deciding not to disturb the teenager on my left, who has propped her backpack against the window to use as a pillow and fallen fast asleep. After we have sipped our drinks, I ask Edith to tell me about her husband and her eyes light up as she sings his praises. How handsome her Walter was. How kind her Walter was. How breathtaking he looked in his uniform the day he came home from the war.

"We were married for close to sixty years, and the entire time, Walter spoiled me rotten," Edith says proudly. "Just look at all this jewelry." She extends her arms so that I can admire her treasures, turning one of the many bracelets on her wrist full circle to show off its design.

"It's beautiful," I tell Edith, not only because that's what she wants to hear, but because it really is.

Edith nods in agreement. "Every birthday, every anniversary, every Christmas, Walter gave me something lovely he picked out all by himself. Except for Valentine's Day. He never gave me anything on Valentine's Day."

"Why not?" I ask. "He seems like such a romantic."

"That's just the point," Edith says as if this should be obvious. "According to Walter, at our house every day was Valentine's Day."

"That's so sweet," I say, genuinely touched. "You're very lucky to have been so well loved."

"I know." Edith blinks rapidly, tears forming in her eyes once more. But before they fall, she smiles and leans forward with one hand on my arm. "Look at my Iris. Isn't she a hoot?" she asks as Iris stands and reaches up, revealing a tan swath of belly between the bottom of her sweater and the waistband of her skintight black leather jeans. She opens the overhead compartment above her seat and pulls down some kind of hard case, big as the extra-large cat carrier Allie and I force Mishmosh into once a year when he has to go see the vet.

"She's going to do her face now," Edith says in a stage whisper, her voice full of excitement, as if a show is about to begin. And Iris does indeed put on a show as she sits down with her makeup case on her lap, props open a mirror the size of a dinner plate, and unpacks brushes, puffs, sponges, cotton balls, and a makeup palette with enough colors on it to make any artist green with envy. Then with a whisk of something here and a dab of something there, Iris creates cheekbones that were nowhere near her face a moment ago, lips that are suddenly pouty instead of thin, and eyes wide and mesmerizing as those of a young, startled, and mascara-laden Liza Minnelli.

"Anybody else want her face done?" Iris asks, looking around at our fellow travelers, who are either still engrossed in their various activities or pretending to be. "How about hair? Step right up, I'm open for business."

"She's good, too," Edith says, squeezing my arm. "Why, look at me. I have a face only a daughter could love." Edith laughs at her own joke. "If it weren't for my Iris and her bag of tricks there, they probably wouldn't have even let me on the plane."

"No takers? Last call," Iris announces loudly. When no one responds, she shrugs and puts her things away.

"Too bad," Edith says. "You all don't know what you're missing." She removes her hand from my arm to cover a yawn. "What time is it, honey?"

I glance at the two watches on my wrist. "Half past two on the West Coast, half past five back east. We have about an hour and a half to go."

"Isn't that clever?" Edith studies my arm for a minute, then shuts her eyes. "I think I'll take a little rest now, if you don't mind, dear."

"Go right ahead," I say, relieved to have a little peace and quiet myself. Edith takes my hand again, intertwining my fingers with her own, and lets her head fall against the back of her seat. Almost immediately she begins to snore.

Why is it always so easy for me to be kind to other people's mothers, and so impossible for me to be kind to my own, I wonder as I too shut my eyes. I'll find out soon enough, I remind myself, and then my eyes fly open as a startling thought crosses my mind: it is entirely possible that while I've been up in the air comforting Edith like a daughter, my own mother has taken her very last breath.

Foolish as a child, I lean forward to stare out the window, as if I might catch a glimpse of my mother in a billowy white nightgown, her hair streaming behind her as she floats past us on her way up to heaven. All I see is an endless bed of puffy clouds below us, and two planes off in the bright blue distance, looking small as a pair of birds soaring across the sky. I lean back and shut my eyes again, keenly aware of

Edith's hand grasped firmly in mine, the hardness of her rings digging into the space between my fingers, her warm papery flesh rubbing softly against my palm. If my mother has indeed left us for the great beyond, I hope she did so with somebody else's daughter holding tightly to her hand and comforting her in all the ways that I never could.

❖

IF YOU CAN'T *stand the heat, get out of the kitchen* is the cliché that springs to mind as I step out of the air-conditioned airport and drag my suitcase over to the taxi line. Even though it's late in the afternoon, the smoggy Los Angeles air is so warm, it feels like I am being blasted in the face with a blow-dryer turned to its highest, hottest setting. Drops of sweat trickle down my back even after I shrug my arms out of my winter coat and sling it over my shoulder.

The taxi line is long and moves slowly but no one seems to be in much of a hurry. Most of the people around me have put on sunglasses and are standing with their faces raised toward the sky to get a head start on their tans as if they haven't got a care in the world. A young woman in front of me crouches down to let her toddler plunk a pair of Mickey Mouse ears onto her head, and laughs as her daughter claps her hands in glee. Their obvious joy in one another fills me with such sadness, I have to look away. But there's no escape: as soon as they vanish from my line of vision, another mother/daughter duo comes into view. This pair is older; the mother looks to be about my age and her daughter is a teenager. But not a surly, eye-rolling, impatient adolescent who spits out the word "mother" with all the disdain she can muster. No, this girl actually seems glad to be on vacation with her mom. She's dressed just like her, in white jeans and a rhinestone-studded T-shirt, and stands close beside her, with her arm across her shoulder. The two chatter away happily, their heads bent close together as they study a pleated map of movie-star homes that the mother is holding out stiffly in front of her like someone just learning to play the accordion.

I sigh a jealous little sigh that unfortunately reaches the ears of a balding man standing off to my left. He's right out of central casting, dressed in a bright Hawaiian shirt patterned with parrots, and a large, heavy-looking camera draped around his neck. "C'mon, now," he says as he catches my eye. "Cheer up. Let's see a little smile." He demonstrates, pointing to his own mouth which grins widely, showing off two rows of crooked yellow teeth. "You can do it, I know you can," he coaxes, as if his goal in life is to take away my sadness. "Say cheese." He lifts his camera and clicks his tongue as he pretends to snap my picture. "You're in L.A. now. You know, La La Land. City of Angels. California dreamin'. So whatever is bothering you, it can't be all that bad."

"How do you know?" I ask in what I think is a curious tone but must come off as hostile because the man's face quickly slams shut before he stalks off, throwing the word "bitch" at me over his shoulder.

Turning around to face front, I am more than relieved to see the taxi dispatcher frantically waving her arms in my direction. I hurry over to a waiting cab, stash my suitcase in the trunk, and then collapse in the backseat and give the driver the address of the hotel where I will be staying along with my father and Jack.

"Very far," the driver says in a thick accent that lets me know English is not his first language.

"How far?"

"Twenty minutes, thirty minutes," he says cheerfully, as though this is good news. Which for him I suppose it is. He steers away from the curb, merges onto the freeway, and before I can say another word, starts jabbering away on his cell phone in a foreign language that is musical and soothing to my ear. I vaguely remember Jack saying something about the hotel and hospital being outside the city limits, so after taking a twenty-dollar bill out of my wallet and folding it into my fist, I settle back and try to relax. Might as well enjoy these last few moments of peace and quiet before I am thrown into the family fray.

As I stare out the window at an endless stream of speeding cars, my eyelids begin to droop and I guess I must fall asleep, because the next thing I know the taxi is idling at the entrance of the Meridian Hotel, my door is being opened by a bellhop in a navy blue uniform, and I am wiping a spot of drool off my chin with the back of my hand.

"Welcome to California," the bellhop says with a wide smile. I force myself to smile back, though I imagine my expression is more of a grimace as I unfold my stiff legs and climb out of the car. After paying the driver, I follow the bellhop into the lobby and up to the registration desk, where he parks my suitcase and steps back with a little bow.

"Checking in?" A young girl who looks fresh out of high school raises her eyebrows and swings her waist-length blond hair at me. I stare at her and for a split second I am sixteen again and jealous that her hair is so shiny and straight while mine is so dull and frizzy. She's wearing a sleeveless white turtleneck tucked tightly into a short blue skirt and I can't help but stare at her stomach, which is as flat and hard as the countertop between us. Without even thinking, I try to hide my soft, round, inferior belly from her eyes by folding my coat over my arm and holding it in front of me like a shield. I know I am being ridiculous and that this teenager couldn't care less about my no-longer-girlish figure. It amazes me how just being in the vicinity of my nuclear family brings back all my insecurities, even the ones outdated by several decades. *Don't be absurd*, I berate myself. *You can't compare yourself with someone who looks like that. For God's sake, you're old enough to be her mother*, a thought that is instantly reinforced by the next word the girl utters to me. "Ma'am?"

"Oh, I'm sorry." I snap out of it. "Yes, I'm checking in. My name is Lydia Pinkowitz."

The clerk whose name tag says, "Hello, my name is Melissa" with a daisy drawn over the "i" clicks her long French-manicured fingernails against her computer keys while I look around the lobby. A large urn filled with pink, white, and purple hyacinths sits upon a smooth marble table planted atop a thick Oriental rug. Several olive green couches are placed in front of the floral arrangement, positioned in a horseshoe around a long coffee table piled with newspapers and magazines. Off to the left are a gift shop, a concierge desk, and the entrance to a restaurant. The lobby is fairly deserted; I imagine everyone is out sightseeing or taking a dip in one of the hotel's three heated outdoor pools.

"Ma'am?"

I turn back around to sign my registration slip and receive the key to room 716. As I head toward the elevators, the smiling bellhop appears beside me, my suitcase in tow. He steers me in the right direction, chattering away about the various tours the hotel offers. Disneyland. Universal Studios. La Brea Tar Pits. Beverly Hills. The Getty Museum. I'd like to tell him to save his breath; I am not here to play tourist and he doesn't have to try so hard. I will still give him a good tip. But I bite my tongue and let him ramble on until we reach the seventh floor.

After hoisting my suitcase onto the luggage rack, opening the curtains, and turning on my air conditioner, the bellhop finally takes his tip and his leave and at long last I am alone. A nap would be nice, but unfortunately it's out of the question. The watches on my wrist tell me that it is quarter past five here in L.A., and quarter past eight back home, and since I have no idea what time visiting hours end at the hospital, I best be on my way. Then again, what difference would five minutes make? I need to call Allie to tell her I've arrived safely, plus, I wouldn't mind being fortified by the sound of her voice before I head to the hospital. But it is my own voice I hear on our answering machine, telling me that I, along with Allie, am not home.

"Hi, Allie, it's me," I say after the beep. "Are you there? What about you, Moisheleh?" The Yiddish nickname I've bestowed upon Mishmosh hangs in the air without eliciting a response. "Okay, Allie," I say, after a few seconds have passed. "I guess you're not there. I just wanted to let you know that I got to the hotel okay and I'm leaving now to go to the hospital. I'll call you when I get back if it's not too late. Love you. Bye."

Disappointed, and annoyed again at Allie for refusing to carry a cell phone, I hang up and toss my cell phone back in my purse. Before going back downstairs, I stop in the bathroom to freshen up a bit. The mirror hanging over the sink is surrounded by bright lightbulbs and all lit up like a backstage Hollywood dressing room, and the reflection in it that stares back at me looks like a movie star who is several decades past her prime. My hair is all matted on one side from sleeping in the taxi, and most of my lipstick has been bitten off. I sure could use Iris and her oversized bag of tricks right about now, I think as I unwrap a bar of hotel soap and splash cold water on my face. Briefly I consider taking a shower, but even I know that would be stalling. Besides, for the first time in her life, I imagine my mother won't care about my appearance; after all, she's got a few other things on her mind. But still, just in case, I run a brush through my hair and reapply my makeup so she won't have anything to criticize before I take the elevator downstairs and ask the concierge to get me a taxi.

"Where are you off to, miss?" he asks, endearing himself to me forever by not calling me "ma'am" like his friend Melissa across the lobby.

"Holy Family Hospital," I say, the irony of the name not lost on me. "I've got the address." I unzip my pocketbook to get out the notebook in which I've written all my vital information. "I think it's pretty close by."

"Very close. Only two miles. Eduardo will take you." The concierge picks up the phone on his desk, speaks rapidly in Spanish, and hangs up. "He'll be outside in a minute. Compliments of the hotel."

"Thank you." I turn and walk through the lobby and sure enough, by the time I reach the exit, a gleaming white van is waiting for me right outside the door. The minute I step out into the sunshine, Eduardo the driver comes around to greet me. He is all Hollywood, sharply dressed, perfectly tanned, and wearing a stylish pair of dark glasses that hide his eyes and are completely unnecessary since the sun has already begun to set in the pink-streaked California sky.

"You are going to the hospital?" Eduardo asks, flashing me a dazzling movie-star smile. His studied English is as perfect as his even white teeth.

"Yes, please." I assume Eduardo has acting aspirations—doesn't everyone who lives this close to Hollywood?—but I don't have the energy to ask. Eduardo slides open the side door of the van and places a small stool in front of it. As I step up, he reaches for my elbow to help me inside. Normally I would protest; though I am pushing fifty, I don't think I'm anywhere near the little-old-lady-who-needs-help-crossing-the-street stage. Yet. But I'm actually grateful for Eduardo's help; his kindness almost moves me to tears.

"Someone is sick?" Eduardo shifts the van into reverse and glances at me over his shoulder as I buckle up. His tone is so sincere, either his acting lessons have already paid off, or he really does want to know.

"My mother." I give him the benefit of the doubt, relieved to finally unburden myself.

"Oh, I am sorry," Eduardo says as we pull away from the curb.

"Thank you." I study the back of his head as we turn a corner and start up a hill. "Do you know my father? Max Pinkowitz. He's been staying at the hotel and going to the hospital every day."

"Yes, yes, Mr. Pinkowitz." Eduardo nods with excitement. "He is here with the younger man with the long hair. Your brother, yes?"

"Sort of."

"He is a very handsome man, your father. A very nice man. I drive him every morning. He loves his wife very much."

"He does?" The two words fly out of my mouth before I can stop them.

Eduardo takes a left at the top of the hill and slows for a stop sign. "I am sorry for your father. He is a very sad man. His heart is broken. Every day he hopes his wife will be better. And every day she is the same. But your mother will get well now that you are here. You are her best medicine. Mothers and daughters are like that, yes?"

Some mothers and daughters, I think, but don't say out loud.

All too soon we pull up in front of the main entrance of the hospital. "Here you are," Eduardo says, putting the van into park. He gets out and comes around to open my door with his step stool in hand.

"Your mother will be all right now," he says, helping me down. "I can feel it here." He touches his heart.

"I hope so," I say, handing him a five dollar bill from my wallet. He flashes me his trademark dizzying smile before going around to the driver's side of the van. Then he gets behind the wheel, waves, and pulls away, leaving me feeling more alone and abandoned than I've ever felt in my entire life.

❖

A HOSPITAL IS no place to get well, I remember my mother telling me, which is odd, because as far as I know, the only time she's ever been in a hospital up until now was the day she gave birth to me. But that's my mother. Just because she hasn't had an experience doesn't mean she doesn't have an opinion about it. A strong opinion. But this place doesn't look so bad. In fact, the lobby doesn't look all that different than the hotel, though the decor isn't quite as fancy. There's a lumpy-looking brown couch in the corner beside two orange straight-back chairs that are facing each other as though deep in conversation. The windows behind the furniture reach from floor to ceiling, and dozens of plants hang in baskets in front of them. Most of them are spider plants, but there are also two wandering Jews in the lobby (actually three, including me). Out of the corner of my eye, I see the entrance to a gift shop with a sign taped to the door that reads, "Closed." Directly in front of me is a reception desk, which is being run by an elderly woman wearing a green smock with a red heart-shaped "Volunteer" badge pinned to the pocket.

"May I help you?" she asks as I step toward her.

"I'm looking for Doris Pinkowitz." I state my mother's name loudly and with great confidence, as though doing so ensures that she is alive and well, or at the very least alive.

"Doris Pinkowitz." The receptionist lifts the reading glasses dangling from a beaded chain around her neck and peers through them at the first page of a spiral notebook lying open on her desk. "Pinkowitz, Pinkowitz…" She runs down the list before her, then licks the tip of her index finger and uses it to turn the page. "Pinkowitz, Doris. Here she is. Intensive Care Unit. Fourth floor." The woman leans back against her seat, drops her glasses onto her ample bosom, and points. "The elevators are right behind you."

"Thanks." I cross the lobby and press the elevator button. As I stand there waiting, a nun appears by my side. I don't hear her approach; it's as though she simply materializes out of thin air. The nun is dressed in a black habit and barely comes up to my shoulder. Her weathered face is wrinkled as the apple dolls they sell at fall festivals back home in Maine, and the blue eyes behind her wire-rimmed glasses look magnified and kind. She smiles at me and I smile back, the first real smile I've given anybody all day. Her presence seems like an omen or maybe it's just wishful thinking, but for the first time since I've left home, I entertain the remote possibility that everything might turn out fine.

When I was growing up, I had an enormous fascination with nuns. Since I never wanted to get married and have children, becoming a nun seemed like my only viable option. As a child, I imagined myself capering about with Sally Field, the flying nun, or Debbie Reynolds, the singing nun. Never mind that being a Jew disqualified me from the outset; I was never one to let a small detail like that stop me. Allie attended Catholic school when she was growing up, and over the years I've asked her endless questions about it. Were the nuns really as cruel as everybody says they were? Did they really make you kneel on cheese graters? What do they wear under those habits? Allie indulged my curiosity, though she didn't have very interesting stories to tell. She had once gotten her knuckles rapped by a nun wielding a wooden ruler, and she imagined that underneath their habits, nuns wore underwear and bras just like everybody else.

When the elevator arrives, the nun enters first and I follow behind her close as a shadow. As the doors close, we press the buttons for our respective floors and then both step back and face forward. When we start to ascend, I have the strange feeling that I am in a confessional. Not that I've ever been in one. But standing beside this tiny nun makes me want to throw myself at her feet and unburden my heart. *Sister, I long to tell her, in my worst moments, I've been so angry I've wished my mother dead, and now here she is, possibly dying. Is it all my fault? Will you forgive me? More importantly, do you think God will forgive me? And most important of all, do you think my mother will forgive me for being such a failure of a daughter?* I let out a deep sigh and the sound completely fills the small enclosed space the nun and I are sharing.

The elevator stops at the third floor and the nun steps forward as the doors slide open. "Good night," she says before floating away soundlessly as a ghost.

"Good night, Sister," I call, sorry to see her go.

The doors close and a few seconds later they open again, this time on the fourth floor, my final destination. A sign on the wall in front of me says "Intensive Care Unit" and points to the right. I turn a corner and walk quietly down a deserted corridor. When I come to a doorway on my left, I peek in to discover a lounge furnished with a stained navy blue couch, several worn leather armchairs, and a long, low coffee table scattered with magazines, crayons, coloring books, tissue boxes, half a hot dog, and several abandoned containers of greasy French fries. In the middle of the debris, a white Styrofoam cup whose rim is bitten down and stained with screaming red lipstick lies on its side like something that has just keeled over and died. A television set hanging from the ceiling looks down at this depressing scene, silently blaring the evening news. I keep walking until the hallway stops at two double doors. An intercom on the wall instructs me to press a button, so I do.

"Yes?"

"I'm here to see Doris Pinkowitz," I say to the wall.

"Name?"

"Doris Pinkowitz," I repeat, louder.

"*Your* name," the faceless voice instructs me gruffly.

"Oh, sorry," I say, duly chastised. "Lydia Pinkowitz. I'm her daughter."

A loud buzz unlocks the entrance to the Intensive Care Unit and I burst through the swinging double doors like a sharpshooter entering a saloon.

"Lydia?" My father looks up, his face a mask of disbelief, and then rushes over to pull me into a hug with his skinny arms, which are surprisingly strong. I drop my pocketbook and lean against him, burying my face in his sharp, bony shoulder. He strokes my hair and I start to dissolve, my whole body shaking with soft, muffled sobs. Immediately my father stiffens, pushes me away and raises one finger in the air. "No crying," he says in the stern voice he admonished me with when I was growing up. "I mean it, Lydia. I'm not letting you in there until you stop crying."

I instantly go into shock mode, which is how I spent my entire childhood. Emotions were not allowed then and clearly they're not allowed now. I can practically feel my grief, anger, fear, and sadness closing themselves off, in the same way a dying woman must feel her heart, lungs, kidneys, and liver shutting down.

"Where is she?" I ask my father.

"In there." He points his chin toward a doorway.

"Alone? Why aren't you in there with her?"

"She's not alone, Lydia. A nurse is with her, getting her ready for the night."

"I'm going in." As I take a step toward my mother, my father grabs my arm right below the shoulder and squeezes it. Tightly. His fingers dig into my flesh and I am rendered immobile. "Hold it, Lydia. For God's sake, pull yourself together." He keeps a firm grasp on my arm for a few seconds—presumably so I can pull myself together—and then releases me. "And let's wait for Jack."

Jack. I forgot all about him. "Where is he?" I ask, rubbing my upper arm briskly, like I am trying to erase my father's fingerprints from my sleeve.

"He went down to get a soda. Now listen. I didn't tell your mother you were coming—"

"What?" I stare at my father, unblinking and unbelieving. "Why not?"

"I didn't want to upset her."

"You didn't want to upset her?" I study my father intently, trying to comprehend the way his mind works. It is a complete and utter mystery to me. "Dad, don't you think she's already upset? She's in the hospital and she—"

"I know exactly where she is, Lydia. Now get a hold of yourself.

Here." He leans down and hands me my purse. "I don't want your mother to see you crying, all right? I mean it. I'm warning you…"

What does he think he's going to do, send me to bed without any supper? I shut my eyes and lift both hands to my temples, pressing my fingertips against my skull and moving them in small circles trying to stave off the headache I feel coming on. I am already regretting my decision to fly to California and it's still only the first day.

My father clasps his hands behind his back and leans against the wall, positioning himself between me and the rest of the Intensive Care Unit. As usual, he is impeccably dressed. His brown and gold striped shirt is not wrinkled in the least and perfectly matches his brown pants and shoes. Except for the tired look in his eyes, he seems no worse for the wear. He probably looks better than I do in my road-weary, jet-lagged state. I still have on the outfit I spent the day traveling in and now I realize I should have taken the time to change. My pants are all bagged out and my top is full of lint. Plus, I am dressed in black, which my mother finds depressing.

"So what's new, Lydia?" my father asks, trying to make conversation.

"What's new? Let's see." I pretend to ponder. *Well, for one thing, my mother's in the hospital, and for another thing…*

Before I can think of how to answer my father's question, the double doors fly open and Jack bangs through them. "Here's your soda, Uncle Max," he says, and then following my father's eyes, notices me. "Oh, look who's finally here."

"Hi, Jack," I say, keeping my voice neutral. "Can we go in now?" I ask my father.

He steps aside to make room for a nurse pushing a wheeled hamper full of sheets in front of her. "Your wife is all set," she says to my father, who nods and then leads the way into the first room on the left, directly across from the nurse's station. It isn't a room, really; it's more like a cubicle, with no door at the entryway, just a door-shaped opening surrounded on either side by glass. The area inside is largely filled with a hospital bed that is largely filled with my mother. Her eyes are closed and she is attached to all kinds of medical paraphernalia. A thick blue pleated tube disappears inside her mouth, a clear narrow tube vanishes up her nose, a shunt of some kind is taped to her neck, a white clip is fastened onto her left middle finger, and a blood pressure cuff encircles her right upper arm. Worst of all, strips of white cloth tie both of her swollen hands to the railings of her hospital bed.

"Doris." My father puts his drink down on the counter near a sink in the corner and steps up to my mother. "Doris," he says again, bending over and speaking softly into her ear. "Lydia's here."

My mother's eyes fly open to glance at my father, a look of intense anger on her face, as if she's furious that he would say such a ridiculous thing to her. When he points across the room, my mother's gaze follows his finger, and the second she catches sight of me actually standing there, her eyes widen with shock. Watching her, it becomes very clear to me why my father didn't tell her I was coming; he was trying to protect her from disappointment in case I didn't show. This realization cuts me to the quick, but I squelch my feelings, for now anyway, and try to act normal, whatever that means. "Hi, Mom," I say, trying to sound casual, ludicrous as that is. "I'm here. I just got in." I clutch the straps of my shoulder bag tightly, as though I'd fall if I let go of them, and walk up the other side of the bed, staring at my mother. She stares back. Her eyes fill with tears and so do mine.

"Ahem." My father clears his throat. Translation: *no crying*. "Doris, I spoke to Selma. She sends her love and she's taking in the mail for us. And everyone in the office sends their love, too."

My mother wrenches her eyes away from me to study my father. "All right," he says. "C'mon now. Everything's going to be fine." My mother glares fiercely, giving him her famous Evil Eye, and he takes a step back, as though she has physically wounded him. "Don't be mad at me," he says. "This isn't my fault."

"You're going to be fine, Aunt Doris," Jack echoes in support of my father. "We're going to take you home soon," he says loudly, as though my mother has suddenly gone completely deaf. "Don't worry, Aunt Doris. Everything's fine."

My mother shoots Jack a look of frustration, shakes her head almost imperceptibly, and brings her eyes back to me. It's hard to interpret her expression, and she can't speak because her mouth is full of what I now realize is a respirator tube. The machine the blue tube is attached to breathes for her, jarring her body every time it forces air into her lungs with a wheeze and a click. Why didn't anybody tell me things were this bad? She can't breathe on her own—how much worse can it get?

"Mom," I say. "You're tired, aren't you? You need to rest." My mother closes her eyes for a split second and then opens them again. I take this as an expression of agreement. She looks entirely worn out, yet I know she'll do her best to stay awake as long as the three of us are keeping her company. "Listen, Mom, I'm tired, too," I say, letting her see me yawn. "I've been traveling since six o'clock this morning and I'm exhausted. Would you mind if I went back to the hotel and got a good night's sleep?" My mother closes her eyes and opens them again, and again I take this as a *yes*. "I'll come back first thing tomorrow and spend the whole day with you. Okay? So you just rest. Try and get a good night's sleep and I'll be here first thing in the morning. I promise."

Am I imagining things, or do the creases lining my mother's forehead relax just a little bit? I reach over and smooth back her hair, which feels coarse and greasy, like matted straw upon which a large wet animal has slept. "As soon as you feel better, I'll wash your hair, okay, Mom?" Upon hearing my words, my mother gives me a look of gratitude that speaks volumes. Then she shuts her eyes and does not open them again.

"Good night, Mom. I'll see you in the morning. *Gey schlufen*." I softly murmur the Yiddish words my grandmother used to say when she tucked me in during her visits, and which I now realize she must have also said to my mother when she was a child. Leaning down, I plant a kiss on my mother's forehead and rest my cheek for a minute on her knotted hair. I am so rooted to the spot with sorrow, I fear I may stay here forever, but then my father clears his throat, which I know is a signal for me to straighten up and "pull myself together," so somehow I do.

"See you tomorrow, Mom," I whisper, stroking her hair again. Then tiptoeing backward, I glance at my father and tilt my head toward the hallway, indicating that I'm going out there and I want him to follow. He starts walking and so does Jack. "Stay," I tell my cousin, as if I am commanding a bad dog. Miraculously he obeys.

"How long has she been like this?" I ask my father in a hushed tone.

"Let's see, what's today, Tuesday? She came in early Friday morning, so today is the fifth day."

I know it's useless to chastise my father now for waiting three whole days before he called me, so I file this information away in the section of my brain labeled "things to deal with later." It's like trying to stuff a thick bulky sweater into a suitcase that is already so full, the zipper's busted.

"What does the doctor say about her condition?" I ask him now. "And please don't just tell me she's going to be fine."

"Lydia, you can talk to her doctor tomorrow. He makes his rounds twice a day. And her nurse, Angelina, is very nice. She'll be here in the morning. You can speak to her night nurse if you want." He nods toward a large desk where several staff members mill about, consulting charts, talking on the phone, measuring out doses of medication. "She's over there somewhere, but Angelina is really the one who knows what's what."

"Why is she hooked up to all those tubes?" I ask my father.

He glances in the direction of my mother and then motions for me to follow him out the double doors of the Intensive Care Unit and further down the hall so we can speak freely without being overheard. My mother's hearing is more than sharp; it's legendary. When I was growing up, whenever I wanted to arrange a secret rendezvous with Colleen to sneak off someplace I wasn't allowed to go, I'd tiptoe upstairs to my bedroom, shut the door, and whisper our plans as softly as I could into the pink receiver of my rotary Princess phone. It didn't matter. As soon as I opened the door and sauntered downstairs into the kitchen, my mother, without even looking up from the magazine she was reading or the crossword puzzle she was solving, said, "Call Colleen back. You're not going anywhere."

My father stops outside the doorway of the visitor's lounge and leans his shoulder against the light blue hospital wall. I've heard the color blue is supposed to be soothing so I lean against the wall too, as if I could absorb its calming essence through my clothes into my skin. "So what are all the tubes for?" I repeat, folding my arms and continuing our disrupted conversation.

"The tube in her mouth is a respirator to help her breathe," my father says softly, though we both know there's really no need for him to keep his voice down. "The tube in her nose is to feed her so she won't starve to death. The port in her neck is for all her medication. And the catheter is for..." My father looks down, embarrassed. "Well, you know what a catheter is for."

I didn't even notice the catheter. This is even worse than I had imagined. "Dad," I say, quietly, not because my mother might hear, but because what I have to say is difficult. "Do the doctors think she's going to pull out of this? Have they told you what her chances are?"

My father keeps looking at his shoes, so I look at them, too. "Fifty-fifty," he says in a voice so low I have to lean toward him to catch his words. "Those are the odds."

"Fifty-fifty?" I ask, making sure I heard him correctly. When he nods, I shut my eyes for a minute in order to digest this new information. Then I open them and take a step closer to him. "Dad, do you think this is what Mom wants?"

"This? What do you mean, this?"

This fate worse than death, I think, but do not dare say aloud. "All this," I wave my hand in the air.

"Lydia, there was no choice," my father says, his voice defensive. "She collapsed and couldn't catch her breath. The doctor said that it hurt her so much to breathe that she would simply stop if we didn't do anything. I had to let them put her on a respirator. I had no choice."

"But do you think she wants to be on it? She seems really mad at you."

My father sighs deeply and a pained expression crosses his face. "I know why she's mad at me, Lydia. She never wanted to come on this trip in the first place. She didn't say a word but she knew she wasn't well enough to go. I wanted to go so she did it for me." My father's voice cracks and his whole body sags against the wall. "We never should have come and now it's too late."

"It's not too late." I give my father empty words to hang his hopes on. "She could get better. She's a fighter. She might make it."

"What are you talking about, Lydia? She *might* make it? Of course she's going to make it." Jack has tracked us down in the hallway, and now draws near, staring at me with a scowl on his face and a glare in his eye. "Don't listen to her, Uncle Max. Aunt Doris is going to be fine. We'll take her home in a day or two. You'll see."

I study Jack, whom I haven't seen since last May. He looks the way he always looks, hastily put together and itching for a fight. His stringy gray ponytail is longer than ever, and he wears jeans that could use a washing, scuffed-up sneakers that have come untied, and a T-shirt that says, "We're all here because we're not all there."

"Jack, I'd like to finish this conversation with my father in private, if you don't mind. Can't you stay inside for a minute so my mother isn't left alone?"

"Lydia, I've been in that room for hours and I just needed some air, all right?" Jack asks though I'm sure he isn't really seeking my approval. "I've been sitting in there all day, not to mention yesterday too, and the day before that and the day before that—"

"Jack, the reason I didn't get here sooner is because no one told me to come." I defend myself from his unspoken but very clear accusation.

"Lydia, the reason no one told you to come is because no one wanted you to—"

"Never mind." I hold up one hand to stop any further words from coming out of Jack's mouth. It is definitely time to take my leave. I feel almost dizzy from the strain of the day, and if I stay much longer, I'm sure to say something I'll live to regret. "I'm going back to the hotel. What are you going to do?" I ask my father.

"We'll stay for a little while," he says, glancing at his watch.

"We usually stick around until eight, then take a cab back and eat dinner in the hotel's restaurant." Jack fills me in on what has already become their daily routine.

"Do you want to eat with us, Lydia?" my father asks.

"I'm really tired, Dad." I beg off, knowing my limits. Dinner with my father and Jack after the day I've had would definitely send me right over the top.

"Take a cab back, Lydia." My father waves some money at me, which I ignore. "Meet us in the hotel lobby tomorrow morning at half past seven. We'll take the van over together and have breakfast in the cafeteria. Okay?"

"Okay." I take a step toward the exit and my father stops me by pulling me into a vise-like hug. "Thanks for coming," he says, his voice thick with emotion.

"She's going to be fine," I respond, giving my father the words he needs to hear and which all of us—including me—so desperately want to believe.

❖

I'M TOO HUNGRY to eat, too tired to sleep, and too freaked out to think. When I get back to the hotel, I barely make it up to the seventh floor before my chin starts trembling and tears begin to flow. I hurry out of the elevator and fly down the hallway, afraid I might break down into a sobbing, wailing mess right out there in the open for all the world to see. All I want to do is collapse onto my king-sized bed and bawl like a baby, but my hands are shaking so badly, I can't unlock the door to my room. Over and over I insert my plastic key card into its intended slot, pull it out quickly as instructed, and push down on the door handle. But it won't move. Instead, a blinking red light appears on the panel above it, letting me know that I can't go inside.

"Shoot," I mutter, which is what my mother always says instead of "Shit." Stubbornly, I keep pushing on the door handle, which just as stubbornly refuses to budge. Did Melissa give me the wrong key, or forget to activate it? I hope not, because I really don't feel like trudging back down to the lobby and dealing with her or anyone else right now.

I stare at the card in my hand, turn it over, and try again. Nothing. What on earth was I thinking when I told Allie not to come with me to California? What an idiot I am. If Allie were here, she'd know what to do. I'm sure she'd be able to figure out how to work this lock with no problem at all. Or if for some reason she couldn't, she'd simply yank the entire door off its hinges in true butch fashion and fling it aside over her shoulder. I should have begged her to come, I think as I slump against the wall outside my room, finally giving in to the self-pity that's been threatening to engulf me all afternoon. Where in the world did I get the silly idea that I had the strength to do this all alone? Though I hate to admit it to anyone, especially myself, the truth is that right now without Allie by my side, I'm nothing but a hopeless, helpless femme.

As I slip further down the wall, and contemplate collapsing onto the worn green carpet at my feet, I hear my father's voice inside my head. *Oh for God's sake, Lydia, pull yourself together.* And that patronizing command is all it takes to transform me from a damsel in distress into Wonder Woman. "I'll open this damn door if it's the last thing I do," I vow, straightening up and jamming the plastic card into its waiting slot like I'm stabbing a Bad Guy in the gut. Miraculously, a green light starts to blink, the door handle gives under my hand, and I stumble inside the cold, dark room.

"It's freezing in here," I tell no one as I switch on all the lights and check out my home away from home. It's your basic hotel room, nothing fancy but it will do. It has everything I need: a boat-sized bed covered with an ugly flowered bedspread, two night tables, one of which I'm sure contains a Bible in its top drawer, a wooden bureau that I don't intend on using since I'm not planning on being here long enough to unpack, a TV, a couch, a desk, and several telephones, including one mounted on the wall behind the toilet in the bathroom. Above the bed hangs a painting of a clown wearing a costume patterned with orange and purple diamonds, grinning from ear to ear, and stepping down a cobblestone street with a monkey on his shoulder. I suppose it was put there to make the room cheerful, but it doesn't. I hate clowns.

I also hate air-conditioning, so I cross the room to shut it off and let some fresh air into the room by opening a sliding glass door that I see leads to my own private little balcony. Then I fall back onto the bed and stare up at the ceiling.

Projected on the white spackled plaster above me as though it were a movie screen is the image of my mother's weary face wrapped around her breathing tube. I blink several times, but the image does not fade. Nor does it blur as I begin to cry, sniffling softly at first and then sobbing more and more loudly. The depth and power of my grief surprises me; the sounds escaping my throat are raw and jagged, and my whole body is shaking and chilled to the bone. I turn onto my side and gather the bedspread tightly around me, hoping for some comfort or at least a bit of warmth. Wrapped in the coverlet, I sob a while longer and then slowly, of its own accord, my body quiets down. I wipe my wet eyes on the pillowcase beneath my head and turn the pillow over. God, I miss Allie and wish she were here to take care of me. I know she would help me change out of the smelly clothes I've been wearing all day into fresh, clean pajamas, and call room service to send up something soothing to eat. I also know I can do these things for myself but even the thought of making such an effort is too overwhelming. I'll just close my eyes and rest for a few minutes, I decide, and then I'll get up and take care of business. But exhaustion trumps the best laid plans and soon I drift off to sleep.

When a loud ringing jars me awake, I call out, "Five minutes, people," which is the first thing Allie says every morning as she slaps our alarm clock into silence. But Allie is not here and it's not an alarm clock that's ringing; it's a telephone, which I fumble for on the nightstand.

"Lydia?"

"Allie?" For a delicious second I don't remember where I am, but the smiling clown hanging above the bed quickly reminds me. "I must have fallen asleep. What time is it?"

"It's a little after midnight here. How are you?"

"I'm a total mess," I say, sitting up in bed and rubbing my eyes. "How are you? How's Mishmosh? Where were you when I called?"

"I was in the basement."

"What were you doing down there?"

"Working on something."

Instantly I am fully awake and on top of that, suspicious. Allie never goes down to her workshop during the week after putting in a full day at the lumberyard. "What were you working on?" I ask her.

"Um…" She hesitates and immediately gives herself away.

"Allie? What are you up to?" Usually I find Allie's inability to keep a secret from me endearing, as more often than not it involves a present she's bought for me or a mystery date she's been planning on the sly. But I can tell that whatever Allie's hiding from me right now is not good news from her tone of voice and the way my stomach clutches with worry. "Allie, what is it? What's wrong?"

"Lydia, I wasn't going to tell you this because I didn't want to upset you. But since you asked…our pipes froze."

"Oh no," I groan. Not frozen pipes, the bane of our New England existence. Here in balmy California with the AC turned off, I'm actually in a bit of a sweat and it's hard to imagine such a thing. "What happened?" I ask, kicking the bedspread off my feet.

I hear one of our kitchen chairs squeak against the linoleum as Allie pulls it out to sit at the table. "As soon as you left, the temperature plunged about twenty degrees," she tells me. "It's some kind of arctic blast coming in from Canada. I had turned the heat way down because you weren't going to be home all day. And I didn't know it was going to get this cold, so I didn't leave the kitchen faucet dripping. And then when I got home and turned on the water, nothing came out and I knew we were in trouble."

"Poor you," I say, in a voice that I hope conveys sympathy. Even though I did ask, it's hard for me to care very much about frozen pipes right now. "So what did you do?"

"I put my coat back on and got into the car and drove downtown to buy a blow-dryer because I couldn't find yours—"

"That's because I brought it with me."

"Yeah, well I finally figured that out. Lydia, why did you bother taking it when I told you not to? All hotels have hair dryers in their rooms nowadays."

"I know, but I always take mine just in case."

"Well your just-in-case almost cost us a burst pipe," Allie says, her voice full of frustration. "And then we would have had another flood like we did last year and it would have been a real mess."

"Okay, okay, I'm sorry, Allie." I hug one of the seven pillows on the bed to my chest and apologize. "You're right. I should have left it home."

"Lydia, why don't you ever listen to me?" Allie punctuates her question with a long huff of exasperation. "I had to go to two drugstores before I found one that had some in stock, and then by the time I got back, it was almost too late. I've been standing up on a stepladder in the basement for over an hour thawing out the pipes with this tiny little travel dryer because it was the only one I could find."

"All right, all right, I said I was sorry. My God, you're acting like I did it on purpose." As a rule, talking to Allie always cheers me up, but this conversation is making me feel worse than I did before I got on the phone. And considering my circumstances, that's no easy task. "It's not my fault that it got so cold and our pipes froze, Allie. I had no idea—"

"I didn't say it was your fault." Allie interrupts me to defend herself. "I just—"

"Well, you're acting like it's my fault," I cut her off, my voice starting to rise. "What do you want me to do, Allie? Walk around L.A. until I find a post office that's open at this hour so I can mail my stupid blow-dryer back to you? Crawl across the entire country on my hands and knees so I can personally deliver it?" I am really yelling now. "Pardon me for packing my blow-dryer so my hair would look good for my mother who happens to be lying in a hospital bed all hooked up to a ventilator and a feeding tube, and who may very well die before morning without ever setting eyes on her only daughter again." My voice breaks on the word "again" as the last syllable disintegrates into a sob that racks my body anew with grief. "I don't care about the goddamn pipes," I shriek, heaving the phone across the bed. The receiver bounces on its cord twice, like a bungee jumper being jerked through the air, before it lands on its side next to my knee and lies perfectly still.

"Lydia? Lydia?" Allie's voice coming through the phone is barely audible over my wailing. "Lydia, I'm sorry. Lydia, talk to me. Hello? Lydia, are you still there?"

"No," I scream toward the phone, crying even harder.

"Lydia, shh, it's all right. Hush now. Come on." I pick up the phone, but don't say anything as Allie continues speaking. "Lydia, listen to me. Everything's going to be all right. Really. I promise." Allie talks to me in a soothing voice, the same voice she uses to calm Mishmosh during thunderstorms when our poor boy scurries around the house panting with fright, his tail bent and tucked between his legs. "Okay, now, Lydia? C'mon. Take a few deep breaths. Let me hear them. C'mon. Breathe." Allie's voice always works on Mishmosh and it works on me, too. I follow her advice, inhaling and exhaling deeply until my body's shuddering slows to a halt.

"Allie?" I'm still crying and her name comes out as a hiccup. "I'm sorry."

"No, Lydia, I'm sorry. It's my fault." As I reach for a tissue from the box on the nightstand to blow my nose, I picture Allie sitting at the kitchen table, raking her fingers through her dark buzzed hair and then holding her head in her hand. "I didn't mean to yell at you," she says quietly. "It's been a very tough day, and I just lost it, that's all. And I miss you."

I twirl the telephone cord around my right pinky the same way Allie sometimes takes a ringlet of my hair and curls it around one of her fingers. "I know," I say, my voice almost back to normal. "I miss you, too."

"I'm sorry, Lyddie," Allie says again. "It's just that everything is so much easier with two. If you were here we could have taken turns thawing out the pipes. My arm is killing me."

"Poor you," I say, meaning it this time. "I'm sorry I wasn't there to help." In the silence that follows, I imagine myself down in our drafty basement balancing on a rickety stepladder, arms raised, aiming a blow-dryer at a cold copper pipe. Allie would be standing close to me, hugging my thighs from behind and resting her head against my butt. Afterward I'd make us big mugs of steaming hot chocolate and we'd cuddle on the couch and congratulate ourselves for being such smart, savvy homeowners. "I wish I was home with you and Mishmosh, Allie," I say, sniffling. "Believe me, nothing would make me happier."

"How's everything going?"

"Awful. Worse than awful." I prop a pillow behind my back and sink into its downy softness. "My mother's all hooked up to a million tubes and machines and she can't talk or eat or anything. They say she has a fifty percent chance of pulling through this. And if that isn't bad enough, my father and Jack are being..." I pause, searching for the right words, but there aren't any. "My father and Jack are being...well, they're being my father and Jack."

"That's unfortunate."

"You're not kidding. Allie, I was so stupid not to let you come with me."

"No, I'm the one who was stupid not to come. I should just jump on a plane right now. Wait, hold on a second." I hear Allie put the phone down on the table and shuffle off in her slippers to another room. "Mishmosh! Cut it out." She claps her hands sharply and then lets loose a string of Spanish words that must make Mishmosh stop whatever he's doing because a minute later she returns to the phone.

"What was he up to?" I ask.

"Chewing on the rubber plant. He misses you, too, Lydia. He's been following me around like a puppy, getting under my feet all evening, and the minute I stop paying attention to him, he starts acting out."

"Poor Mishy." I press my hand against my chest to try and quell the strong fist of loneliness that's squeezing my heart so tightly it feels like it might burst. "I'll be home soon, Allie."

"How soon?"

"I don't know yet. I'll know more tomorrow after I speak with the doctor."

"It's tomorrow here already," Allie says with a yawn. "I better go to bed if I'm going to be able to get up on time. Call me when you know what's going on. I want to hear everything. And Lydia, I'm very sorry I yelled at you. I was just cranky. You know how I get when I'm hungry and cold."

"Turn up the heat if you're cold. And why are you hungry?" I swing my legs over the side of the bed, resting my elbow on my knee and my chin in my hand. "What did you eat for supper tonight?" Silence on the other end of the phone, which is not a good sign. Allie's eating habits aren't exactly the greatest. Before we were a couple, her idea of dinner was a hot fudge sundae with a bag of plantain chips on the side. "Allie, what did you eat?"

"Nothing," Allie says in the voice of a child who knows she's been naughty.

"Allie-e-e-e." I stretch her name into a groan. "Why didn't you have something? There's plenty of food in the house. I went shopping, remember?"

"I know, I know. But I got all involved with the pipes and then I looked through the mail and scooped out the kitty litter and got undressed and read the paper, and by then it was eleven o'clock and food was just too much to deal with."

"You won't sleep well if you're hungry," I remind her.

"I won't sleep well without you in my arms," she reminds me.

"You have to eat something before you go to sleep. Have a bowl of cereal. Or a sandwich."

"I don't want a bowl of cereal or a sandwich."

"What then?"

Allie thinks for a minute. "I'll make myself some rice and beans. You know. Puerto Rican comfort food."

"I wish I was there to have some, too."

"Why, Lydia?" Allie's voice rises with suspicion. "Didn't you eat any supper?"

"No."

"Lyd-i-a." Allie stretches out my name in the same tone of voice I used to stretch out hers. "You need to keep up your strength. Promise me you'll have a decent breakfast tomorrow. I don't want to have to worry about you not eating."

"Allie, you don't have to worry. I'll eat, I'll eat, I promise. God, we're pathetic."

Allie agrees. "We just don't do well when we're apart."

"I'll come home as soon as I can, Allie. And I'm sorry I didn't listen to you about the blow-dryer. I'll leave it home next time."

"Blow-dryer? What blow-dryer? What are you talking about?"

That's my Allie, I think with a smile. "I love you," I tell her. "A lot."

"*Te quiero mucho.* I love you, too. Good night."

"Good night." As soon as I hang up the phone, the room becomes deathly silent and a tidal wave of loneliness washes over me and pulls me under. Sadly, I crawl between the sheets, gather a pillow into my arms as though it were Allie's soft warm body, and shut my eyes to sleep.

❖

WHY DID THE MAN throw the clock out the window? He wanted to see time fly. It was the very first joke I ever learned, and I remember repeating it to my mother, my father, my school bus driver, even the mail carrier, but despite my enthusiastic delivery, the silly question with its even sillier answer never got a laugh out of anyone. And I certainly don't find it funny now as I lie still as a stone and stare through the darkness at the red numbers of the digital clock on the night stand next to my bed. Two-twelve...two-thirteen...two-fourteen... It feels like an infinity passes between each minute and the one that follows it, and I am absolutely convinced that this night will never end.

It's no surprise that sleep is impossible to come by, three thousand miles away from home in a strange hotel room without Allie nestled beside me and Mishmosh slumbering at my feet, using my toes as a pillow for his great mottled head. Still, I'd do anything to make time fly, even carry the damn clock across the room out to the balcony and hurl it over the railing with all my might, if I thought that would do any good. In my sleep-deprived state, I imagine I'd get a great deal of satisfaction watching the instrument of my torture sail through the air in a graceful arc before plummeting seven stories to smash into a hundred pieces on the sidewalk below. If nothing else, at least the act would kill some time—a minute, maybe two—before I'd crawl back into bed and resume my lonely vigil, waiting for morning to come.

I rotate the clock away from me so its obnoxious little numbers are facing the wall, try a different pillow, roll onto my belly, squeeze my eyes shut, and after what seems like an hour, open my eyes and pull the clock toward me to check the time again. Two-nineteen…two-twenty…two-twenty-one… As I moan and groan and toss and turn and stare through the darkness at the maddening red numbers of the digital clock, I remember another time I found myself wide awake when I should have been sound asleep, staring at something glowing and red:

I am standing in the doorway of our dark kitchen sometime after midnight, my pudgy eight-year-old body encased in flannel feet pajamas, my small hand reaching up along the wall in search of the switch that turns on the light. I have come downstairs for a drink of water, but the glowing red circle, small as a Cheerio, is like a tiny stop sign, freezing me in my tracks. The small sphere blazes for an instant like a summer sun whose color intensifies right before it sinks below the horizon. Then it moves through the darkness, tracing a narrow arc down, up and back down again. I stand silently and watch it for a moment, until thirst wins out and I turn on the light. But I still don't move because what I see now roots me to the spot: my mother, sitting at the kitchen table wearing her blue fuzzy bathrobe and a white protective hairnet that encircles her head like a cloud. A cigarette is held between the second and third fingers of her right hand, which rests on the table between a green overflowing ashtray shaped like a leaf and a shiny silver lighter. Our eyes meet and we stare at each other, my mother's gaze fixed, serious, and slightly curious as if I am a strange creature that she's never seen before. I feel a nervous giggle start to form in my belly and I'm afraid I'm going to laugh the way I always do when Colleen and I have staring contests on the school bus, which try as I might, I always lose. But I know laughing right now would be a big mistake, so I swallow hard, forcing myself to remain still, still looking deeply into my mother's eyes. I wait for her to say something or do something or simply look away. But she remains just as she is: unmoving and silent as the chair she is sitting on. Even the cigarette at her side seems to be holding its breath.

Finally my hand, as though it is something separate and apart from the rest of my motionless body, wanders up the wall again and pulls the light switch downward, returning the room to darkness. The red circle of my mother's cigarette travels upward and glows more brightly as she brings it to her lips once more. Quietly, I remain where I am for another minute before backing out of the room on tiptoe and then turning to make my way down the hall, up the stairs, and into my room, where I crawl between the sheets and pull the covers over my head. I know I have seen something I shouldn't have, like the time last year when bored with my Sunday morning cartoons and impatient for breakfast, I opened my parents' bedroom door and caught a glimpse of them thrashing about on their big king-sized bed. "What the hell is wrong with you?" my father yelled, yanking the blankets around himself and my mother as I backed away and pulled shut their bedroom door. Tonight I have done something wrong again, though I don't know what it is. I do know, however, that it is not something to mention to my mother. Ever. I don't have to be told that I am not supposed to know my mother sits by herself at the kitchen table in the middle of the night staring into the dark. Once upon a time this was her secret. Now it is ours.

I haven't thought about this in years, but now that the memory has surfaced during my own sleepless state, I can't help but wonder. What did my mother think about, sitting all alone in the dark kitchen while her husband and child slept upstairs in their respective beds? Did she daydream about what could have been and what still might be? Did she regret the choices she had made and consider other options? How did she feel, sitting there with no one keeping her company except a pack of cigarettes, a lighter, and a sky full of stars? Was she lonely? Sad? Angry? Or unlikely as it seems, content? Maybe she was just enjoying a little peace and quiet in the middle of the night when there was no one making demands of her: *Mommy, can I have a drink of water? Will you play Chinese checkers with me? Doris, where are my good shoes? Have you seen my blue-and-white striped tie?*

I roll over and glance at the clock again. Two-thirty-three...two-thirty-four...two-thirty-five West Coast time translates to five-thirty-five Allie time, way too early for me to give her a call. But maybe it isn't too early to check in with Vera.

The thought of hearing the familiar voice of someone who loves me propels me out of bed to cross the room, rummage through my purse for my cell phone, and slide open the glass door to step out onto my tiny balcony. The fresh air feels good—it's brisk but not chilly—and I breathe in deeply. For some reason I feel better standing outside in my stockinged feet and pink tiger-striped pajamas, staring up at the dark, velvety, star-scattered sky. Corny as it sounds, I know that across the country the very same sky hovers over Allie and Mishmosh, and that offers a small degree of comfort.

I turn on my phone and speed-dial Vera's cell number. She answers on the first ring. "Good morning, Sunshine," I sing out with false cheer as I lean my elbows on the cold, metal railing of the balcony. "Where are you? Did I wake you?"

"I'm at Serena's. And no, you didn't wake me. You'll have to try much harder to do that. I'm already on my fourth cup of coffee." The sound of Vera's husky voice wraps itself around me like a warm blanket, soothing me instantly. "I'm glad you called, Lydia. How's it going out there?"

"Oh, Vera." I say her name as if it contains all the sadness of the world. "My mother's on life support."

"She is? Oh, Lydia, that's awful. I am so, so sorry." Vera easily offers the sympathy I need as desperately as my mother needs the oxygen that is being pumped into her lungs. "How are you doing? Are you holding up all right?"

"I don't know. I guess so. No, not really. Allie and I had a fight on the phone." I fill Vera in on the details but she doesn't seem all that interested.

"You and Allie are fine," Vera assures me, almost impatiently. "You just had a little spat because you're both stressed out, that's all. She wishes you were home and you wish she was in L.A. No big deal. Tell me more about your mother. And about how you're feeling."

"I can't even figure out how I'm feeling." I lean over the balcony to take another deep breath of fresh California pre-dawn air and then straighten up to do something I hate: get in touch with my emotions. "I'm sad, of course," I state the obvious. "And tired. And right now I'm kind of numb."

"That's understandable," Vera says. "How's it going with your father and Jack?"

"Pretty bad. Jack is hostile as ever and my father is trying to control everything, including me. He won't let me cry in front of my mother and—"

"Whoa. Stop right there." Vera cuts me off sharply. "What do you mean your father won't let you cry?"

"I mean he won't let me cry." I don't know how to explain it any better. "He doesn't want me to get my mother upset."

"I would think she'd be more upset to see that you're not crying," Vera points out.

"What do you mean?" I turn away from the sky to lean my back against the wrought-iron railing and stare through the glass door at the disheveled bed in the middle of my room.

"Lydia," Vera says. "How will your mother know that you care about her if she doesn't see you cry?"

"I don't know," I tell Vera. It's a good question, even if I don't have the answer to it.

"Have you spent any time alone with her?"

"Not yet. I don't know if I'll be able to." I exhale loudly and push a wayward curl off my forehead. "My father is acting like her personal bodyguard. He won't let me go in to see her by myself."

"Lydia, why are you behaving like a child?" Vera asks, her tone stern.

"Because I feel like one," I reply in a tiny voice that sounds remarkably like a five-year-old's.

"Well, you happen to be an adult," Vera states firmly. "No matter how your father treats you. You don't have to listen to him, you know."

"I don't?" I ask, as if this is news to me.

"No," Vera says. "You don't." She pauses and I hear her take a sip of coffee. "Have you decided what you have to say to your mother yet, Lydia?"

I step off the balcony and head back to the island of my bed, diving into the safety of the blankets. "No."

"Well, it might be a good idea to give it some thought. It's now or never, as they say. And lucky for you, Serena won't be up for hours. I've got plenty of time. And plenty of coffee."

"I hate it when you pull your tough-love act on me, Vera."

"I know you do. I can practically hear you pouting." Vera falls silent, and I listen as she pours herself a warm-up and opens the door of Serena's refrigerator. If I know Vera—and I do—she's searching her daughter's shelves for some half-and-half, among the cartons of soy milk and no-fat or low-fat diary products that real coffee lovers like the two of us regard with disgust.

"I'm stumped, Vera, I really am." I sit up to pull a strand of hair forward, looking for split ends before I realize what I'm doing and stop.

"Lydia, this is so unlike you. I don't think I've ever known you to be at a loss for words."

"Well, there's always a first time," I say with a lightheartedness I don't feel. "I can't say what I've wanted to tell her for years: that she was a rotten mother and I've been pissed off at her for decades. She's so weak and frail now, even I'm not mean enough to do that."

"Why don't you tell me?" Vera asks. "Tell me all the ways she's been rotten to you."

"You've heard it all before, Vera. You've been hearing about it ever since we met."

"I know, Lydia. But I want to hear it again. Really."

"You do? Okay. Here goes." I hug my knees to my chest and start reciting the long litany of all the ways that my mother has failed me: how she never held me or kissed me or told me she loved me when I was a child, how she never called me or visited me or told me she was proud of me as an adult. As usual, giving voice to all my hurt makes me blubber like a baby. "How can you stand being friends with such an unlovable person?" I wail when I am done.

"You're not an unlovable person, Lydia," Vera states emphatically. "Not by a long shot. What you are is a very hurt person."

"I am," I howl into the phone as yet more sobs rise up from my throat. "I am a very hurt person and now it's too late to do anything about it." I let it all out until my tears are spent, and then use the edge of my sleeve to wipe my runny nose.

"Listen, Lydia, you're right. It may very well be too late to get what you need from your mother," Vera says once I am quiet. It's times like these I wish my old friend knew how to mince words. "That's the bad news," she continues. "But the good news is, it may not be too late for your mother to get what she needs from you."

"What are you talking about, Vera?" I lean back against the headboard and draw the covers up to my chin. "What could my mother possibly need from me?"

"What do you want from her?" Vera, in true therapist fashion, answers my question with one of her own.

"I just want her to love me," I say, pathetic as that sounds.

"I imagine she just wants you to love her," Vera counters. "The one thing you can give her that nobody else in the world can is a daughter's love. The hurt goes both ways, Lydia. As can the healing."

There is silence across the telephone wires between us while I think this over. "But I don't even know if I do love her," I say, baring my very soul. "Maybe I just feel sorry for her because she's so sick right now."

"Nonsense, Lydia. Of course you love her. If you didn't, you wouldn't be so upset. The opposite of love isn't hate. It's not caring. And you do care. Clearly. A lot."

"But what if I don't know how to love her?" I ask. "And what if she doesn't want my love?"

"Good questions." Vera gives me her highest words of praise, as she often did when I was a student sitting in her classroom. "You can't do anything about the latter, but I'm not sure I agree with you about the former. You know how to love, Lydia. You love me. You love Allie."

"But I don't have a lifetime of baggage attached to either one of you," I argue.

"No, but maybe it's time to forget all that."

"Forget all that?" I repeat Vera's words slowly, like they're a phrase uttered in a foreign language I've never heard before. "How?"

"Be in the moment with her. I know it sounds preposterous, but just give it a shot, Lydia. Come to think of it, didn't you once go through a Buddhist phase?"

"Yeah. it was pretty short-lived, though. Oh, I do remember one thing. Ommm." I wedge the phone between my neck and shoulder so I can clasp my hands in my lap and chant the syllable that always began the meditation sessions at the Zen center where I halfheartedly practiced many years ago.

"What if you acted as if there was no past and no future?" Vera asks as my monotone fades away. "Isn't that what the Buddhists teach? What if when you go to the hospital tomorrow, you act as though your mother was someone you'd never met before?" By Vera's tone of voice, I can tell she's warming up to the idea. "Pretend you have no past history with her. And you don't want anything from her in the future. If this was the very first time you were meeting her, and you saw her lying there suffering in that hospital bed, what would you feel for her? Nothing but compassion."

"It's a theory, Vera." I unbend my neck and switch the phone to my other ear. "Maybe. If I was a saint. Or a holy person. Which in case you haven't noticed, I'm not."

"Well, I thought it was a good idea," Vera says, defending herself. "But okay. We'll scratch that and move on to our own tradition."

"You're kidding. This I've got to hear." As long as I've known her, Vera has always been one of those religion-is-the-opiate-of-the-people types. Desperate times call for desperate measures, I suppose.

"Didn't some famous rabbi or other say that we should be kind to everyone we meet because anyone could be the Messiah?" Vera wonders out loud.

I groan and fling aside the blankets. "Vera, if my mother's the Messiah, not only am I in trouble, we're all in trouble. Nice try, though." I get out of bed, cross the room, and step out onto the balcony again to stare into the darkness.

"Okay, here's my last suggestion," Vera offers. "Lydia, I want you to think of one good memory from your childhood that involves your mother."

"There aren't any."

"Well, I want you to come up with one anyway. Just humor me, okay?" Vera waits until I agree before she goes on. "You're going to be sitting around with a lot of time to think. That's one thing hospitals are good for. So that's your homework. And rest assured, there will be a test."

"Vera, let's change tacks here," I say, being less than thrilled with my assignment. "What if you were lying in a hospital bed about to die—"

"God forbid."

"God forbid," I agree, "and Serena came to see you? What would you want her to say to you?"

Vera doesn't hesitate. "I'd want her to tell me that she was happy."

"Really?" This gives me pause. "That's it?"

"Yes. I think so." Vera mulls over her answer, then adds to it. "I'd want to know that she was happy, and that she was loved. And that there would be people around to take care of her after I was gone."

"Wow." My eyes focus on the lights of an airplane as it streaks across the sky. "You wouldn't want her to tell you how much she loves you, how much she was going to miss you?"

"No," Vera says matter-of-factly. "I know all that already. And besides, I'm her mother, Lydia. Her welfare comes before mine."

"Even on your deathbed?"

"Especially on my deathbed."

"Vera, you're a really great parent," I tell her, not for the first time. "Does Serena know how lucky she is?"

"I think so. Though I wish she would show her gratitude by keeping an extra carton of cream in the house when her old mother comes to visit. She knows I go through it like water. Whoever invented two-percent milk is no hero of mine. But enough about me." I hear Vera close the refrigerator. "Back to you."

"What about me?"

"Was this useful at all? Do you have a better idea about what you want to tell your mother?"

"Frankly, no."

Vera sighs. "I'm sorry I wasn't more helpful, Lydia."

"You have nothing to apologize for, Vera. You tried. I'm just a hopeless case."

"No, you're not. You're just attached to the idea of being a hopeless case." Vera pauses and clears her throat. "How would your life be different if you resolved your issues with your mother, Lydia? Who would you be?"

"I can't imagine." The idea seems as far out of reach as the stars twinkling overhead in the dark California sky.

"Well, think about it. And think fast. Your mother is on life support. I hate to be the one to say it, but that means she could die at any moment. Which means there's no time like the present."

"I know." I close my eyes and once again the image of my mother in her hospital bed all hooked up to machines rises to the surface of my mind. "I'll talk to her, Vera. Today. This morning. But I think I'm going to have to play it by ear. Like you said, be here now. Trust that whatever words fly out of my mouth are exactly the ones I need her to hear."

"Do you think that's wise?" Vera asks, not unkindly.

"I don't know," I answer truthfully. "But right now it's about the best that I can do."

❖

"LADIES AND JELLYBEANS. Please get up, get washed, get dressed, and come to the children's dining room." This is how my father woke me every weekday morning when I was growing up, and I hear his voice in my head now as I dash around my hotel room getting ready to go to the hospital. If there's one thing my father hates, it's tardiness. Lucky for him, I inherited his punctuality gene; I am showered, dressed, made up, and out the door at exactly seven-nineteen, giving me a full eleven minutes to ride the elevator down from the seventh floor to the first floor, which is a good ten minutes more than necessary.

Stepping into the hotel lobby, I glance around and immediately catch sight of my father standing in front of the reception desk engaged in a lively conversation with Melissa, who is staring up at him with her big blue eyes and nodding continuously, like one of those toy dogs with the bobbing heads people keep on their dashboards. Today Melissa's nails are painted a glittery hot pink and her long shiny hair is fixed in a heavy-looking braid draped over her shoulder. The tip of her braid resembles a paintbrush and rests on the counter between her and my father. He keeps glancing down at it with interest, as though he were trying to figure out a way to grab it and tuck it away for safekeeping like a lucky rabbit's foot shoved deep inside his pocket.

"Dad?" I approach him cautiously, as though I am barging in on something I have no business interrupting.

"Lydia, there you are. Let's go, let's go." My father snaps to attention, spinning around and looking pointedly at his watch to show me how annoyed he is that I am only ten minutes early, which in his book is the equivalent of being twenty minutes late. "C'mon, the van is waiting for us. You have everything?" He looks me over quickly and gives a short nod of approval at what he sees: his adult daughter who is trying her best to feel and act like an adult, dressed neatly in a white jersey and gray slacks with a yellow sweater draped over her arm and her pocketbook slung over her shoulder.

"Thank you, doll. I appreciate it," my father calls to Melissa as he hustles me through the lobby. I wonder what Melissa has done to warrant his gratitude but decide it's probably best not to ask.

"Nice girl, that Melissa," my father says as he puts his hand on my waist and steers me toward the exit. "Very pretty, too."

I ignore my father's appraisal of Melissa as a bellhop steps back with a little bow and pulls open the glass door for us. My father takes my elbow as though he owns it and propels me outside into sunlight so bright it makes us raise our hands to our foreheads in unison as though we are saluting an invisible superior officer standing in front of us instead of merely shielding our eyes.

"Where's the van?" my father asks, as if I am responsible for its absence.

"Beats me." I shrug, draping my sweater across my shoulders. Despite the bright sunshine, the early morning air is still a bit cool. I glance up the street but Eduardo's vehicle is nowhere in sight. My father searches the traffic coming toward us from both directions, his head swiveling back and forth on his scrawny neck quickly as though he is watching a professional tennis match. "Oh for God's sake," he finally yells, throwing up his hands in disgust. "I told them seven-thirty. Is that too much to ask? Bunch of *momsers*. Why is it so difficult for people to be on time?"

"Relax, Dad," I say, suggesting he do something the man finds impossible. "It's just about seven-thirty now." I look down at my wrist and the sight of my small rhinestone–decorated watch snuggled up to Allie's larger timepiece fills me with so much longing I fear I might collapse on the spot. Instead, I lean back against a large concrete planter filled with various flowering shrubs and look up the street again. "I'm sure it'll be here any minute now. And besides," I add, "Jack's not down yet anyway."

"Jack's meeting us later," my father says, beginning to pace.

"He is?" I ask, surprised. "Why?"

"He had a rough night. He's still sleeping."

I almost laugh. "Sleeping? Or sleeping it off?"

My question stops my father in his tracks. "Don't be nasty, Lydia. This is very hard on Jack."

"Oh really?" I wrinkle my brow and nod slightly as if I am pondering this. "As opposed to this being very easy on me?"

"Lydia, don't start with me, all right?" My father looks me full in the face for the first time all morning. "I was up for most of the night myself. Jack cried out in his sleep practically every hour on the hour and I had to keep waking him up and calming him down."

"Really?" I ask again, my voice curious, not cynical this time. "What does he cry out?"

My father shakes his head to signal he doesn't want to tell me, and glances back toward the hotel. I know he is just about at the end of his rope—according to my West Coast watch it is now seven-thirty-three—and that he is seriously considering storming back inside and giving the concierge a piece of his mind. And a scene like that is just about the last thing I need.

"Dad," I say, trying to distract him. "What does Jack cry out in his sleep?"

"Lydia—" My father hesitates, looks back toward the hotel once more, and then for some reason decides to tell me. "Sometimes he calls out, 'Mommy.' Sometimes he just yells, 'No.' And sometimes he whimpers like a baby." My father looks away from me, as if he is embarrassed on Jack's behalf for his non-macho behavior. "All this is very difficult for Jack," my father informs me again. "You know your mother and your aunt Beatrice were very close. Not to mention identical. To the freckle. I'm sure Jack hasn't stopped thinking about his own mother since the minute he got here. And dreaming about her, too. Considering how much Jack hates hospitals it was very nice of him to come at all. And now that you've finally arrived, I thought I'd let him get a little extra rest. Believe me, he needs it."

As my father resumes his manic pacing, I study my shoes and think about Jack. It's easy for me to forget that underneath that extremely annoying exterior lies someone who hasn't had a mother for a very long time. And before my aunt Beatrice died, she lay curled in a coma for close to a year. I stare down at my feet picturing the young Jack before he had a long gray ponytail and a beer belly, vegging out in front of the television set at our house, where he spent a great deal of time trying to deny that his mother was in the hospital clinging to life and his father was off somewhere clinging to the woman whom he would run off with several months before Jack's mother died. If it's this difficult for me to contemplate losing my mother at the ripe old age of forty-nine, I imagine it must have been a hundred times harder for the teenaged Jack to face losing his. For the first time ever, I feel something that resembles compassion toward my cousin, and I vow to be nicer to him. Or at least to try.

"Here he is. Come on." My father grabs my arm and pushes me toward Eduardo's glistening white van, which has just appeared at the curb. Eduardo, looking very dapper in his freshly pressed clothes and wrap-around sunglasses, gets out and comes around to the passenger side, his step stool in hand, his lips curved upward into a charming grin. I smile back at him, inwardly bracing myself for the onslaught of my father's famous temper, which I am sure is about to be unleashed at the poor guy just because he committed the unforgivable crime of being a few minutes late.

"Hey, Eddie," my father calls, all smiles. *"Buenos días."*

I am shocked at my father's pleasantness, and at the same time mortified at his condescending words. I can't believe he has the gall to give Eduardo an anglicized nickname, and on top of that, add insult to injury by tossing a Spanish phrase out to him as though he knows the language.

"Dad," I say, tapping his arm to get his attention. "You really shouldn't—"

"Hola, Señor Pinkowitz." Eduardo calls back before I can finish my sentence. *"Cómo está usted?"*

"Muy bien, muy bien." My father nods, and then, since this is about the extent of his Spanish vocabulary, he switches to English to introduce us. "Have you met my daughter, Lydia?"

"Yes, I drove her yesterday." Eduardo places his stool at my feet and slides open the van's door. "Good morning."

"Good morning," I say, allowing him to help me up. He makes sure my father gets in all right and then slides the door closed and goes around to the driver's side of the van.

"You are going to the hospital?" Eduardo asks, once he is back behind the wheel.

"Sí," says my father, removing his wallet from his back pocket. He pulls out a five dollar bill—Eduardo's tip, I presume—and folds it into his hand before leaning back against the seat.

"Where is the young señor this morning?" Eduardo wonders out loud as he steers us into traffic.

"Taking a *siesta*," my father answers, pleased that he has remembered another Spanish word.

"And how is the señora?"

"Oy," my father sighs deeply, and then brightens. "You know what *oy* means, Eddie?"

"No, señor. What does it mean?" I can't tell if Eduardo thinks humoring my father is part of his job description or if he's just an extraordinarily nice person. Maybe both.

"Oy means…" My father pauses, thinking. "Well, first of all, it's

a Yiddish word. Yiddish is the language the Jews of Eastern Europe spoke many years ago. My parents both spoke it. They were from Russia, from Odessa, which is right near the sea."

I am stunned that my father is speaking to Eduardo like this. He never talks about his parents, both of whom died before I was born. I didn't even know they were from Odessa.

"*Oy* is a very hard word to translate," my father continues. "It means…" He hesitates and stares out the window as we come to the stop sign that lets me know we are almost at the hospital. "I'll use it in a sentence," he says, leaning forward. "*Oy*, am I happy. *Oy*, am I sad. *Oy*, am I hungry. *Oy*, was that close. *Oy*, now what am I going to do?"

"Ah." Eduardo pulls into the circular driveway of the hospital and turns around to face us. "In Spanish, we say, *ay*. *Ay*, what is the matter? *Ay*, I am not feeling well. *Ay*, what did you do? Sometimes we say, *Ay, ay, ay*."

My father chuckles. "Sometimes we say *oy, oy, oy*. You see, Lydia," he turns to me as if this whole lesson in linguistics was solely for my benefit, "people are the same all over. Wherever you go, you meet nice people, you meet not-so-nice people…" He reaches over the front seat to give Eduardo the five-spot folded in his hand. "*Por favor*. Here you go, Eddie. *Gracias*."

"*De nada*, Señor Pinkowitz. It is always a pleasure." Eduardo gets out of the van and slides open the passenger door so we can disembark. My father steps down on the stool Eduardo provides and moves aside so I can do the same. Eduardo closes the door with a rushing noise and bids us farewell. "Maybe the señora will be better today," he says. "I hope so."

My father blinks his eyes rapidly, then pulls out a long white handkerchief from his back pocket and brings it up to his face to loudly blow his nose. "*Que sera, sera*, Eddie," he says, his voice so full of sorrow my heart turns over. "Whatever will be, will be."

❖

A PROMISE IS a promise, and since I promised Allie I would eat a good breakfast this morning, I follow my father past the reception desk where he makes the elderly volunteer blush like a schoolgirl just by saying hello to her, down the hallway and into the hospital cafeteria.

"Here, Lydia." He hands me a warm, wet brown plastic tray, takes one for himself, and leads me to the food line. "Hey, Malika." My father greets the woman standing behind the steam tables with a warm smile, as if they have known each other for years. "What's cooking this morning?"

Malika grins widely, revealing a large gap between her two front teeth. "Good morning, Mr. Pinkowitz. Look what I have for you." She waves the metal serving spoon she is holding in her dark hand toward the bins of food in front of her. "Scrambled eggs, bacon, sausage, pancakes, oatmeal, home fries. Whatever you like."

"How about some bacon and eggs?"

"Very good." Malika nods her approval as she heaps some food onto a white china plate. She holds it out toward my father but when he bends forward to grab it, she snatches it back. "What's wrong with my pancakes this morning?" she asks, insulted by his small breakfast order. "What's the matter with my oatmeal, my home fries, my nice fresh sausage?"

"I'm in training, Malika. I told you. I need to get down to my fighting weight." My father pats his flat belly and reaches for his food again but Malika whips it away from him.

"One pancake, Mr. Pinkowitz. Just a small one. Or else Malika will worry about you all morning." She adds a pancake that could hardly be called small to his plate and only then allows my father to take it from her.

"All right, you win again, Malika." He lowers the dish onto his tray, starts moving down the line, and then stops. "Come on, Lydia," he says, the impatience in his voice trying to mask the fact that he'd momentarily forgotten all about me. "Malika," he says, almost as an afterthought, "this is my daughter, Lydia."

"Nice to meet you, Malika," I say, studying the ID badge clipped to her white uniform. "Your name is so pretty. Does it mean something?"

Malika stands up tall and proud. "It is African," she says. "It means queen."

"Oh, just like my middle name," I tell her, continuing my father's early morning language lesson. "In English, my middle name is Marilyn, but in Hebrew it's Malka. And Malka means queen."

Malika steps back into a slight curtsey and bows her head in respect. "What can Queen Malika get Queen Lydia to eat this morning?"

"Do you have some toast or a bagel or something like that?" I ask. "It all looks very good," I hastily add, not wanting to hurt her feelings. "I'm just not a big breakfast eater."

Malika places her hands on her abundant hips and frowns in disapproval. "No eggs? No oatmeal?" She clicks her tongue against the roof of her mouth and shakes her head as if she is my mother and doesn't know what to do with me. "You don't want to lose that nice figure of yours," she says, nodding her chin in my direction. "It is no good for a queen to be skinny, right, Mr. Pinkowitz? Over there." She points her spoon toward a self-service station. "Toast, bagels, juice, coffee, tea. If you don't see what you want, you come and tell me. Malika will get it for you."

"Thank you," I tell her, lifting my tray.

"Have a nice day, Your Highness." She bows again before turning to wait on her next customer.

My father and I take our trays over to the far corner where carafes of coffee and bags of bread products await us. I place the two halves of a pre-sliced English muffin onto the wire racks of an industrial toaster and nod when my father tells me he'll pay for our meals and meet me at a table. While I wait for my muffin to toast, I glance around the cafeteria, which looks similar to the one Vera and I ate our meals in during the conference we attended last October. But instead of dozens of Women's Studies scholars clustered around tables waving their arms around with excitement and expounding with great passion about their latest research projects, I see various configurations of diners eating their food gravely, hardly a word exchanged among them. Medical personnel wearing white lab coats, orderlies in green uniforms, nurses in pastel-colored smocks and pants, all with ID badges pinned to their pockets, chew quietly, all deep in thought.

And then there are the families. People dressed in civilian clothes like my father and me, all bleary-eyed and looking worn out and resigned as they gaze woodenly at the plates of food or coffee cups in front of them. Over by the window a dark-haired woman wrapped in a bright yellow sari sits alone at a table, dunking a tea bag into a cup of hot water over and over. I wonder if her husband is a patient here. Or perhaps it's one of her parents, or her sibling, or her child. At the table behind her, a man cuts up a waffle for the small girl hunched across from him. The child sits perfectly still and stares straight ahead, her face set in an expression much too serious for someone so young.

Isn't there anyone here for a happy occasion? Isn't anybody's wife having a baby? Isn't someone here to take home a loved one who's had a miraculous recovery? As my English muffin drops off the wire toaster rack and slides onto the metal tray beneath it, I study the ID tag of the nurse standing next to me pouring herself a cup of coffee and come up with a brilliant idea: visitors should be given ID badges, too. "Sister going through chemo." "Spouse having heart surgery." "Brother getting a new knee." "Child with meningitis." If I'd been wearing a badge that said "Mother on life support" when I got off the plane yesterday, that man with the camera never would have bothered me. At least here in the hospital we're all in the same boat, so I don't have to worry about someone trying to get me to smile. Which makes me wish that somebody would. Where's the little nun I saw yesterday, I wonder as I spread butter on my muffin and add cream to my coffee. Seeing her kind old face again would surely lift my spirits. I pick up my tray and do another quick scan of the room but do not catch sight of her. Instead I see my father sitting alone at a table in the corner, so I carry my meager breakfast—a meal hardly fit for a queen—across the cafeteria to join him.

"Sit down, Lydia," he says when I approach, as though I need an invitation. I place my tray across from his and drop into a seat. My father downs his coffee in two large gulps and digs into his scrambled eggs with gusto while I chew a small bite of English muffin and force myself to swallow. We don't have much to say to each other and I'm surprised to find myself wishing Jack were here eating with us. Unlike me, Jack knows how to converse with my father. If Jack were here, I'm sure the two of them would be easily holding forth about things that interest them: money, sports, business, politics. I, on the other hand, haven't a clue as to how to make small talk with my father, and while this isn't news to me, the longer we sit here in silence, the sadder I become. I have to say something—anything—to alleviate the feeling that I am sharing the table with a virtual stranger. Though if my father were a stranger, there wouldn't be any problem. I know how to talk to strangers. It's easy for me to strike up a conversation with just about anyone: the supermarket cashier who admires the picture of Mishmosh I carry in my wallet as she rings up a dozen cans of cat food; a patient sitting in the waiting room of my doctor's office who tells me more than I ever wanted to know about his recurring kidney stones; a woman in the drugstore who confirms my opinion on waterproof versus water-based mascara; my new friend Edith, who sat next to me on the airplane yesterday, sobbing over the loss of her beloved Walter. If my father were an actual stranger, I could ask him where he was from, what kind of work he does, whom he was here to see. Obviously I know the answers to all those questions, and try as I might, I can't think of any others to ask.

But being the *habladora* that Allie knows and loves, having nothing to say rarely stops me from chattering away. Surely if I just start talking, my father and I will stumble across some common ground. "So, Dad," I begin, but before I can think of another word to utter, a loud crackling noise fills the air.

"Shh, Lydia." My father holds one finger against his lips and then points it up toward the ceiling.

"Good morning," a male voice booms above our heads. Who can it be, God? More static rustles, as if someone is crumpling a paper bag right up against a microphone. The noise reminds me of my high school days when the principal's voice came over the crackly public address system during homeroom every morning in order to make the day's announcements and ask several students who were in trouble—usually including me—to immediately report to his office.

"This is Father O'Connor," says the voice, followed by a piercing shriek of feedback that makes me and several other breakfast eaters cringe and cover our ears. "Today is Wednesday, January 11th, 2006. Here is the thought of the day." All around me diners pat their mouths with their napkins and put down their plastic knives and forks, so out of respect, I do the same. Father O'Connor continues. "Do to no one what is distasteful to yourself. Give to the hungry some of your bread, and to the naked some of your clothing. Seek counsel from every wise man. At all times bless the Lord…"

Father O'Connor loses me when he says "every wise man" instead of "every wise person" but I see he has my father's undivided attention. If I had any doubt that my father was a total stranger before the priest's voice descended upon us, now I am sure of it. My father does not have one religious molecule in his body. When I was growing up he *schlepped* my mother and me to synagogue only twice a year: on Rosh

Hashanah and Yom Kippur. And as I recall, he fell asleep just minutes after the High Holiday services began, thoroughly embarrassing me and disturbing those seated near us with his loud, rattling snores.

"Now let us pray." Father O'Connor has finished his thought of the day, but he is not through with us yet. As my own father clasps his hands and shuts his eyes, I can't help but wonder if he really is someone I've never met before. Maybe I've been transported to Bizarro World, a place featured in the Superman comic books Jack loved as a child. In Bizarro World, everything was the opposite of what you would expect: Superman was a big klutz, Lois Lane was ugly, and it was a crime to do anything well. Has my father turned into Bizarro Dad? That would explain a lot, I think as the priest concludes, "Oh God, come to my aid. O Lord, make haste to help me. Glory be to the Father, the Son, and the Holy Spirit, as it was in the beginning, as it is now, and as it ever shall be, world without end. Amen."

"Amen," says my father. Then he catches me looking at him and shrugs. "It can't be bad, Lydia. A little religion never hurt anyone."

A little religion never hurt anyone? I consider my father's statement, which ordinarily would propel me into a long, passionate diatribe against the Catholic Church's sexism and misogyny, not to mention homophobia. But when I open my mouth, feminist rhetoric doesn't fly out of it; instead my last bite of English muffin pops into it. "Whatever gets you through," I mumble to my father as I swallow my food and my opinions. Now I feel like a total stranger to myself. Reaching down for my pocketbook, I extract a small silver case shaped like a sleeping cat that contains a tube of lipstick and a mirror. *And who might you be?* I ask the reflection that stares back at me as I touch up my makeup. *Bizarro Lydia?*

Finished with our breakfast, my father and I rise from the table in unison, dispose of our trash, and leave the cafeteria. The silence between us, which was uncomfortable to begin with, grows heavier with each step we take toward the elevator that will carry us up to the fourth floor to see my mother. No one rides with us, and when we disembark and round the corner, my father's pace quickens. Now he's a man on a mission and I have to hurry to keep up with him. When we reach the doors to the Intensive Care Unit, he pushes the button on the wall and gives me a meaningful look as we wait to be let in. *I hope you're going to behave yourself* are the words I think he would like to say to me, but before he has a chance to do so, a loud buzz sounds and he ushers me inside.

The ICU is much busier this morning, with nurses, doctors, aides, and orderlies all bustling about on their soft-soled shoes, making notations on charts and waving clipboards in the air. No one greets us or pays us any mind, so my father leads the way into my mother's cubicle. She is much the same as we left her last night, still dressed in a light blue johnny, lying on her back tethered to a myriad of equipment, her hands tied with white strips of cloth to the railings on either side of her bed. My mother's hair is tangled and hanks of it are spread across her pillow, going off in different directions like a family of snakes all anxious to crawl away from her head. Her eyes are closed and the color of her complexion is not one I've ever seen on a human being before. Her skin looks gray and waxy, and though I hate to even think it, lifeless. But I know she is breathing; the pleated blue respirator tube stuck down her throat doesn't give her any other choice.

"Doris," my father says softly, leaning close to her ear. "Doris, Lydia and I are here." We wait expectantly but my mother does not open her eyes. "Dorito." My father calls her by a nickname I have not heard him use in many years, but she still does not respond.

"She's sleeping," my father whispers, in case I cannot see this for myself. He nods toward two black vinyl chairs near the bed and we sit down side by side.

"That's her heart rate." My father pokes me on the shoulder to get my attention, then leans forward and points to the TV monitor above my mother's bed. "See the number that's blinking? Seventy-three, seventy-four. That's good. Anything below fifty or above one hundred would be a problem." He nods, pleased to be showing off the medical facts he's recently learned. "Your mother has always had a good strong heart. Look at her EKG." He moves one hand up and down through the air as if he is practicing how to conduct an orchestra. "And that's her blood pressure, see the two numbers with the slash? The cuff on her arm takes it automatically. Every hour. Right now it's one-fifty-four over eighty-nine. That's a little high, but not bad, not bad at all." My father gives me a backhanded slap on the arm to make sure I'm still following him, then points at the screen again. "That other number there is measuring her oxygen. They measure it with that white clip on her finger. Looks like it's ninety-seven percent. That's excellent.

Of course that's with the ventilator. The tricky part will be when they take her off it." He inhales deeply and then exhales slowly, as if he's demonstrating to my mother how to breathe on her own. Then he falls quiet for a moment, and I listen to the respirator whirring and clicking, and something beeping loudly, like a garbage truck backing up out in the hall. "They were supposed to get her off that thing by now," my father says, gesturing toward the cumbersome machine in the corner. "I don't know what the hell is taking so long." He keeps his voice low, but his tone is filled with annoyance, as though my mother's situation is the result of an incompetent nurse or doctor who has fallen behind schedule. "It's been six days already, Lydia. I don't know how much more of this I can take."

So leave, I want to tell him, suddenly filled with anger. *If it's too much for you, just go*. All I want out of life—my life and my mother's life, whatever's left of it—is for my father to take a hike so I can have a few private moments with her for the first time since I left home thirty-one years ago. But I know better than to ask him to step outside. I'm sure he's afraid to leave my mother and me alone without a chaperone. What does he think I'm going to do, pull the plug? Tell her how sick she is, as if she doesn't already know?

I fold my arms against the chill in the room and try to come up with a plan. My father slouches down in his seat, rests his cheek on his fist, and lets out a long, loud yawn without bothering to cover his mouth. "You tired, Dad?" I ask, though the answer is obvious. "I know you didn't sleep well last night. Why don't you go down the hall to the lounge and stretch out on the couch? I'll come get you when she wakes up."

"No, Lydia, I'm fine." My father rubs his eyes with the thumb and forefinger of one hand and straightens up in his chair.

Now what? I look around the room, noticing the box of latex gloves on the counter near the sink, the receptacle for biohazardous materials mounted on the wall, the bedside table on wheels rolled into the corner upon which rests a Styrofoam water pitcher along with a stack of cups. The light in here is dim, as if the florescent tube above our head needs changing. It's hard to tell if it's day or night; the tiny window behind my mother's bed reveals only the back wall of another hospital wing. I turn my head and look through the glass wall that faces the rest of the Intensive Care Unit. A bin of dirty laundry parked right outside my mother's doorway gives me an idea.

"How are things at work, Dad?" I ask, not because I have developed a sudden interest in the dry-cleaning and tailoring business, but because my father, like me, is a classic Type A personality and I know it is just killing him to be spending so much time away from the office.

"I didn't get a chance to speak to them yesterday," my father says, frowning. "I was going to call this morning from the room, but I didn't want to wake up Jack."

"Here." I reach inside my bag, find my cell phone, and extend it toward him. "Why don't you call them now?"

"Lydia, what are you, crazy? Put that thing away." My father looks around in a panic, as though I've just pulled a loaded handgun out of my purse. "You can't use a cell phone in here. What's the matter with you? Didn't you see the signs?"

"Take it outside." I wave the phone in front of him like I'm teasing a little boy with a piece of his favorite candy. "I'll be here in case she wakes up. You won't be on long."

My father stares at the phone, a lifeline to the outside world, and I can tell this is a tough one for him. I'm sure he feels guilty for even thinking about the office at a time like this, but then again, the opportunity to check up on things at home—on his daughter's dime no less—is an offer too good to refuse.

"What if she wakes up while I'm gone?" my father asks, though I imagine he's thinking just the opposite: *What if she doesn't wake up while I'm gone? What if she never wakes up again?*

"Don't worry. I'll come find you." I can see that he's starting to weaken. The words "lead us not into temptation" flit through my mind, but I ignore them while my father thinks things over. *Just go*, I implore him silently. Before Jack gets here and I never have this chance again.

"I guess a quick call would be okay." At last my father takes the bait and rises. "How do you use this thing?" He turns the phone over in his hand and studies it, two sharp lines creasing his brow. "It's different than mine."

I give him a quick lesson in Cell Phones for Dummies and then practically shove him out the door, giddy with success. I know my father is completely incapable of making a quick call to the office. Once he makes contact, he'll want his secretary to read his mail to him, go over his phone messages, give him an update on what's been going on. I'm good for twenty minutes, half an hour, at least.

I wait until I hear the doors of the Intensive Care Unit whoosh open and shut and then return to stand by the head of my mother's bed. Her forehead is creased with worry lines that deepen every time the respirator forces air into her lungs, jarring her body so that it rises slightly before thudding back against the bed. The johnny she is wearing has slipped off one shoulder and I can see several electrode patches stuck onto her chest, one right next to a large brown mole I remember her always trying to hide underneath the top of her bathing suit when I was a child. A sob catches in my throat as I stand there watching her. "Mommy?" I offer a word my mother hasn't heard me say in over forty years and one I'm sure she gave up all hope of ever hearing again.

Instantly she opens her eyes.

"Hi," I whisper, meeting her gaze and holding it steady. My mother's eyes are light brown with flecks of gold in them just like mine. As I stand there watching her, she starts to cry. And since there is no one around telling me not to, I cry, too. We don't speak to each other: she is rendered mute by the breathing tube stuck down her throat, and I am too overcome with emotion to utter a single word. *This is my mother,* I think, staring into her eyes. The only one I will ever have. The woman who gave birth to me. The woman who clothed me and fed me and took care of me the best way she knew how. She wasn't a perfect mother— not by a long shot—but looking at her now, it's hard to believe she was the monster I've always made her out to be, either.

I look into my mother's eyes in a way that I never have before: openly, honestly, frankly, while tears silently stream down my cheeks. Things that would ordinarily make me queasy—the feeding tube inserted into her left nostril, the needle jabbed into her neck attached to the port that dispenses her meds, the large and alarming purple bruises on her arms—do not even register with me. Everything recedes except for my mother's wet, red-rimmed, rheumy eyes. They are filled to the brim with sadness and sorrow and longing. And something else. Something I fail to recognize at first because I don't remember ever seeing it before. But there it is, and there's no mistaking it. Love. Pure and simple. Though I know as well as anyone that love—especially between a mother and daughter—is always messy and complicated.

But not today. Today there is nothing but unadulterated, unlimited, unconditional love flowing from my mother's eyes into mine.

"Mom," I whisper, taking her hand and swallowing hard. "I have some things I need to tell you."

My mother looks at me attentively and I hold her gaze. Here it is, the moment I've waited for all my life. My mother and I are alone and she is lying speechless before me, with no choice other than to hear what I have to say. I decide to begin with a gift.

"Mom, I love you, you know that, right?" My mother squeezes my hand tightly, with much more strength than I thought was left in her weak, tired body. "And I know you love me, too." She squeezes my hand even harder. We stare into each other's eyes again, the room silent except for the rhythmic whirr and click of the respirator. Maybe that's enough, I think, still watching my mother's face. Maybe that's all I have to say. I dare to break my mother's gaze for a moment, and when I do, again I remember the discussion I had with Vera early this morning, though it seems like a lifetime ago.

"Mom, I want you to know that I'm happy. Really happy. I wake up glad to be alive every single day." When in doubt, I always follow Vera's lead, and even though the words seem forced at first, as I continue to speak, I realize they are absolutely true. "Allie adores me and is really good to me. I have a lot of wonderful friends who care about me and are always there when I need them. I know it took a long time, but I finally figured out what makes me happy and how to create that for myself. So you don't have to worry about me. Just do what's best for you. I love my job and my home and my community and..." My voice falters as I observe the change in my mother's face. A look of peace has come over her. Like someone who has finally completed a long, arduous task she never in a million years thought she'd be able to finish. And as I stand there studying her, I realize something else: There was a method to my mother's madness. She was tough with me on purpose so that I would grow up to be independent and free. And not wind up like her. Tied to a man as surely as she is tied to the railings of her hospital bed. Unable to be on her own the same way that right now she is unable to breathe on her own.

"I get it now, Mom. I could never have put together the amazing life I have now, if it weren't for you. You did good by me," I say, though never in my wildest dreams did I ever imagine such words would ever leave my lips. "You were a good mother. A very good mother. You did a good job."

My mother shuts her eyes tightly, opens them again and then, using all the strength she has left, slowly nods her head up and down, letting me know she agrees with me. She faintly squeezes my hand one last time and then releases it.

"Why don't you rest now, Mom?" I ask, stroking her forearm lightly. Her skin feels dry and hot. "I'll sit right in that chair and keep an eye on you. I won't go anywhere. Okay?"

No one comes in or out as I sit in the semi-dark and semi-quiet, watching my mother sleep. The only thing that exists is this room, this moment, each breath my mother is forced to take. We are completely cut off from the world outside the hospital, the world outside the Intensive Care Unit, the world outside this cubicle. We are alone together, suspended in time and space, just my mother and me. I listen to the steady whir and click of the respirator, the soft inhale and exhale of my own breath, and I feel almost peaceful except for the thought that keeps flickering through my mind: My mother is going to die. I don't know how I know this, but I do. I can feel it with every fiber of my being. She waited for me to come and now that I'm here and I've made peace with her, I can feel her getting ready to go. My little mother. She looks so worn out and helpless lying here with tubes and needles pumping air and nutrients and drugs into her body, it would be a blessing to release her from all this suffering and pain. *Mom, I know you're tough, but you don't have to fight anymore. You can stop struggling,* I silently tell her. *You can go. But oh, how I wish you would stay.*

❖

SHE IS THE QUINTESSENTIAL MOM. Average height and average weight, though I would bet anything she'd love to lose ten pounds, and has probably tried Weight Watchers, Jenny Craig, and the South Beach Diet many times. Straight ash blond hair cut to a sensible length and held back with a silver clip at the nape of her neck. Pale skin despite the blush brushed on her cheeks that is a bit too pink and was probably bought from a neighbor or a co-worker moonlighting as an Avon Lady. Lipstick peach instead of red, mascara brown instead of black. A plain gold wedding band around the fourth finger of her left hand and small sapphire posts that lie flat against her earlobes and are probably her birthstone and a recent gift from her husband. A mother-and-child charm hanging from a gold chain around her neck, which she fingers from time to time without realizing she is doing so. She wears no perfume, but if she did it would carry the odor of freshly baked cookies, lemon furniture polish, sheets hot from the dryer, moist coconut cream that she smoothes on her hands. She is Angelina, my mother's angel of a nurse, and I am half out of my mind in love with her. If anyone can make my mother well it is Angelina, whose very being exudes calmness, capability, and TLC.

She breezes into the room, her white crepe-sole shoes not making a sound, and goes straight to her patient, nodding briefly in my direction to let me know that before we can chat, she needs to attend to the business at hand: reading the numbers and graphs on the monitor, checking the fluid level of the bag attached to my mother's feeding tube, measuring the ounces of urine in the receptacle attached to my mother's catheter hanging near the foot of her bed. I can tell by the way Angelina moves about the room briskly that she has done this a thousand times before, but I can also tell from the sympathy in her eyes that she cares about every patient she has ever attended, and my mother is no exception. When she finishes her tasks, I tell my mother that I'll be right back and follow Angelina out into the hall.

"I'm Lydia," I say, extending my hand. "Her daughter. We spoke on the phone a few days ago."

"Oh, nice to meet you. I'm glad you're here. Come." Angelina leads me to two office chairs parked in front of a desk with an old blue clunky typewriter on it and gestures for me to sit down. The nurse's station is quiet at the moment; I imagine all the members of the medical staff are busy attending their patients.

"How does my mother seem to you?" I ask, trying to keep the new, ever-present note of fear out of my voice.

"She's holding her own," Angelina says, careful not to give anything away. "She had a bit of a rough time last night so she got something to help her sleep early this morning, at about five o'clock, before I came in. She won't open her eyes before noon."

That's what you think, I say to myself, feeling even more grateful that my mother and I had a chance to talk a few minutes ago. "How long do you think she'll stay on the respirator?" I ask.

Angelina frowns slightly and I see that her lipstick has feathered below the right corner of her mouth. "You'll be able to speak with Dr. Harte this morning. He'll be in for his rounds soon."

"Dr. Heart?"

"H-A-R-T-E," Angelina spells out. "I know. We used to have a doctor who worked here named Dr. Payne. P-A-Y-N-E. He was a great doctor, but not many patients were happy to meet him." Angelina laughs and I am struck by how unfamiliar the sound is. I feel like I haven't heard anyone laugh in years.

"Why are her hands so swollen? And why are they tied to the bed?" I ask, fighting to keep my voice neutral. "Is that really necessary?"

"In your mother's case, I'm afraid it is," Angelina says, folding her own hands and resting them on her light blue polyester lap. Her nails are polished a pale, translucent pink. "Her hands are swollen from the steroids the doctor gave her. And they're tied for her own safety, so she won't pull out all her tubes and needles."

"Did she try and do that?" I ask, though I can guess the answer.

"Oh yeah." Angelina's green eyes widen. "She's quite a fighter, your mother."

I smile, feeling oddly proud. "You don't know the half of it."

"When she woke up from her anesthesia, your mother was not very happy, believe me. She kept trying to pull everything out. So I'm sorry, but we had to restrain her." Angelina hesitates, studying me as if she's trying to make a decision. "You can untie her hands while you're in the room," she finally says, "as long as you promise to keep an eye on her. But at night, we'll have to tie them up again."

"Thank you." I accept this small gift gratefully. Then I force myself to ask the first of what I imagine are going to be many difficult questions in the days ahead. "Angelina, do you think my mother would prefer not to be on life support?"

Angelina shifts her weight around; clearly my question has made her uncomfortable. "I have something for you," she says, getting up and going over to a neighboring desk. She plucks a folder out of a wire basket wedged between a computer and a fax machine and sits back down next to me. "The first few days your mother was here, she was able to write a little," Angelina informs me as she flips through the folder. "But lately, all she's been able to come up with is this." She shows me a piece of paper with meaningless penciled curlicues whirling down the page. "Then yesterday, she made it clear to me that she wanted to try to write again."

"Was she able to?"

Angelina silently hands me another piece of paper, also covered with a continuous loop of circles that remind me of the silver Slinky toy Jack stole from me when I was a child. The sight of those circles momentarily comforts me; they look just like the doodles my mother always drew on paper napkins when she was sitting at the kitchen table talking on the phone. Maybe she's just scribbling to pass the time, like she used to do when she was put on hold, waiting for the plumber, the electrician, the gardener, or the car mechanic to come back on the line. But my denial is shattered when I see, underneath the penciled coil that rolls off the page, one distinct word that try as I might, I can't pretend isn't there.

"Kill?" I read aloud.

Angelina nods, looking from the page to me.

The shaky letters swim before my eyes, but I blink my tears away. "Kill," I say again, the word not a question this time. "Angelina, did you by any chance show this to my father?"

"And your brother."

"Cousin." I correct her. "What did they say?"

"Not much."

"That figures. Do you know if they talked to my mother about it?"

Angelina shakes her head. "I doubt it. Your father is having an extremely difficult time with this, Lydia. He's a man who likes to be very much in control, isn't he?"

I raise my eyebrows. "Tell me about it."

"It's very hard for men like that to feel so powerless. Your father is afraid, and I'm sure that's not a feeling he likes to have." Angelina looks to me for confirmation; I nod. "Your dad wants this all to go away so he can have his wife back, just the way she was before. So he doesn't want to hear or think about anything that might upset or scare him."

"Such as?"

"Such as the possibility that your mother might die."

Hot beads of sweat collect under my armpits and I can smell a sour odor rising up from beneath my clothes. I recognize the scent at once; it is the smell of fear. I wonder if Angelina can detect it. A tremor begins in my chest and moves up to my skull, increasing in intensity until my whole body is shaking and I feel like my head is about to shatter. It's one thing for me to think that my mother is going to die; it's quite another thing to hear someone else say it. I stare at my mother's nurse and force myself to ask her the second hard question of the day. "Do you really think my mother is going to die?"

A shadow crosses Angelina's face as though she is suddenly aware that she's said too much. A phone rings loudly on a nearby desk, and she waits for another nurse to pick it up before she speaks. "Lydia, your mother is seriously ill." Angelina is obviously choosing her words carefully. "At the moment she is unable to breathe on her own. There's always a chance that someone in her situation won't pull through. But there's also a chance—a very good chance—that she will."

"What if she doesn't want to?" I study the word written on the page before me whose four uneven letters look like they were printed by a small child just learning her ABC's instead of a woman who once worked briefly as a stenographer and takes great pride in her meticulous, even handwriting.

"Motivation is definitely a factor in recovery," Angelina says, looking directly at me. "Having so many family members around is bound to lift her spirits. You'll have to wait and see."

"May I keep this?" I ask Angelina, who nods and rises as I fold the page and tuck it inside my pocket. I get up from my chair, too, and when Angelina gives me a motherly pat on the shoulder, it takes everything I have not to throw myself into her arms, rest my head on her soft, inviting bosom, shut my eyes, and weep.

"SO SOFT, SMOOTH, and young looking, even their hands won't give them away," said the male voice-over while the image of two fresh-faced smiling women filled the screen of our large, bulky console TV. As a teenager, whenever this particular skin cream commercial came on, I always stopped what I was doing and paid close attention, even though I had seen the ad many times before. Both women had shiny brown hair smoothed into Marlo Thomas *That Girl* flips that I could never master, and their smiles never once faltered as they held their matching hands up to the camera as though they were a recently won, much coveted prize. The women turned their palms this way and that, fanned their fingers like the tentacles of an exotic, graceful sea anemone, and then with an almost obscene amount of pleasure, each one used her right hand to caress the flawless, unwrinkled flesh of her left. Which was the mother and which was the daughter? It was impossible to tell, and that was the point of the whole thing. But that isn't what held my attention— they always identified who was who at the end of the sixty-second spot anyway, making both women dissolve into identical peals of helpless laughter. No, what fascinated me was that this mother/daughter duo, or any such pair, actually looked like they were happy to be together, on national TV, sitting in their bright sunny kitchen, showing off their perfect, creamy hands.

The commercial comes flooding back to me when I return to my mother's room and catch sight of her once beautiful hands, now tied with fraying strips of white cloth to the railings on either side of her hospital bed. I have always been jealous of my mother's hands; often she remarks that they are her very best feature. When she was a young woman, my mother's hands were slim and elegant with long tapered fingers. They looked like they belonged at the end of someone else's arms, someone taller, thinner, and more refined than any female member of our short, pudgy family. When I was growing up, my mother's weekly manicure appointments—Tuesday afternoons at three o'clock—were sacred and she would not miss them for anything, even to pick me up from school the day the bus got a flat tire (Colleen's mother drove me home). Doing the dishes was out of the question, of course; my mother wasn't going to spend all that good money on manicures just to have them ruined by hot, soapy water. And since the idea of rinsing off a bowl or plate would never even occur to my father, the job naturally fell to me. Though my mother's hands are now dotted with age spots and her skin is less firm than it once was, she still takes special care of her hands. I don't think I've ever seen her with her nails unpolished. Even now they are filed into perfect ovals and painted a warm, shiny red.

As gently as I can, I tug at the knot on the white strip of cloth that anchors my mother's left hand to the railing of her bed. When it loosens, I slide it out from under her wrist and lay her hand down against her side, being careful not to disturb the white clip attached to her middle finger that measures her oxygen level. Then I walk around the bed and do the same for her right hand. My mother continues to sleep and I continue to study her swollen hands. The jewelry that she always wears—the white gold wedding band and matching engagement ring on her left hand and a ruby and diamond cocktail ring on her right—look like they are cutting into her puffy flesh and I wonder why no one thought to remove them. Now they lie trapped beneath her enlarged knuckles and there's no way anyone will be able to slip them off. I hope they won't have to be cut away eventually. The thought of someone taking a knife to the rings my mother has worn on her delicate hands for over fifty years is almost more than I can bear.

"Still sleeping?" My father comes back into the room, his face more relaxed than it's been since I've arrived. His arms are full of newspapers, which he piles onto one of the chairs beside my mother's bed after removing my pocketbook from the seat and dropping it to the floor. He drops himself into the other chair and settles in for the duration. "Want part of the paper, Lydia?" he asks, and when I decline, he disappears behind the business section of the *New York Times* as he did every Sunday morning of my childhood after he'd had his fill of coffee, bagels, cream cheese, and lox.

I stay where I am, watching my mother's body jerk in time to the respirator as she sleeps, the one-word note she wrote yesterday burning a hole in my pocket. What does it mean? Does she want us to kill her? And if so, will we be able to grant her wish? And if not—though I can't imagine what else she might mean by the word "kill"—will we be able to keep her alive? I am seized with a desire that is completely unfamiliar to me: a desire to do whatever it is my mother wants, if only I can figure out what that is. As I hover near her bed, my breathing slows on its own, until I am inhaling and exhaling along with the even rhythm of the noisy respirator. Off to the side, my father clears his throat and turns a page. My mother's eyes flutter and she moves her head slightly to the right. I look at the watch on my wrist I keep set to West Coast time and am stunned to see it is not even ten o'clock. It's going to be a very long day.

Might as well make myself comfortable, I think, lifting the stack of newspapers off the chair so I can sit back down beside my father. Now he is reading the sports section. I skim the front pages of *The New York Times*, *The Los Angeles Times*, and *The Wall Street Journal*, pretending interest in the headlines while I wait for my father to finish reading the scores. When he does so, he drops the newspaper onto the floor and extends his hand to me, palm up. I know he wants and expects me to pass him another section of the paper, but instead I hand him the page upon which my mother has scrawled the word "kill."

"What's this?" He lifts the white sheet of paper closer to his face, recognizes it, and then turns his head and holds it as far away as possible, as if it repulses him. "Lydia, where did you get this?"

"Angelina gave it to me. Why didn't you tell me about it?"

"Why should I? There's nothing to tell."

"Dad, there's plenty to tell. This is important. Very important. I'm going to talk to Mom about it."

"No, you're not," my father says. "Lydia, If you dare, I'll—" But before he can finish his threat, I snatch the note from his hand, drop all the newspapers from my lap onto the floor, and return to the side of my mother's bed.

"Mom, are you sleeping?" I ask, bending close to her ear. She opens her eyes, startled, but when she sees my face, her expression calms. "Mom, you can understand me, right?" I ask. She nods, a tiny, almost imperceptible motion.

My father stands close behind me, a great menacing bear about to attack. I ignore him as best I can. "Mom, your nurse showed me what you wrote yesterday." I hold the page in front of her eyes. "I have to ask you a really hard question, okay?" Another slight nod. "What did you mean by this? Do you want to die? Do you want us…" I swallow hard, "…to kill you?"

"Oh for God's sake, Lydia," my father explodes. "What kind of question is that? Doris, you're going to be fine. Nobody's dying here. Nobody's killing anyone. We're all going home. Soon. Very soon. I promise."

My mother glares at my father like she wants to kill *him*. He flinches at her gaze, shuts his mouth, and takes a big step back.

"Mom." I look directly into her eyes and smooth a tendril of sweaty hair off her forehead. "Tell me what you want. I'm listening. Do you want to die?"

The room seems to hold its breath while I wait for my mother to answer. She locks eyes with me and shakes her head. My sigh of relief is drowned out by the respirator's loud belch.

"All right," I say, folding the paper and putting it away. "I'm sorry I had to ask you that, but I really needed to know. Now that you've told me, I'm going to do everything I can to help you get better. Okay?"

My mother nods again.

"But why did you write 'kill'?"

"Lydia, please." My father is at my back again. "I mean it now. Enough."

"Dad, this is important. She's trying to tell us something." But what, I wonder. I look at my mother again and she starts bobbing her right hand up and down in a frantic motion. "Is your hand hurting you?" I ask, and then glance over my shoulder at my father. "Angelina said I could untie her," I inform him before he can yell at me for doing so. "Is that it?" I bring my attention back to my mother. "Is your wrist sore from being tied to the bed?"

My mother shakes her head, then waves her hand again.

"She wants to write something," my father says, moving across the room to fetch a clipboard that has a white pad pinned underneath its clasp and a pencil attached to it with a long white string. "Here, Doris. Here you go."

My mother lifts her right hand and grasps the pencil my father offers firmly. He holds the clipboard steady as she tries to write. All she can manage is a wiggly line that crawls across the paper in a downhill slope until it falls off the end of the page. She makes another feeble attempt, but the result is the same.

"Why don't you rest now, Doris?" My father takes the pencil out of her hand and tucks the clipboard under his arm. "Just take it easy. You can try again later."

"Can I have that?" I ask, pointing to the pencil and pad he is about to put down on the counter by the sink. My father hands everything over, though I can tell he doesn't want to. I turn to a fresh page and start printing out the alphabet in large, clear letters. Like many a good feminist, I've held plenty of human services jobs—it's how I supported myself while I earned both my master's and doctorate degrees. My parents made it clear they would pay for med school or law school but not some "crazy *meshugeneh* Women's Studies program." So while I was a student, I took care of several disabled people, including one who couldn't speak but communicated instead with a letter board, similar to the one I am creating now. I finish the alphabet, add the words "yes" and "no" to the bottom of the page, and hold it up with a flourish.

"*Voilà*," I say, and then explain. "It's a letter board, Mom. Maybe it will be easier for you to point to the letters instead of writing them. To spell out what you want to say."

"Would you look at that," my father marvels. "How clever." I think this is the first thing I've ever done in my adult life that has truly impressed him. "Doris, Lydia wrote out the alphabet for you, so you can point to the letters. Point." My father jabs his forefinger in the air to demonstrate. My mother studies the alphabet I've written with interest and then raises her right hand.

"H." I read the letter I think she is indicating, and my mother nods. "O." She moves her manicured finger across the page without lifting it in a smooth, sweeping motion, the same way Colleen and I used to steer the small wooden pointer across her Ouija board when we were in junior high, asking it to answer our questions about what we would be and who we would marry when we grew up. "Is that an N?" I ask my mother. "No? Do you mean M? Okay. H-O-M..." My mother's finger moves slowly to the left. "E," I say aloud. "H-O-M-E."

"Home," my father proclaims.

"Is that it?" I ask my mother. "Home? You want to go home?"

She nods emphatically.

"We're going home, Doris. In a day or two. As soon as they take the respirator out." My father is talking loudly again, although my mother hears better than he does. Better than I do. "The respirator," he repeats, pointing to his own throat. "They have to take it out."

My mother shoots him her Evil Eye and he throws his hands up in the air and holds them there in a gesture of surrender. "What'd I do, Doris? Please. I'm trying as hard as I can to get you out of here. I really am. Aren't I, Lydia?" He turns to me for support.

"Do you want to say anything else, Mom?" I offer her the alphabet again. She stabs at a letter with her red nail and her finger slides off the page.

I urge her to try again, but she is too weak to lift her hand and I feel guilty for wearing her out. "You seem tired, Mom. Rest a little and we'll try again later. Okay?" She nods and closes her eyes.

My father and I resume our positions on the two chairs off to the side of the room, but before we can get comfortable, Jack barges in, strands of his long white hair flying. "Did I miss anything?" he asks, as if he has just raced into a movie theater, afraid that the coming attractions have ended and the main feature has already begun.

"No, Jack." My father gestures toward my mother's hospital bed. "Everything's still the same."

"Phew." He brushes the hair out of his face and starts unsnapping the navy blue windbreaker he has on.

"Is it still cool outside?" I ask, just to make conversation.

"A little," Jack answers, shrugging off his jacket.

"Oh my God, Jack, what is wrong with you?" I say as loudly as I dare, the vow I made this morning to be nicer to him flying out the window. "I can't believe how rude you are."

"What?" Jack asks, clueless. "I didn't even say anything yet."

"Your shirt." I point to his apparel. "I can't believe you're wearing that. In a hospital, no less. That is so offensive on so many levels, I don't even know where to begin."

My cousin looks down at his chest, which is covered with the words "I'm not a gynecologist, but I'll take a look" and says, "Oops," with a apologetic shrug and a sheepish grin.

"Jack." I try and fail to contain my fury. "What the hell were you thinking?"

"Lydia, I wasn't thinking, okay?" Now Jack is furious, too. "Crystal wasn't around to help me pack so I just grabbed a pile of T-shirts and jeans, threw everything into a suitcase, and caught the first plane I could, unlike a certain someone who took her own sweet time getting her big fat ass out here—"

"Children, children." Though Jack and I are middle-aged adults, my father reprimands us as if we are still the pre-adolescents we once were when my cousin and his parents visited us every Saturday afternoon. Jack and I pretty much spent the whole day arguing about anything and everything: what game we wanted to play, who got to set it up, who got to go first, who got to keep score. "If you must fight, take it outside," my father says, jerking his thumb over his shoulder and banishing us from the room, just as he did when we were young. "I don't want you disturbing her." He nods his chin in my mother's direction. "She needs her beauty sleep."

"Sorry," I mumble to my father. "But Jack, I'm serious," I say, keeping my voice low. "You cannot wear that T-shirt in here."

"What would you like me to do, Lydia?" Jack stage-whispers. "Take it off? Run around naked?"

"You can turn your shirt inside out, or you can put your jacket back on," I tell my cousin, giving him the illusion that he has a choice in the matter. "It's entirely up to you."

Jack opts to put his jacket back on and then leaves in search of another chair to bring back to the room. A few minutes after he returns, Angelina comes to check on my mother. She examines the monitor, the fluids, and the various contraptions attached to my mother's hand, chest, face, and neck before turning to us. "How's she doing?"

"Great," Jack says. "Wonderful. She just finished a tap dance."

Angelina ignores him and looks at me. "She was conscious for a little while and she knew we were here," I say, "but now she's sleeping again."

"It's normal for her to go in and out," Angelina tells us. "The doctor will stop by to see her soon."

"Nice girl, that Angelina," my father says as soon as she leaves the room. "Very attractive, too," he adds, as I knew he would. At least he's consistent, I think, as he picks up the newspaper again.

The longest day of my life continues to crawl by one endless moment at a time. Every hour on the hour, the blood pressure cuff wrapped around my mother's arm automatically tightens, causing her to screw up her face and loudly moan. Technicians come and go, sticking my mother with needles, adjusting her tubes, recording her vital signs. A little before noon Dr. Harte comes in. Tall, thin, and slightly balding, with pronounced cheekbones and a long skinny nose set in the palest face I've ever seen, he reminds me of the actor who played the father in the old *Patty Duke Show*. He spends a few minutes reading through my mother's chart, nodding thoughtfully as he flips through the pages. Then he glances briefly at her monitor and even more briefly at her before proclaiming that she "looks good" and there's nothing to be done at the moment; just like Angelina said earlier, all we can do is wait and see.

After the doctor leaves, I notice the room seems colder, and gather the two sides of my sweater together in one hand, bunching them tightly under my neck. "Why is it so cold in here?" I ask my father. "I'm chilled to the bone."

"It's for the machines," Jack informs me. "They won't work right if they get too hot. Right, Uncle Max?"

As my father nods, I see movement out of the corner of my eye. My mother is gesturing with her right hand again. I am up and at her side in an instant.

"Do you want to write something, Mom?" I ask. She shakes her head. "Do you want to try pointing to the alphabet?" Again, no. "What, then?" She flaps her fingers against her palm quickly as if she wants me to come even closer, and when I do, she takes hold of my hand, plasters it to her right side and covers it with her own. Instantly I understand, and lean over her, careful not to disturb all the tubes and needles, and offer my other hand. She grips it tightly, pressing it against her left side, warming me as best she can with the heat of her body, all she has to offer. As I stand there, carefully shifting my weight so I don't topple over her, I hear Vera's voice in my head, reminding me: *She's a mother. She wants to mother you.* My eyes well up with tears, and I turn my head so my father won't see. And as I stand there hanging in the balance, my hands heating against my mother's hips, I remember a saying I saw on a bumper sticker years ago that I didn't believe back then but now know is true: It's never too late to have a happy childhood.

❖

WHAT A DIFFERENCE a day makes... As the afternoon wears on and I continue my mother's bedside vigil, the title of an old song appears in my head out of nowhere, though I don't remember who sang it or any of the words. All I know is the hard thrilling truth of that phrase and I am reeling with it. A new day is dawning. My mother and I have made up. I have given her what I've always wanted to get from her: acknowledgment, validation, and love. And that simple though not easy act has changed everything completely.

For the first time ever, I understand what is meant when people say they have had a change of heart, because my heart is lighter, and free as a bird that's been let out of its cage. My whole body seems lighter, too, and not because I ate a tiny breakfast and could only manage to choke down a few bites of the lunch my father brought upstairs for me. Corny as it sounds, I feel like a great weight has been lifted off my shoulders, a weight I've been carrying around for years and years and years. I feel altered and transformed; I am not the same person I was yesterday, or even several hours ago. I have molted but instead of skin, what I have shed is a lifetime of sadness, resentment, anger, and grief. I could never have predicted that I would be able to let go of all my pain so easily. But it has truly vanished like a puff of my mother's bygone cigarette smoke disappearing into thin air.

Though I feel energized and ecstatic by all the day's events, underneath it all, I am also utterly exhausted. Everything aches with fatigue: my brain, my bones, my fingernails, even my eyelashes. I wonder if they can bring a cot in here so I can lie down, I think, mentally rearranging the furniture of my mother's room. If we took out the bedside table, which we're not using anyway, and angled the respirator a little to the left, there might just be enough space. I know I could go down the hall to one of the visitor lounges and stretch out on a couch as Jack has done, but I have no desire to move. Cocooned in my mother's cubicle is like being wrapped in a warm fuzzy blanket on a cold blustery day. I feel cozy and safe and protected, and I want to stay here forever.

But Angelina has other ideas. When she comes in at three o'clock to check on my mother, she takes one look at me and says, "Out, Lydia. Now."

"Why?" I ask. "And what about him?" I point to my father, who is slumped down in the chair beside me, snoring lightly. "Why do I have to leave if he doesn't?"

"Because he went downstairs for lunch and you've been in here all day without a break since eight o'clock this morning."

"That's all right. I'm used to working long hours," I tell Angelina, trying to joke with her. "If you can handle a twelve-hour shift, so can I."

But Angelina is not in a joking mood. "Lydia, you need to stretch your legs and you need some fresh air," she says, her voice stern. "And besides," she adds, seeing I'm not convinced, "if you fall apart, you won't be any help to your mother at all. If you don't want to do it for yourself, do it for her." I've got to hand it to Angelina. She's smart—too smart. She knows the one and only thing to say that will persuade me to vacate the premises.

"Okay, okay," I say, giving in at last. "But just for a few minutes." Rising from my chair, I place my hands on my hips and look over my shoulder, twisting my back first to one side and then to the other. My spine makes small crackling noises, and I have to admit Angelina is right: it does feel good to get up and move. I pull the straps of my purse up over my arm and tap my father on the shoulder. "Dad?"

"What? What's the matter?" His eyes pop open and he startles awake. "What is it? What happened, Lydia?"

"Nothing, Dad. Calm down. Everything's okay. Mom's still sleeping." We both glance over in her direction to make sure that what I've said is true. "I'm just going downstairs for a few minutes to get some air. Do you want me to bring you anything from the cafeteria?"

"No, I'm fine." He waves my question away and then uses the back of his hand to cover a large yawn that halfway out of his mouth changes to a tired groan.

"See you soon." I head out of the room but take only two steps before turning back. "Can I have my cell phone?" I ask, holding out my hand. My father pats his various pockets until he finds the phone and returns it to me. Before I am out of the room again, he has fallen back to sleep.

I push my way through the swinging doors of the ICU and stride down the hallway. When I pass the visitor's lounge, I peek my head in to see Jack splayed across the couch like a lifeless rag doll, his head propped up on one armrest, his dirty sneakers dangling over the other. His long gray ponytail spills over the side of the couch, its uneven ends brushing the floor, and his glazed eyes are glued to the TV set mounted overhead. He is watching some game on ESPN that involves very large men chasing a small ball of some sort, and doesn't see me standing in the doorway. I decide not to bother him and continue on my way downstairs.

The world outside Holy Family Hospital is so bright, it shocks me, and as I push open the glass door, I fumble in my purse for a pair of sunglasses to quickly shove onto my face like a movie star fresh out of rehab who doesn't want to be recognized. Though I know I should take Angelina's advice and go for a short walk, an empty wooden bench next to the building beckons me, and I lower myself onto it instead. Leaning back, I close my eyes and raise my face to the sun, hoping to bake out the chill that has lodged inside me. The hot, dry Los Angeles air feels like a blessing after being cooped up inside and freezing all day.

After a few minutes, I am warm enough to remove my sweater. After a few more minutes, I feel refreshed enough to open my eyes and look around. It's amazing to me that there's still a world out here that hasn't changed all that much since the last time I saw it early this morning. Cars wend their way up the street one after another, birds chirp in the trees, a teenage boy zips by on a shiny silver bike. Off to the side, I see three nurses sitting on a bench similar to the one I have claimed; two of them puff away on cigarettes and one munches handfuls of potato chips, her hand reaching into the bag on her lap and rising to her mouth in a continuous motion as if her arm is an automated lever. Across the street a young woman with a baby carriage stands on the corner waiting for the traffic light to change. She turns her head and hides her face in the crook of her arm as a bus zooms by, spewing a dark cloud of smoke behind it. Clearly life goes on. If you're lucky. Will my mother be so lucky? I wish I knew the answer.

"I have an idea. Let's call Allie," I say aloud, as if there is a group of people sitting on the bench with me, eagerly awaiting instruction. And in a way there is. In addition to forty-nine-year-old Lydia, there's thirtysomething Lydia, twentysomething Lydia, teenage Lydia, little girl Lydia, and baby Lydia all contained inside me, each one clamoring to be taken care of and reassured that she isn't about to become what once upon a time she longed to be: an orphan. My mind fills with the scene in the movie *Peter Pan* when all the Lost Boys meet Wendy for the first time and crowd around her to sing with great delight, "We have a mother. At last we have a mother." I sing the same words softly to myself—to all my selves—keeping my voice low so the nurses perched nearby won't hear me. It's true: I have a mother, at last I have a mother. But for how long? Another minute, another hour, another day?

I continue sitting in the sun while my mind ping-pongs back and forth and my heart beats out equal amounts of joy and sadness each time it thunks heavily inside my chest. A quartet of teenage girls saunters by, their eight flip-flops making a clipped, syncopated racket slapping against the soles of their feet, and I remember a fight about footwear my mother and I had when I was a teenager. It was Yom Kippur and I was determined to follow all the strict rules of the holiday to the letter. So in addition to fasting and not doing any work or riding in a car, I was also going to refrain from wearing leather to show respect to the animals who sacrifice their lives to feed and clothe us. When I got ready to go to synagogue that morning, I put on a knee-length purple dress that my mother had approved of, but instead of the fancy black patent leather flats that went with it, I decided to wear a pair of yellow flip-flops instead. I can still hear the shriek my mother gave when she caught sight of me. "You are not leaving the house like that," she yelled, pointing at my feet. I responded by yelling back, "You are so goddamned hypocritical," which only proved my own hypocrisy, as I was taking the Lord's name in vain not just on any day, but on the holiest day of the year. My mother didn't give in so much as give up, and she, my father, and I walked the mile and a half to synagogue without saying a word. On the way home, a painful water blister formed on the inside of my left big toe, which only made me yell at my mother again, this time for allowing me to wear the flimsy flip-flops, which offered no support. "What kind of mother are you?" I believe I even shouted. Now I smile at the memory, and then grin at how amused I am by it. Yesterday the memory would have filled me with self-righteous indignation; today it merely makes me chuckle.

I dig out my cell phone, eager to discuss all this with Allie, my darling creature of habit, who always comes right home after work and eats her dinner at six o'clock. But when I turn on my phone, I see I have one missed call—a message from Allie—so I listen to it first.

"Hi, Lyddie, it's me." At the sound of Allie's voice, I feel my insides start to melt, like a carton of ice cream left out on the kitchen counter. "I just wanted to let you know I probably won't be home tonight when you try to call. I'm going on a little shopping excursion right after work. To check out a birthday present for a certain special someone. I know, I know, your birthday's not until August, but this is a big one and I want to do it up right. I'm just starting to look around, okay? So don't ask me where I'm going or what I'm looking at because I'm not going to tell you. I mean it, Lydia. I miss you terribly and so does Mishmosh. Bye."

"Bye," I echo, saving her message so I can listen to it again later.

Briefly I think of calling Vera, but I'm starting to get a bit antsy out here. Twenty minutes have passed since I've been away from my mother, and in that short period of time, anything might have happened. As I gather up my things, I remember something Colleen said to me years ago, soon after her first child, a daughter, was born. "I can't stand to be apart from her, even for a minute, even to go to the bathroom," she told me early one morning, her sleep-deprived voice sounding groggy and blissful over the phone. "At night, I keep getting up to check on her. If I can't see her, I get this actual pain in my chest, this ache, this longing to be with her. I call it phantom baby pain. It's like part of me is gone if I'm not in the same room with her." This is how I feel about my mother, I realize, as I rise and stretch and crack my bones like I've just woken up from a long winter nap. Who would ever have imagined such a thing?

I move toward the door of the hospital and as I open it, I see the little nun I met yesterday—was it really only yesterday?—scuttling ahead of me. She moves fast, bringing the White Rabbit of *Alice in Wonderland* to mind. *I'm late, I'm late for a very important date.* I hurry after her, walking quickly and quietly as a private eye in an old detective movie from the fifties, but I still have trouble keeping up. Why I'm trailing her, I can't say, but I feel a mysterious need to go after her, so when she passes the elevator bank and turns right, toward the cafeteria, I do, too.

The nun stops in front of a heavy-looking wooden door, and using all her weight, which can't be more than eighty pounds, she pulls it open and steps inside. Without a word, I follow her and see that we have entered the hospital's chapel, a bright, airy room with a high ceiling, lined with wooden pews leading up to an altar upon which hangs a large cross with a very lifelike Jesus nailed to it. Sunlight pouring through two stained glass windows spills fragments of blue, red, yellow, and green onto the white walls. The nun takes a seat in the second row and I slip in beside her.

"Good afternoon, Sister," I say, and even though I keep my voice hushed, it echoes loudly through the spacious room.

"Good afternoon," she replies, holding out her hand. "I'm Sister Grace."

"I'm Lydia," I tell her, taking her hand. "Lydia Pinkowitz."

"Did you come here to pray?" Sister Grace asks, peering up at me through her thick glasses. Her eyes are just as I remember them, blue and kind.

"Maybe. I guess so." I don't really know why I've followed Sister Grace into the chapel but I don't feel comfortable telling her that.

"Forgive me," Sister Grace says, clasping her hands onto her lap. "I'm too old to kneel."

"That's all right," I assure her. "I'm too Jewish to kneel."

She smiles. "He was Jewish, too," she says, pointing to the figure on the cross with a finger crooked from arthritis.

"I know. A Jewish carpenter." An oxymoron if I've ever heard one, since all the Jewish men I know, upon hearing the word "screwdriver," think of vodka and orange juice instead of a tool.

"Whom are you here to see?" Sister Grace studies my face, her eyes magnified and curious behind her thick glasses.

"My mother," I say with a little sigh. "She's in the Intensive Care Unit. She's very sick."

"I'm sorry, my child," Sister Grace says and the words "my child" wash over me like holy water. "But remember, God doesn't give us more than we can handle. He takes care of all His children. Including your mother. And including you." She nods her head and turns from me to face forward. "Come, Lydia," she says, patting my knee lightly. "Let us pray."

I clasp my hands and bow my head slightly, just as Sister Grace does, remembering the words my father spoke earlier this morning: *a little religion never hurt anyone.* And while that certainly isn't true, I do feel a sense of calmness as I sit here with Sister Grace even though I know I need to be getting back to my mother. I steal a glance at the nun next to me who is so tiny I feel like an awkward giant sitting beside her. She is still as the statue on the altar before us, and I hesitate to disturb her. I wonder what she thinks about when she prays. Or maybe she isn't praying at all. Maybe her mind is spinning in circles the way mine usually does. What is prayer anyway? And does it really do any good? Is anyone up there listening? To think that all those years of Hebrew school have culminated in this moment: Lydia Marilyn Pinkowitz, known to all her teachers as Leah Malka, sitting on a pew in a Christian chapel of all places, doubting the existence of God.

"*Sh'ma, Yisroael, Adonai Elohanu, Adonai Echad.*" I move my lips and whisper the one prayer I remember, the most important one, the one every Jew is supposed to say first thing in the morning and last thing at night so if we die in our sleep, those will be the very last words that pass through our lips as we leave this lifetime and enter whatever follows. *Hear O Israel, the Lord our God, the Lord is One.* I can't believe I've just said these words, which praise a God whom I don't particularly like or believe in: the Biblical God who I was told was just and merciful but who seemed to me to be unfair and unkind. I prefer the nurturing, maternal, loving Goddess myself, but I say the words anyway, just in case. Plus even though I hate to admit it, the age-old Hebrew feels familiar on my tongue and that offers comfort. I wonder if I should say the ancient, holy words for my mother when I go back upstairs since she can't say them herself. And if I do so and she dies, will they still count?

"Sister Grace, I have to go," I say, rising. "Thank you."

"Peace be with you." She grasps one of my hands in both her own, and I notice a gold wedding band circling the fourth finger of her left hand. Bride of Christ meets Bride of Allie, I think, wondering how Sister Grace would feel if she knew I was a lesbian. I decide it doesn't really matter and take my leave. But I can't get up to the fourth floor right away; the hallway is jammed with gridlock. Several EMTs are rushing about, barking orders loudly and wheeling a patient on a stretcher surrounded by IV poles and other medical contraptions onto the elevators.

"What's going on?" I ask the receptionist, who has a concerned look on her face.

"A terrible car accident," she says. "Some poor Mexican fellow was driving. It looks bad."

"Are there stairs somewhere?" The woman points to the left and I hurry off, more anxious than ever to get back up to my mother. But I can't get anywhere near the swinging doors that lead to the Intensive Care Unit. The staff is in full-blown emergency mode and all I can do is stay out of their way. I duck inside the visitor's lounge, which is filled to overflowing with members of a large family that span four generations at least. Jack is nowhere in sight, and neither is my father. I'm glad of this; the faces of the Mexican family from the smallest infant to the oldest great-grandparent are grave, and I'm sure they are in no mood to put up with some well-meaning yet invasive white person's Spanish banter. Though I doubt even my father would be insensitive enough to say *"Buenos días"* at a time like this.

I try not to stare at the dark brown faces before me, one more beautiful than the next, as we all wait for someone to come tell us we can go inside. But it is not a doctor or a nurse that comes to summon the Mexican family; it is a priest, and as they all file out behind him, a loud wailing begins, and builds, swelling like a tsunami. I follow them inside and see that whoever has been injured has been placed in the cubicle next to my mother's. The priest disappears into the room, and the family crowds around him, spilling all the way out to the nurse's station.

"What's happening?" I ask Angelina, whom I finally catch sight of leaning her hip against a file cabinet and holding a folder in one hand.

"He's not going to make it," she says, her voice full of sorrow. "He lost control of his truck and smashed head-on into a telephone pole. He never had a chance. They're giving him his last rites now." As if on cue, the accident victim's family grows quiet and the priest's voice rises out of the silence. "May the Lord Jesus Christ protect you and lead you to eternal life…"

I have always been told that hearing is the last to go, but I pray to God—any God—that my mother is not listening to what's going on right now. I slip inside her room where Jack and my father sit, their eyes full of shock, their faces green.

"Mom," I say, but she does not respond. "Mom?" I repeat, a bit louder.

"Lydia, don't wake her up," my father whispers.

"I won't. I just wanted to make sure she was asleep," I tell him, backing away from my mother and taking a seat next to Jack. The three of us maintain a respectful silence until the priest is through and the bereaved family files out, their sobs and moans tearing apart my heart.

Except for the involuntary up-and-down motion of her body caused by the respirator, my mother doesn't stir for the rest of the afternoon. She doesn't even wake when the blood pressure cuff around her arm inflates itself every hour on the hour to carry out its own special brand of torture. Each time it starts strangling her arm, Jack and my father swivel their heads to the monitor, as if the figures that appear there are the winning numbers of a lottery ticket they are holding. Which in a way I guess they are.

I don't care about numbers and graphs, though I know they're important; all I care about is the look on my mother's face. Her expression is blank and I can't tell what that means. As I study her, a disturbing thought enters my mind: what if I blew it? What if she's at peace now and is all ready to go? I know it's not uncommon for someone who is dying to hang on longer than expected as they anticipate an important occasion, such as a birthday, an anniversary, or just the arrival of someone they need to see in order to tie up loose ends. What if the only thing that had been tethering my mother to this life was her unresolved relationship with me? Now that it feels like there is some sort of peace between us, might she feel her work here is finished and that it's time for her to leave this earth and enter the world to come?

I stare at my mother's face for hours, memorizing her flaccid cheeks, the cleft in her chin, the two deep lines that run from her nostrils to the outer edges of her lips, the beauty mark below her nose. And then all too soon, it is eight o'clock, the end of visiting hours, and we have to go. And difficult as this day has been, now comes the hardest part of all: though I don't want to, I must place one heavy foot in front of the other and drag myself out of the hospital, each step I take putting more distance between me and my mother, whom I may never see alive again.

❖

"TODAY IS THE FIRST day of the rest of your mother's life." Angelina is all smiles when she greets me with these uplifting words the next morning as I enter the Intensive Care Unit with Jack and my father trailing close behind.

"What do you mean?" I ask, my heart cautiously fluttering with hope.

"I mean," Angelina's smile widens, "your mother turned the corner last night and we're taking the respirator out. In about an hour."

"Oh, thank God," my father says, and his knees actually buckle, causing him to stagger backward and fall.

Jack catches him with both hands under one elbow as he sags against the wall and stands him on his feet. "Take it easy, Uncle Max. C'mon, let's go sit down."

"We're prepping her, so you can't go in there yet," Angelina says, nodding toward my mother's room. "Why don't you go wait in the lounge until I call you?"

My father, Jack, and I troop off, our mood nothing short of jubilant. We enter the empty lounge and arrange ourselves on the couch, all three of us crossing our left legs over our right at the same time like we're performing a comedy routine. "Didn't I tell you she'd be fine?" my father asks, taking careful aim before punching me lightly on the shoulder. I don't argue with him because for once in my life I'm glad that he's right.

"I wonder when they'll release her," Jack muses, lifting the remote control off the coffee table to turn on the TV. After flipping through the channels twice, he settles on an old *I Love Lucy* episode. As he and my father lift their heads to watch the Ricardos and the Mertzes pumping their fists in the air and arguing loudly, I consider going downstairs to call Allie and tell her the good news. Because of the three-hour time difference, we're still playing our frustrating game of phone tag and haven't managed to speak to each other directly since the day before yesterday. I've left her several messages and she's done the same, letting me know that she's fine, Mishmosh is fine, and the pipes are fine (she wrapped them in special heating tape so they won't freeze again). In addition, Allie, knowing how neurotic I am, left me a very long message going over my mail, which was mostly junk, and my email, which was mostly spam. At least my mother was considerate enough to get sick in January during my break, I thought after I hung up the phone. If this had happened right in the middle of the semester, I don't know what I would have done.

When the grating noise of canned laughter becomes too much for me to bear, I rise from the couch, my hand already reaching into my purse, rooting around for my cell phone. Telling my father I'll be right back, I step out into the hallway, but before I make it halfway to the elevator, the doors to the ICU slap open and Angelina bursts out of them, hurrying toward me.

"Your mother is pretty upset at the moment," Angelina says when she catches up to me, her voice breathless and urgent. "I think you should come."

"Should I get my father?" I glance inside the visitor's lounge as Angelina hustles me past its doorway.

"No. I asked her if she wanted him, but she said she only wanted you."

"She did?" I can't help feeling pleased as Angelina and I speedwalk toward the ICU, but my pleasure at being wanted is quickly overshadowed by concern. "Why is she upset?" I take hold of Angelina's arm to stop her for a moment. "The respirator is coming out. That's good news, isn't it?"

"It's very good news," Angelina assures me as I study her worried face. Today she is all dressed in light purple and wears tiny round amethyst posts in her ears that reflect the florescent lights above us. "But she's been hooked up to it for seven days now, and even though she's uncomfortable, she's used to it. Sometimes patients get very frightened when they're about to undergo a change in treatment, even when we explain to them that their health has improved and the change is for the better."

I follow Angelina back into the Intensive Care Unit, patting my hair, straightening my yellow cap-sleeved pullover, and smoothing my black pants as I go. Though I'm sure my appearance is the very last thing on my mother's mind, old habits die hard and since I am trained to expect her criticism, my natural response is to do everything I can to prevent it. But when I enter my mother's room and she catches sight of me, her eyes do not narrow in judgment; they widen with relief instead.

"What's wrong, Mom?" I take her hand and cover her one exposed shoulder with the fresh pink johnny she is wearing, careful not to disturb the electrode patches stuck to her chest or the port going into her neck before turning to Angelina. "Why is she tied to the bed again?"

"Because she fought with the nurse who was on duty before me this morning," Angela tells me. "When she tried to draw some blood, your mother twisted her arm."

"Oh Mom," I say, though it's hard to blame her, especially given the fresh purple bruises on her own arm. Like me, she has always had small veins that are very difficult to puncture, and she's probably had just about enough.

"Can I untie my mother's hands now? I'll stay here with her," I promise Angelina, who hesitates before nodding her assent. The minute my mother's hands are free, she motions that she wants to write.

"Wait a minute, Mom. Here." I go in search of the clipboard and bring it over to the bed. "Do you want to use the letters?" I hold the alphabet up to her but she waves it away with impatience. "You want to write something? Here." I turn to a fresh page just as my father and Jack sweep into the room.

"Hi, Aunt Doris," Jack calls, flopping into a chair. "They said we could come in for a few minutes, just to say good morning."

"Doris, they're taking the tube out." My father makes a pulling motion at the base of his throat right in front of his crisp blue collar. "The tube. They're taking it out. Isn't that good?"

My mother looks at him as if she can't understand how she wound up married to someone who's so clueless, and shakes her head.

"What, it's not good?" My father sits down beside Jack and leans forward in his chair, resting his elbows on his knees. "You'll be able to breathe on your own. You'll be able to talk. You'll be able to eat. You'll be able to yell at me. That's not good?"

My mother shakes her head again and starts to write on the pad I am holding for her. I see she is concentrating hard, but just like yesterday, all she can manage is a meaningless looping scribble.

"Here, Mom. Let's try the letters."

My father and Jack come to stand beside me as my mother points with her red nail. "H," I read. "O. Home? You want to go home?" My mother nods.

"Soon," my father tells her. "Very soon."

My mother clenches her eyes shut for a moment and I can practically feel the heat of her rage. I know she is incredibly frustrated and I imagine she is using everything she has to gather up her strength, determined to make us understand whatever it is she is trying to say. She opens her eyes and lifts her finger again.

"N," I say. "O?" She nods. "W. Now. Home now."

"You want to go home now?" Jack asks.

My mother points at Jack and then touches her own nose as if she is saying *bingo!*

"You want to go home now?" my father asks. "You can't go home now, Doris. Not until they take the tube out."

Upon hearing his words my mother shakes her head violently and I fear she is going to dislodge everything attached to her throat, her nose, her neck, and her arm.

"What, you don't want them to take the tube out?" my father asks, incredulous. "They have to take it out, Doris. You know that. Don't worry, you'll be okay."

Again my mother shakes her head.

"Put the letters away and let her rest, Lydia." My father grabs the clipboard out of my hand. "They'll be coming in soon and I don't think it's good for you to be upsetting her so much."

"I'm not the one upsetting her," I state, furious that my father is blaming me, but too distracted by the look on my mother's face to really start an argument. As she watches him cross the room, carrying the pad and pencil out of reach, her eyes fill with a terrible panic. She looks like someone lost at sea whose small lifeboat—her only hope—is swiftly drifting away. Searching the room frantically, my mother motions for Jack to come closer and he does so immediately, happy to be summoned forth. "What, Aunt Doris? What can I get you?" She waves her hand again, indicating that she wants him to come even nearer. Jack moves my body to the right like a piece of bulky furniture that's gotten in his way, and then steps in front of me. His long gray hair sweeps across my face, tickling my nose, and I impatiently brush it aside.

"I'm here, Aunt Doris," Jack says. My mother scans his T-shirt, which begs the question, "Why be difficult when with a little more effort you can be impossible?" and then raises one red fingernail and stabs him in the belly.

"Oof." Jack collapses in on himself and then straightens up, my mother's finger still poking him in the stomach.

"P," I say, as I realize what my mother is doing, and then pause as if I am a contestant in the final round of the national spelling bee, trying to conjure up the letters of a word that is particularly challenging. "L," I call out as my mother continues pointing. "A." Pause. "N. Plan? You want us to make a plan?" My mother scowls and moves her finger across Jack's chest. He is standing up tall and proud with his stomach in and his shoulders back, like he's lined up for an official roll call.

"E," I announce. "Plane? You want to get on a plane? Now? And go home?"

"Soon, Doris," my father says again, but before she can even glare at him, Angelina enters the room.

"It's time," she says and then claps her hands twice. "Everybody out." My father and Jack leave; I linger in the doorway, looking back at my mother, who is clearly frightened out of her mind. She forms her mouth into the shape of an "O" around the respirator tube, and opens her eyes as widely as she can until her expression resembles the distraught figure in Edvard Munch's painting *The Scream*.

"Mom, I'll be right outside. Right here." I show her that I'm not going very far, but she starts thrashing about on the bed and I'm afraid she's going to hurt herself. "Give us a minute, Angelina," I plead, desperate to find out what is causing my mother this much distress.

"Here, Mom. Let's try again." I bring her the clipboard and she tears the sheet with the alphabet off the pad. Using every ounce of strength she has, my mother grips the pencil firmly and writes a full sentence. When she's done, she hands it to me.

"They want to kill me and make a mosaic out of my remains," I read aloud and now I am incredulous. "Is this what you meant the other day when you wrote the word 'kill'?" My mother nods with satisfaction; finally someone understands what she has been trying so hard to communicate. "Okay," I say thoughtfully. "I get it now," I assure her even though I don't get it at all. In addition to affecting her lungs, is my mother's illness also making her lose her mind?

"Listen, Mom, promise me you won't pull out anything and I'll be right back. Will you promise?" My mother nods again, and even though I don't completely believe she will behave herself, I take the piece of paper out of the room and race off in search of Angelina. Instead I find Dr. Harte sitting at a desk at the nurse's station going over some notes.

"Dr. Harte," I say, trying to control the waver in my voice.

"Lydia, right?" he asks. "Your mother's doing fine. They're taking her off the respirator any minute now."

"Look at this." I show him the sentence that she wrote. "My mother has never been paranoid before. What's going on? Has something happened to her brain?"

The doctor reads my mother's words and is completely unfazed by them. "It's nothing to worry about," he says. "Just a little ICU-induced psychosis. That's all."

"My mother's psychotic?" I ask, my voice rising.

"It's actually quite common," Dr. Harte continues in his dry, detached manner. "After about five or six days in here, patients lose touch with reality. They don't know if it's day or night. They don't sleep well. They aren't eating. They're on very powerful drugs. And the combination of all that wreaks havoc with the mind."

"Will she recover from it?" I ask, my voice still trembling.

"Oh yes. She'll be fine. In fact, she won't remember any of this at all." Dr. Harte waves his hand around the area.

"That's a relief," I tell him. "Thank you." I head back to my mother's room, where Jack and my father have returned to attend her.

"What did the doctor say, Lydia? Did she write something?" Before I can hide the piece of paper, my father catches sight of it and snatches it from my hand. He reads what is written there aloud and punctuates my mother's sentence with an exasperated groan. "Doris, what are you, crazy? Nobody wants to kill you. Don't be ridiculous. C'mon now. Stop the nonsense."

My mother frowns at him with her eyes and rolls her head away.

"Mom." I step up to her bed and stand directly in front of her. "It's all right. I understand now. I know you're in a lot of danger here and I am going to do everything I can to protect you."

"Lydia." My father's voice is full of warning.

"Dad." My voice is just as threatening, as is the look I throw in his direction. "Mom," I turn back to her. "I promise I will take care of you. You know I'm a strong woman. Just like you, right? I'm going to protect you. I'm not going to let anything bad happen to you."

My mother actually seems to take comfort from my words; Jack and my father are rendered mute. Angelina comes in again, bustles about for a few minutes, and then orders us to leave. I stand right by the doorway, making sure I am in my mother's line of vision. Another nurse joins Angelina, and as they approach my mother's bed, she puffs herself up as large as she can, like a cat ready to lash out at anything that dares come near. The two nurses close in on her and though I crane my neck, their backs prevent me from seeing exactly what goes on.

"Mrs. Pinkowitz," I hear Angelina's co-worker say. "This will only take a minute. Now I want you to—ouch!"

"Mrs. Pinkowitz, this isn't going to hurt," Angelina tries to reassure her. "We just have to—" I hear some scuffling and then Angelina's voice again. "Hold up a minute. I don't think this is going to work."

A long moment passes and then Angelina pokes her head out of the doorway. "Lydia," she says, "I asked your mother if she wanted you to come in and she nodded yes. Usually we don't allow family members to be present during this procedure, but your mother is so agitated, I think it would help, so I'm willing to make an exception."

"Does she want me, too?" My father takes a step toward Angelina, eager to go inside. I can tell his question puts her in a tough spot, and so can Jack because he takes my father's arm to distract him.

"Let Lydia go, Uncle Max," he says. "This is women's work."

My father takes a minute to think this over and then nods, as if he needs to give me permission before we can proceed.

"Thanks Dad," I say, suddenly feeling sorry for him. Angelina beckons me to follow her back into my mother's room and as I approach her bed, I see how utterly exhausted she is. *Stop fighting, Mom*, I want to tell her, but I know that isn't what she wants to hear, and besides, it would be useless since the word "surrender" does not exist in my mother's vocabulary.

"I'm here, Mom," I tell her, stroking her sweaty forehead. "I'm right here and I'm not going anywhere, all right? Can they take the tube out now?"

My mother gazes at me as though her heart is breaking and I can see by her expression that she thinks she is not long for this world. "I love you, Mom," I say. "I'm staying right here."

Angelina comes up behind me and my mother glances in her direction and holds up a finger: *wait*. Angelina freezes in her tracks and my mother lifts both hands, points to the rings, and then points to me.

"Your rings, Mom? They can't get them off, your hands are too swollen."

My mother shakes her head and points to her rings again and then again to me.

"You want me to have your rings, Mom? All right. I understand."

My mother nods and then, like a woman pumped up on adrenaline lifting an automobile off her injured child, she sits up and yanks her engagement and wedding rings off her left hand and her ruby and diamond cocktail ring off her right. I don't know how in the world she manages to pull those unyielding bands of metal up over her fingers, which at the moment are four times their normal size, but somehow she accomplishes this superhuman feat before our unbelieving eyes.

"I'll keep your rings until you want them back, Mom," I say and when she drops them into my hands, I slide them onto my fingers and hold them up for her to see. "I'll take good care of them, Mom. I promise."

My mother lies back and shuts her eyes, worn out and resigned. I nod to the nurses, step out of their way, and turn my back, afraid I'll pass out if I actually have to witness them pulling the long blue tube out of my mother's throat. It doesn't take more than a few minutes for them to remove it along with the feeding tube going up her nose, and then the room is filled with the sound of my mother gulping for air.

"Breathe, Mrs. Pinkowitz. Inhale, exhale," Angelina instructs her. "You're all right. You're doing fine." My mother's gasps sound like those of a badly wounded animal and I find myself panting along with her. *Breathe, breathe, breathe*, I silently coax her. My mother is working hard to catch her breath; everything else is irrelevant now. Her chest heaves up and down with effort and she is perspiring heavily.

"Oxygen," Angelina says, and the other nurse tries to strap a mask to my mother's face, but she fights her off again.

"Try the nasal cannula," Angelina instructs and this time my mother lets her insert a plastic prong into each of her nostrils and tuck the tubing they're attached to up around her ears. The oxygen is a great help and soon my mother's breathing, while still labored, becomes steadier and easier. When she seems stable, the nurse pulls the tape off my mother's neck that's holding her med port in place and slides the needle away. It looks like it all hurts like hell, but my mother doesn't complain. "I'll put a new port in her arm later," the nurse tells me before she leaves the room.

Jack and my father return and the sight of my mother sitting up and being off the respirator brings them enormous relief. "Doris, you look much better. Much much better," my father says and for once my mother does not glower at him. Encouraged, my father says, "I love you," then musters up the courage to ask, "Do you love me?" My mother nods and his whole face lights up.

"Her blood pressure is good," Jack says, checking the monitor. "Everything looks great, Aunt Doris."

My mother doesn't respond—she is still using all her energy just to pull air into her lungs—and a few minutes later Dr. Harte enters the room.

"How's everything going?" he asks, standing at the foot of my mother's bed. "You look good, Mrs. Pinkowitz. You're coming along just fine."

My mother opens her mouth to speak but no sound comes out.

"Your throat is going to be very sore for a few days," the doctor tells her. "Don't try to talk now. Just rest your voice. It'll come back soon. You're doing fine," he repeats but my mother shakes her head and motions for the pad and pencil. I bring it to her and she writes down one word: *liar*. Then she hastily writes a sentence and motions for me to show it to my father.

"Don't pay him anything," my father reads aloud and laughs. "Okay, Doris. I won't. Don't worry. He won't get a nickel out of me. Not one lousy dime."

My mother nods with satisfaction as Dr. Harte leaves the room and then indicates she wants to write more so I return the clipboard to her. "One-fifty. Joe," I read aloud. "What's does that mean?"

"One-fifty for Joe?" my father asks her. "You remember that?" My mother nods and again I ask what she's talking about. "While we were on the trip, there were two snowstorms back home," my father explains, "and Joe plowed our driveway out. Selma told her over the phone." He turns back to my mother. "I'll pay Joe, don't worry. I'll send him a check the minute we get home. I'm all over it. You know me." My father shakes his head in wonder. "That's what you're thinking about, Doris? Paying Joe?"

Of course that's what she's thinking about, I want to tell him. She wants her life back. She wants to be in control. My mother is writing again; this time she prints only a number: 914. "What does that mean, Dad?"

"I know, I know, Doris," my father says. "It's all taken care of."

"What's taken care of?" I ask.

My father locks eyes with my mother. "Can I tell her?"

"Tell me what?" I study my mother, who thinks for a moment before she nods.

"There's a safety deposit box at the bank with a bank book in it," my father explains. "It's box number 914. Your mother opened up a savings account before you were born, as soon as she knew she was pregnant, and she's put money into it every week since without fail.

Sometimes a ten, sometimes a twenty, once in a while a fifty. Take it from me, Lydia, you're a very wealthy dame."

"Oh, Mom." I turn to her, afraid I'm going to weep. I can't believe that all this time, through all the years I've fought with her, rejected her, and turned my back on her, my mother has been quietly and steadily, in her own way, taking care of me.

Luckily Angelina comes in before I have a chance to break down completely. "Is your mouth dry, Mrs. Pinkowitz?" she asks. My mother nods. "Here. This might help." She unwraps a small green sponge that is fastened onto a stick like a Popsicle. "It's soaked in mouthwash," she explains, inserting it between my mother's lips. My mother makes a face and Angelina smiles an apology. "I know, I know. It doesn't taste very good, but it will help with the dryness. In a little while we'll give you some ice chips." She hands me a few moist sponges wrapped in plastic and tells me that my mother can have one whenever she wants.

"I'll be back." Angelina gives a little wave and leaves the room. The four of us sit quietly in the cubicle for a while, until my mother points to my father's watch. When he tells her it's just about noon, she asks for the clipboard and writes one word upon it: *eat.*

"You want some lunch, Mom?" I ask. "I'll see if they can bring you some food." My mother shakes her head and points to my father and Jack. "You want us to get something to eat?" She nods and I feel a bit smug that I am the one who best understands what she means.

"We're okay, Doris," my father tells her. My mother shakes her head and points again to the word "eat."

I know what she's doing; she's trying to take care of us. She's a wife, mother, and aunt, and her role is to nurture her family. "Let's go down and get some lunch, Dad. It won't take long," I say, even though I'm not hungry. But I want to carry out my mother's wishes and return her to her rightful position as head of household. "C'mon, Jack."

I rise to leave the room, but my mother shakes her head. She points first to Jack, then to my father, and then to the doorway, instructing them to go. Then she points to me and starts writing on her clipboard.

"What is it, Mom?" I read the word she has put down on the page aloud. "Lollipop." She has me stumped for a minute but then I understand. "This?" I ask, holding up a green sponge attached to a stick that does indeed look like a lollipop. "You want to rinse out your mouth again?" My mother shakes her head and points to me. "What?" I ask. "You want me to use it?" I know this isn't what my mother wants and my ego deflates at not being able to figure out what she's trying to say. She points to the word again, then to me, and then to one of the chairs near the foot of her bed. When it's clear I still don't get it, she writes down another word: *stay.*

"Lollipop stay?" I think hard and then the tears well up, unstoppable, as the one positive memory from my childhood I've been searching for rushes forward. Lollipop. The pet name my mother used to call me a hundred years ago. "Lollipop, there you are! What color is my Lollipop today?" she'd ask when she lifted me up out of my crib in the morning. "Red? Green? Yellow?" Whatever color I chose to be, my mother assured me that was her favorite by smacking her lips and then licking and nibbling my chubby little fingers while I shrieked with delight. Other times she'd make me dissolve into giggles by singing that old song from the fifties, "Lollipop, lollipop, oh lolli, lolli, lolli…" Lollipop. Her Lollipop. The name she called me until the day I told her it was too babyish and ordered her to stop. "Moth-er!" I spat the word out as though it left a bad taste in my mouth. "Don't call me that. I'm not your lollipop." But I was wrong. I was and I am and I always will be.

"I'll stay, Mom," I say, pushing the words past the hard lump in my throat. "Dad and Jack can bring me something to eat. I'll sit with you. I won't leave you alone. Is that what you want?"

My mother nods and then opens her arms wide to gather me up as I tumble headlong into them.

SHE LOVES ME, *she loves me not. She loves me, she loves me not.* Of course when I was growing up, it was *he* loves me, *he* loves me not, but budding lesbian that I was, I always managed to finagle things so I ended on "he loves me *not*," much to Colleen's disappointment and my great relief. Not that it mattered much anyway, since I never had anyone specific in mind, unlike Colleen, who had a mad crush on a new boy every other week.

"She loves me, she loves me not. She loves me, she loves me not." It's seven-thirty Friday morning, and being the über-punctual

Pinkowitzes that my father and I are, and despite Jack's slothful tendencies, we have somehow managed to arrive at the hospital a good thirty minutes before visiting hours start. Jack and my father are inside eating breakfast in the cafeteria and I am outside sitting on the bench I now think of as mine, getting ready to call Allie, who I know is just about to go on her midmorning break at the lumberyard. In the meantime, I pluck petals off a daisy I found on the ground that must have dropped out of a bouquet bought by some visitor en route to visit a patient.

"She loves me, she loves me not. She loves me," I announce to the world at large, holding up one last white petal in triumph. Contrary to popular belief, I am not mooning over my very own Allie, Martina Navratilova, or some other drop-dead-gorgeous butch who makes me drool with desire. No, believe it or not, I am swooning over my mother, who loves me, as I tell Allie the minute she picks up the phone.

"It's a miracle, Allie. Everything is different now. My mother loves me. She really *loves* me. In a very deep way. Like a…like a… like a mother," I say, and then burst out laughing, startling a tiny brown bird that has just hopped up to peck at some bread crumbs near my feet. "She's been saving all this money for me, and she wouldn't let them take out the breathing tube unless I was in the room with her, and she gave me her rings—just to hold, not to keep—and she warmed up my hands, and—"

"Lyddie, hold on. You're babbling. Slow down. And start at the beginning."

I take a deep breath and try to focus. I feel so far away from home, as if the distance between this bench I am sitting on and the lumberyard where Allie works is much greater than the actual three thousand miles that lie between us. I feel like I'm calling from another planet. From another world. Like Brigadoon maybe. Or Oz. How can I put into words everything that has transpired in the past forty-eight hours between my mother and me? I inhale deeply, exhale slowly, and give it another try.

"I feel like…I feel…" I pause, trying to collect my thoughts. "Allie, this is what it must be like when someone who was adopted finally finds her birth mother. You know how much I've wanted a mother my whole life. And at last I have one. A mother who loves me. Isn't that amazing? And what's more amazing is that I love her, too. A lot. More than a lot. More than I ever knew."

Allie doesn't say anything, and I wonder if I've put the poor girl in shock. "Allie, are you still there? Aren't you happy for me?"

"I'm here, Lydia. And of course I'm happy for you. You know that. It's just a little hard to take in and switch gears, that's all."

"What do you mean?"

"I mean, up until now you've never used the words *mother* and *love* in the same sentence before."

"I haven't?"

"No. The word you always used was *hate*."

"Hate? What are you talking about, Allie? I never said I hated my mother." I quickly lower my voice as if my mother could hear me out here, four floors below her hospital room. "How can you even say such a thing?" I am aghast at the very thought.

"*You* said it, Lydia," Allie reminds me. "You said you hated her for taking you to a diet doctor and making you join Weight Watchers when you were only ten years old. You hated her because she wouldn't let you have a dog or a cat or even a goldfish when you were growing up and you really wanted a pet. You hated her because she made you change out of the pantsuit you'd bought to wear to Jack and Crystal's wedding and made you wear an ugly dress of hers instead. You hated her for being too busy to come to your graduation ceremony when you got your Ph.D. You hated her because—"

"All right, all right." I cut Allie off before she can give me any more examples. "Maybe I said it a few times, but I never meant it, Allie. I was just angry, that's all. I hated some things that she did, but I never hated *her*. And anyway, why are you being so nasty to me?"

"I'm not being nasty to you, Lydia," Allie says, her voice maddeningly calm. "I'm just refreshing your memory."

"My memory doesn't need refreshing, Allie. Everything's different now."

"Good. I hope so."

"What do you mean, you hope so?" I ask, pressing the phone tightly against my ear.

"I mean, I hope so," Allie repeats. "For your sake. I hope everything's different now, Lydia, and maybe it is—"

"It *is*," I insist firmly. "You have no idea what's happened in the last few days, Allie. You're not even here."

"That's not fair," Allie protests. "I offered to come but you said you didn't want me to."

And I'm glad, I think, but don't say aloud.

"I just want you to be careful, that's all, Lydia," Allie continues. "So you don't get hurt all over again."

I lean against the back of my cold stone bench and press against its unyielding hardness. "Why are you being so unsupportive, Allie? Vera thinks this is great. She said it's like I've done four years of therapy in only four days. She's proud of me."

"I'm proud of you, too, Lydia. I'm always proud of you. And I don't think I'm being unsupportive. I'm being realistic."

"Allie." I let the sound of her name hover in the space between us while I gather my thoughts, desperate to make her understand. An ICU nurse passes by on her way in to work and looks at me with a question in her eyes, her worry no doubt a reaction to the frown on my face. I give a little wave signaling that everything's okay before turning back to Allie's and my conversation. "Listen to me, Allie. My mother and I are on good terms for the first time in my entire adult life and you are not going to spoil it for me. Even if I am being unrealistic. Even if I'm dreaming. I don't care." I refuse to let Allie's words burst my bubble, and concentrate hard to recapture the feeling I had before I dialed her number. When I first got out here only a few moments ago, I felt punchy, woozy, light-headed, like I could float away if I wasn't gripping the edge of the bench I was sitting on tightly with both hands. The last time I felt this way was seventeen years ago when I fell madly in love with Allie, and when I realize this, I tell her so.

"I feel that way every day that I'm lucky enough to wake up next to you," Allie says her voice tinged with sadness.

"Oh Allie, I miss you, too. I do. It's just that I'm in another world out here." Again I try to explain. "I sat in my mother's room for twelve hours yesterday and it was like being transported to another dimension. Time is different, space is different. It's like everything else just faded away and nothing else matters."

"Nothing else matters? What about me? What about Mishmosh? What about," Allie clears her throat purposefully, "the birthday present I went shopping for last night?"

This is my cue to start playing twenty questions with Allie in order to guess what she's thinking of buying for me. And under normal circumstances, such a game would fill me with delight. But these are hardly normal circumstances, and at the moment something even as monumental as my forthcoming fiftieth birthday seems trivial in comparison with what I've been going through. "Of course you matter," I hastily assure Allie, glad that she can't see my right foot jiggling up and down with impatience. It's almost eight o'clock and I'm dying to get upstairs. "You matter a lot, Allie. It's just that I'm a little preoccupied right now." I wait, but Allie doesn't acknowledge this or say anything further until I change the subject and remember to ask, "So how are you doing?"

"I'm all right," she says without much conviction.

"What's wrong?" I probe, trying to hide my restlessness by injecting a heavy dose of concern into my voice.

"Nothing's wrong, Lydia. I'm just lonely for you, that's all. The house feels so empty with only me and Mishmosh rattling around inside it. And on top of that, the weather's been just awful. It's been snowing like crazy for the past couple of days and the temperature still hasn't risen above my shoe size."

"Wow, it must be freezing." Allie has what she calls "tiny Puerto Rican feet," which means it can't be more than six degrees back home. "I'm sorry," I say, as if the lousy weather Allie is experiencing is somehow my fault. I don't dare tell her that it's a beautiful morning here in L.A. The sky is a brilliant cloud-free blue and it's already so warm, I'm comfortable sitting out here in just the bottom part of my sweater set: a sleeveless lilac camisole that matches the cardigan I've taken off and neatly folded on the bench beside me.

"So is your mother any better?" Allie asks after another minute. "Is she still in intensive care?"

"She was when we left last night." I shield my eyes from the sun and look up toward the fourth floor of the hospital, though of course I can't make out what's going on inside. "They said if she's still improving they might move her out today."

"Well, that's good news. Any idea when they'll send her home?"

"Not yet."

"Any idea when they'll send you home?"

"No."

There is another long, loud silence on the other end of the phone. "Allie," I finally say. "I'll get on a plane as soon as I can. But I can't leave right now. My mother needs me."

"I know that, Lydia. Of course she needs you. It's just that I need you, too."

"I'm sorry, Allie. I just can't come home right now."

"I know that, Lydia," Allie says again. "I wasn't asking you to come home. I was just trying to say that I miss you."

Allie's neediness puzzles me. We've been apart for three days before. For four days, five days, a week once when I was a guest scholar-in-residence at Vera's university. And Allie's always done fine on her own. She's even teased me about how much fun she's had playing bachlorette: not making the bed, letting unwashed dishes pile up in the sink, eating frozen dinners in front of the television, leaving her dirty laundry in a heap on the floor. No, something else must be wrong. As I mull this over, it suddenly dawns on me that what I'm going through must remind Allie that she will never have this chance again, the chance to sit at her mother's bedside and tell her that she loves her.

"Allie, is this hard for you because my mother's still alive and yours isn't?" I ask softly.

"Oh my God, no, Lydia. Where did you get that crazy idea? What kind of person do you think I am?" Allie's tone is a mixture of hurt and indignation. "I'm not jealous of you and your mother. I just hope the peace between you lasts, that's all."

"It will, Allie. You'll see."

"Lydia, sometimes during a crisis people don't act the way they usually do, and then when everything settles down, they revert back to their old behaviors. That's all I'm saying."

"This is different, Allie," I insist stubbornly. "And anyway, I have to go." I jump up, grab my pocketbook, and fold my sweater over my arm. "It's after eight o'clock and I want to get upstairs and see my mother."

"Okay. I have to get back to work, too."

"I'll call you soon, all right?"

"All right. Bye."

I snap my cell phone shut and try to ignore the uneasy feeling that's growing in the pit of my stomach. I can't remember the last time Allie and I hung up the phone without saying "I love you" to each other and I almost call her back to say it. And to hear it. But I'm afraid that continuing our conversation might only make things worse, and besides, now it's already seven minutes after eight and I'm eager to see my mother and anxious to get up to her cubicle ahead of my father and Jack. I walk over to the hospital entrance, pull open the door, and step inside the lobby, only to see my father and my cousin standing by the elevator. As we wait for it to arrive, I marvel once more at my father's immaculate clothing and wonder how he manages to look so fresh every morning. His tan shirt is completely free of wrinkles, as are his brown cuffed slacks. He should share some of his dry-cleaning tricks of the trade with Jack, I think as I study my cousin who, in his usual unkempt manner, has his long gray hair half in and half out of a ratty-looking ponytail, and is wearing a pair of faded jeans ripped at the knee. Today's quote of the day imprinted on his T-shirt reads "Somebody has to be a bad example," which for once is rather fitting, and furthermore, a statement with which I cannot argue.

The elevator arrives and we ride up as a unit, make our way to the fourth floor, and after getting buzzed in, rush into my mother's cubicle. She is lying in bed, her head propped up by two pillows, her eyes darting about wildly. Upon catching sight of the three of us, she bursts into tears.

"Doris, what is it? What's the matter, baby?" My father is beside her at once, pushing her scraggly hair back from her forehead and kissing the tears dripping down her cheeks.

"I thought…I thought…" My mother can hardly get the words out and her voice is scratchy and barely audible. I imagine that her throat is still sore from being on the respirator. "I thought I'd never see you again," she finally manages to whisper.

"No, no, Doris. We're here. We're right here. They don't let us in until eight o'clock, that's all. It's okay. *Shah.*" To my astonishment, my father is breaking his own rule and allowing himself to cry. As am I. Jack has turned his back to us, so perhaps he is crying, too.

"Hi, Mom," I say, once we've all calmed down. "How did you sleep?"

"Not so good," she croaks. "I was hungry."

"Can you eat yet? Did they bring you any food?"

My mother points to a tray on her bedside table, upon which rest individual servings of applesauce and Jell-O.

"Good morning, everyone," Angelina says as she sails into the room and stops at the foot of my mother's bed. "How are you, Mrs. Pinkowitz?" My mother lifts one hand and shimmies it in the air, *comme çi, comme ça.*

"She says she's hungry," I tell Angelina.

"She can eat." Angelina pulls open the tin foil lid of the plastic Jell-O cup. "Do you want some Jell-O? I think it's strawberry. Or maybe raspberry. You taste it and tell me."

My mother shakes her head and points in my direction.

"You want me to eat it?" I ask. "Mom, you know I hate Jell-O. And applesauce," I remind her in case she has the notion to offer me any.

"You do?" Jack pipes up. "Me, too. How about pudding?"

"Blech." I make a face and Jack gives me a smile and a thumbs up, pleased to find out at long last that the two of us have something in common. "I'll eat something later, Mom. I don't want to take your food."

My mother shakes her head again, points to the white plastic spoon Angelina is holding and then points to my hand. "Oh, I get it. You want me to feed you. Is that it?" My mother nods.

"Here you go." Angelina turns everything over to me.

"It's nothing personal," I tell her, stepping toward my mother.

"It's okay. She doesn't trust me, and why should she?" Angelina asks. "She hardly knows me. She knows you."

I scoop a small bit of Jell-O onto the spoon and lift it toward my mother, who opens her mouth eagerly as a newborn bird. Bite after bite disappears between her lips and after the Jell-O is gone, I feed her the applesauce, too. When she's full, she turns her head away like a baby who's had enough.

"Why don't you take a rest now, Mom?" She immediately follows my suggestion by leaning back against the pillow and closing her eyes. My father, Jack, and I take up residence in our usual chairs and commence our usual activities. My father reads one of the newspapers he bought at the hotel's gift shop, Jack studies the numbers on my mother's monitor announcing any changes that occur like a sportscaster at a ballgame, and I watch my mother sleep. When noontime arrives, my father and Jack rise to go to lunch and again my mother asks me to stay. She beckons me to come close with one finger curled in the air. "You're the only one who understands me," she says, as I bend down in order to hear her better. "I would be dead if you hadn't come," she tells me, her raspy words startling and amazing to hear.

At around two o'clock, Angelina comes in bearing good news: my mother is well enough to leave the Intensive Care Unit and move down the hall. The worst has passed; now she has to rest and get her strength back. "Don't worry, Mrs. Pinkowitz, you'll be in good hands over there," Angelina says in response to the worried look that crosses my mother's face. "Everyone across the hall is very nice and very competent. You'll have a new nurse and a physical therapist and a respiratory therapist and they'll all take good care of you."

"What about Dr. Harte?" my father asks, his voice full of concern.

"He'll still be her doctor," Angelina says. "There's nothing to worry about," she reassures my mother again. "You won't have to do anything. We'll move you right in this bed."

Sure enough, a few minutes later, two burly attendants in green scrubs hustle into my mother's room. "You need to wait outside," the larger of the two tells us. Like yesterday, Jack and my father obey orders and I ignore them, even though the fellow barking commands is huge and looks like a bouncer at a bar whom no one who had any brains whatsoever would dare to mess around with. "You need to wait outside," he repeats firmly.

"I'll move as soon as you do," I tell him, stepping out of the way but not out of the room. My mother's eyes have grown fearful again and I will not desert her.

The attendants busy themselves with unhooking things and checking things and then wheeling my mother away. "I'm right here, Mom," I say, jogging behind her bed, being careful to stay back far enough so that I don't get in the way, but near enough so she knows that I'm still close at hand. The attendants wheel her into room 403 and while they settle her in and hook her up to new machines, I lean against the doorjamb and chatter away, filling the airwaves with whatever meaningless small talk comes to mind. Without pausing for breath, I yak about the weather here in L.A. and back home, the grilled vegetable sandwich my father brought me from the cafeteria for lunch, and the chef's salad I ordered from room service last night for supper. As I blab on and on, I realize I sound very much like my mother, whose chitchat has always been met by me with criticism and scorn. There's a time and a place for everything, I guess, moving from food to fashion as I tell my mother all about the outfit I am wearing, including where I bought it and how much it cost. Right now my purpose is not to impress anyone with my wit or intelligence; it is to soothe my mother with the sound of my voice as she is being pulled and prodded by strangers who seem to be taking an awfully long time to arrange her body in a position suitable to their liking.

"Okay, she's all yours," the attendant finally tells me as he and his companion step into the hallway and leave. My father, Jack, and I file inside and admire my mother's new digs, a real room with a large picture window, a television hanging from the ceiling, a telephone right next to the bed, and best of all, her own private bathroom.

"Hey, not bad, not bad at all," my father says, taking a good look around. "They've already brought in three chairs for us. That was very nice of them. This is great, Doris. You'll be a lot more comfortable in here."

"Want to watch TV, Aunt Doris?" Jack asks, searching for the remote.

"She has it," I tell Jack. "That's it, Mom. It's attached to your bed."

Before my mother can turn on the television, a nurse enters the room. She is wearing a yellow-flowered smock over white polyester pants, and her thick, dyed auburn hair is pulled back into a ponytail that is almost as long as Jack's. She has five gold hoops of varying sizes hanging from each ear and her fingernails are long, square-tipped, and painted a shocking electric blue with a bolt of glittery silver lightning slashed across each one.

"Good afternoon, everyone," she says briskly, like she is standing center stage and welcoming us to a matinee. She has a strong Spanish accent and I pray that my father will not presume that all people of Spanish descent are acquainted with one another and ask if she knows Eduardo, our van driver. "My name is Margarita—"

"Like the drink?" Jack quips, trying to be funny. Or charming. Or something.

"Like the drink." Margarita places her hands on her hips, drums those glittering nails against her smock, and shoots him a look that says *don't interrupt me again.* "You must be Ms. Pinkowitz," she says to my mother.

"Mrs.," I correct her.

"I always say Ms.," Margarita informs me. "I never assume a patient wants to be called Mrs."

"In this case you can assume," I say, throwing thirty-plus years of feminist training right out the window. Maybe this will make up for the countless times I've sent my mother birthday cards addressed to "Ms. Doris Pinkowitz" in defiance of her preference to be addressed not as Mrs. Doris Pinkowitz, which in my opinion is bad enough, but Mrs. Max Pinkowitz, which is even worse.

"All right, Mrs. Pinkowitz," Margarita corrects herself. "I'm your nurse. Any time you need me, you just press this." She shows my mother a red call button attached to a small white plastic rectangle hooked to her bed. "This rings the nurse's station. If I'm busy with another patient, someone else will come."

"How many other patients do you have?" my father asks. I can tell he misses Angelina already.

"Five," Margarita answers. "This moves your bed up and down." She shows my mother another gadget. "And this is for your TV." She hands my mother the remote. "And you can only make local calls on your telephone. Unless you have a calling card." My mother waves one hand in the direction of the telephone, dismissing it and letting us know she's not in the mood to talk to anybody besides the people in this room. "Your respiratory therapist will come in soon, and then your physical therapist," Margarita continues. "We want to get you up and walking as quickly as possible. As soon as you can make it to the bathroom, we'll take your catheter out." My mother's eyes travel to the bathroom door and I can tell by the look in her eyes, it seems not miles, but light-years away. Margarita notices my mother's expression, too. "Don't worry, Mrs. Pinkowitz. Every day you'll get a little bit stronger. You'll be up and around before you—wait. What's the matter? What is it, honey?" Margarita's whole manner changes at the sight of my mother wincing in pain. "What's wrong?" she asks again.

"It's the blood pressure machine," I tell her, pointing to my mother's arm, which is being squeezed tightly yet again. "Look, her skin is tearing right there under the cuff. Can't you do something about that?"

"I can move it to her other arm," Margarita says. "Or to her leg. Whatever she'd like."

"Does it have to be taken every hour now that she's out of the ICU?" I ask. "It's really bothering her. Can't it be taken every two hours? Or every three?"

"Let me check with the doctor. I'll be right back." Margarita scuttles out of the room and a few minutes later scuttles back. "We can change it to once every two hours, Mrs. Pinkowitz," she says, and my mother turns away from her to throw me a look of gratitude. "Do you want me to put it on your leg or your other arm?"

My mother lifts her left arm, which is the color of an eggplant from her wrist to her elbow. "When will those purple marks go away?" I ask Margarita as she pries apart the Velcro and slides away the cuff.

"In a week or two. Don't worry, Mrs. Pinkowitz. When you get out of here, you'll be as good as new." She switches the dreaded blood pressure cuff to my mother's other arm and then holds up a pair of white plastic boots with Velcro straps attached to them. "These are for your feet," Margarita explains, already reaching for my mother's right foot. "To help with your circulation. To prevent blood clots."

My mother pulls back her leg, as if she is about to give Margarita a good, swift kick in the belly. "No," she says, thrusting her foot under the blankets.

"They don't hurt, Mrs. Pinkowitz." Margarita, against her better judgment, reaches for my mother's leg again. "They just might make you a little warm."

"Don't," my mother says, raising one finger in the air. "I mean it."

"Does she have to wear them?" I ask, running interference.

"It's a good idea," Margarita advises. "You don't want her to get blood clots."

"Mom?"

"No, Lydia," my mother says, in a voice that lets me know her word is final.

"Her feet get really hot," I explain to Margarita, though this has not always been the case. When I was growing up, my mother constantly complained that her feet were freezing cold. Jack and I even got her battery-operated electric socks for her birthday the year he moved in with us, a gift we were sure would please my hard-to-buy-for mother, but by that time her body temperature had risen—with menopause, I now realize—and her feet have been hot ever since. Come to think of it, just like mine.

Margarita looks at my mother, looks at me, and then shrugs as if to say, *hey, it's your funeral*, before tucking the boots under her arm and taking her leave. My mother closes her eyes, exhausted. I don't see how she's going to handle her various therapies any time soon and I decide to go find Dr. Harte and tell him so. After listening to me plead my case, he nods thoughtfully and says he'll give her a break and start everything tomorrow. Maybe I should have been a lawyer, I think as I return to my mother's room to give her an update. She is fast asleep in her bed, with Jack and my father draped across their chairs, snoring close beside her.

The sight of the three of them snoozing away rivets me to the spot. I lean my back against the doorway, struck by the vulnerability of my small, fragile family. A feeling of tenderness washes over me as I look at each of them in turn, my mother, my father, even Jack. There's one empty chair in the room and I try to picture Allie sitting in it, but it's an image that eludes me. I just can't envision her here, and this makes my stomach grip with worry. The empty chair is for me and me alone, and I tiptoe over to it and sit down as quietly as possible. There doesn't seem to be a place for Allie here, and not only because there isn't enough space to squeeze one more chair between the window and the bed. I've replaced the family I've come from with the family I've created for so long, it's hard to imagine being part of them both. Now that I have my old family back, will I have to sacrifice my new one? When Allie and I first became a couple, one of the things we bonded over was being all alone in the world: Allie's biological family was dead and I was barely speaking to mine. Will Allie be able to understand and adjust to everything that's changed since I've been away? Will I? Or might I have to choose? These are questions I don't have the answers to and would rather not think about, so when my eyelids grow heavy, I slump down in my seat and like the rest of my family, gratefully give myself over to sleep.

❖

No REST FOR the weary, I think as my six a.m. wake-up call shatters the silence of my hotel room. It's Saturday morning and if I were home that would mean sleeping in all snuggled up next to Allie under a nice warm quilt, both of us curled on our left sides, her arm tucked under mine and wrapped around my stomach. Even Mishmosh knows the difference between a weekend and a weekday morning and is kind enough not to meow in my face on Saturdays and Sundays before nine o'clock. But that's irrelevant in L.A. Here in my new life, one day is like any other, which means I better rise and shine and get my butt moving. Even though my father's parting words to me last night were "See you in the lobby at seven-thirty," I know he really meant seven o'clock, since he has been going downstairs earlier and earlier every morning. When I arrive at six-fifty-five, he's already there, standing at the front desk in perfectly pressed gray slacks and a short-sleeved maroon shirt, a thick folded newspaper clamped under his arm. I, on the other hand, have run out of clean clothes and have resorted to mixing and matching, pairing the black slacks I wore on the flight out here five days ago with my lavender camisole and yellow cardigan. Not one of my better outfits, but today it will have to do.

"Hi, Dad," I call as I approach, but he lifts one hand in my direction, warning me to stay back. I stop where I am, wondering what's wrong. My father's face is red with anger and Melissa, who is working alone behind the front desk this morning, looks a bit shell-shocked and like she's just about to cry.

"Now you listen to me," my father says, wagging a finger in her face. He is keeping his voice low but I can tell it's an effort for him to control it. "My wife is sick, you understand? She's in the hospital. I don't know how long we'll be here. I told you that before. We're in room 523 and room 716. We've been here all week."

"Yes, Mr. Pinkowitz. I know," Melissa says, keeping her eyes transfixed upon the computer screen in front of her instead of looking up at him. Today Melissa has pulled her hair back in some sort of elaborate French twist, which she probably thinks makes her look older. But the sophisticated hairdo along with her heavy makeup does just the opposite; she reminds me of a little girl dressed up in her mother's fancy clothes and high heel shoes. She clicks her nails halfheartedly on her keyboard and then speaks again to my father. "We have a wedding coming in today. All the rooms in the hotel are booked. I'd do something if I could, but we're completely full, Mr. Pinkowitz. I'm sorry."

"What the hell is wrong with you people?" My father roars as I knew he would. "What the hell do you want me to do? My wife is sick. She's sick, I'm telling you. We don't know when she'll be able to get on an airplane and fly across the entire country. What do you want us to do? Sleep out on the goddamn street? Fine." He slams his hand down on the counter, unleashing the fury he's been holding in check for more than a week. I know my father has been oozing with anger for days now: he's mad at the hospital for not making my mother better fast enough; he's mad at himself for dragging my mother on a trip he knows he should never have taken her on; and who knows, he may even be mad at my mother herself, for getting sick in the first place. Mostly he's mad because he isn't in control of the situation, a feeling I can certainly sympathize with. But still, that's no reason to take out all his frustrations on poor little Melissa, who is only an eager to please, wide-eyed, gum-cracking teenage girl trying to do her job.

"Dad." I touch his arm, which he lifts abruptly, flinging me aside like an annoying fly. When I was a child, my father's anger terrified me, but as I've learned in the past few days, I may still be *his* child, but I'm not a child any longer. "Stop it," I say, coming back up to him like a novice boxer who has been knocked back against the ropes by the reigning champ but doesn't know enough to get out of the ring.

"Lydia, be quiet." My father shakes me off again. "Now you listen carefully, Melissa. I am not leaving my room and my daughter is not leaving her room. Case closed. Is that clear?" my father thunders. "You got that?" If Melissa was a guy, I'm sure he would grab her by the collar with both hands and shake her until her teeth rattled, lifting her clear off her feet in the process.

Stick to your guns, I think, trying to meet Melissa's gaze and send a silent message to her. *Don't let him intimidate you. Kick us out. Go ahead.* Not that I have any desire to sleep on the streets of L.A. this evening; I just don't want my father to win. But he gets his way, of course. It's a man's world after all, and young Melissa is no match for the mighty Max Pinkowitz. Visibly rattled, she disappears through a doorway and returns a few minutes later with an apologetic manager who rewards my father's temper tantrum by moving some incoming guests around and allowing us to remain in our rooms. Satisfied, my father becomes Prince Charming again, shaking hands with the manager and smiling warmly at Melissa. "Enjoy your day," he has the nerve to say to her. "Thank you, sweetheart. Thank you very much."

Invigorated from winning his battle, my father pivots on his heel and briskly crosses the lobby to the concierge's desk, just as the elevator doors open and spit out Jack. I could swear he's wearing the same jeans he wore yesterday and the day before that and the day before that as well. Today his T-shirt asks the world, "If I got smart with you, how would you know?" A question to which I don't have the answer.

This morning Eduardo is off duty, and our new driver is the strong, silent type. We arrive at the hospital without a word, eat Malika's breakfast, listen to Father O'Connor's prayer of the day, and make our way up to my mother's room, arriving at eight o'clock sharp. She smiles at the sight of us, and points to her breakfast tray. "I waited for you to feed me," she says with effort, her voice still weak and gravelly. She looks tired, and the sight of the nasal cannula inserted into her nose unsettles me. Two clear plastic tubes stretch from my mother's nostrils across her cheekbones and are tucked behind her ears to hold them in place. Then they meet under her chin and merge into one long tube, the end of which is connected to her oxygen supply, which comes out of the wall. She has a fresh IV inserted into her arm, and the white clip that measures her oxygen level remains pinched to her finger. She still looks like a patient and I realize now that I didn't expect this. I expected her to look simply like my mother.

"What do you have there?" I ask, turning from her face to the plate on her tray, which boasts three lumpy mounds of unidentifiable food, one pale yellow, one grayish-white, and one a muddy brown.

"Eggs. Toast. Potatoes. It's all pureed," my mother explains in a scratchy whisper. "My throat is still sore." She fumbles with the controls lying on top of the sheets, tossing aside the red nurse's call button, which I notice is the same shade as her nail polish, and finds another panel, which moves her bed up and down. She raises herself into a sitting position and says, "Lydia, you look very nice this morning."

I glance down at my less-than-clean, hastily slapped together outfit, hardly the height of fashion by anybody's standards. "I do?"

"Your hair looks pretty today. Have you cut it recently?"

"No." My hand automatically travels upward to feel my freshly washed, still damp curls. I can't ever remember the last time my mother has complimented me on my appearance. What are they feeding her through the IV in her arm? Ground-up happy pills?

"My hair is such a mess," my mother sighs.

"I'll see if I can wash it for you today," I tell her.

"I don't know, Lydia. How will I make it over there?" I look across the room, my mother's simple question breaking my heart. There's no way she'll be able to walk to the sink, much less bend her head down under the faucet, and we both know this. She hasn't even gotten out of bed yet.

"Aunt Doris, they probably have dry shampoo," Jack says, opening a cabinet and poking around. "You know, it comes in a can like hair spray and you just comb it through. We use it on wigs all the time. In the industry."

"What a good idea." My mother beams at Jack as if he has just invented the product himself. "Maybe later."

"Let's try some of this, Mom," I say, wheeling her breakfast table closer to the bed. Her meal looks like baby food and after two bites she turns up her nose and shakes her head: *no more*. I don't blame her; this breakfast is about as appetizing as the soggy canned food I serve Mishmosh back home every morning.

Margarita buzzes into the room and then stops short, as if she is surprised to see that my mother has company. "Oh," she says, quickly recovering. "Good morning."

"*Buenos días*, Rita," my father says from his chair, in a lame attempt to be friendly.

The nurse snaps her head in his direction and looks at him sharply. "Mar-gar-i-ta," she says, pausing briefly between each syllable. "Are you Spanish?"

"No." My father shakes his head sheepishly. "Only by association." Margarita keeps staring at him, her fiery eyes demanding an explanation. "My daughter-in-law is Spanish," he tells her.

"Crystal is Spanish?" I ask Jack. "I never knew that."

"Crystal?" my father says, looking at me as though I've lost my mind. "I'm not talking about Crystal. I'm talking about Allie. That's short for Alicia," he tells Margarita.

"Where is Alicia from?" Margarita asks. My father nods his chin at me, confirming my suspicion that despite knowing her for seventeen years, he has absolutely no idea.

"Puerto Rico," I remind my father and inform the nurse.

"Ah, she is Latina like me," Margarita says, a note of pride in her voice. Then she turns her back on us, signaling that the discussion is over. Which is fine with me because I need a minute here to absorb my father's words. I can't believe he just referred to Allie as his daughter-in-law. I try to digest this amazing fact as I watch Margarita whirl into action, checking my mother's IV tubes, blood pressure cuff, nasal cannula, and oxygen clip.

"Mrs. Pinkowitz," Margarita says, satisfied that all is in order. "You need to eat some breakfast."

"*Feh*," my mother says, raising one hand and giving the air two backhanded slaps as if she's pushing aside something she finds extremely distasteful. It's one of her trademark gestures and I know it well. It means, *Please. Just leave me alone.*

"You've got to eat, and you've got to drink." Margarita looks down at the bag of urine hanging at the foot of the bed. "More input and more output, Mrs. Pinkowitz. Otherwise you won't be able to go home."

"Any idea when she will be able to go home?" I ask.

"That's up to the doctor. He calls the shots around here. He's in charge."

"I thought you were in charge," I say to Margarita.

She responds with a sound that is halfway between a snort and a chuckle. "I should be," she says and then turns to address my mother. "Mrs. Pinkowitz, your physical therapist and your respiratory therapist will be in soon. We're going to get you up today."

My mother does not look thrilled at this prospect. Margarita tells us again that my mother needs to eat more and then exits the room. I watch my father keep his eyes focused on her shapely retreating figure and wait for his appraisal of it. But he makes no comment, which I believe is a first.

"Dad." I can't help myself. "Don't you think Margarita is pretty?"

"I wouldn't say pretty, exactly," my father responds. "But she's one tough cookie, that's for sure."

I guess you can't be pretty and tough at the same time, I think, turning toward my mother's breakfast to resume feeding her. But Jack beats me to it.

"Here, Aunt Doris." He picks up the spoon I've discarded on the tray and scoops up a small mound of egg, which in addition to being pureed is now ice cold and thus even less appealing. "Open wide, Aunt Doris. Here comes the airplane." Jack zigzags the food through the air and presses it against my mother's closed mouth. "Knock, knock, anybody home? Open up," Jack persists. "Abra cadabra. Hocus pocus. Open sesame."

"Jack, leave her alone," I say, feeling a great need to protect my mother. "She doesn't want it."

"Lydia, didn't you hear the nurse? She needs to eat," he says, scraping up a little more food with the edge of the spoon. "C'mon now, Aunt Doris. Eat up. Eat it 'cause it's good for you," he singsongs in a mocking voice.

"Jack, your bedside manner leaves a lot to be desired," I tell him, folding my arms.

"This is how she used to feed Bethany when she was a baby, right, Aunt Doris?" Jack asks, the spoonful of food still hovering in the air.

"How is Bethany?" I wonder out loud. My mother perks up and looks at Jack with interest.

"Ah, Bethany...and I use the word loosely...Joy." Jack rolls his eyes in perfect imitation of his teenage daughter, who has elevated the gesture into a form of high art. "How should I know how she is? I'm only her father. I'd be the last person on earth to know. Except maybe her mother. Ask the manager of The Gap. Or Macy's. Or Jennifer's Nail Salon. That's where she spends all her time. At least according to my credit cards."

"Home," my mother rasps out the word with one finger pointing skyward like Spielberg's famous bug-eyed alien, E.T.

"I know, Doris. You want to go home. Soon," my father says absently from behind the pages of his newspaper.

My mother shakes her head and points her raised finger at Jack. "Home," she repeats. Jack and I look at her and then lock eyes with each other, still uncomprehending. A few seconds pass and then we blink in unison as we both figure out what my mother means, the realization filling both our hearts with gladness.

"You want me to go home?" Jack asks, not bothering to hide the thrill in his voice at the thought of being dismissed.

"Bethany," my mother whispers.

"Here, Mom, drink some apple juice. That'll soothe your throat and make your voice better," I tell her. My mother refuses the drink but accepts some ice chips, which I slide into her mouth with a clean plastic spoon.

"Crystal is home with Bethany. She can hold down the fort," Jack says. I imagine he feels he has to put up a good front and protest at least a little, pretending that he wants to stay.

My mother shakes her head and holds up two fingers in the shape of the letter V.

"Peace, brother," Jack says, holding up his own fingers like the hippie he once was and would still like to be.

My mother shakes her head again, lowers her hand, and then raises first one finger and then another. One, two.

"Two?" I ask. My mother nods. I know what she's trying to say. My mother is nothing if not traditional. "Two parents, is that what you mean, Mom?" She nods once more and I translate for Jack. "She's saying that you should go home because Bethany needs both a mother and a father to take care of her."

"Right," my mother whispers. Her voice seems to be getting weaker, not stronger.

"Are you sure, Aunt Doris?" Jack asks. "What do you think, Uncle Max?"

No response from the peanut gallery. "Dad?" I say loudly.

"What?" asks my father, who clearly has not been paying attention to the discussion going on around him. He lowers his newspaper and looks at us.

"Jack's considering going home. To be with Crystal and Bethany. What do you think?"

My father ponders this. "What about you, Lydia. Can you stay?"

I don't even hesitate. "I'll stay until you can go home. Okay, Mom?" She nods, not surprised in the least by my answer. I, on the other hand, am stunned. As I'm sure Allie will be, but I just can't think about that right now.

"Great. Let me run downstairs and see when I can catch a flight." Jack practically flies out of the room, so great is his joy. In a little while he comes back and tells us he's booked on a plane leaving later that afternoon, and has to head back to the hotel to gather up his things and grab a cab to the airport.

"Bye, Aunt Doris." Jack bends down to kiss her, and she cups his face with one hand in a loving gesture. "Be good, *tateleh*," she whispers, calling him by the Yiddish endearment she used when he was a boy.

"Bye, Uncle Max." Jack holds out his hand, but my father gets up and pulls him into a tight embrace. "Take care of yourself," he says, and I can hear by his voice that he's struggling not to cry. "Thanks for everything, Jack."

My turn. I wonder how Jack is going to bid me farewell, and to my surprise, he gestures for me to follow him out into the hallway. "Listen, Lydia," he says, once we are out of ear shot. "I want you to keep in touch and let me know what's going on. You can call collect if you need to. Okay?"

I ignore his snotty reference to the enormous difference in our income brackets and simply say, "Sure, Jack, thanks for coming," as if I am a hostess escorting a party guest I've been dying to get rid of all evening out the door.

"Let me know if you need anything. I'll check on their house when I get back, make sure everything's kosher."

"All right. Thanks, Jack." We stand there for another minute in an awkward silence, like two teenagers on a first date who aren't sure if we should shake hands, hug each other, or risk a good-night kiss. "You better go," I finally tell him. "You've got a plane to catch."

"Lydia," he says, looking down at his untied sneakers. "Listen, I know I can be kind of gruff. Crystal tells me so all the time. But it's just an act. Underneath it all, I'm not such a bad person, really. Actually, I'm a pretty decent person. You should know that."

"How, Jack?" I ask, dipping my head to try and catch his eye. "How would I know that? All I see is the act. We don't really know each other."

"No, we don't. Well, you'll have to take my word for it, I guess. Tell Allie I said hello," he says, and then extends his hand. "Friends?"

"Relatives," I say, and he laughs.

"Whatever."

We shake on it and then he turns, gives a little wave, and with his hands jammed into his pockets, heads down the hallway, leaving me in his wake. I watch him strut down the corridor, his hair switching back and forth like a straggly horse's tail, until he gets to the elevator bank. He pushes the button and stands there, whistling. When the elevator arrives, he steps into it and a second later, sticks his head out to check that I'm watching. Then with the rest of his body hidden from sight, Jack reaches up with one hand and grabs his own neck as if he is choking himself. With a terrified look on his face, he gasps, bugs out his eyes and gags as he pulls his own head into the elevator. It's something we used to do as teenagers to make each other laugh: stand partially behind a door or a wall and pretend to be a victim in a horror movie being strangled by a gruesome stranger. Jack leans out of the elevator one last time, smiling, and I smile back, wiggling my fingers at him in a final farewell. Believe it or not, I'm actually going to miss the guy.

❖

MY MOTHER IS sharing her bed with a stranger and my father doesn't seem to care or even notice. But I do and I don't like it one bit. "Hello," I call out, announcing my arrival loudly as I come back into her room after saying good-bye to Jack. "Who are you?"

"I'm Alec. The respiratory therapist," the young man sitting by my mother's feet answers. He is extremely good-looking and strikes me as the kind of person who knows this about himself. He is tall and lanky and perfectly at ease with his body, which is now taking up a good portion of my mother's bed. His dark hair is a mass of curls that just begs to be affectionately tousled, and his big brown eyes have a perpetual wink in them. He can't be more than twenty-five.

"I'm Lydia. Her daughter," I tell him, and then gesture toward the open newspaper being held up in the corner of the room. "And that's my father. Hey, Dad?"

"What, Lydia?" he asks, closing the business section, but keeping his place with one finger. "Good God, Doris." My father points toward Alec with the paper, his voice full of indignation and shock. "Why is that handsome young gentleman sitting on your bed?"

"Why not?" my mother asks in her new, deep sexy voice, punctuating her question with a coy shrug that makes her johnny slip halfway off one shoulder.

I laugh as Alec makes himself even more comfortable, pushing himself back on the bed and stretching his long legs out in front of him. "I'm here to teach you how to breathe," he tells my mother. "Okay?" he asks, putting one hand on her bare shin. She nods, staring at him intently. She is all ears.

"Let's see. Your oxygen is set at six liters per minute. We're going to give you less in a little while but there's nothing to worry about. If your monitor registers that your oxygen level falls below ninety percent, it'll beep and we'll increase it again. It's measured by this white clip on your middle finger, they told you that, right?"

"Yes," my mother whispers, holding up her left hand.

"How's your finger? Is the clip bothering you?" My mother scrunches up her face in an expression of pain, and Alec takes her hand tenderly in his, looking deeply into her eyes as if he is about to propose. "Would you like me to move it for you? I can put it on your ear." Alec removes the clip and my mother holds her hand straight out in front of her, wrinkling her nose in disgust at the sight of her middle fingernail, which unlike her nine others is naked and unpolished.

"Mom, you can get a manicure as soon as you get home," I assure her.

"They had to take the polish off that nail in order to get an accurate reading," Alec says, gently tucking a strand of my mother's hair behind her ear and fastening the clip to her lobe. He is still playing the suitor, only now he is wooing her with an expensive earring. "How's that?" he asks.

"Stunning, I'm sure," my mother squeaks out. I smile, thrilled that her sense of humor is back. Sitting down next to my father, I poke him in the arm and insist that he pay attention as Alec teaches my mother the finer points of inhaling and exhaling, something he says we all need to learn.

"Nobody really knows how to breathe correctly," Alec tells us. "Nobody uses their lungs to full capacity." He shakes his head as though he thinks this is a crying shame. "Now, Mrs. Pinkowitz, this is a little breathing test." He holds up a round plastic contraption with a tube sticking up on one end. "You breathe in here—in, in, in—just like you're sucking on a straw. You've just about finished your milkshake and you want to get every last drop." He demonstrates and as he inhales deeply, a little ball rises to the top of the apparatus. I think of the first summer that Allie and I were together, when she took me to the Paradise County Fair, determined to win me a stuffed animal at the "Test Your Strength" booth. She raised a heavy mallet with both hands and brought it down hard on a small lever that sent a metal weight racing up a vertical track toward the bell hanging high overhead that taunted her, waiting to be rung. It took Allie several tries but she finally choked up on the mallet and did it, winning me a stuffed animal we named Amelia Bearhart and still display proudly in our living room.

My mother has far less luck than Allie, though. Despite several attempts, which I can tell are an effort for her, she is hardly able to move the ball in the breathing test device at all. After only breathing into it three times, she offers the apparatus back to Alec. "I'm done."

"For now," Alec says, taking the instrument from her and putting it on a shelf near the bed. "We'll try again later. Meanwhile, I want you to take deep, deep breaths, to exercise your lungs. Like this. In…out. In…out." Alec's whole body puffs up with pride as he inhales, and sags with exaggeration every time he lets out his breath. "Got that?" he asks my mother, and then without waiting for a reply, he launches into an explanation about the various inhalers he's brought for her to use, both of which contain medicine which will cut down on her inflammation and open up her lungs. One needs to be used twice a day, one puff each time; and the other needs to be used four times a day, three puffs each time. Or is it twice a day, three puffs each time; and four times a day, one puff each time? I ask Alec to repeat everything he says while I write it all down.

"I'll be your secretary, Mom." I show her the notes I've taken on the small pad I keep in my pocketbook. "I'll help you keep it all straight."

"Now for your nebulizer," Alec says, springing off the bed. He hums a wordless tune as he makes some adjustments on a machine attached to the wall. "This might feel a little strange," he says, "but it will really help you. I'm going to take you off your oxygen and put this mask over your face. It's going to fill with mist and I want you to breathe it in as deeply as you can. It will last for about twenty minutes and then when you're through, I'll put you back on your oxygen again."

Alec approaches my mother mask-first, but before he can hold it up to her face and stretch the elastic band over her head, she grabs it from him and does it herself. He nods in approval and then steps back to turn on the mist. My mother breathes in once, coughs violently, and whips the mask away.

"Mrs. Pinkowitz, you have to keep it on," Alec insists. "Be a good girl, now," he pleads, tilting his head in what I'm sure he thinks is an adorable angle. "Please, Mrs. Pinkowitz?" He slaps his palms together and holds his hands up to his chest, his long skinny fingers pointing at my mother in a beseeching manner. "Please," he begs again, staring at her with his big brown eyes. "Do it for me?"

My mother gives him a look that says, *You've got to be kidding*, but nevertheless brings the mask up to her face once more. I know she wants to get well, but I'm sure she never thought it would require this much work. She takes a hesitant breath, and tolerates the mist better this time, not coughing as much as before. When the twenty minutes are up, Alec takes the mask from my mother and helps her place the prongs of her nasal cannula back into her nostrils before he adjusts her oxygen, and lopes out the door with a friendly wave, letting us know that he'll be back again later.

"Is that a promise or a threat?" I ask my mother, who holds both of her hands up to the sky, a gesture which means, *Do I know?* and acknowledges my attempt to make her laugh at the same time.

We have just settled back for a little rest, my mother lowering her bed so she can lie flat and my father and I perched in our seats, when someone new bounces through the doorway.

"Hi, I'm Cathy," the young woman sings out as if this is the best news we've heard all day. "I'm your physical therapist." She is so perky, I half expect her to do a cartwheel and a handspring as she makes her way across the room. "Are you ready to get up, Mrs. Pinkowitz? I bet you're tired of lying there," she says, gesturing toward the jumbled sheets on my mother's bed with a heavy-looking white cloth belt she holds in both hands.

"I'm Lydia, her daughter," I introduce myself and help my mother stall for time. "And the gentleman in the corner is her husband."

"Hello there," my father says, taking in Cathy's athletic good looks. She is a real California girl: tanned, bleach blond, and blue-eyed, her figure boyish and leggy. Dressed all in white with a terrycloth sweatband encircling her non-sweaty forehead, she looks like she just leaped over a net, shook hands with her opponent, and stepped off a tennis court. "Sunny" is the word I'd use to describe her.

"Have you been out of that bed at all, Mrs. Pinkowitz?" Cathy asks.

"No," my mother says. "I'm not ready."

"Sure you are," Cathy argues. "I'll get something to help you." She drops the white cloth belt onto my mother's bed, leaves the room, and returns a minute later carrying a folded metal walker. "You might need this for a few days," Cathy says, pulling out the legs of the walker, which have bright green tennis balls attached to their ends. "We'll see if you can manage a few steps. If not, you can just stand and lean on it."

"Not today," says my mother.

But her lack of motivation does not discourage Cathy in the least. She reaches across my mother for the button that controls her bed's position and presses it so that my mother has no choice but to sit up. "There. Very good." Cathy praises my mother as if she's already accomplished something. "Now let's just move your legs so they're dangling over the side of the bed. Can you do that for me?"

My mother does not move.

"Mrs. Pinkowitz." Cathy places her hands on her nonexistent hips in an attempt to appear stern. "You have to work with me here. Okay?"

"It's *Shabbos*," my mother states. "The Jewish Sabbath. We don't work on Saturdays."

"Nice try, Mom," I acknowledge. "But we're not exactly religious."

My mother frowns at me for betraying her and looks to my father for support.

"C'mon, Doris," he says. "How am I going to take you dancing if you don't get out of bed?"

"What about if you just sit up by yourself, without leaning against your pillows? Try that for a minute," Cathy suggests.

"That's a good idea, Mom. If you can sit up for a little while, I'll be able to shampoo your hair. With the dry shampoo that Margarita brought us."

My mother nods and considers her options. She looks at all of us in turn and I imagine she's thinking, *Three against one. What choice do I have?* Plus she knows she's going to have to get up sooner or later. With great effort, she wiggles herself around until she is facing my father and me, and then drops her legs over the side of the bed.

"Doris, pull your *shmatte* down." My father points to my mother's lap. Her johnny is all bunched up, exposing her pale white knees.

My mother shrugs, not bothered by this. "Hey, if you've got it, flaunt it," she says. My father puts his hands in front of his own knees and pantomimes covering them with an invisible blanket. "Don't worry, Max," my mother says, nonplussed. "They've seen it all, believe me. They've seen things you haven't even seen," she tells him, her words making my father turn red with embarrassment. Still, Cathy helps my mother straighten out her johnny and then steps back to watch how she does, sitting up and breathing.

"How are you feeling?" Cathy asks after a moment.

"Swell," pants my mother.

Cathy beams, oblivious to my mother's sense of irony. "Let's try standing up," she chirps, moving the walker closer to my mother's bed. Before my mother can gather up the strength to protest, Cathy has tied her thick white belt around my mother's waist and used it to pull her to her feet.

"Hold on, Mrs. Pinkowitz. Hold on to the walker," Cathy instructs, as she holds on to her.

"Doris, you're up. Hooray." My father cheers and claps his hands. Briefly, I wonder if he had the same reaction the first day I managed to stand on my own two feet. I doubt it; most likely he was working at his office when the momentous event occurred.

My mother's body is trembling, and I'm afraid she's going to faint. "Don't you think she should sit down?" I ask Cathy. "She looks pretty unsteady."

"She's doing fine," says the unrelentingly upbeat physical therapist, who I'm beginning to think has a streak of sadism running underneath that peppy cheerleader façade. "We're going to take a few steps now."

My mother shakes her head and looks at Cathy. Translation: maybe *you're* going to take a few steps, but *I'm* not.

"One step, Mrs. Pinkowitz? Just one?"

"No," says my mother. Clearly Cathy's bubbly charms do not work as well as those that belong to the handsome Alec. "I want to sit down."

"Okay. Let me help you." Cathy guides my mother off her feet and back into bed. "You did very well, Mrs. Pinkowitz. Your oxygen didn't fall below ninety percent and that's a very good sign. I'll be back after lunch to work with you again. Okay?"

"Don't hurry," my mother tells her as Cathy packs up her walker and her belt and waves good-bye.

"Lunchtime," Margarita says, gliding into the room.

"It's like Grand Central Station in here," my father notes, dazed by the constant activity.

"I have to test your blood sugar, Mrs. Pinkowitz," Margarita says, showing her the small, square machine she is carrying. "That means I have to prick your finger."

"Why?" my mother wants to know. "I'm not diabetic."

"I know, honey. It's because of all the steroids you've been on. That can throw your sugar off. I'm sorry I have to do this." She lifts my mother's hand, swipes her middle finger with an alcohol swab, and then jabs it quickly, making my mother, my father, and I all jump. "I'm sorry," Margarita says again, smearing a drop of my mother's blood on a slide and inserting it into her contraption. "This will just take a minute. Let's see. Your blood sugar is ninety-eight. That's normal. I'm going to tell them to bring you some solid food for lunch. Okay?"

My mother brightens at the prospect. She hasn't had a real meal in more than a week.

"What's the last thing you remember eating, Mom?" I ask her after Margarita leaves.

My mother thinks for a minute, then looks to my father for the answer.

"We both had lamb chops at that nice restaurant, what was the name of it? You know, where we ate dinner right before the lecture. They had that really good salad dressing with the poppy seeds in it that you like. You remember." My mother stares at him blankly. My father sits up and leans forward. My mother is like an elephant: she never forgets. Anything. Least of all the details of a meal. "You don't remember, Doris? They brought us that delicious cheesecake for dessert, with all the different toppings. Strawberry, blueberry, raspberry…"

"It sounds good," my mother says. "But I don't remember."

"Do you remember the lecture, Doris? They were talking about all the Broadway shows, *Fiddler on the Roof*, *Funny Girl*, *I Can Get It For You Wholesale*, *Hello Dolly*…"

My father glances at me for a split second, letting me know how much this concerns him. I tell my parents I'll be right back and leave the room heading for the nurse's station. Behind the desk sits my old friend, Dr. Harte. When I tell him my latest worry—that my mother has lost her long-term memory—he assures me again that this is normal. "She'll be sharp as a tack in a day or so," he tells me. "I'll go in and see her." He rises from his chair and follows me back into the room. "Mrs. Pinkowitz," he says and much to my surprise, my mother smiles at him warmly. I guess she's already forgotten how she called him a liar and told my father to stiff him. "How are you today?"

"Better."

"Good. Let's take a listen." The doctor plugs the ends of his stethoscope into his ears and places the round metal disk against my mother's chest. "Breathe in for me as deeply as you can. Now breathe out. Again. Very good." Dr. Harte nods, detaches himself from his stethoscope and steps back. "You're doing very well, dear. Now you have to get stronger. Has the respiratory therapist been in?" My mother nods. "The physical therapist?" She nods again. "Excellent. You'll be out of here before you know it."

"When?" I ask, moving out of the way as an orderly brings in my mother's lunch tray.

"Not until she gets out of bed and goes to the bathroom by herself. And we're sure that everything is stable. Oh, and you'll need to call the airlines about the oxygen she'll require on the plane."

"*I* need to do that?"

Dr. Harte raises his eyebrows, letting me know that *he's* certainly not going to spend his precious time on hold with the airlines, listening to Muzak and waiting for an actual person to come on the line and speak to him to set this up. "You'll have to call the oxygen company, too, eventually. But don't worry about that now. That all comes later." Dr. Harte turns back toward my mother. "You're doing beautifully," he tells her.

"Thank you, Doctor," my father says. "You know, my daughter's a doctor, too."

"Really?" Dr. Harte stares at me with new respect in his eyes. "What do you specialize in?"

"I'm not a medical doctor," I rush to clarify. "I'm a professor."

"She has her Ph.D.," my father brags. "She holds a doctorate in Jewish Studies."

"That's wonderful," Dr. Harte says, just as his pager goes off. "Excuse me," he says, hurrying away.

"Um, Dad." There are some things I can let slide, but this is definitely not one of them. "I'm not a professor of Jewish Studies. I'm a professor of Women's Studies."

"No, you're not."

"Yes, I am." How can he argue this with me? "Where did you even get that idea?"

"From you. You told me you were teaching Jewish Studies."

"I never said that."

"Yes, you did, Lydia, don't you remember?" My father's question implies that my memory, like my mother's, is suddenly on the blink.

"You told me that you were teaching a course about women and the Holocaust. A few years ago. Remember?"

"Of course I remember," I tell my father. "But that class wasn't taught through the Jewish Studies department. It was taught through the Women's Studies department. Because I am a Women's Studies professor. Because I got my doctorate in Women's Studies." Can I be any clearer than that?

"What's for lunch?" My mother, who has always had a knack for changing the subject whenever the conversation gets too unpleasant, points to the tray sitting on her bedside table. I bring it over to her and lift the metal cover off her steaming plate.

"It looks like some kind of stew." I study the food, which reminds me of past high school lunches that I always took one bite of and then threw in the trash. "It's like chicken pot pie without the pie. You want some?" I unwrap my mother's plastic utensils and hand her a spoon. "Why don't you try feeding yourself?" My mother is game, but when she lifts the spoon halfway to her mouth, her hand begins to shake like someone with Parkinson's Disease. I take the spoon from her before she spills its contents all over her lap and pull up a chair to feed her. She eats everything on her plate—chicken, string beans, and chocolate pudding—and I am encouraged that her appetite has returned. But she is so weak. The effort of all the morning's tasks has exhausted her and soon after her meal, she closes her eyes and falls asleep. Watching her, I wonder how in the world she will ever have the strength to fly from California to New York, an arduous trip for anyone, even those of us in perfect health. Will the Holy Family Hospital ever loosen its clutches and release my own holy family from its tight, unyielding grasp?

❖

MOE, LARRY, AND CURLY. The Three Musketeers. Three Blind Mice. Snap, Crackle, Pop. The Pinkowitz Trio has taken Los Angeles by storm and it looks like we are a huge success. Every day my mother grows stronger. A lot stronger. Dr. Harte attributes it to the fact that she's now getting a good night's sleep—her room is much quieter than her ICU cubicle—and she's eating well, too. Still, the speed of her progress amazes me. On Saturday afternoon, with the aid of a walker, she surprises herself by taking her very first step, and by Sunday morning she makes her way across the entire room. Jack's chair has been replaced by a commode, a substitution that amuses me no end and horrifies my mother so much that she makes it her business to be able to use the bathroom by Sunday afternoon. On Monday, my mother feeds herself breakfast, lunch, and supper, and in between all her various therapies, she is able to sit up in a chair for over an hour, making it possible for me to brush out her hair and wash it with dry shampoo. And while she is long overdue for an appointment with her colorist and stylist, much to my relief, she is finally beginning to look like her old self.

Inside my mother's body, things have gotten better, too. She's been using her inhalers faithfully and practicing her breathing, and is now able to make the ball in the breathing test apparatus rise halfway to the top of its plastic container. Her oxygen has been lowered to four liters per minute, her blood pressure only has to be checked once every four hours, and her last IV has been removed.

And finally, in addition to her physical improvement, my mother's mental capacities have made their own show-stopping comeback, too. Clever girl that I am, I've discovered a way to test how well her brain cells are functioning, by asking her to help me out with the crossword puzzles I've torn from my father's discarded day-old newspapers. The first time I asked my mother for the solution to a simple clue, a five-letter word meaning "pancake," the answer *crepe* eluded her, though she did come up with *blintz* which, while one letter too long, was a perfectly logical guess. But a few puzzles later, she was able to provide me with a six-letter word for "no longer reliant on mother" (weaned); a ten-letter word for "non-human" (mechanical), and the name of the actress who played Nora Charles in *The Thin Man* (Myrna Loy). She was even able to figure out the answer to a clue that I should have known but had me stumped, "Sappho's last letter."

"Wasn't she Greek?" my mother asked as I sat across from her, pencil poised above a little white square.

"Yes, Mom. She was a poet. She lived on the island of Lesbos," I told her, as if my mother and I talked about such matters all the time.

"Then her last letter would be omega," my mother said just as matter-of-factly, and lo and behold she was right.

On Tuesday morning, Margarita bustles through the doorway, having been off duty on Sunday and Monday. "How is she?" she asks, nodding her chin at my mother.

"Coming along fine," says my father, lowering his ever-present reading material.

"Why don't you ask her yourself? These days she's a regular *habladora*," I say, and then inwardly wince, horrified that I've behaved just as badly as my father by casually tossing around Spanish words when I have no business doing so. But Margarita surprises me with a hearty laugh; I had expected her to bite my head off. "*Habladora*? Where did you learn that?" she chuckles.

"My spouse is Puerto Rican," I remind her, though of course she has no way of knowing this. My father didn't specify whom his Puerto Rican daughter-in-law was married to, and for all Margarita knows, my parents have a son somewhere who is blissfully married to the aforementioned Alicia.

But Margarita is more concerned with her patient than with the ethnic makeup of my family, and rightly so. "How are you, Mrs. Pinkowitz?" she asks my mother directly. The nurse has obviously spent some, if not most of her time during her two days off having an extreme makeover at a trendy salon. Her hair, while still auburn, has been lightened several shades and is now woven into dozens of braids that hang down her back, many of them decorated with brightly colored beads and shells that clack together musically whenever she turns her head. And her formerly blue, square fingernails are now shaped into ovals and polished a deep magenta, with a tiny glittering jewel embedded in the middle of each one.

"I like your nails," my mother says, leaning forward to get a closer look.

"I like yours," Margarita counters. "How are you feeling? Better?"

"Much better." My mother's voice is just about back to normal. "My daughter washed my hair yesterday."

"It looks nice." Margarita compliments her again. "Would you like me to braid it for you? Like mine?"

"Yes, but not so many." My mother wriggles herself across the bed to make some room. Margarita climbs aboard, kneels behind her, and weaves her hair into two French braids, which she joins together with a purple scrunchie at the back of her neck. Finished, she hops up to admire her handiwork. "Very glamorous," she says with approval. "I think you're going to be ready to go home soon."

"What do we have to do to make that happen?" I ask.

"The doctor will tell you," Margarita answers. "Let's go see if we can find him."

Margarita and I step out into the hall and locate Dr. Harte sitting at a desk behind the nurse's station, slurping coffee out of a white Styrofoam cup and scribbling notes on a patient's chart. Out of respect for his position, Margarita stands quietly with her hands clasped behind her back, waiting for him to look up and acknowledge her presence before she speaks. "Doctor, Lydia would like to speak with you about the steps she needs to take to get her mother home."

"Ah, yes." He puts down his pen and studies me as if he's assessing whether or not I am up to the task. "You'll need to call the airlines and ask them the maximum amount of oxygen they can give her on the plane. You'll need to call the oxygen company to set up oxygen for her on the way to the airport, at the airport, on the way home from the airport, and at home. You'll need to have an appointment set up with her primary care physician within a week of her return. I'll make a copy of her chart for you to bring to him."

"Or her," Margarita and I chorus automatically and then laugh.

Dr. Harte frowns at us both and continues. "Here's the name and number of the oxygen company." He scribbles the information across the top sheet of a prescription pad, rips it off, and hands it to me. "But call the airlines first." He turns his attention back to the chart on the desk in front of him, signaling that we are dismissed.

"Dr. Harte," I say, lingering at his desk though Margarita has walked away. Just because the doctor is through with me does not mean that I am through with him. "What exactly is my mother's prognosis?" I ask. "Will she recover from this?"

The doctor keeps writing as if I have not spoken, but I stand my ground. He takes his own sweet time, but eventually finishes with his notes, closes the chart, and swivels his seat around to face me.

"Her lungs aren't as damaged as I thought they were at first. She will recover from the bronchitis, but the emphysema will remain," he tells me, his voice a dull, flat monotone. "She may need to stay on the oxygen, or over time she may be able to dispense with it, or just use it when she's sleeping, or as needed. She has a strong constitution and she seems very motivated, which is due largely in part to you and your dad." The doctor gives me just the faintest hint of a smile. "Not many patients have such a loving family willing to devote so much time to their care. Your mother is very lucky to have a daughter like you."

"Thank you, Dr. Harte," I say, truly humbled even though I'm sure the doctor has no idea how much his words mean to me.

I return to my mother's room to tell my parents what's going on, just as Alec and Cathy are on their way inside. They collide in the doorway, bumping their hips together, and then step back and laugh.

"You go first," Alec says.

"No you." Cathy stares up at him and giggles.

"No, you. I insist," Alec looks down at her and smiles. They hold each other's gaze for just a split second longer than necessary, letting me know that the two of them are definitely an item and a fairly new one at that.

"After you," Cathy says.

"No, after you," argues Alec, draping his arm across his stomach and bowing from the waist like a perfect English gentleman.

"How about after me? Age before beauty," I say, nudging them both out of the way with a phrase that was said to me by an elderly lady not that long ago. I enter the room with the two lovebirds twittering behind me to tell my father about my conversation with Dr. Harte. "Dad, I have to call the airlines and the oxygen company to make some arrangements. I think I might need your credit card." He hands it over without argument (unlike the many times I begged him for it when I was a teenager en route to the mall) and then returns to his newspaper. A moment later, as I stand in front of the elevator bank, he joins me in the hallway.

"Lydia, I'm concerned," he begins, just as he did many times when I was growing up and had done something that displeased him.

"About what?" I reply just as I did back then.

"About flying home," he says, "and what will happen once we get there."

"What do you mean?" I ask as the elevator arrives. The doors slide open but I don't step inside and a few seconds later they slide back shut.

"I mean what if something happens on the way to the airport? Or on the plane? Or once we get off the plane? And no one's been home for a month. There's no food in the house, the heat hasn't been turned on…" My father's voice fades and he avoids my eye. We are so alike in so many ways that I know immediately what is going on here. Indirectly, my father is asking for help, something he finds incredibly difficult to do. Especially from his daughter.

"Dad." I study him and decide to put the poor man out of his misery. "Do you want me to fly home with you and Mom?"

"Would you, Lydia?" He looks at me, relief and gratitude written all over his face. "That would be great. I'm sure we could use a pair of extra hands. It would only be for a few days. Until I get your mother settled."

"All right. Let me go call the airlines." *And Allie*, I think as I push the elevator button again. Who I'm sure will be less than thrilled at this news. But really, what choice do I have?

I go downstairs to use the pay phone rather than do my business in my mother's crowded room. As expected, I am put on hold for a long time, first with the travel agent, who it turns out cannot help me; then with a representative from the airlines who informs me that with forty-eight hours' notice they can provide my mother with up to eight liters of oxygen a minute during the flight; and then with someone from the oxygen company, who gives me a list of the facts they require in order to provide my mother with everything she needs. I write everything down in my notebook, tromp back upstairs, speak to the doctor again, ride the elevator back down, and make yet more phone calls. I keep my mother informed every step of the way and she listens closely and watches me carefully, admiration streaming from her eyes. "You could be a nurse," she tells me. "Or a social worker. You're very well organized."

"Thanks, Mom, but I like my job," I say, unable to keep a note of defensiveness out of my voice. My parents have never supported my choice of occupation, my father having no interest in "women's lib," as he still calls it, and my mother seeing no need for it. "I don't have to be liberated," she told me once. "Your father lets me do whatever I want."

After Dr. Harte gives me the okay, I set up a flight for the three of us that leaves early Friday morning, and arrange for the airline to fax all the information we need to the front desk of our hotel. We have to be at the airport four hours before the flight from Los Angeles to New York because of my mother's special needs, and the oxygen company promises to deliver the necessary tanks the evening before we leave. I explain all this to my father; my mother is fast asleep.

That evening back in my hotel room, I eat a light supper, take a hot bath, change into my pajamas, and watch a bit of the evening news, knowing that what I'm really doing is avoiding the inevitable: calling

Allie and telling her my new plans. As I take my cell phone out onto the little terrace to dial our number, I find myself hoping she won't be home so I can just leave a message, and of course I feel horribly guilty about that. I'm just rehearsing a little speech in my head when Allie picks up the phone.

"Hi, Lydia."

"Hi, Allie." I make sure no trace of disappointment is evident in my voice. "How are you?"

"Okay. What's going on?"

"Not much. Except I'm flying home on Friday."

"You are?" Allie's tone instantly lightens with the news. "Mishmosh, do you hear that?" Allie calls out to our cat, her voice bursting with happiness. "Your *mamacita* is coming home. What time does your plane get in, Lyddie? What time should I pick you up?"

Oops. Of course *home* means our home to Allie. "Um, Allie? I'm not flying home-home. I'm going home with my parents. To help them out. Just for a few days."

"You are?" Allie asks glumly. Then her voice perks up. "I'll just meet you there," she says, brightening. "I can come down Saturday morning and take a few days off work next week. Then when you're ready we'll drive home together."

"Let me think about that," I say, my eyes searching the sky as I stall for time. For some reason, I feel hesitant about integrating Allie into my new family life. My parents are like brand new toys that I've barely taken out of the box, and I'm not ready to share them with anybody just yet.

"What's the matter, Lydia?" Allie asks. "Don't you want me to come?"

"Of course I want you to come. It's not me, it's my parents," I tell her, thinking fast. "I'm not sure that my mother will want to see anyone right away. She's very weak and she isn't herself. Plus she looks terrible. Her hair is a mess, her arms are all black and blue, and her face is puffed up to twice its size. You know how vain my mother is. I think she'd feel too embarrassed to let anyone she knows see her looking like that."

"I suppose so," Allie says, with a sigh of defeat. "Well, just do what you want," she adds, as if she doesn't really care when she gets to see me again. Which makes me suddenly miss her.

"Allie, maybe I should just fly home," I say. "Or maybe I'll just stay one night with my parents and then you can come get me. What do you think?"

"Whatever," she says, unwilling to commit herself. "It's your decision, Lydia."

We talk a bit longer with Allie filling me in on which bills she's paid, and reading me some of my more important email before we say good-bye and hang up. As soon as we do so, my fingers immediately dial Vera's number. And thank God, she's there. After I bring her up to date on my mother, I start in on what I really need to talk about: what's going on with me and Allie.

"When I ask her how she is, she says, 'okay,'" I tell Vera. "When I ask her how Mishmosh is, she says, 'fine.' She reminds me of me when I was a teenager and gave my mother snotty one-word answers. 'Where are you going?' 'Out.' 'Who are you going with?' 'People.'" I collapse into a metal chair and rest my feet up on the balcony railing. "It's so weird, Vera. My mother used to feel like a stranger, and now Allie's the one who does."

"Why does anyone have to feel like a stranger?" Vera asks pointedly. "Lydia, with everything you're going through, it doesn't surprise me that you feel distant from Allie."

"She doesn't even believe that my mother and I are okay now," I say, sinking down lower in my chair with dejection. "She thinks this is just a passing phase." As I say this aloud a new thought occurs to me. "Is that what you think, Vera?"

"Time will tell, Lydia," Vera says, in her usual rational way. "I think you've made some major progress here, and there also might be some backsliding. You know, two steps forward and three steps back. Or is it three steps forward and two steps back?"

I walk two fingers up and down my thigh as if they are miniature legs doing a little dance and then give up. "I don't know, Vera. I can never remember."

"Me neither. Well, never mind. You'll just have to wait and see. And Lydia?"

"Yes, Vera?"

"Don't be so hard on Allie. I don't think it's that she doesn't believe you. I think it's that she loves you and she's trying to protect you. After all, Allie more than anyone has seen firsthand how much your mother has hurt you over the years."

As usual, Vera is right. "I suppose so."

"And forgive me for saying this, but most people your age are more mature than you are—"

"Hey, thanks a lot."

"And what I mean by that," Vera ignores my sarcasm, "is most people in their forties have already learned how to integrate the various roles they play: being someone's spouse, being someone's child. You haven't developed that skill because your parents haven't really been a part of your life. So when you're with them, you're still a little girl emotionally. And it's hard for you to feel like an adult at the same time. Besides, you and Allie have never been good at being apart."

"That's true." I take my feet down from the railing and stare out into the distance, remembering back to the time when Allie and I started seeing each other and the difficulties we had during that period of time (eleven months and seventeen days, to be exact) before we moved in together. At the end of each workday, Allie wanted to go home to her apartment, I wanted to go home to mine, but being newly and madly in love, we couldn't stand spending even one night away from each other. What to do? Finally we compromised on a rotating schedule: Mondays, Wednesdays, and Fridays at Allie's house and Tuesdays, Thursdays, and Saturdays at mine (we'd flip a coin for Sundays). This pleased neither of us, though we both had to admit that it was fair. If we had such a hard time negotiating the measly half a dozen blocks between our living spaces back then, it's no wonder that we're having such a hard time figuring out how to manage being three thousand miles apart.

"Plus you're used to having conflict in your life between you and your biological family," Vera continues, in full-fledged therapist mode. "Now that that's not happening, you're creating conflict in your chosen family. Without that conflict, you probably feel out of balance. You're a textbook case, Lydia," Vera proclaims. "But don't worry. You and Allie have a very strong foundation and a lot of love between you. I predict everything is going to turn out just fine."

"You really think so, Vera?" I ask, hardly convinced.

"Lydia, try not to worry so much. Trust me. This will all be over soon and you and Allie will be your old romantic selves again," Vera says and then before we get off the phone, she tries to lighten my mood by warning me that if I keep calling her for support and advice, she's going to have to start charging me for long-distance therapy. "And believe me, Lydia," Vera chuckles. "I may be good, but I'm certainly not cheap."

The next morning, back at the hospital, I fill my mother in on our plans, since she fell asleep yesterday before we had a chance to do so. "Good news, Mom," I announce, waltzing into her room behind my father. "We're getting out of here two days from now, on Friday. Your plane leaves at eight o'clock."

My mother is sitting up in bed, holding a cup of tea in both hands. "Are you coming with us to the airport, Lydia? What time does your flight leave?"

"I'm flying to New York with you," I tell her, sitting down in my customary seat next to her bed. "To help out. Until you get back on your feet."

"Isn't that great, Doris?" my father asks, sinking down beside me and leaning forward, resting his elbows on his knees. "Lydia can go to the store for us, do some shopping—"

"No." My mother silences him with one word then turns to me. "You're not coming home with us."

"I'm not?" I thought she'd be thrilled at the idea. "Why not?"

"Because," she says flatly.

"Because why?" I ask, reverting to my adolescent behavior.

"Because I said so," my mother answers, also falling back to the answers she gave me when I was a child. "It's not necessary, Lydia. Your father and I will be fine. We don't need your help."

I look at my father and by the expression on his face I can tell he's not so sure but doesn't dare argue. "I know it's not necessary, Mom," I say, since like me, my mother hates to feel helpless. "I know I don't need to come. But what if I want to come?"

"No, Lydia."

"What if I just get on the plane?" I try a different approach. "I have a ticket. What if I follow you back to the house in a cab? What are you going to do, leave me out there in the cold?"

My mother lifts one finger and points it at me with a scowl. "Don't give me a hard time, Lydia. I mean it. You have your own life and you need to get back to it. I've bothered you enough."

"It hasn't been a bother."

"Stop." My mother holds one hand up, as if she's halting oncoming traffic. "I don't need your help. Your father and I are perfectly capable of taking care of ourselves. I want you to pick up the phone and change your flight, Lydia. Now."

"But—"

"No buts." My mother's voice is firm and when she gets like this, I know from experience that the conversation is over.

After glancing at my father, whose look tells me to do as I am told, I pick up the phone and call the airlines. There are two flights going from Los Angeles to Maine on Friday; the first one leaves an hour after my parents take off, and the second one departs three hours after that. I decide I better take the later flight, just in case something happens and my parents get delayed. After everything is arranged, I hang up the phone and turn to my mother. "I'm going downstairs to call Allie," I tell her. "I'll be back very soon."

"Take your time." My mother waves me off. "I'm not going anywhere."

Outside the hospital, I sit on my bench and dial Allie's work number. According to her watch, it's half past eleven at home, which means she hasn't left on her lunch break yet. When the lumberyard's receptionist answers the phone and tells me that Allie is busy, I tell her it's an emergency and five seconds later Allie picks up the phone.

"What is it?" she pants, a little out of breath.

"I'm coming home. To you. For real," I say, suddenly happy at the prospect. "I changed my flight. I'll be home Friday night."

"Oh my God. Finally," Allie says, her voice full of joy. "What time?"

"I get in at eleven-eleven." I scan the itinerary I scrawled on a scrap of paper and give her my flight number. "If that's too late for you to pick me up, I can take a cab."

Allie is quiet for a long moment. "Lydia, do you *want* to take a cab home?" she asks, all the happiness gone from her voice.

"No, Allie, I just didn't want to bother you."

"Bother me?" I can tell by her tone that Allie is shaking her head. "Lydia, what's come over you? Don't you know it's me, Alicia Maria Taraza, the butch of your dreams? Don't you know I'd come get you even if your plane landed at four in the morning in the middle of a blizzard with whiteout conditions and all the roads closed? Don't you know I'd walk through the snow barefoot and carry you home on my back if I had to? Lyddie, Lyddie, Lyddie, what's gotten into you?"

Allie's declaration of undying love melts the frozen tundra of my heart and I smile in spite of myself. "I don't know, Allie," I say, my voice starting to quiver. "I just feel so far away from you."

"That's because you are far away from me, silly girl. But you're coming home soon. And I can't wait to see you."

"I can't wait to see you either," I say, hoping Allie can tell by my voice that I mean it. "And Mishmosh, too. Do you think he missed me? Do you think he even remembers me?"

"Remember you? Are you kidding? Every day when I come home from work, I find him curled up on the couch in your study, and he sleeps on your pillow every night."

"He does?" All at once I wish I could beam myself home like a Star Trek character. "I'll see you soon, Allie. Okay?"

"Okay," Allie says, happily. "*Te quiero mucho. Hasta la vista*, baby."

The rest of the day flies by with my mother's "staff" keeping her constantly occupied with all her various therapies. Thursday passes quickly as well, and in the evening, right after my mother finishes her supper, a delivery man appears in her doorway with several bulky green oxygen tanks and a small metal dolly.

"This is what you'll need to take to the airport," the man from the oxygen company tells us, pointing. "The dolly can hold two tanks side by side, and the third one that she's using can rest between her legs in her wheelchair," he explains. Like everyone else I have met on this trip, he is young, definitely not more than thirty, and seems to be in a big hurry. "Let's see, you've got the tanks, the nasal cannula, the gauge, the wrench. You're all set."

"Wait a minute," I stop him by grabbing his sleeve. "What wrench?"

"This wrench, see?" He holds up a black plastic tool. "You turn this counterclockwise like so, to open up the tank. The needle on the gauge will tell you when you're almost out of oxygen and here's where you set how many liters per minute you need. See?" He demonstrates quickly and then says again, "Okay. You're all set."

"Oh no," I say, putting both hands on either side of the doorjamb to block his exit in case he tries to make a quick getaway. "Let me explain something to you. These are oxygen tanks," I say, which of course he already knows. "My mother's oxygen tanks. That means her life depends on my father knowing how to use them correctly. You can't just spit out three sentences in two seconds and then be on your merry way. You're talking to a man," I nod toward my father, "whose entire tool kit consists of a bobby pin and a butter knife."

"Lydia, I beg your pardon." My father throws out a feeble protest, but I can tell he is intimidated by the task that lies ahead of him. If he goofs this up, my mother will not be able to breathe.

"How long does each tank last?" I ask.

"Let's see. On her dosage," he does a quick mental calculation, "each tank will last for three hours."

I do my math out loud. "It's an hour to the airport, and we have to get there four hours early. So that's five hours right there. Dad, you're going to have to change tanks at least once. So you need to learn how to do this."

My father hangs on every word like a model student while the delivery fellow, under my watchful eye, shows him how to read the gauge, how to transfer it from one tank to the next, how to attach the bottom end of the nasal cannula tube to the oxygen supply, how to set the correct dosage, and how to check that the oxygen is flowing. I make him try it a few times without any help, hoping he will catch on and build his confidence. He's still a little shaky after doing it several times, but I see that my mother, who is somewhat mechanically inclined, is paying close attention. I am very tempted to suggest that I change my flight reservations back again, but I bite my tongue because I know my mother will not allow that. Between the two of them I'm going to have to trust that they'll be able to figure out the oxygen and be fine.

As visiting hours draw to an end, Margarita enters the room to say good night. And good-bye, since she won't be seeing us in the morning. After she bids farewell to my parents, I ask her to step out into the hall with me to have a little talk.

Margarita takes me over to the nurse's station and finds two chairs for us. She has a huge leopard print tote bag hanging over her shoulder and a black sweater slung across her arm. I know it's the end of her shift and I feel bad about detaining her, but I have a few things that I need to say.

"I just wanted to let you know that I can't thank you enough for everything you've done for my mother," I start out in a trembling voice as two tears slide down my cheeks.

Margarita's eyes fill, too, and this does not surprise me. All along, I knew that underneath that tough exterior, she was nothing but a marshmallow. "No need to thank me, Lydia," she says, her entire arm disappearing inside her enormous bag until she comes up with a pack of tissues. "Your mother's recovery is all the thanks I need. I'm just doing my job."

"Well, you did a very good job," I say, dabbing my eyes. "But I want to know your opinion. You've spent a lot more time with her than the doctor has. Do you think she's going to be okay? I was going to fly home with my parents to help them out but then I changed my flight and now I'm thinking maybe I should change it back."

Margarita narrows her eyes and squints at me. "Lydia, how old are you?" she asks.

"Forty-nine," I tell her, having never been the kind of woman who lies about her age.

"Ooh, girl, you're looking good." Margarita nods and gives me an exaggerated once-over. "You have a family?"

"Yes," I say, thinking of Allie and Mishmosh, and feeling grateful for the tactful way Margarita phrased her question. Even though she doesn't strike me as someone who would have a problem with me being a lesbian, one can never tell.

"Listen, honey." Margarita leans closer to me and puts her hand on my arm as if she is about to share something very private and confidential. "You're a very pretty woman, but this kind of thing can wear you out and make you ugly real fast. Your mother is stubborn. Trust me. She's going to live a long time. You have your own life and your own family. Don't ever forget that." I nod, listening intently. "There will be more crises and more emergencies. That's one thing I can guarantee," Margarita says, looking straight at me. "This thing ain't over yet. You've got to pace yourself. Your parents have made it this far in life without your help. They're going to do just fine."

"Thanks, Margarita." We stand and she pulls me into a hug. When we step apart, I think to ask, "Do you have a family?"

"Two girls," she answers proudly. "Ten and twelve, both of them going on twenty-one." I wait a beat but she does not mention a husband or partner.

"Your daughters are very lucky to have you as a mother," I say as we start walking down the hall. "Tell them I said so."

"They won't believe you." Margarita shakes her head, sending all her braids flying.

"Maybe not now," I say. "But give them a year or two. Or ten. Or forty. Someday they'll learn to appreciate you." I stop outside my mother's room and smile as she looks up from her bed expectantly. "Take it from me. I am one who knows."

❖

HOME SWEET HOME. Home is where the heart is. Home is where you hang your hat. There's no place like home…there's no place like home. Finally I am homeward bound and so happy about it, I don't even mind the long day's journey into night I have to undertake in order to get there.

Of course I am already up, showered, dressed, and packed when the phone rings at three a.m. with my wake-up call. Now it's half past three and I am leaving my room for the last time. I softly shut the door and make my way down the hall, pulling my suitcase behind me. Halfway to the elevator, I stop, overcome by a feeling that I've forgotten something. But what? Suitcase, carry-on bag, purse…winter coat. That's it. I dash back to my room to retrieve it and then ride the elevator down to the first floor.

The lobby is deserted as is the front desk, and I have to call out, "Hello? Anybody here?" three times before a sleepy clerk with a bad case of teenage acne drags himself out from a back room and comes over to check me out. As I stand in front of him drumming the edge of my credit card lightly against the counter and dreading the amount of the bill, my father joins me, shadowed by a bellhop pushing a cart loaded down with all of his and my mother's luggage.

"Room 716?" The clerk hunts and pecks at his keyboard, peers at the computer screen, and then says, "You're all set," not bothering to cover his mouth, which gapes open in a wide yawn.

"I am?" I turn away from him to face my father, who is also

clicking the corner of his credit card against the desk. "Dad, you don't have to pay my bill."

"I didn't pay your bill, Lydia. I haven't checked out yet. Room 523," he tells the clerk.

"You're all set as well, sir."

"I am?" my father asks, surprised.

"Yes sir. Both these rooms have been paid for by a Mr. Jack Gutman."

"Well, what do you know?" My father chuckles. "He's all right, that Jack. Thank you," he says to the clerk as he slips his credit card back into his wallet. "Come on, Lydia."

We step outside, and I am relieved that the van we arranged for last night is already waiting for us but disappointed that Eduardo is not behind the wheel; I would have liked to say good-bye to him. Our driver helps us load everything into the back, and then steers his way through the dark, empty streets of L.A., pulling up to the hospital in record time. A guard buzzes us in and we ride up to the fourth floor, where my mother awaits us.

"Hi, Mom." I step into the room and greet her, keeping my voice to a whisper out of habit because it is the middle of the night. Bending down, I kiss her on the cheek and then step back. "You look great," I say, and she does. Even though she is still tethered to an oxygen tank and sitting in a wheelchair, she is finally out of a hospital johnny and into her own clothes, a pair of gray slacks and a cream-colored sweater. She also wears a delicate necklace of light blue cloisonné beads and matching earrings, the sight of which reminds me that I haven't given back her jewelry yet.

"Here, Mom." I pull her rings off my fingers. "Take these."

"Thank you, Lydia." My mother slides her wedding band and her engagement ring onto the fourth finger of her left hand. Then she studies her ruby and diamond cocktail ring for a minute, almost as if she doesn't recognize it, before holding it out to me. "Keep it, Lydia. As a thank you for what a big help you've been."

"Oh Mom." There go my hopes of getting through just one day of this trip without crying. "You don't have to give me your ring."

"I know I don't have to, Lydia. I want to. Besides, sooner or later it will be yours anyway."

I ignore the implications of that statement and slip the ring back onto my right hand. "It's beautiful," I say, kissing her on the cheek again. "Thank you."

"You're welcome."

"Let's go, ladies. The van is waiting," my father says, always tense before a flight, even one that leaves five hours from now. "All set?"

My mother nods and we begin the journey, a night nurse we've never met before wheeling her out of the room, with my father and me trailing close behind, in charge of the extra oxygen tanks. As we wait for the elevator for the very last time, the doors to the Intensive Care Unit burst open and Angelina flies out of them.

"I heard you were leaving," she says, hurrying toward us.

"Angelina, what are you doing here in the middle of the night?" I ask. "Don't you work the day shift?"

"I switch on and off. Mrs. Pinkowitz, it's so good to see you up and about." Angelina places both hands on the armrests of my mother's wheelchair and bends down to look her in the eye.

"It's good to see you, too," my mother replies in a polite voice that lets me know she has no idea who this woman is.

"Mom, it's Angelina. She took care of you in the ICU. Don't you remember her?"

My mother studies the nurse's face but I can see that it doesn't register. "I'm sorry," she says.

"It's all right." Angelina straightens up. "You must be glad to be going home."

"Very glad," my mother says. "Good-bye."

"Good luck to all of you," Angelina stays with us until we get on the elevator, and then waves as the door closes. We make our way downstairs, through the lobby, and out the door, where our van driver is waiting for us, chatting on his cell phone and smoking a cigarette. He drops his butt on the ground and stubs it out the second he catches sight of my mother with her oxygen tank.

"All set?" he asks, opening the door to the van. The nurse holds the wheelchair steady as my father helps my mother climb out of it and up into the vehicle. I crawl over her to sit beside her and my father takes his place up front next to the driver. We settle in, buckle our seat belts, and watch the nurse push the now-empty wheelchair back toward the hospital, a place I am relieved I will never have to enter again.

As soon as the van pulls away from the curb, my father half turns in his seat and glances at my mother. "Everything okay, Doris?" he asks.

"Fine," she says. "Don't worry about me. I'm all right."

He swivels back around and though he is facing away from me, I see him pull his flight itinerary along with his license out of his jacket pocket, and grasp them firmly in his fist, just as I have done.

"Look, Dad," I say, holding up the flight documents and ID that I won't need for at least another six hours.

He laughs. "What do you know? You got my *shtick*, kid."

I laugh, too. "I always wondered where I got it."

Soon we are at the airport, pulling up to the curb outside Terminal One. The van barely stops before my father leaps out and hurries off to find a skycap with a wheelchair. We get my mother settled and my father pushes her inside the terminal with me following with the oxygen tanks and another skycap behind me with our luggage. After all our quiet days in the hospital, the hustle and bustle of the airport is more than a little overwhelming. Even at this early, ungodly hour, it is full of people racing about: businessmen in suits swinging briefcases and barking into cell phones; parents dodging through the crowd chasing their running, laughing children; pairs of carefully groomed flight attendants speedwalking on their high heels while sipping large cups of coffee. Because my mother is clearly a special-needs customer, we are brought to the front of the line and checked in quickly. My parents' luggage disappears and they receive their boarding passes without a problem.

"What about this bag?" the man who has checked them in asks me.

"That's mine," I tell him. "I'm on a different flight."

"What is your flight number?" he asks.

"I'm on a different airline," I tell him. "Can you watch this for me while I bring them through security?"

"No, miss, I'm afraid not," he says, and though I argue with him briefly, he remains firm.

"Mom." I find my parents, who have moved off to the side and out of harm's way. "I can't come through security with you because of my suitcase. I have to go check in at my own airline. It's in a different terminal. I'll do that and then come find you."

My mother's face shatters with this news. "Lydia." She reaches up and tenderly cradles my cheeks in both hands as if my head is fragile as an antique china teacup. "Remember, the safety deposit box. Number 914. Everything in it is for you."

"Mom." The noise and frenzied activity of the airport fade away and all I see are my mother's worried eyes. "It's not a big deal. I'll find you. And you're going to be fine. I'll meet you at your gate. I promise."

"Hurry back, Lydia," my father says, his frightened glance wandering toward the gauge on my mother's oxygen tank.

"I will," I say, and then stand there waving as they disappear into the crowd. Once they are out of sight, I run toward the exit and flag down a taxi to take me to Terminal Nine, too much in a hurry to wait for the free shuttle. Luckily there are only three people ahead of me in line and it doesn't take long for me to step up to the counter. A brunette version of Melissa, complete with French-manicured nails and a too-heavily-made-up face, types my flight number into her computer.

"That flight doesn't leave for another six hours," she informs me. "You can't check in until four hours before the flight."

"Can I just check this bag?" I motion toward the large suitcase beside me, which I would gladly abandon if I could figure out a way to do so without raising suspicion. "I have to go help my parents in another terminal. My mother's on oxygen and they can't manage by themselves."

"I'm sorry," the airline worker says. "Those are the rules."

"You don't understand," I tell her, my voice cracking and the tears I never seem to run out of starting to flow. "My mother's on oxygen," I repeat, openly weeping now. "If I don't help her change her tank in an hour, she won't be able to breathe. She will die," I wail, not caring that people are starting to murmur and stare.

"Let me get the manager," the woman says, disappearing through a door in the wall behind her. I can't believe I'm finally having the meltdown I've managed to hold at bay ever since I left home eleven days ago. I sob for a few more minutes and then pull myself together just as the door in the wall opens and a man comes out of it and walks briskly over to me.

"What seems to be the problem?" he asks, his voice professional yet kind. I explain the entire situation to him and he takes care of everything: putting me on an earlier flight so that I can check my luggage through and assuring me that if I miss that flight, there will still be a space for me on my original, later one. Then he issues me a special pass that will allow me to return to Terminal One, go through security, and meet my parents at their gate.

"I made it," I announce, once I finally find them.

"Oh look, Doris. Lydia's here," my father says casually, as if we are meeting for lunch at a neighborhood diner.

"See, Mom, I told you there was nothing to worry about." Her wheelchair is parked at the end of a row of seats and I sit down next to her and take her hand. "Are you feeling okay?"

"I'm all right," she says, but her voice lacks confidence.

"Do you want something to eat?"

"Maybe something small. A muffin. Blueberry if they have it. But no coffee. I don't want to have to go to the bathroom."

"I'll have coffee," my father says. "And a copy of the *Times* if you can find one."

I head off toward the newsstands and food court and return bearing breakfast and the morning paper. My mother takes her food and watches me spread a thick slab of cream cheese across one half of the onion bagel I've bought for myself.

"Not so much," she says, frowning. "You've lost some weight, Lydia, that's the only good thing that's come out of this. It would be a shame if you gained it all back."

"Mom," I groan, spreading the cream cheese on even thicker, for spite. "I like my body the way it is. I don't want to lose any weight."

"Lydia, you may feel that way now but take it from me, as you get older it's much harder to—"

"Mom, please. Drop it." I've never spoken to my mother like this before and am shocked when she actually obeys my request. Though she does get the last word in by shrugging one shoulder as if to say, *Okay, Lydia, but don't say I didn't warn you...*

Soon the waiting area is crowded to overflowing with other passengers flying to New York. After we finish breakfast, I look down at my mother's oxygen tank and notice that the needle of its gauge has just hit the red zone, signaling that the supply is getting low.

"Hey, Dad?" I poke the front page of the newspaper he is holding up in front of him.

"What is it, Lydia?"

"You need to change Mom's oxygen tank."

"Now?"

"Yes, now."

My father exhales heavily, knowing that his moment of truth has arrived. He bends down and studies the tank, trying to remember everything he has recently learned about it. "I turn the wrench this way?" he asks me, twisting it to the left.

"I'm not helping," I answer, folding my arms. "I'm not going home with you. You need to figure it out yourself."

"All right." He sets to work and as far as I can tell, after a few false starts, does everything the way he's supposed to. When he finishes he looks at my mother anxiously. "All set, Doris? Are you getting the oxygen?"

"No," she says. "I'm not getting anything." She takes the nasal cannula out of her nose, checks the two prongs, and inserts them into her nostrils again. "No," she says again, shaking her head. "Nothing."

"What do you mean nothing? You're not getting anything? I did it right." My father checks everything again. "Are you sure, Doris?"

She throws him a look and says, "I'm sure," her own anxiety clearly rising. Both my parents turn to me but I just shake my head and refold my arms. My mother sighs, knowing that the time has come to take matters into her own hands, and she does so literally, checking the gauge, and the dosage knob, and then pulling on the tubing of her nasal cannula, the bottom end of which she soon discovers has come loose and is no longer fastened to the tank. "Um, Max," my mother says, holding up the end of the clear plastic tube like someone showing her baffled spouse why the toaster or the television set is no longer working: it isn't plugged in.

"Whoops." My father attaches the tube where it belongs, underneath the gauge. "How's that?" My mother waits a minute and then nods, once again back in the saddle. Now that the problem is solved, all three of us relax and breathe a little easier.

All too soon a flight attendant comes over to help my parents onto the plane before general boarding begins. She instructs me to leave the extra oxygen tanks behind the desk for the medical supply company to pick up later, and then it is really time to say good-bye.

"Lydia." My father grabs me into a fierce hug and squeezes me like he never wants to let go. "I can't thank you enough. Really. You were terrific. We wouldn't have survived without you." When he straightens up and pushes me away, I see that his eyes are wet.

"Good-bye, Dad," I say, offering him a tissue, which he takes and turns away to use, embarrassed that once again I've seen him cry.

"Good-bye, Mom." I bend down to embrace my mother, who seems so small in my arms. "I love you."

"I love you, too, sweetheart," my mother says. "Have a good trip home. And tell Allie I said thank you for letting me borrow you for so long."

"I will. You have a good trip, too. Don't forget the oxygen company will be at your gate with more tanks as soon as you get off the plane. And Jack will meet you at baggage claim and drive you home."

The flight attendant waits politely as we hug and kiss one last time, and when we are finally through, she wheels my mother away, my father trailing behind them. A minute later the woman comes back out, pushing the wheelchair in front of her, now empty of my mother. Balanced on the seat instead is her clunky green oxygen tank. The sight of it undoes me and all I can think of is the day we put Princess, the poodle we had when I was growing up, to sleep. We brought the poor old pooch to the vet, who took her in his arms and disappeared into his back office, only to return to the waiting area a few moments later bearing her tags, leash, and collar. I sobbed then, and I sob now, just as shamelessly.

"Your parents are all set," the flight attendant tells me, awkwardly patting my back. "They're sitting right in the front, and your mother is all hooked up. Don't worry. There's plenty of oxygen on the plane. She'll be fine."

I thank the flight attendant and, having no other choice, take her word for it. Standing at the plate glass window still sniffling, I look out at my parents' plane, hoping to catch a glimpse of them, but of course that's impossible. Now that they're on board, there's nothing left for me to do but make my way back to my own terminal, which I do, though not in time to catch my re-booked earlier flight. I wait around the airport for several hours, and then once I finally do board, I doze the whole first leg of the journey, sleepwalk my way through the Chicago airport, change planes, and snooze through the second flight, too. Then before I know it, I am rising from my seat, shuffling down the aisle behind my fellow travelers, and then racing through the terminal in search of Allie, who is standing as close as she can behind the security checkpoint, her eyes scanning the faces of all the passengers streaming toward her. I push my way through the crowd and at last the distance between us—both real and imagined—disappears as I throw myself, sobbing yet again, though this time with tears of relief, into her waiting arms.

"It's okay," Allie murmurs, holding me close and stroking my back. "Everything's all right now. You're safe. You're home."

"I'm sorry, Allie," I mumble, my mouth pressed against the sleeve of her puffy ski jacket.

"Sorry? For what?" She looks down and lifts my chin with one finger.

"For being so mean to you. On the phone. When I was away."

"Lydia, you were all stressed out. Don't you think I know that? It's okay. All is forgiven."

"Really?" I ask tearfully. Sometimes being loved so completely is almost too much to take. "You're not mad at me?"

"Of course not," says Allie. "Are you mad at me?"

"No."

"Well, then. I'm glad that's settled. Here." Allie digs into her pocket and pulls out my little wooden heart. "Want this?" she asks, offering it to me on the flat of her palm.

"Of course." I take back my charm and then unstrap the black leather band circling my wrist. "You can have this, too."

Allie buckles her grandfather's watch around her arm and then hand in hand we ride the escalator down to baggage claim, with me chattering away and Allie grinning from ear to ear, so happy to have her *habladora* back. Having slept for most of the day and still on West Coast time, I am not tired in the least, so I babble on as we wait at carousel number nine along with the rest of the passengers who have just arrived from Chicago. Soon it is obvious that our luggage has been delayed, so we look around for a place to sit down but there isn't any. The terminal grows hot and stuffy despite the frigid temperature outside—right before we landed the pilot informed us that it was, in his words, a "balmy eleven degrees"—so Allie and I both open and remove our coats.

"Hey, you've lost weight." Allie looks me over with a disapproving frown. "Didn't you eat when you were out there?"

"Not so much. I was too upset," I tell her. "This morning my mother noticed I lost weight, too. She said that was the one good thing that came out of all this." I sigh, as if I am hearing her comment for the first time all over again. "I guess the honeymoon is over."

"After only seventeen years? Hardly," Allie says, wrapping her arms around me and giving me a luxurious kiss that proves my statement wrong and makes people stare.

Finally the luggage arrives but my suitcase does not appear with the others on the conveyor belt. It is then that I remember that in L.A. my bag was checked through on the earlier flight, so we go into the office to claim it.

Forty-five minutes later we pull into our driveway, and a minute after that I am wandering around our house searching for Mishmosh, who is nowhere to be found. "Mishy. Moisheleh. Mishman," I call, to no avail. Finally I spy him under the bed, his green eyes completely dilated as he stares at me with a shocked look on his face as though he is seeing a ghost. "Mishmosh, it's me," I whine, holding out my hand for him to sniff. Cautiously he smells my fingertips, and then recognizing my scent, crawls out from underneath the bed, bangs his head affectionately against my leg, and then slinks by me and trots into the kitchen to get himself something to eat.

"Hey, has he lost weight, too?" I ask Allie as I study my boy.

"He went on a little hunger strike while you were gone," Allie replies, hanging her head with guilt when I chastise her for keeping this a secret from me. "I didn't want to worry you, Lydia. You had enough going on out there. And besides, look at him." She motions toward our cat, who is now noisily chowing down. "He's still pretty hefty, don't you think? He probably could still stand to lose a few pounds. Unlike you." Allie turns toward me and holds out her hand. "Come on. Let's go to sleep."

A few minutes later I am all tucked in, with Allie snuggled up beside me and Mishmosh on the pillow I consider mine and he obviously thinks belongs to him, his furry body perched atop my head like it is an egg he is determined to hatch. Allie wraps herself around me and pulls me against her even more tightly, as Mishmosh kneads my hair with his two front paws and purrs louder than the engine of the plane I just flew in on. I shut my eyes and in no time at all, drift off to sleep feeling as lucky and loved as a homecoming queen.

❖

THE FIRST FIFTY YEARS were a prelude to my life," Vera says, kissing me on the cheek. "You know who said that, Lydia? Yoko Ono." Vera is the first guest to arrive at my fiftieth birthday party, which we are holding in our very own backyard, and she flounces across the lawn in a long flowered sundress and strappy sandals, looking spectacular and glamorous as always. Though this summer has been the rainiest on record, the second Saturday in August, which happens to be my actual birthday, arrives made to order: warm but not hot, breezy but not windy, a bit humid, but not unbearably so. Our property has been transformed into the perfect site for a garden party with brightly colored Japanese lanterns strung from one end of the yard to the other; round tables covered with white tablecloths scattered about, a glass vase filled with black-eyed Susans, Queen Anne's lace, and tiger lilies cut from the garden centered on each one; and a bar and buffet of cold seafood and salads set up in the back corner over by Allie's roses, which though a bit past their peak, still look and smell absolutely glorious.

"And who was it that said 'youth is wasted on the young'?" Vera continues musing out loud. "Never mind all that, Lydia. Fifty is the new forty. Maybe even the new thirty-five. Trust me, I'm here in the sagging flesh to tell you not to worry. As they say, the best is yet to come."

"Thanks, Vera. I'll take your word for it." I laugh, throwing my arms around her and pulling her into a real hug. "But as far as I'm concerned, the best is already here. I'm so glad *you* could come."

"Are you kidding? I wouldn't have missed this for the world. You look beautiful." Vera appreciates my outfit from head to toe, making an especially big fuss over my antique white crocheted dress with the flutter sleeves and scalloped hem, which she knows I spent weeks shopping for. "Is this from Allie?" she asks, lifting my hand to examine the diamond and ruby ring on my finger.

"No, that's the ring my mother gave me. This is from Allie." I crane my neck so Vera can admire the locket I am wearing. It is also adorned with diamonds, which are after all a girl's best friend, and several small rubies.

When Vera finishes admiring my necklace, I drop my chin to my chest and hold the locket out to study it myself. "Isn't it gorgeous?" I ask.

"It's absolutely stunning. I must say, Allie's got darn good taste. In jewelry *and* in women. So where is she, anyway?"

"Inside, doing some last-minute thing. She'll be out soon. But meanwhile, where is the alleged entourage you said you were bringing?" Vera had been the first to return her R.S.V.P. card, letting me know that of course she'd be there to celebrate my big day, and asking, would I mind if she brought along not one, but two dates? This request from my old friend, who does not believe in romance—at least for herself—and who has never been coupled with anyone in all the time I've known her, struck me as so odd that I simply said it was fine. Perhaps in her dotage Vera had discovered the joys of nonmonogamy?

"My mystery guests are over there somewhere." Vera waves her arm toward the front of the house, where a tall woman in a long yellow dress stands with her back to me, examining a branch of our lilac tree.

"One of your dates is Serena? How perfect." I take Vera's arm and cross the lawn to greet her. "Hi, Serena." Vera's daughter turns and practically knocks me over with her enormous, taut, protruding belly. I can't believe it. She looks like she's six months gone. At least. "Oh my God, Serena, you're pregnant!" I hug her as best as I can, laughing with delight. "Two guests, huh? One inside the other. Now I get it," I say as Vera and I both bring Serena over to a table, insist that she sit down with her feet propped up on a folding chair, and then go off to get her a drink. "Vera, why didn't you say anything?"

"Oh, Lydia, I've been thinking about it and I wanted to, honestly I did." Vera stops in front of the bar, and asks the caterer standing behind it for a tall glass of lemonade before turning back to me. "But Serena wanted to keep it a secret for a while, and then…well, to tell you the truth, I was a little nervous about how you'd react. With all the issues you have about mothers and daughters, I wasn't sure that you'd be happy for me."

"Really, Vera?" I take her arm again as we head back toward Serena. "Am I really such a terrible friend?"

"No, Lydia." Vera ducks her head to take a sip of Serena's drink. "It's just that in the past you've had, shall we say mixed feelings when other women you know have become mothers? So I wasn't sure how you would take this. I just thought it might trigger you, as we therapists like to say. That's all. And anyway, now you know."

"Serena's going to be a mother and you're going to be a *bubbe*." I stop walking as if I need to stand still to absorb it all. "Wow, Vera. *Mazel tov*. This is really something. You're right, though. I'm not happy for you." I look my friend squarely in the eye. "I'm overjoyed." I squeeze Vera's hand and hold on to it as we meander back to her daughter. "Does Serena know if it's a boy or a girl?"

"No. She doesn't want to know."

"Is there another parent in the picture? Some type of partner or spouse?"

"No," Vera says again. "Unless you count the turkey baster."

"She's a single parent by choice?" I ask, though the question has already been answered.

Vera smiles and shrugs. "What can I say, Lydia? The apple does not fall far from the tree."

"What prompted all this?"

Vera shrugs. "Serena turned forty and realized it was now or never, so she decided to go for it. And she was very, very lucky and got pregnant right on her first try."

"Like mother, like daughter," I point out. "Only you were ten years younger when you got pregnant with Serena."

"See? Forty *is* the new thirty." We reach Serena's table and Vera places her lemonade down in front of her. "Here, honey. If it gets too warm in the sun, let me know. I have a hat for you in the car. Or we can go sit in the shade."

"I'm okay for now, Mom. Thanks." Serena smiles, sips, and gazes off into the distance with one hand draped lightly across her belly, looking, well…"serene" is the word that comes to mind.

Ever the gracious hostess, I excuse myself to greet more guests. Some colleagues from the Women's Studies Department arrive next and present me with a "Wise Woman's Care Packet" that contains among other things, a package of adult diapers, a tube of denture cream, a pair of funky yellow polka-dot reading glasses, a fake hearing aid, a real bottle of prune juice, and the latest issue of *AARP* magazine.

"What's this?" I pull one more item out of the box: a small, pleated fan, which I unfold and hold up for all to see. It has a delicate pattern of pink chrysanthemums on it and is decorated with a matching silk tassel.

"That's for your hot flashes," the secretary of my department informs me.

"You mean her power surges," another colleague calls out. "Lydia, have you had any yet?"

"Nope." I fold the fan back up and place it inside the box. "But when I do, I'm sure this will come in handy."

"And here's one more thing." Emmeline steps up and plunks a crimson fedora decorated with a large purple feather on top of my head. "Even though I'm not old enough to join yet, my elders have been gracious enough to allow me to officially induct you into the Red Hat Society."

"Thank you, one and all. Who says feminists don't have a sense of humor?" I ask, looking around at my dear friends. It is then that I notice that Emmeline has stepped back and is now holding hands with someone I have never met before and who is the most androgynous-looking person I have ever seen. He or she is dressed in white linen pants and a beige button-down shirt, has short-cropped silver hair, and wears not a speck of makeup or jewelry. "Lydia, this is Rob," Emmeline says, her voice soft and dreamy. Rob shakes my hand firmly and then drifts off to fetch Emmeline something to eat from the buffet and something to drink from the bar.

"Rob, huh?" I poke Emmeline in the ribs with my elbow as we both stare at her date's attractive, retreating figure. I know it shouldn't matter and is politically incorrect besides, but still, I can't help but wonder which team Emmeline is currently playing on. Besides, I turned fifty exactly seven hours ago, which means, at least to my mind, that I've earned the right to stop being politically correct. "So, Emmeline," I say ultra casually. "Is that Rob as in Roberta or Rob as in Robert?"

"That's Rob as in robbing the cradle," Emmeline answers without answering before she, too, ambles away.

More and more people arrive and soon the party is in full swing with all of my friends eating, drinking, laughing, and catching up on the latest lesbian gossip. Allie is leading a small group of guests around our property, giving them a walking tour of her garden. Early this morning we set up a badminton net and some exercise mats, and now a horde of children of various ages, shapes, and sizes are running, shouting, and tumbling all over our lawn. And across the grass, an impromptu game of softball is just getting underway, with Aurora's moms acting as coaches, trying to teach their miniature Ms. and all her friends exactly how to "throw like a girl."

As I stand there taking everything in, Allie shows up at my side, wraps her arm around my waist, and plants a kiss below my left ear. "Why don't you come sit down with me and eat something, birthday girl?" she asks. "Before all the good stuff is gone."

"Okay." I let Allie lead me away but before we get very far, she stops and points toward the street.

"Hey, look," she says, watching a long white limo pull up in front of our house. "Is that the president?"

My gaze follows her fingertip. "God, I hope not."

"Who, then? Ed McMahon? Have we finally won the Publisher's Clearinghouse Sweepstake?"

"No, silly. You know who that is, Allie." And off I go to greet the guests I have been awaiting to make my party complete.

"Hi, Mom. Hi, Dad," I say as they climb out of the car.

"Happy birthday, Lydia." My father, who is dressed in a jazzy pin-striped summer suit, kisses me lightly on the forehead and passes me an envelope. "Don't lose that," he warns, which is his way of letting me know that in addition to a birthday card, there's a check tucked inside.

"I won't. Thanks, Dad."

"You're very welcome. Is this your house? Say, this is nice." My parents have never visited Allie and me before, and the surprise in my father's voice tells me he never expected that Allie and I would be the proud owners of such a nice little place. I wonder what he was expecting our home to look like, but luckily before I can ask him, my mother grabs me by the shoulders and hugs me tight.

"Hi, sweetheart," she says as we cling to each other and both start to weep. "No," she says, pushing me gently away and holding up one finger. "No crying today. I'm here. I made it. Without oxygen no less."

"Really, Mom? You don't need it anymore?"

"I need it sometimes. You know, I have good days and not-so-good days. There's some in the car, and I have a small tank right here." She holds up a bright turquoise mesh tote bag that perfectly matches her outfit. "Just in case."

"Hey, Lydia." Jack gets out next, and I am amazed to see that he's all dressed up in a button-down white shirt, pleated black pants, and a red bow tie. His hair is still long but it is braided neatly and tied down at the end with a piece of rawhide string.

"Hey, Jack, you clean up pretty good," I tell him. "Thanks for dressing up for my party."

Jack shrugs like it's no big deal. "Don't thank me, Lydia," he says, motioning toward the car. "Thank Crystal. This was all her idea. Hey." He pokes his head inside the car. "You girls coming or what?"

"Hold your horses, Jack," a voice says before Crystal emerges. She kicks one long leg and then the other out of the limo like a movie star at the premiere of her latest film, and then takes Jack's hand, rises, and stands still for a moment so we can all admire her. Crystal is wearing a tiny red skirt and halter top, along with matching three-inch heels that sink slightly into the ground as she takes a few steps across the lawn toward me. "Happy birthday, Lydia," she says, bending her long, lithe frame in half and leaning forward to buss the air around my cheek.

"Thanks, Crystal. I like your new do." Crystal has done away with the spiky look and now styles her hair like Cleopatra, complete with black bangs cut straight across her forehead and chin-length hair that curls slightly under.

"Thank you," Crystal says, and then turns her back on us and calls into the car. "Bethany Joy Gutman, I am not telling you again. Get your butt out of that car. Right now."

"Okay, okay, *okay*," says Bethany, making sure that everyone knows she doesn't want to do as she's told. Especially by her mother. Sighing deeply, like she's just been asked to lift the car off the ground single-handedly instead of merely lug her body out of it, she glumly steps out onto the lawn. "Hi, Lydia."

"Bethany?"

"It's B.J.," she says sharply. I stare at her, trying not to be obvious about it as I take in the amazing transformation of Jack and Crystal's fifteen-year-old daughter. True, I haven't seen her in over a year, but still, it's hard to believe that this is the same girl who, last I heard, was following in her mother's stylishly clad footsteps and spending practically every waking weekend and after-school moment at the mall, the spa, and the tanning salon. Gone are the makeup, the long nails, the hairstyle blow-dried within an inch of its life, the expensive jewelry and the designer clothing. Bethany—or B.J., as I must remember she now wants to be called—has taken grunge to a new level. Her hair looks like it hasn't seen a brush or a comb since the beginning of summer, and her jeans are patched and torn. She wears two different colored flip-flops on her feet and her toes are far from clean.

"I like your T-shirt," I tell her. It is several sizes too large and reads, "Two parents for sale. Cheap!"

"See?" B.J. née Bethany spits out the word at her mother. "I told you she would like it."

"Why don't you go join those kids over there?" Jack motions toward the side of the house where some of our friends and their offspring are still playing badminton, while others have set up and started a rousing game of croquet.

"You're not serious, are you?" B.J. says in a voice that makes it clear to all within hearing range that she would never, under any circumstances even dream of stooping so low.

"I have a better idea," Crystal says. "Why don't you go take a long walk…off a short pier?"

"That's so funny I forgot to laugh," B.J. says before thrusting her fists into her pockets and storming off.

"Wow," I say, as we watch her stomp away. It's been a while since I've witnessed such teenage hostility—and even longer since I spewed it myself—and in an odd way it's refreshing to see that some things never change.

"That's our darling daughter," Jack says, shaking his head. "Miss Congeniality."

"Don't worry, Jack." My mother puts her hand on his arm. "All teenagers go through a phase of hating their parents. It's perfectly normal."

"How long does it last?" Jack wants to know.

My mother shrugs. "Some of them get over it sooner, some of them get over it later. It lasts as long as it lasts. But eventually," my mother gives me a meaningful look, "they all come around."

"Why don't we go into the backyard?" I make a move to steer my newly arrived guests toward the party. "I want you to meet everyone." Leading the way proudly as if I am escorting royalty, I bring my family over to a table where we all sit down except for Crystal, who excuses herself and takes off immediately in search of a drink. Allie joins us, hovering at my side, and Vera appears instantly, eager to be introduced.

"This is Vera, my best friend," I tell my mother, hardly believing that after all this time the two of them are meeting face-to-face at last.

My mother contradicts me. "She's not your best friend."

"Yes, she is."

"No, she isn't." My mother shakes her head and points a long red fingernail at Allie. "*She's* your best friend. Just like your father is my best friend."

"I've wanted to meet you for such a long time," says Vera, who isn't concerned in the least about being demoted to the position of second fiddle. She extends her hand, which my mother takes, and then utters the one thing I pleaded with her not to say. "I've heard so much about you."

"Really?" My mother looks at her with interest. "Anything good?"

Vera laughs. "Everything good. Only good. You have a very special daughter."

"I know," my mother says, making me wonder if this is all a dream.

"Hey, Lydia, here, I brought you something." Jack reaches into his back pocket and shoves an envelope across the table. "Open it."

"Presents go over there." I indicate a table over by Allie's favorite hydrangea plant, which is bursting all over with giant white flowers almost as big as volleyballs. "I'm not opening them now."

"Please?" Jack asks. "Can't you just open mine?"

"Why?"

"Trust me. You'll see."

"Oh, all right, but you'll have to wait a minute. I have something for you, too." Jack and I were born a mere two weeks apart and I thought it only fair for me to give him a gift to acknowledge his upcoming special day.

"I'll get it," Allie says, striding across the lawn toward the house. She comes back a few minutes later carrying a tray of iced tea for my parents, with Jack's present tucked under her arm.

"Why, Lydia, you shouldn't have." Jack is obviously surprised and pleased by the present, which is all wrapped up in shiny green paper and tied with a silver bow. "Thanks a lot."

"Maybe you better wait and see what it is first before you thank me," I say, tearing open the envelope he gave me. "Oh my God, Jack."

"What is it?" Allie asks, peering over my shoulder.

"Not one, but two tickets to the Barbra Streisand concert at Madison Square Garden. Wow, Jack, I can't believe it."

"May I point out that those are orchestra seats?" Jack says, making sure I fully appreciate his gift. Which I do.

"Jack, I am truly, truly impressed," I say, putting the tickets back in their envelope and handing them to Allie. "You better lock these up in our safe," I tell her. "I'm sure they're worth a small fortune."

Satisfied, Jack shrugs like it was nothing. "Hey, what can I say? That's what you get when your cousin works in the industry. My turn." He tears the wrapping paper off his present, opens it, and holds up the T-shirt I had made especially for him at our local copy shop, reading out loud: "My sister turned fifty and all I got was this lousy T-shirt." Jack chuckles and then looks from the shirt to me with one eyebrow raised. "Sister?" he asks.

"Sister," I answer. "The correct word for 'female sibling.' Which is what I am to you, since we do share a set of parents." I smile at him warmly. "Do you like it?"

"I love it," he says, planting a sloppy kiss on my cheek. "Thanks a lot, Sis."

"You're very welcome, Bro."

The party goes on, lasting well into the late afternoon and early evening, and everyone continues to enjoy themselves. I look around, happy and relieved that even my family seems to be having a good time: my father is explaining to the caterer how to get red wine stains out of white tablecloths (cold water and salt is the trick) and my mother has attached herself to Vera and Serena and is telling them how to cure the heartburn that pregnancy brings (eat a few almonds every hour). Jack is handing out business cards to all the lesbian mothers and urging them to bring their kids in for a screen test, and Crystal, wineglass in hand, is flirting with the handsome caterer serving drinks behind the bar. All my guests taken care of, I scan the crowd for Allie, but instead my eyes fall upon someone sitting by herself on the steps of our side porch who is staring down at her hands, not enjoying herself at all. Horrified that one of my guests is having such a terrible time, I go to her immediately.

"Hi, B.J.," I say, sinking down beside her on the porch. "You're not having any fun at all, are you?"

"No, but what else is new? And anyway, it's not your fault."

"Whose fault is it?" I ask, already guessing the answer. Whose fault is everything when you're an adolescent girl? Your mother's. Proving me correct, B.J. glances sideways and scowls with disdain in the direction of Crystal, who is now holding court at a table of pre-teens whose mothers all veer toward this side of butch and know next to nothing about hair care, clothing, and makeup. "She never, ever listens to me." B.J. explodes with the intensity and passion only a teenager can muster. "She won't even call me B.J. It's my *name* and that's what she should call me. But she won't. Just because she's my mother, she thinks she knows *everything*. She doesn't care about my opinions. She doesn't care about what I have to say. She doesn't care about me at all. And neither does my father."

"I'm sure they care about you, even if they don't always show it. But it's hard, isn't it?" I put a tentative arm around B.J.'s shoulder as she cringes at the mere sound of her mother's high-pitched laughter.

"She wishes I was like *them*." B.J. indicates the admiring girly-girls swarming around Crystal with disgust. "Well, I used to be, but I'm not anymore, okay?"

"Okay," I say, which makes B.J. turn toward me with surprise. "I think you're fine just the way you are."

"You do?"

"Sure, B.J. I think you're great. There's nothing wrong with you."

B.J. stares down at her hands again, pondering this. "You grew up with my father, right?" she asks me, looking up after a minute. I hold her gaze and nod. "What was he like when he was my age?"

A Nazi, I think, remembering all the ways Jack tortured me when we were young, because of the way I looked, the way I acted, the way I thought. But I don't think it's a good idea to tell B.J. that. "He was sad," I say after a minute, which is really more the truth. "His mother died when he was just about your age, you know, and his father just took off. Talk about not caring. Jack had a pretty rough time."

B.J. considers this. "Did you know my mother's parents kicked her out of the house when she was sixteen?"

"No, I didn't know that." I look across the yard over at Crystal. "What happened?"

"I don't know." B.J. shrugs her bony little shoulders. "I don't think she meant to tell me. But one day when she was yelling at me for something, she said if I didn't change my lousy attitude she'd throw me out on the street just like her parents had done to her."

"Wow." I keep staring at Crystal, who must sense she's being studied, because she looks over and raises her glass in our direction in a silent toast. "You know, B.J., nobody gets off easy. Everyone has a rough childhood. I'm sure your mom was devastated when they kicked her out."

"I guess. But…" As I wait for B.J. to continue, I study her face, noticing how pretty she is, despite her lack of grooming and personal hygiene. She is her mother's daughter after all, complete with those supermodel cheekbones, dimpled chin, and large green eyes. "You're a feminist, right, Lydia?"

"You betcha." Raising my right fist high, I shout, "Sisterhood is powerful," and pound the air twice as if I am hammering an invisible nail into an invisible wall.

B.J. looks at me like I'm the weirdest person she has ever met, so I sheepishly lower my arm. "It's just something we feminists used to do," I tell her. "In the good old days when we were fighting the good fight. Which, by the way, we still are."

"Is that why you don't have any children?" she asks me.

"Oh no, B.J. You can be a feminist and a mother at the same time," I assure her. "I just never wanted to be a parent, that's all."

"But how come?"

I look out over my party as I think about how to answer B.J. and my gaze falls on Vera, whose hand is resting on Serena's swollen stomach. From the expression of sheer bliss that has taken over her face, I know she has just felt the baby kick. "I guess I've always known I'm not really mommy material," I admit to B.J. and to myself. "I'm not the kind of person who can give up everything you have to give up in order to be a good parent. I mean, it's not all sacrifice; you do give up a lot but you get a lot, too. At least, that's what I've been told. But still, it's just not right for me. Though you know what I would like to be?" I turn to look at B.J. "This might sound kind of strange, but what I'd really like is to be a grandmother. Without being a mother. But I haven't figured out a way to do that yet. Can you?"

B.J. takes my question seriously. "No," she says after thinking it over. "I don't think you can be a grandmother if you aren't a mother first. But I know something else you can be."

"What's that?" I try to catch her eye but she looks away.

"You could be like a really cool aunt or something," she says softly, her face turning just the faintest shade of pink as she mumbles her suggestion.

"Hmm," I hold my chin in my hand and nod a few times. "I think I could probably do that. On one condition, though."

"What's that?"

"Only if you'll be my really cool niece. Deal?" I hold out my hand.

"Deal," B.J. says, giving me a firm shake.

"Lydia, can you come over here for a minute?" Allie calls from the midst of the party.

"I think I'm wanted. Come with me." I stand and reach for B.J.'s hand. We walk toward Allie, who is pouring glasses of champagne and handing them out to everyone. I accept one from her and ask for another. "But just fill it halfway. Not even. This much." I hold my thumb and forefinger two inches apart.

"Like so?" Allie asks.

"That's good. Thank you," I say, taking the glass from her and, in my first official act as B.J.'s really cool aunt, hand it to my recently acquired niece with a flourish.

"For me?" she asks, widening her eyes and obviously so pleased that she momentarily drops her disgruntled, sullen teenager persona. "Gee, thanks, Aunt Lydia."

"You're welcome, B.J.," I say, the sound of my new handle uttered in her sweet young voice music to my ears.

Once the champagne is distributed, and some flattering and embarrassing toasts have been made, a breathless and breathtaking Marilyn Monroe impersonator shows up to deliver a silly singing telegram sent by Colleen, who couldn't leave her brood to join the fun. When she is through crooning, everyone turns to me and soon a cry goes up. "Speech! Speech!" my guests all chorus. I look to Allie for help but she doesn't offer any.

"Oh, okay, if you insist," I say, pretending that I mind being the center of all this attention. "I'm going to keep this very short and sweet."

"Like you," someone calls out.

"Like me," I acknowledge, overwhelmed by so much love. "Thank you all for coming. It means the world to me. There aren't that many people whose friends are their family and whose family are their friends." I look around until I catch my mother's eye. She smiles at me with pride. "I feel very, very lucky."

More champagne is poured as I raise my glass high. "To the next fifty years," I say.

"Hear, hear."

"Salud."

"L'chaim."

A large sheet cake covered with white icing appears out of nowhere and is placed in front of me, blazing with fifty red candles. "Oh my God," I say, stepping back from the heat. "Is it hot in here or is it me?" At first I am joking, but then I realize that the warmth I feel spreading from my chest up to my neck and face is coming from somewhere deep inside me.

"She's having her first hot flash," Vera announces to the crowd like a proud mother. *"Mazel tov,* Lydia!" Laughing, she hands me my fan, which I take gratefully and then flutter in front of my flushed face in a vain attempt to cool down. Then, with B.J.'s help, I blow out all of my candles, not even bothering to make a wish because everything I could possibly hope for has already come true.

❖

"YOU DON'T LOOK a day over fifty," Allie says the next morning the split second I open my eyes.

I roll over on my side to look at her, sending a miffed Mishmosh tumbling off my stomach and out of bed. "How long have you been awake, staring at me and waiting to say that?"

"A while, sleepyhead." Allie props herself up on one elbow and smiles at me. "Did you like your party?"

"I loved my party. Except I didn't get to see very much of you. Thanks for being such a big help."

Allie shrugs one shoulder. "Hey, I was only doing my job. What else are butches for? But the party isn't over yet."

"It isn't?"

"Nope." As Allie gazes at me, her eyes darken with a look I know well. The look of desire. "What about having a little celebration for just the two of us right now?"

"Great idea." I reach up for her and just as she takes me in her arms and the festivities begin, wouldn't you know it—the phone starts to ring.

"Oh no," Allie groans in my ear. "Why does it always do that? How does it know?"

"Shh, Let me listen." I cover her mouth softly, just as our answering machine clicks on.

"Hi, Lollipop, it's Mom."

"Lollipop?" Allie asks, nibbling my fingers. I clamp my hand over her mouth to shush her again.

"I'm just calling because you asked me to let you know that your father and I got home safe, which we did. Jack's driver dropped us off late last night, just after midnight. All right? So now you can stop worrying about me, and let me start worrying about you. That's the way it's supposed to be, the mother worrying about the daughter, not the other way around." My mother stops speaking, clears her throat, and then coughs, a dry hacking sound that strikes terror into my heart. Did I find my mother so late in life, only to turn around and lose her? "It's nothing, Lydia. It's only a tickle in my throat," she continues as if she can hear my thoughts. "Listen, I'm no spring chicken, what can I tell you. When you get to be my age, you get a little ache, a little pain, a little cough, that's all. It's nothing to be concerned about. I'm fine. I mean it. Even the doctor says so, okay? He says I'll have days, and I'll have days. So don't worry about me. Just enjoy. Happy birthday again, sweetheart. I love you. And I'll speak to you during the week."

"All right now?" Allie asks once the machine clicks off.

"All right," I say nuzzling into her arms.

Much much later, after hunger propels us out of bed, I play my mother's message again. And again. And again. Allie complains, but I don't care. I'm making up for lost time. A lot of lost time.

It took me half a century to find my mother.

She was well worth the wait.

Author's Note

The care, love, generosity, and wisdom of many extraordinary people sustained me during the writing of this book. I am grateful to:

My family, whose unconditional love and support have made all the difference each and every day of my entire life;

My remarkable friends, each of whom I adore and could not live without (you know exactly who you are!);

The talented members of my precious writing group: Ann Turner, Anna Kirwan, Barbara Diamond Goldin, Corinne Demas, Ellen Wittlinger, Jane Yolen, and Patricia MacLachlan, who gave me invaluable insight and feedback on various drafts of this book;

Other very special writers and friends whose support and/or feedback were extraodinarily helpful: Tzivia Gover, Joann Kobin, Suzanne Strempek Shea, Martha Nelson Patrick, Lynn Matteson, Beth Spong, Marilyn Eve Silberglied, Meryl Cohn, and Janet Feld;

My wonderful agent, Elizabeth Harding of Curtis Brown, Ltd. for her unflagging enthusiasm, sharp eye, and ceaseless support, and her extremely intelligent, not to mention utterly fabulous colleague, Mitchell Waters;

All the amazing people at Bold Strokes Books who do such fine work, especially Radclyffe, the powerhouse behind it all, and Stacia Seaman, who never misses the opportunity to insert or delete a comma;

My dream research team: Sister Factoid who was available 24/7 to Google anything and everything, and the extremely knowledgeable Julie Sulinski, R.N., B.S.N., who gave so generously of her time and expertise, answering my endless medical questions with intelligence, enthusiasm, wit, and good cheer;

And finally, I am grateful beyond words to Mary Grace Newman Vazquez, who blesses my life each and every day with her own special brand of joy.

About the Author

Lesléa Newman has published more than fifty books, including the novels *Good Enough to Eat* and *In Every Laugh a Tear*; the short story collections *A Letter to Harvey Milk* and *Girls Will be Girls*; the poetry collections *Still Life with Buddy* and *Signs of Love*; the middle grade novels *Hachiko Waits* and *Fat Chance*; and the children's books *The Boy Who Cried Fabulous*, *A Fire Engine for Ruthie*, *The Best Cat in the World*, and *Heather Has Two Mommies*. She has received numerous literary awards including poetry fellowships from the Massachusetts Artists Fellowship Foundation and the National Endowment for the Arts, the Highlights for Children Fiction Writing Award, a Parents' Choice Silver Medal, the James Baldwin Award for Cultural Achievement, and four Pushcart Prize Nominations. Nine of her books have been Lambda Literary Award finalists. Currently, she is the Poet Laureate of Northampton, Massachusetts. Lesléa's work often addresses lesbian identity and Jewish identity, and how the two intersect and how they collide. Her most recent books include a new volume of poetry entitled *Nobody's Mother*, and the first board books for children with same sex parents: *Mommy, Mama, and Me*, and *Daddy, Papa, and Me*.

Books Available From Bold Strokes Books

The Seduction of Moxie by Colette Moody. When 1930s Broadway actress Violet London meets speakeasy singer Moxie Valette, she is instantly attracted and her Hollywood trip takes an unexpected turn. (978-1-60282-114-9)

Goldenseal by Gill McKnight. When Amy Fortune returns to her childhood home, she discovers something sinister in the air—but is former lover Leone Garoul stalking her or protecting her? (978-1-60282-115-6)

Romantic Interludes 2: Secrets edited by Radclyffe and Stacia Seaman. An anthology of sensual lesbian love stories: passion, surprises, and secret desires. (978-1-60282-116-3)

Femme Noir by Clara Nipper. Nora Delaney meets her match in Max Abbott, a sex-crazed dame who may or may not have the information Nora needs to solve a murder—but can she contain her lust for Max long enough to find out? (978-1-60282-117-0)

The Reluctant Daughter by Lesléa Newman. Heartwarming, heartbreaking, and ultimately triumphant—the story every daughter recognizes of the lifelong struggle for our mothers to really see us. (978-1-60282-118-7)

Erosistible by Gill McKnight. When Win Martin arrives at a luxurious Greek hotel for a much-anticipated week of sun and sex with her new girlfriend, she is stunned to find her ex-girlfriend, Benny, is the proprietor. Aeros Ebook. (978-1-60282-134-7)

Looking Glass Lives by Felice Picano. Cousins Roger and Alistair become lifelong friends and discover their sexuality amidst the backdrop of twentieth-century gay culture. (978-1-60282-089-0)

Breaking the Ice by Kim Baldwin. Nothing is easy about life above the Arctic Circle—except, perhaps, falling in love. At least that's what pilot Bryson Faulkner hopes when she meets Karla Edwards. (978-1-60282-087-6)

It Should Be a Crime by Carsen Taite. Two women fulfill their mutual desire with a night of passion, neither expecting more until law professor Morgan Bradley and student Parker Casey meet again…in the classroom. (978-1-60282-086-9)

Rough Trade edited by Todd Gregory. Top male erotica writers pen their own hot, sexy versions of the term "rough trade," producing some of the hottest, nastiest, and most dangerous fiction ever published. (978-1-60282-092-0)

The High Priest and the Idol by Jane Fletcher. Jemeryl and Tevi's relationship is put to the test when the Guardian sends Jemeryl on a mission that puts her not only in harm's way, but back into the sights of a previous lover. (978-1-60282-085-2)

Point of Ignition by Erin Dutton. Amid a blaze that threatens to consume them both, firefighter Kate Chambers and property owner Alexi Clark redefine love and trust. (978-1-60282-084-5)

Secrets in the Stone by Radclyffe. Reclusive sculptor Rooke Tyler suddenly finds herself the object of two very different women's affections, and choosing between them will change her life forever. (978-1-60282-083-8)

Dark Garden by Jennifer Fulton. Vienna Blake and Mason Cavender are sworn enemies—who can't resist each other. Something has to give. (978-1-60282-036-4)

Late in the Season by Felice Picano. Set on Fire Island, this is the story of an unlikely pair of friends—a gay composer in his late thirties and an eighteen-year-old schoolgirl. (978-1-60282-082-1)

Punishment with Kisses by Diane Anderson-Minshall. Will Megan find the answers she seeks about her sister Ashley's murder or will her growing relationship with one of Ash's exes blind her to the real truth? (978-1-60282-081-4)

September Canvas by Gun Brooke. When Deanna Moore meets TV personality Faythe she is reluctantly attracted to her, but will Faythe side with the people spreading rumors about Deanna? (978-1-60282-080-7)

No Leavin' Love by Larkin Rose. Beautiful, successful Mercedes Miller thinks she can resume her affair with ranch foreman Sydney Campbell, but the rules have changed. (978-1-60282-079-1)

Between the Lines by Bobbi Marolt. When romance writer Gail Prescott meets actress Tannen Albright, she develops feelings that she usually only experiences through her characters. (978-1-60282-078-4)

Blue Skies by Ali Vali. Commander Berkley Levine leads an elite group of pilots on missions ordered by her ex-lover Captain Aidan Sullivan and everything is on the line—including love. (978-1-60282-077-7)

The Lure by Felice Picano. When Noel Cummings is recruited by the police to go undercover to find a killer, his life will never be the same. (978-1-60282-076-0)

Death of a Dying Man by J.M. Redmann. Mickey Knight, Private Eye and partner of Dr. Cordelia James, doesn't need a drop-dead gorgeous assistant—not until nature steps in. (978-1-60282-075-3)

Justice for All by Radclyffe. Dell Mitchell goes undercover to expose a human traffic ring and ends up in the middle of an even deadlier conspiracy. (978-1-60282-074-6)

Sanctuary by I. Beacham. Cate Canton faces one major obstacle to her goal of crushing her business rival, Dita Newton—her uncontrollable attraction to Dita. (978-1-60282-055-5)

The Sublime and Spirited Voyage of Original Sin by Colette Moody. Pirate Gayle Malvern finds the presence of an abducted seamstress, Celia Pierce, a welcome distraction until the captive comes to mean more to her than is wise. (978-1-60282-054-8)

Suspect Passions by VK Powell. Can two women, a city attorney and a beat cop, put aside their differences long enough to see that they're perfect for each other? (978-1-60282-053-1)

Just Business by Julie Cannon. Two women who come together—each for her own selfish needs—discover that love can never be as simple as a business transaction. (978-1-60282-052-4)

Sistine Heresy by Justine Saracen. Adrianna Borgia, survivor of the Borgia court, presents Michelangelo with the greatest temptations of his life while struggling with soul-threatening desires for the painter Raphaela. (978-1-60282-051-7)

Radical Encounters by Radclyffe. An out-of-bounds, outside-the-lines collection of provocative, superheated erotica by award-winning romance and erotica author Radclyffe. (978-1-60282-050-0)

Thief of Always by Kim Baldwin & Xenia Alexiou. Stealing a diamond to save the world should be easy for Elite Operative Mishael Taylor, but she didn't figure on love getting in the way. (978-1-60282-049-4)

X by JD Glass. When X-hacker Charlie Riven is framed for a crime she didn't commit, she accepts help from an unlikely source—sexy Treasury Agent Elaine Harper. (978-1-60282-048-7)

The Middle of Somewhere by Clifford Henderson. Eadie T. Pratt sets out on a road trip in search of a new life and ends up in the middle of somewhere she never expected. (978-1-60282-047-0)

Paybacks by Gabrielle Goldsby. Cameron Howard wants to avoid her old nemesis Mackenzie Brandt but their high school reunion brings up more than just memories. (978-1-60282-046-3)

Uncross My Heart by Andrews & Austin. When a radio talk show diva sets out to interview a female priest, the two women end up at odds and neither heaven nor earth is safe from their feelings. (978-1-60282-045-6)

Fireside by Cate Culpepper. Mac, a therapist, and Abby, a nurse, fall in love against the backdrop of friendship, healing, and defending one's own within the Fireside shelter. (978-1-60282-044-9)

A Pirate's Heart by Catherine Friend. When rare book librarian Emma Boyd searches for a long-lost treasure map, she learns the hard way that pirates still exist in today's world—some modern pirates steal maps, others steal hearts. (978-1-60282-040-1)

The Limits of Justice by John Morgan Wilson. Benjamin Justice and reporter Alexandra Templeton search for a killer in a mysterious compound in the remote California desert. (978-1-60282-060-9)

Trails Merge by Rachel Spangler. Parker Riley escapes the high-powered world of politics to Campbell Carson's ski resort—and their mutual attraction produces anything but smooth running. (978-1-60282-039-5)

Dreams of Bali by C.J. Harte. Madison Barnes worships work, power, and success, and she's never allowed anyone to interfere—that is, until she runs into Karlie Henderson Stockard. Aeros EBook (978-1-60282-070-8)

Designed for Love by Erin Dutton. Jillian Sealy and Wil Johnson don't much like each other, but they do have to work together—and what they desire most is not what either of them had planned. (978-1-60282-038-8)

Calling the Dead by Ali Vali. Six months after Hurricane Katrina, NOLA Detective Sept Savoie is a cop who thinks making a relationship work is harder than catching a serial killer—but her current case may prove her wrong. (978-1-60282-037-1)

Shots Fired by MJ Williamz. Kyla and Echo seem to have the perfect relationship and the perfect life until someone shoots at Kyla—and Echo is the most likely suspect. (978-1-60282-035-7)

truelesbianlove.com by Carsen Taite. Mackenzie Lewis and Dr. Jordan Wagner have very different ideas about love, but they discover that truelesbianlove is closer than a click away. Aeros EBook (978-1-60282-069-2)

Justice at Risk by John Morgan Wilson. Benjamin Justice's blind date leads to a rare opportunity for legitimate work, but a reckless risk changes his life forever. (978-1-60282-059-3)

Run to Me by Lisa Girolami. Burned by the four-letter word called love, the only thing Beth Standish wants to do is run for—or maybe from—her life. (978-1-60282-034-0)

Split the Aces by Jove Belle. In the neon glare of Sin City, two women ride a wave of passion that threatens to consume them in a world of fast money and fast times. (978-1-60282-033-3)

Uncharted Passage by Julie Cannon. Two women on a vacation that turns deadly face down one of nature's most ruthless killers—and find themselves falling in love. (978-1-60282-032-6)

Night Call by Radclyffe. All medevac helicopter pilot Jett McNally wants to do is fly and forget about the horror and heartbreak she left behind in the Middle East, but anesthesiologist Tristan Holmes has other plans. (978-1-60282-031-9)

Lake Effect Snow by C.P. Rowlands. News correspondent Annie T. Booker and FBI Agent Sarah Moore struggle to stay one step ahead of disaster as Annie's life becomes the war zone she once reported on. Aeros EBook (978-1-60282-068-5)

I Dare You by Larkin Rose. Stripper by night, corporate raider by day, Kelsey's only looking for sex and power, until she meets a woman who stirs her heart and her body. (978-1-60282-030-2)

Truth Behind the Mask by Lesley Davis. Erith Baylor is drawn to Sentinel Pagan Osborne's quiet strength, but the secrets between them strain duty and family ties. (978-1-60282-029-6)

Cooper's Deale by KI Thompson. Two would-be lovers and a decidedly inopportune murder spell trouble for Addy Cooper, no matter which way the cards fall. (978-1-60282-028-9)

Romantic Interludes 1: Discovery ed. by Radclyffe and Stacia Seaman. An anthology of sensual, erotic contemporary love stories from the best-selling Bold Strokes authors. (978-1-60282-027-2)

A Guarded Heart by Jennifer Fulton. The last place FBI Special Agent Pat Roussel expects to find herself is assigned to an illicit private security gig baby-sitting a celebrity. (Ebook) (978-1-60282-067-8)

Saving Grace by Jennifer Fulton. Champion swimmer Dawn Beaumont, injured in a car crash she caused, flees to Moon Island, where scientist Grace Ramsay welcomes her. (Ebook) (978-1-60282-066-1)

The Sacred Shore by Jennifer Fulton. Successful tech industry survivor Merris Randall does not believe in love at first sight until she meets Olivia Pearce. (Ebook) (978-1-60282-065-4)